I was awakened from a sound sleep and charged with a murder I didn't commit...but how could I prove it?

"Police, motherfucker!" someone shouted. "Hands where we can see 'em!"

I raised my hands and awaited further instruction. Someone found the light switch, and I winced at the sudden brightness. When my eyes adjusted, I counted six rifles trained on me, the men holding them in helmets and body armor. The man directly across from me lowered his rifle. With a gloved hand he picked up my gun from the bed and bagged it. The huge man nearest me took a step closer, his sneer visible through his plastic face shield, and drove his rifle stock into the left side of my skull. Within half a second, the pain began, radiating from my right ear to my eyes. It took me several heartbeats to realize I'd bitten my tongue. Blood trickled into the back of my throat as I tried to match my breathing to the murderous pulsing. If the space between the platform bed and the wall had been wider than two feet, I'd have slumped to the floor instead of leaning on the edge of the bed and struggling to keep from sliding off. I squeezed my eyes shut and grasped the bedspread, keeping my hands where they could be seen.

"Enough, Berko!"

Somebody banged into my dresser as if shoved. The voice had sounded familiar. I forced myself to open my eyes. Standing above me, bald head bare and torso sheathed in Kevlar, Terry Chalmers holstered his service pistol and unhooked handcuffs from his belt. Beside him was Rafael Pinero, gun still in hand, his brown fedora an odd-looking accessory for his vest. Chalmers hauled me up onto the bed face down, cuffing my hands behind me.

"Gideon Rimes," Pinero said, "you are under arrest for the murder of Kenneth Carnahan. You have the right to remain silent..."

Kenny, dead?

Buffalo, New York, private investigator Gideon Rimes, a black Iraq-war vet and retired army CID detective, is hired to protect blues singer Indigo Waters from her ex-boyfriend, a police officer who serves as a driver and personal bodyguard for Buffalo Mayor Ophelia Green. When the boyfriend is murdered, Rimes is the prime suspect. He's arrested but police are forced to release him due to a lack of evidence. As the cops search for clues to tie Rimes to the murder, he begins his own hunt for the killer, uncovering a plot that involves city leaders, a wealthy business owner, corrupt cops, access to control of a half-billion-dollar project—and a dark family secret that someone will do anything to keep hidden, regardless of who they have to kill...

KUDOS for *Nickel City Blues*

In *Nickel City Blues* by Gary Earl Ross, Gideon Rimes is a Black Iraq-war vet, a former military CID cop, and current PI who gets a gig to protect a blues singer from her stalker boyfriend, a cop on the mayor's protection detail. Rimes and the cop have a few words when the cop violates a restraining order the singer has on him, so when the cop ends up dead, Rimes is the prime suspect. Released due to lack of evidence after a brutal middle of the night arrest, Rimes is determined to find the killer and clear his name. But what he finds is corruption, ruthless mercenaries, and dark secrets. Now the only question is can he stay alive long enough to bring the killer to justice. The story is tense, intriguing, and well written—a fast-paced, action-filled tale of cops, private investigators, attorneys, and politicians that will have you turning pages from beginning to end. ~ *Taylor Jones, The Review Team of Taylor Jones & Regan Murphy.*

Nickel City Blues by Gary Earl Ross is the story of a former army vet and military cop turned private eye. Gideon Rimes is a PI in Buffalo, New York, who's hired to protect a colored blues singer from her stalker cop ex-boyfriend. Acting as a bodyguard, Gideon follows the singer to the nightclub where she works, and when the boyfriend shows up, Gideon and the bouncers convince the man to leave, but not before the cop and Gideon get into an altercation. Later when the cop turns up dead, Gideon is arrested, but there's no evidence he had anything to do with it. So the cops let him go. Reluctantly. Then Gideon is hired by the singer, the mayor, and the dead cop's parents to find his killer. As Gideon investigates he discovers that there is much more to the story than a cop who didn't want to break up with his girlfriend and ended up dead. Nickel City Blues is hard hitting, fast paced, and tension filled. This one will keep you glued to the edge of your seat. If you like books you can't put down, you're going to love this one. ~ *Regan Murphy, The Review Team of Taylor Jones & Regan Murphy*

ACKNOWLEDGEMENTS

As solitary a profession as writing is, no writer is an island. A novelist succeeds because of the family, friends, and colleagues who offer inspiration, become character models, or serve as first readers. A novel maintains its credibility because of the various experts and professionals who, knowingly or unknowingly, provide the novelist with the realities and details of the world under construction. Finally, a book is shaped by an editor whose professional distance from the emotions of the work guides the author to a stronger final product. For *Nickel City Blues* I am indebted to the following, who may or may not know why they are being acknowledged: my police officer son David and his colleague John Chapman; my brother Steve for sharing his extensive knowledge of firearms; my sisters Renee and Lori, my brother Rob, and my cousin Bobby; Satya Popuri and Adam Tudor; Dennis and Suzette Hollins; Duane and Shelia Crockett; Scott and Glo Williams; Amrom and Linda Chodos; Ramona Alsace; Juan and Nancy Alsace; Ralph and Christine Alsace; Alan and Marlene Jacobson; Jack and Nancy Adler; Murry Galloway; the Just Buffalo Literary Center, especially Laurie Dean Torrell and Barbara Cole; the JBLC Writers' Critique group, especially Khalil Nieves and Susan Solomon, author of the Emlyn Goode mysteries; Buffalo Mayor Byron Brown; Patty Mac, owner of the fondly remembered Shadow Lounge; my editors at Black Opal Books; and, finally, Tamara Alsace. Thank you all.

Nickel
City
Blues

A Gideon Rimes Mystery

Gary Earl Ross

A Black Opal Books Publication

DEDICATION

For Tammy,
who met me in that space where anything can happen
and made me a better man.

Chapter 1

Indigo Waters held the wireless microphone in her left hand as she moved amid tables full of wings, sandwiches, and pitchers of beer. She was small and curvy, with short black hair and skin like whipped chocolate. Her huge amber eyes glittered like the sequins on her clinging copper gown, even in the muted light of the Anchor Bar. The voice that shook the autographed celebrity photos on the walls of the nominal birthplace of the chicken wing had extraordinary range and clarity.

It seemed too big to come out of such a small woman, too old to belong to someone barely twenty-five. Some of the patrons this Friday night in early October moved their lips along with her on "Night Time is the Right Time." Fingers tapped table tops, others kept time with the band. But most of them just watched Indigo in rapt silence.

The crowd was a mixture of young and old, black and white and brown, sports jerseys and sports jackets, tight jeans and casual dresses. Several were obviously suburban, having driven into downtown Buffalo from Amherst or Williamsville for a night of theater before stopping off for a snack. Others wearing hockey jerseys and carrying foam fingers looked as if they had come from the Sabres victory at Key Arena.

There were college kids, gangster-rap wannabes, old-timers who couldn't shake an outdated pimp look, and tourists who couldn't stop staring at the antique toys, sports gear, and musical instruments hanging from the ceilings, the multistate license plates on the walls, or the vintage motorcycles mounted high on special brackets.

As far as I could tell, it was an ordinary Friday night in one of the Nickel City's best loved establishments.

I sat alone at a small table opposite the bandstand, nursing a Corona and picking over the last of my suicide wings. I was in a perfect place to watch the main dining hall, the bar beyond it, and the parking lot entrance, as well as the emergency exit at the front of the building. My positioning was no accident. I had been hired to keep an eye out for the man stalking Indigo Waters.

"He's a big guy," she'd said in my Elmwood Avenue office the day before. In jeans and a print top, she was seated in one of the metal-frame client chairs in front of my desk. "I mean, you're no midget—and you'd look a lot scarier bald instead of having those big salt and pepper curls—but he's bigger than you, and he doesn't wear glasses, and he's younger."

"Young men can be dangerous," I said. "Especially when they don't wear glasses."

She ignored my stab at humor. "He's a real cop, so you being black won't matter to him either." Her southern accent gave an inescapable whisper of music to her speaking voice. I wasn't surprised. I'd seen her sing before.

"Mr. Rimes is a real cop," her lawyer said. "Or he was." Navy suit tailored to fit her tall, thin frame and medium-length black hair tied back to reveal the oval of her face, Phoenix Trinidad sat in the chair beside Indigo's. Though we had never met before she led her client into my office, each of us had known of the other because my godfather, Bobby Chance, was good friends with her mentor and law partner, Jonah Landsburgh. But it was apparent she knew more about me than I did about her. "He was career army. An MP. He served two tours in Iraq then went to work for the CID and earned an advanced degree in criminology before he retired."

"What's CID?" Indigo asked.

"Criminal Investigation Division," I said. "Army detectives."

Indigo scrutinized me closely, considering.

"He came home and took a campus police job at Buffalo State," Ms. Trinidad said.

"You went from army detective to rent-a-cop?" Indigo asked me.

Ms. Trinidad shook her head. "State University police have exactly the same training as New York State police. But Mr. Rimes didn't stay long." She hesitated. "After two years, he left and got a PI license."

Indigo shifted her gaze from her lawyer to me and back, as if waiting for more.

I leaned forward and looked directly at Ms. Trinidad. "You might as well tell her the rest of it." I hoped she would, because I didn't like talking about it.

Deep brown eyes never leaving mine, she smiled sadly, almost apologetically. I found myself appreciating the contrast between her apricot lipstick and light cinnamon skin.

"Mr. Rimes resigned from the campus police force after a shooting incident left two dead and a police officer paralyzed."

Indigo's already large eyes widened. "You killed somebody?"

"Yes," I said.

"Who? A student?"

"No." I sat back.

"Mr. Rimes did what he was trained to do," Ms. Trinidad said. "He neutralized the threat." She paused, and I thought I saw sympathy flicker in her eyes. "He killed the killer."

"*One* of the killers," I said. "The other one survived."

"You shot them both?"

"Yes."

Indigo looked at Ms. Trinidad. "When did all this happen?"

"About three years ago, before you came to Buffalo." She patted Indigo's forearm. "So this man is the real deal. He can protect you."

Indigo looked at the Real Deal again, curly hair, glasses, and all. I considered smiling but decided not to. We studied each other several seconds before she asked, "Who was he?"

"His name was Marv Tull," I said, resigned that I would have to talk about it—think about it—after all. I pulled off my stainless steel frames and tapped my lower lip with one of the stems. "He and his cousin Jasper went on a killing spree in Pennsylvania and were on the run to Canada when they stopped here. They ditched a stolen car in Delaware Park, behind the art gallery, and crossed over to Buff State. They were in a campus lot jacking a replacement when my partner and I rolled up on them."

"I think I heard about that…"

For a moment she looked past me, processing all she'd been told as I tried not to think of Solange Aucoin with a bullet in her left eye or Jimmy on his belly, lips kissing asphalt, as blood pooled around his midsection. The daughter of Parisian professors, Mademoiselle Aucoin had come to Buffalo State for graduate study in special education and was, by all accounts, delighted to have picked up a used yellow Hyundai two days before she died.

Jimmy Doran had slipped into his uniform and duty belt early that morning, kissed Peggy Ann goodbye, and walked through his front door for the last time. I seldom thought of the other victims of the shooting spree, Tull's parole officer and the people who died for their cars: the seventh grade teacher waiting at a red light in Pittsburgh, the vacationing Kansas couple in Erie, the old woman and her ten-year-old grandson in Jamestown.

The split second it took me to read the emptiness in Tull's eyes had not cost them their lives or their ability to walk. Sometimes that split-second felt like a century. The only thing that shortened it was the indignation I felt whenever I remembered that Jasper Hellman tried to sue me from prison over his colostomy bag.

Lower lip caught between my teeth, I slid my glasses back on.

"He's still bigger than you," Indigo said. "And younger."

"And a real cop," I said. I looked at the lawyer. "So why me? Why not go to his district commander or file an order of protection?"

Ms. Trinidad smiled again—beautiful white teeth, a gotcha smile if I ever saw one. "I hoped you'd want to help somebody you care about avoid embarrassment at a critical time. You see, the man bothering my client is Kenneth Carnahan, body-guard and personal driver to a friend of yours, Mayor Ophelia Green."

Chapter 2

Around midnight, the Jazz Blues Alliance finished their last set, Indigo's powerhouse "At Last" bringing diners and drinkers to their feet. The applause and whistles lasted a full five minutes. There were calls for an encore but there would be no encore. More restaurant than bar and more famous than the average neighborhood tavern or bottom-feeder pick-up joint, the Anchor did not remain open until four, closing time just about everywhere else in the Nickel City. When the clapping finally faded, the crowd began to file out, and the band packed their instruments.

Indi, as she had told me to call her when she led me to my table three hours earlier, dropped into the chair across from me, her forehead glistening.

"Etta James, eat your heart out," I said, my lips still tingling from the wings. "I don't know where you hide that voice."

Somewhat breathless, she half-smiled and thanked me. Then she began to fan herself with a menu from the table. "I always sweat like this by the end," she said. "But it's clean sweat, like sex."

I ignored the smile in her eyes and handed her the glass of ice water I got just before service stopped. She drained it.

"He swore he would see me tonight," she said. She set down the glass, and her fiery nails caught the overhead light. "But he didn't come." She sounded disappointed.

"No, he didn't." I sat back, discreetly adjusting the nylon Blackhawk shoulder rig that held my compact Glock 26 beneath my black leather jacket.

"Do you think it's because you called the mayor?"

"Maybe."

"What did she say?"

"She said she'd have a talk with him and settle this before it turned into a problem." A problem she could hardly afford with a tight election in less than a month. Ophelia had thanked me for the heads-up about one of her security staff and said it had been too long since we'd shared a beer and a game of darts. As soon as this election was over, she promised, we'd get together.

"You don't believe her?"

"I do believe her. Ophelia generally does what she says, but I also believe in being sure." I watched Indi for a moment. "Did you want him to come?"

She hesitated. "Maybe I just want to know it's over."

I nodded.

"What now?"

"I'm yours for the weekend," I said. "I take you home, check your place, and make sure you lock yourself in when I go. My associate watches your building all night, and I come pick you up in the morning."

She cocked her head. "You don't have to go, do you? Like home to your wife?"

"Don't have a wife," I said. I'd been married once but never shared that part of my life with clients. "I can sleep on your sofa if you'd feel safer."

"Rimes and Waters. We sound good together, like a drink." Her voice softened. She reached out to trace my mustache with her finger. "I got a real big bed."

"Then you can stretch out as much as you like," I said.

Full claret-colored lips pursing in a pout, she looked crestfallen. "You don't think I'm...worth it?"

"You are, but I can't look out *for* you if I spend all night looking *at* you and all day tomorrow falling asleep. Besides, I'm old enough to be your father."

"Young father maybe."

"Father is still the operative word. But thanks for the pretty thought." Her expression hovered somewhere between hurt and uncertainty. Clearly, she was used to hearing yes from men. "Look, isn't this what got you in trouble in the first place?" I said. "Kenny spent a couple months with you and couldn't let go." I chuckled and shook my head. "Maybe you *would* be the best lay of my life, and maybe I'd stalk you myself. Two stalkers with guns. You have to be smarter than that."

She lowered her eyes and looked away, perhaps embarrassed.

The pianist walked over. A dark, wiry man of medium height, he looked to be in his mid-sixties. He had a salt and pepper mustache, wire-rimmed glasses, thinning gray hair, and extraordinarily long fingers, which he held out to me. "Doc Rogers," he said, shaking my hand. His voice was as crisp as his tan suit.

"Gideon Rimes," I said.

"So you the brother Miss Trinidad got lookin' out for our little girl here."

Indi's cheeks darkened. "Doc."

"Doing my best," I said.

Doc pulled out a chair and sat. "Miss Indi here got a great future. Other girls her age just get stuck on hip-hop, but Indi got the good stuff in her blood." He gestured toward the other musicians. "Me and the fellas just one station on the way. Talent like hers got to break out and leave us old-timers behind. A year from now she'll have a contract with somebody—if the internet don't finish killin' the music business first." He looked at Indi. "That fella I know in New York'll be in town next month. We got to put on a dynamite show that night."

Indi took a deep breath. "Thanks, Doc." Then she stood, kissed his cheek, and went to the ladies' room to change.

The other musicians in the JBA drifted over, beers in hand, and grabbed chairs. Doc introduced us. Big Willy Simmons, the tenor sax player, was carrying two beers and put one in front of Doc. His forehead a sheen of sweat, Big Willy simply touched the bill of his black Breton cap. He was about Doc's age, had four inches on me, and wore an olive suit that would have been a perfect fit for a man thirty-five pounds heavier.

His smile was pleasant, despite uneven nicotine-stained teeth. Teddy Evans was a flat-faced old-school blues man, shorter than his bass. He had a full head of white hair and wore a black and tan tropical dress shirt over dark trousers. He knocked back half his beer before he shook my hand. The only white guy was drummer Dix Danishovsky, who looked perhaps ten years younger than the others. In a vest and slacks from a navy three-piece, he had a receding hairline and a neatly trimmed goatee shot through with gray.

After Doc explained why I was there, no one's face registered surprise that Indi was having man trouble. I made a mental note of that, wondering if she had caused any tension among the band or if they simply sensed she was the kind of woman who'd have man trouble. I asked if anyone knew anything about the men she dated, especially the one she'd been seeing lately. I watched their faces for a reaction, for flickers of jealousy, longing, or regret. I saw none. Also, though Dix recalled seeing "a big white boy" help her into a big black Chevy one Friday night last month, no one seemed to know her dating habits, and no one mentioned the mayor or her driver. Ophelia would be relieved.

"She's kind of private," Dix said, and the others bobbed their heads in agreement. "And we really don't have the time to share a lot of personal stuff. I mean, it may seem like we're having a good time up there—and we are—but this is work. We really don't hang out with each other all that often because we got day gigs—me and Teddy—and even if we had the time to fool around, Indi's kinda young. Man, my wife'd have my ass."

Teddy laughed. "Mine too."

"Me and Big Willy are retired," Doc said. "We practice at my house a couple nights a week. We play at different places most Saturdays, sometimes the Colored Musicians Club or a Canalside bar or a place near one of the colleges. Every summer we get a Wednesday at Larkinville. But *here* almost every Friday night is ours. Been that way a lot of years. I saw Indi sing at her college a few years back and invited her to audition for us after Nona died."

I remembered Nona Swanson from coming to the Anchor with Bobby now and again when I was on leave. A big-breasted light-skinned diva in her late seventies, she was a local legend who'd sung with some of the great names in blues and jazz. For fifteen years, she had rocked the Anchor Bar every Friday night with a combination of wild wigs, glittery gowns, sultry singing, a sweat-soaked handkerchief in her left hand, and raunchy double entendres directed at the men in the audience.

"Everybody knew Indi was special the minute she opened her mouth," Doc said. "We got a good thing here and she's a big part of it. If we knew she was havin' problems, we'd try to look out for her, same as we did for Nona when she couldn't get around so good."

Everyone nodded. I looked from face to face, convinced of their avuncular sincerity.

Arms folded atop the back of the chair he straddled, Teddy eyed me through tinted lenses. "So you think baby girl's in real danger?"

"*She* thinks so," I said.

"She be the one to know," Doc said.

"That's why her lawyer brought her to me."

Big Willy snorted then coughed, hard. Doc patted him on the back. "'Course she in real danger." Even as he tried to clear it, Big Willy's voice was a rumble deep enough to nudge a Richter needle. "Man, you know how we get when we young, dumb, and fulla come and *finally* get the one woman put everybody else to shame. That is *real* danger."

Dix and Teddy both laughed, but Doc lowered his eyes a bit, as if embarrassed.

"Doc, don't go pretendin' you don't know nothin' 'bout Wonder Pussy," Teddy said. "Bet Rimes here know all about it. Do just about anything to keep tappin' *that* shit."

"Anything," Big Willy said, fleshy lips peeling back in a nicotine grimace.

As Dix nodded and Teddy reached for his beer, Indi emerged from the ladies' room. The band fell silent, exchanging vaguely guilty looks as she moved toward the table. A black garment bag folded over her left arm and a shoe bag hanging from her right hand, she'd changed into jeans, low-cut boots, and a short brown leather jacket.

I stood. "Ready?"

"Yep."

We started out of the dining room.

Before we could cross the barroom, five men stepped inside from the parking lot. Amid bursts of laughter, it sounded as if they were having two simultaneous conversations—until the man in front saw me and stopped, forcing those behind him to stop as well. I shifted Indi behind me and slid my right hand inside my jacket.

The man at the point of the wedge formation facing me was Kenny Carnahan.

Chapter 3

Two of the men reached inside their jackets and one swung his arm behind his back, but Kenny held up a hand. All three froze, as did the two waitresses in my field of vision, the restaurant host at the lectern to my right, the woman behind the counter in the narrow gift shop nook, and the bartender to my left, whiskey glass and dish cloth still in hand.

Glad the men had come inside instead of fanning out in the parking lot—where they could surround us—I studied them in the heartbeat it took someone to speak. In dark jacket and khakis, Kenny was broad-shouldered, about six-three, with flaming red hair. Though he was in his early thirties, his freckled face was that of what he had been before manhood, a good-looking Irish kid, maybe a generation or two removed from South Buffalo to a more affluent part of town. I'd met him at a few public events and, once or twice, at Ophelia's house in North Buffalo. I knew he'd taken a bullet during his time on the Gang Crimes Task Force. We'd never had a chance to talk, and I hadn't formed an opinion of him, but I figured that was about to change.

His companions, in jackets and slacks of various colors, were men I had never seen before. Two—one bald and the color of a burnt chestnut, the other gray-haired and pallid—were taller than Kenny. The bald man wore a loose-fitting dark leather jacket and a black mustache. Gray Hair was the oldest. An outdated brown suit hung on his shoulders, and he had a pocked, angular face I couldn't read. The other men were shorter than Kenny but not by much. The shortest looked Latino, with a thin mustache, thick black hair beneath a brown fedora tilted back on his head, and wide shoulders straining the seams of a rust-colored sports jacket. A wooden toothpick moved from one side of his mouth to the other. Something about him and the bald man said *cop*. The youngest, a redhead in a blue nylon shell, looked as if he and Kenny shared DNA.

"Easy, my brother," the bald man said, trying to make his deep voice soothing. "I don't know what's up, but things don't have to go down this way. You know we're on the job."

"I know," I said.

"If something bad just happened here, nobody needs to get hurt."

"It's nothing like that." I took in a long slow breath and let it out. "Officer, I'm a licensed private investigator and I have a carry permit. I'm working here."

"Detective sergeant," the man corrected me. "What you carrying?"

"Baby Glock," I said.

"You're the mayor's friend, Rimes," Kenny said matter-of-factly. "You were a pallbearer at her husband's funeral. I drove the two of you to a couple of banquets. She said they hired you to bodyguard Indigo."

"Did she tell you to leave Ms. Waters alone?"

The two I had pegged as cops exchanged surprised glances and looked at Kenny, who said, "She did."

"Then why the *fuck*—"

"Indi!" I snapped. When she fell silent, I said, "Doc, keep her with the band." I listened for Doc's footsteps then felt Indi pulled away from me. I didn't look over my shoulder but I sensed the band gathering around her, shuffling back into the dining room. I said to Kenny, "The mayor told you to leave her alone but you're here anyway."

"Indi doesn't need a bodyguard," he said. "Not with me. I'd never hurt her." He angled his head, as if looking past me. "Baby, we can work things out," he called. "I just want to talk to you."

"Even if you lose your job?" I needed to keep him focused on me, and I needed to be the calm side of the conversation so the cops would read things correctly and drag him out before he forced my hand and somebody died.

"So I won't drive the mayor anymore, but my job is safe." He shrugged. "I got a medal says I'm a hero." Then he laughed. "Besides, I belong to the union."

Gray Hair chuckled, and the one who looked like a younger Kenny thrust a fist into the air. "PBA, yeah!"

I was pleased the cops, still frozen, did not react. Their eyes said they were still assessing.

"Who's that next to you?" I asked.

"My brother Lenny."

Kenny and Lenny. *Great*, I thought. *Vaudeville.* "Lenny, you a cop too?"

Lenny waved aside the idea. "Hey, man, I'm just along for moral support." The pitch of his voice placed him around college age, and the slurred words and glazed eyes indicated too many beers. He was nothing more than a kid thrilled to be hanging out with his brother and the big boys. The Latino cop looked at him and frowned, as if annoyed by the same thought.

"My problem, Kenny, is I wasn't hired to let you talk to her. I was hired to keep you from stalking her."

He spread his hands apart to show me he posed no threat. "Seriously, dude, I'm no stalker." He looked at his friends as if expecting them to verbalize their agreement. No one moved. Gray Hair, the unreadable man, appeared to smile faintly.

"She doesn't want to see you anymore. She doesn't want to talk. If you keep trying to make her, you *are* a stalker." I looked past Kenny at the detective sergeant and tried to hold his gaze. "What's the worst kind of call a patrol officer can get?"

"Domestic," he answered without missing a beat. The Latino cop nodded. They might be in plainclothes now but everyone started out in patrol.

"Why?"

"Because the situation is always volatile, totally unpredictable."

"Right," I said. "From smiles to smackdowns in seven seconds."

"Truth," he said.

During my time in the CID, I had investigated the aftermath of on-post domestic disturbances. The childless wife who poisoned her officer husband, then herself, rather than face the loneliness of posting to a new base from which he would begin yet another extended deployment. The colonel who ended his son's long-standing rebelliousness with a .45 caliber bullet. The drill sergeant still at his kitchen table, face frozen in surprise at the meat cleaver embedded in his skull. But I had gone from being an MP in a combat zone to a CID officer on post. I had never answered a domestic disturbance call, never found myself in the charged ribbon of space between battling lovers or angry parents and children where truces could collapse in a heartbeat. Shooting down a decorated cop and getting shot by his peers was hardly how I had envisioned my first time in that DMZ.

"So if you're all carrying and domestics are by nature unpredictable," I said, "you've got to understand how tense I'm feeling right about now."

"I do," the detective said.

"Then do us all a favor and take your friend back to the car. Drive away. Tell him to pick up a six-pack, to go finish getting blitzed with his brother then move on with his life."

Lenny reddened. "Man, he can't talk about you like that," he said. "You're a cop, a real cop." He looked at the others. "You're *all* cops. He's just some no-name security guard. In *glasses*." He turned from them to me. "Shit, *I* could kick your ass, fucker!"

"Somebody talk to Lenny," I said.

Kenny glanced at him. "Be quiet, bro."

"But you could—"

"Shut up!" Kenny said, wheeling on Lenny. Then he shifted his attention back to me but continued to talk to his brother. "Rimes was a cop, in the army and at Buff State. And he served with the mayor's husband in Iraq. He knows what he's doing." Kenny's jaw tightened as if he was considering every possibility. He obviously knew I had killed before, in the service of my country and my state. I hoped the look in my eyes told him he couldn't reason me into standing down, even against these odds. He couldn't get to his gun before I'd have mine out. Even if my death was a certainty—and we both knew it was—I'd probably tag him first, and his little brother might get hurt in the crossfire. After several seconds, Kenny sucked his teeth and looked at Lenny, who was waiting to be told what to do. "Remember those spree killers, Hellman and Tull?"

"Killers?" Lenny was too buzzed to mask his confusion.

"I remember," the Latino cop said. "Shit went down at the college a few years back."

"So what's that got to do with anything?" Lenny said.

Before Kenny could answer, the bald detective cleared his throat. "Rimes is the one who took 'em out, dickhead. Remember, Rafael?"

"Right," the Latino cop said, narrowing his eyes and almost cracking a smile. "You're *that guy*."

Lenny said nothing, just stood there gaping at me.

"He *will* shoot," the detective said. "Believe it."

Lenny blinked repeatedly, as if struggling to bring me into focus. "Fuck!" he breathed.

I couldn't tell whether his exclamation was newfound respect for me or just frustration he wouldn't get to kick my ass after all, that he'd have to show off for the big kids another day.

Eyes on mine, the bald detective relaxed, withdrew his hand from his jacket, and kept his arms at his sides. "Look, this craziness is about to get out of hand for no reason. Kenny, man, I thought I was coming to meet your girl, and you go dragging me into some domestic bullshit. I oughta beat your ass myself." He gave Kenny a playful smack against the back of his head. Then he looked at the other men and settled on me. "We can dial it down, Rimes."

My instinct told me to trust him. I nodded and withdrew my hand as the Latino cop and the unreadable man relaxed. "You're gonna want to see my permit," I said.

"Yeah, I guess I got to."

"Everything is in my front left pocket." I moved toward him, patting my jeans before pulling out my wallet and opening it to the windows with my PI license and gun permit. When I reached him, I handed everything over. He read my credentials, gave a slight nod to the others, and handed the wallet back.

"Terry Chalmers," he said. We shook hands after I slid the wallet away. Then he cocked his head toward the Latino cop. "My partner, Detective Pinero." Pinero snapped two fingers toward me in a reverse salute.

No one had introduced the gray-haired man. That was certainly worth a mental note.

"One more thing," I said, holding my jacket open and positioning myself so that only Chalmers could see me reach into my inside breast pocket for a folded packet of papers with a blue cover. I turned to Kenny and slapped the packet into his hand before he could register what it was. "Order of protection," I said. "Signed by Judge Kayla Baker McQueen. You are not to come within a hundred yards of Indigo Waters. Nor are you permitted to contact her by telephone or any other means. Kenneth Carnahan, you've been served."

I took a few steps back as Kenny looked at the order, his mouth open and his eyes transitioning from surprise to anger. "As of this minute," I said to Chalmers, "your boy is in violation and is subject to arrest."

"Fuck you, Rimes!" Kenny threw the order to the floor and would have stomped up to me if Chalmers and Pinero hadn't held him back. "And fuck that judge! Bitch!"

Chalmers picked up the order, then gripped Kenny's elbow. "Time to go, man."

"Okay, we'll go," Kenny said, shrugging off his friends. "Call it professional courtesy we didn't shoot your ass down like a dog, Rimes." He looked at Lenny. "Besides, Mom and Dad would have my balls on a hoagie roll if something happened to my brother." He laughed at his own joke as Chalmers took hold of his arm again. The others parted so Chalmers could pull him toward the door. "Hey, Indigo, you and me?"

Kenny shouted. "We're still gonna talk, baby. You know you got nothing to be afraid of, not from me. But I can't let you blow me off like we didn't mean something special. That hurts way too much. Hear me?"

Then they were all outside. Gray Hair was the last to leave and glanced back at me as he did so.

I went to the door just in time to see the doors close on a black Chevy Tahoe. The windows were tinted but Kenny must have been driving because it squealed out of the lot.

Just when it seemed that common sense, blood bonds, the brotherhood of the badge, and a court order trumped Wonder Pussy, testosterone had to lift its ugly, stiffening head. *God damn it, Ophelia*, I thought. *Why can't you have happily married old cops in the rotation for your security detail?*

Chapter 4

Indi's apartment was in a light-colored brick building on Linwood Avenue, a quarter mile from the bar. I parked my dark blue Ford Escape beneath a tree near her front entrance then got out and held the door for her. The whole time I looked around for signs of movement inside other parked cars. Nothing.

At the front door I held the garment bag while Indi flipped through the keys on a gold carabiner and slid one into the lock. Wordlessly, she pushed open the door. We passed a row of mailboxes and climbed three flights to her apartment, with Indi so close I could feel her trembling. She seemed as unsettled by the tone of Kenny's voice as I was. Maybe more.

That hurts way too much. Translation: *I'm the victim here.* Corollary: *This is all your fault.* All were lyrics in the universal song of the stalker, the anthem of both the unapologetic abuser and the tearful killer standing over his woman's dead body: *Baby, now look what you made me do!*

Indi unlocked her apartment door. We stepped into a dark room whose oversized window looked out onto Linwood Avenue. I handed back the garment bag and crossed the room. I closed the curtains before I signaled for Indi to turn on the lights. She flicked a wall switch, and two floor lamps revealed we were in a white living room with a hardwood floor, navy curtains, and a dining nook at the far end.

The furnishings were simple: loveseat and armchair, pressboard bookcase, flat screen TV and sound system on separate stands, a two-seater dinette set in the nook with a laptop computer open on the table.

"Lock the door and stand right here," I said.

She nodded, and I noticed her eyes had filled.

"You're safe now," I said. "But I'll stay. Once I check the apartment, I'll call my associate and tell him I won't need him."

Nodding again, she sniffled loudly and wiped her nose with a tissue from her purse. Then she shot the deadbolt, put on the security chain, and faced me again.

"And just so you know, I will be opening your cupboards and closets and drawers."

She sniffed again but this time shook her head.

"It's non-negotiable," I said.

"How come?"

"Because sometimes people leave a little surprise where you least expect it."

"Like a…like a bomb?"

"Could be. Maybe something else, like bleach and ammonia rigged to mix and make poison gas." I paused to let that sink in. "Is Kenny the outdoorsy type?"

"What do you mean?"

"Hunting? Fishing?"

She chewed her lip. "I think he said something once about hunting. Why?"

"Because being in the woods might give him ideas for tokens of his affection. Access to poisonous plants. Or spiders or snakes."

She wrinkled her nose. "Snakes?"

"The Massasauga rattler can be found in the wild in central and western New York and over the border in southern Ontario, all places folks from around here go to hunt or fish."

For a half dozen heartbeats she looked at me as if I were a Massasauga rattler. "How do you know all this shit?"

"I like to read," I said.

"Then check the drawers," she said. "You believe in being sure."

"That's why I wouldn't take the job unless you got a re-straining order."

It was a small apartment with just one entrance and off-white walls in every room—a sliver of a kitchen, a single bed-room, a bathroom with a claw-footed tub and a floor of small hexagonal tiles. I went through everything—kitchen cupboards and drawers, food storage containers, the oven, the noisy fridge, the medicine cabinet. I used a curved umbrella handle to push aside the shoes on the floor of the bedroom closet, a plastic hanger to poke through dresser drawers and the linen closet, and my nose to check cosmetics containers and medi-cine bottles for hints of contamination.

On one corner of the dresser sat a lacquered jewelry box with six drawers of various sizes. Behind the jewelry box was a manila envelope which held a high school diploma from Baxley, Georgia, and a Bachelor's degree from Paine College in Augusta. Around the edges of the large mirror were photo-graphs of Indi with people I had never seen, in places I had never been—likely Baxley and Paine. Some featured a young Indi holding a microphone and singing on what seemed a school stage. Others put her in front of a church choir in gold and blue robes beneath a painting of Jesus surrounded by chil-dren from around the world.

On the floor by the queen-sized bed was a stack of books, from romances and mysteries to self-help guides and celebrity biographies. One title caught my eye. As I decided to ask Indi about it, I opened the nightstand drawers. The upper was clut-tered with nail clippers, aspirin, loose coins, a pen and note-book set, a few bottles of nail polish, and several pieces of cos-tume jewelry. Inside the lower drawer were condoms in a small plastic bowl, tubes of massage oils, fuzzy pink hand-cuffs, edible panties, vibrators, Ben Wa balls, and feather tick-lers. Poor Kenny, I thought. He wanted to deliver her from her experimental phase, to make her want only him, when what *she* wanted most was pleasure itself. The image of Indi's toys working their magic in another man's hands had to hurt.

Always volatile. Totally unpredictable.

She was standing by the door when I returned to the living

room, but the garment bag and shoe bag were on the loveseat.

"No bombs, no snakes, no bedbugs," I said.

She came across the room in two strides and threw her arms around me. "Thank God!" she said. "Thank you!"

Her relief sounded genuine but the press of her jeans into mine made me disengage myself and hold her at arm's length. "I do need to ask you something," I said. "About something I found."

"Oh." For the second time tonight I saw her blush.

"A book in your pile," I said, fighting back a grin. "A privately printed book called *A Vision for the City of Buffalo.*"

"Yeah?"

"It's Republican campaign literature from Richard Merlotta, who's running against Ophelia Green for mayor."

"So?"

"I just find it curious you're being stalked by the mayor's bodyguard and you have a book by the opposition candidate."

Indi frowned.

If I had been younger, less conscientious, and hoping to spend the night in her bed, my chance would have died in that instant.

"Most people look at me like I'm all voice and no brains," she said, her accent gaining ground in the swirl of her anger. "Well, surprise. I like to read too."

"Look, I didn't mean to—"

But I never got the chance to finish my explanation or apology or whatever it would have become. Indi swept past me, scooped up her bags, disappeared into her bedroom, and slammed the door. Later, I heard her come out and go into the bathroom, then start a bath and lock the door. When the drumming of the water stopped, I could hear the strains of soft jazz from an all-night radio program and, I imagined the scented candles I had noticed earlier now flickering on the sink and toilet tank. By the time she finished her soak, turned off the radio, and returned to her room—in a robe or naked I couldn't say because I didn't look—I had used my cell phone to give LJ the night off and had slid the loveseat in front of the door. I settled in the armchair, facing the makeshift barricade. My feet on a small ottoman and the Glock in my lap, I closed my eyes for a combat nap. And still wondered why Indi had Wreck-It Rick Merlotta's book by her bed.

Chapter 5

By the time Indi woke, around eight, I had been up for nearly two hours, drinking instant coffee out of a Barack Obama mug and working the soreness out of my back and legs. After dozing fitfully, I was stiff and tired but only mildly hungry after last night's wings. Indi hadn't eaten late and would likely need something soon. Unfortunately, nothing resembling breakfast food was in the refrigerator or the cupboard. I was standing near the large window when Indi stepped into the living room. A blue robe wrapped around her, she dropped into the armchair, which I had returned to its prior location, and yawned.

"Doesn't taste like Tim Horton's," I said, "but there's coffee in the kitchen."

"Thanks," she said, stretching. "Just give me a minute."

It was a sunny Saturday with few clouds and enough breeze to send fallen red and gold maple leaves skittering about the street. I stared down at Linwood Avenue, as if waiting for a cab, but actually surveying the street for the black Tahoe. Relieved to see no black SUV of any kind, I contemplated my next move. Food for Indi? No problem. Buffalo had no shortage of places for a leisurely weekend breakfast. Then what? Plan how to babysit Indi during the day. At some point call Indi's lawyer to tell her I was glad she had followed both my advice to file a restraining order and my recommendation of a willing judge. Another call to Ophelia, who was already on the ropes in the polls because of an unexpected turn in her East

Side development program. She could ill afford negative publicity, which was why Ms. Trinidad, whose partner was a major contributor, had come to me in the first place.

The coffee would keep me charged awhile but, eventually, I'd need to crash. I would have to stash my client somewhere safe. I couldn't take her to LJ's home because I never intended for them to meet, just that he should watch her place and call me at once if anything seemed wrong. LJ was a senior at Buffalo State, a computer systems major with a criminal justice minor. He still lived with his parents and did me the occasional paid favor. I glanced at Indi. Toenails ablaze, legs longer and more muscled than her height would have suggested, a taut chocolate thigh visible where one edge of the robe had fallen open—or been flipped back. One up-close look at her would send LJ's twenty-one-year-old hormones into hyper drive. His parents would never forgive me.

Indi stood and smiled, the previous night's anger apparently gone. She made a brief show of retying her robe and went into the kitchen. A minute later she returned, sipping from a dark blue mug.

"Tonight the band's at the Shadow Lounge on Hertel," I said.

"Yes. We set up by eight-thirty and start around nine."

"What do you absolutely have to do today?"

She shrugged. "My outfit for tonight is at the dry cleaners."

"Anything else?"

"I have to pull together some activities for my kids on Monday, so I need a little time online." She started to raise the mug then stopped and grimaced. "You don't think he'd come to my regular job, do you?"

Indi worked as a preschool teacher—according to Ms. Trinidad, a very good one—on the ground floor of Hope's Haven, a sprawling Main Street almost-mansion in the University District. All three floors of what once had been the home and medical office of a revered family practitioner had been converted into a comprehensive women's services center, with an emergency shelter, a clinic, a counseling department, GED and job training classes, and a licensed preschool. Established by a bequest from steel heiress Hope Driscoll Osgood, the center was funded by an endowment and grants—and represented in all matters legal by Phoenix Trinidad, Esquire. Would Kenny dare show up at Indi's day gig and make a scene amid children and displaced homemakers?

Always volatile. Totally unpredictable.

"I don't know." I let out a long breath. "But I'll be there to persuade him to leave."

"Better you than our security guards. They're like eighty." She still held the mug a few inches below her chin. "What am I gonna do, Rimes?"

"With any luck, we'll settle it before then." I sidled past her into the kitchen and rinsed the Barack Obama mug. "Meantime, finish your coffee and get dressed." I set the mug in the sink. "I'm taking you to see Bobby for breakfast."

Chapter 6

While many Buffalo retirees abandoned the city and its legendary—often exaggerated—snow, my godfather always felt most at home in the Elmwood Village, a stretch of shops, galleries, restaurants, and bars that began where Buffalo State and the Albright Knox Art Gallery faced each other across Elmwood Avenue and ended in the Allentown district. When he retired from Buff State ten years earlier, Bobby—Robert Chance, PhD—sold the cozy west side house where I'd lived since my father died and bought an Elmwood Avenue apartment house five blocks away. The twelve-unit sandstone property was squeezed between two tall Victorian houses south of West Ferry. A quarter mile from my office, Bobby's building had three stories, flagstone steps leading to a central front door, and large bay windows in the six apartments facing the avenue.

The building was rundown and vacant when Bobby bought it, remodeled a top floor apartment, and moved in. I was stationed in South Korea then and cringed at the first pictures he sent me. Gradually, however, as he invested more and more of Evelyn's life insurance, his photos showed a building in transition. Within a year, the outside had been hydroblasted and the inside fully renovated. Each five-room unit had high filigree ceilings, new cabinets and plumbing fixtures, and red oak wainscoting. Bobby offered his first apartment—ground floor rear—to Sam Wingard, a retiree from Buffalo State's physical plant. Sam lived rent free, his apartment part of his compensation for building maintenance. The remaining units had rented quickly and stayed occupied.

I explained Bobby's building to Indi as we drove from her place to his. What I didn't share was that the apartment below his had become available three months before I left the army, and he'd held it for me. Whatever the outcome of this dance with Kenny Carnahan, I didn't want to answer my door one evening to find Indi wearing nothing but a trench coat.

"How did your parents die?" she asked as I turned onto Lexington. Though leaves had begun to turn and fall, there was still a dense canopy of green overhead.

"My mother had a brain aneurysm," I said. "She died when I was seven, and my dad died after a fall from a ladder, about five years later."

"Oh, that's so sad!" Indi laid her fingers on my right forearm. "I'm sorry."

"Thanks. It was a long time ago. Bobby helped me understand that death, in one way or another, always leads to new life."

Her fingers remained on my arm until I slowed, about halfway down the block, and braked alongside a silver Chrysler Crossfire. Then she withdrew them as I shifted into reverse and spun the wheel to back into a space. I straightened out, inched toward the back of the Crossfire, and turned off the engine.

"So your godparents raised you. Were they friends with your parents?"

"Not at first," I said. "Bobby was a professor at Buffalo State, which had a mostly white faculty then. He didn't have a lot of friends. My dad was the janitor who cleaned his office in the evening. One evening Bobby was working late and my dad got into a discussion with him."

"That's how they became friends?"

"They bonded over books," I said. We climbed out. I pushed the LOCK button on the remote and pocketed my key ring. "My dad was a great reader. Anything he could get his hands on." I joined Indi on the sidewalk and we started toward Elmwood. "For Bobby, my dad was a kindred spirit, and they swapped and discussed books, and then movies and sports and politics. Pretty soon they were fishing and bowling together."

"What about your mother and his wife?"

"They got to be friends too but not as close as my dad and Bobby. After my mother died, I used to go to their house after school while Dad was still at work. I had dinner with them and got help with my homework."

"Did your godparents have children of their own?"

I shook my head but said nothing of Evelyn's repeated miscarriages or the glaze that even now covered Bobby's eyes when he spoke about her. "They took in foster children from time to time, but most of them were short-term placements. They took legal guardianship of only two, me and the woman who became my sister."

"Tell me about her."

"Maybe later. Since you're about to meet Bobby, first I should tell you about *him*. He can help you find stuff to do with your class. I bet he can give you five good ideas before you enter Google."

"Okay," she said, as if doubtful.

So I told her about Bobby. By nature a nurturer, he was, quite simply, the smartest man I'd ever known. It wasn't just that he read three or four books a week and remembered long passages almost verbatim or that he spoke French and Spanish fluently and had studied both Chinese and Swahili. It wasn't that he carried one of his many telescopes up to the roof of his building on clear summer nights to watch the stars, whatever the ambient light of the Village, or that he could discuss with encyclopedic authority almost any subject, from music, law, and architecture to history, science, and the arts. People constantly told him he should go on *Jeopardy* without realizing he had already been there, lasting six days before being upended by a California librarian. No, what made most people see Bobby as brilliant was that his was the most *infectious* intelligence they had ever encountered. He could hold enthralled for an hour or more not only a classroom full of students with a common objective but any ragtag group who stood still long enough to listen to two sentences. And at the end of their time with him, most people felt not just smarter but *cheerfully* so. Part philosopher, part storyteller, and part natural psychologist, Bobby was inspirational, a born teacher. "The kind of man," I said, "whose hemlock cup would have been monogrammed."

"I don't understand," Indi said.

"Like Socrates," I said. "Ancient Greece."

"What did he teach?"

"Socrates?"

She rolled her eyes. "Your godfather."

I smiled as we rounded the corner. "Bobby was an English professor and he still looks the part, but there's nothing absent-minded about him. He just *knows* things, a little bit about everything. Some of his friends call him Bobbypedia."

"Is he where you got the stuff about poisons and rattlesnakes?"

"Some of it. I read a lot too. But I don't always remember where specific things come from."

When we reached the building, I led her up the steps and opened the outer door. Indi followed me into the vestibule. I rang Bobby's bell rather than use my key on the inner door. Presently, the small speaker in the brass intercom crackled: "Yes?"

I held the button. "It's me, Bobby."

Even if I hadn't called ahead, he would have buzzed us in without asking about my key. Despite having what I called the teacher's disease—the need to share everything in his head as if retaining it would lead to a cerebral explosion—Bobby was very discreet.

Bobby and Kayla, in matching white terry robes and wearing their glasses, were waiting for us at the top of the carpeted stairs on the third floor. I hadn't told Indigo about Bobby's longtime lover, Family Court Judge Kayla Baker McQueen, but when I called he hadn't mentioned she was with him. I liked Kayla and thought she was the best thing that had happened to him since he took early retirement a year after Evelyn died. A russet-skinned divorcee with a short black perm and sharp eyes, Kayla was about Bobby's age and a few inches shorter than his five-foot-eight. Despite a reputation as a tough

jurist, she was patient with his chatter and seemed to understand the elliptical spin of his brain. Clearly, she both admired
and cared for him, but I saw her as a necessary balance to his
life. Likewise, he was devoted to her, had traveled with her to
Hawaii, Greece, and Senegal, had even moved into her waterfront condo during her recuperation from surgery two summers
earlier. In their five years together, they had discussed marriage several times, but each seemed to cling to the independ-
ence their arrangement offered. Either way, I was glad they
had each other.

As I led Indi upstairs, Kayla cocked an eyebrow at me, as if
inquiring whether I'd served the order of protection Phoenix
Trinidad had asked her to sign. I offered her a faint nod to confirm I had.

After I introduced Indi to them, Bobby took her hand. "I
can't believe I have Indigo Waters in my home," he said in his
rich tenor voice. Indi's cheeks darkened, and she lowered her
eyes. "We've seen you sing many times," he added. "Haven't
we, Kayla?"

Kayla smiled. "You always bring us to our feet."

"You have a marvelous voice," Bobby continued. "Just
marvelous. I am honored you're here. Welcome." His deep
brown face split into a wide grin. The sparse silver hairs high
on his forehead seemed to ignite with excitement. He led Indi
into his apartment as Kayla and I followed. As instructed, Ms.
Trinidad had used my name when she approached the judge,
but Kayla and I hadn't seen each other in weeks. Now we exchanged catch-up pleasantries on the way into the living room.
She was especially excited her only daughter Alaila, an actress
based in Manhattan, had a small but pivotal part in the touring
company of *Past Imperfect*, a popular Broadway musical coming to the Shea's Performing Arts Center in February.

"Dinner's on me the night we go," I said.

Indi stopped and looked at the ceiling-high bookcases
which occupied two walls and flanked the bay window that
overlooked Elmwood. For a long time, she just stared at the
spines, from rich leather to faded cloth to cracked paper, at the
rolling library ladder attached to a curved steel rail connecting

all the bookcases, at the unabridged dictionary open on a pivoting desktop stand beside Bobby's computer. Never seeming to notice the flat screen TV and sound system in the corner or the matching leather couch and armchair, she turned to my godfather and let her mouth fall open as if in surprise. "He told me you liked to read," she said, jerking a thumb in my direction, "but *damn*!"

Kayla moved to Indi and took her arm. "Dusting them is a real pain. I bought him an iPad last summer but he hardly ever uses it."

"I like the feel of books," Bobby said. "I use the iPad for chess and Scrabble."

"And then there is the problem of book mold," Kayla continued. "Sometimes, if you stay in here too long, you start coughing." She steered Indi toward the kitchen. "You must be hungry." They pushed past the refinished swinging door, and I heard Indi's breath catch at the sight of the modern stainless steel kitchen in which Bobby took great pride.

"We've already made vegetable cheese omelets," Bobby said, beginning to follow, "but if you'd prefer pancakes, I think I can whip some up pretty quickly."

I touched Bobby's arm. He stopped and turned to me. I explained quickly why Indi was with me and what had happened last night. "I need her to stay here for two hours or so while I take care of a couple things."

Bobby narrowed his eyes at me, glasses sliding down a notch. "One of which I hope is sleep."

"Yes."

"Do you need to eat first?"

"I'm hungry but I'll wait. I'll appreciate the food more if I sleep first."

He nodded. "I'll buzz you if she gets restless."

"Thanks, Bobby." I hesitated. "You and Kayla don't have plans, do you?"

"Not apart from spending the day together."

"Good. I'm glad she's here."

I loved the way Bobby's eyes crinkled when he smiled. "Me too," he said.

Once inside my apartment, I called Ophelia on my mobile phone and told her about my encounter with Kenny and Lenny, about Kenny's general lack of concern for his job. "This court order is going to be embarrassing," I said, "but not the freak show you'd have if one of us put the other one down."

"I thought it might come to this," Ophelia said. "You're both stubborn bastards, but *you* don't work for me. You said no the last time I asked."

"And will the next time. I know where I don't belong, Ophelia."

She sighed but the edge remained in her voice. "Do what you gotta do."

"Always," I said as my phone beeped its low battery alert.

After Ophelia hung up I plugged my mobile into its charger and went into my bedroom to call the lawyer on my land line. "Ms. Trinidad?"

"Phoenix," she said. "Call me Phoenix."

I thought about that for a moment. Then I told her about crossing paths with Kenny and my conversation with Ophelia and said I thought Kenny would likely violate the order of protection. "The police won't come in time. One of us is going to have to hurt the other one."

"It's Saturday morning," she said. "I doubt he'll try anything right now but stick with her through this evening. I'll call Marla at Hope's Haven for emergency placement."

"Indi says the guards there are eighty years old."

"To her. The alarm panel has a direct-line panic button to the nearest police station."

"Good." I looked at the radio receiver beside the phone on my nightstand. The red light indicated my own private security link to upstairs was working. If Indi tried to leave, Bobby would push a button and the receiver would buzz loud enough to wake me. "Just so you know," I said, "we're at my building right now."

Phoenix paused to take in a deep breath and let out her exasperation. "What, you didn't think Kenny could figure out where you live?"

"Actually, she's upstairs," I said. "With Judge McQueen."

She was silent a moment. "You like to surprise me, don't you, Gideon?"

I gave her my address and said I would call her later. Then I stripped to my shorts and put my glasses and gun on the nightstand. I crawled into bed and closed my eyes. My last thought before sinking into peace was that, even though just about everyone but Bobby called me G or just plain Rimes, I liked hearing Phoenix Trinidad say my given name.

Chapter 7

Saturday evening I cut the ignition and climbed out of my Escape to survey the half block of Hertel Avenue that separated my front bumper from the Shadow Lounge. Seeing nothing out of the ordinary, I rounded the car and held open the door for Indi, who emerged in jeans and her brown leather jacket and carried her garment bag, shoe bag, and a black clutch purse. As we neared the Shadow, I noted that every table beneath the black awning over the front patio was occupied but none of the diners and early drinkers bore any resemblance to Kenny.

Inside, the overhead lighting was soft, but strings of red LED lights set at various heights along the crimson stucco walls and behind the bar stretched the entire length of the split-level interior. A sizable crowd was already at the bar, to the right of the door, and most of the tables had two or three customers. The air carried sounds of talking and laughing and drinking. I saw Doc Rogers and the JBA setting up in the performance space just past the bar but none of them noticed us. We stopped at the hostess station, tended by a slender, black-clad woman with short blonde hair and a silver nose ring.

"Is Grace here?" I asked. Grace Patterson, the owner, was an old friend of Bobby's.

The woman smiled at me. "Are you Dr. Chance?"

"Rimes," I said. "I'm in Dr. Chance's party." I turned to Indi. "Ms. Waters here sings with the band."

The woman gave me a look that said she knew who Indi

was and led us to a round bar table right across from where the
band would play. She took the hand-lettered RESERVED sign
from the red tablecloth. Before returning to the hostess station,
she steered a freckle-faced server with spiked hair and a tight
skirt toward me. Unzipping my jacket only part way to keep
my Glock hidden, I ordered a Corona with lime. As Indi disappeared into the ladies' room, I slid onto one of the four bar
chairs that semi-circled the table. I sat with the door on my
right and my back to an elevated dining area. To my left were
restrooms, more dining tables, the kitchen door, and another
elevated section against the rear wall. With minimal effort I
could watch the entire room, even when the floor thickened
with dancing.

When my Corona came, I pushed the lime wedge into the
bottle and took a swig.

Having exchanged a greeting with Indi, Doc came over and
shook my hand. His suit tonight was pearl gray, his tie deep
red. "Glad to see ya, Rimes," he said. Then he leaned close
enough for me to smell his Old Spice and lowered his voice.
"Man, things got wild last night." He furrowed his brow.
"You'da shot that boy if you had to, wouldn't ya?"

"It all worked out."

"Just the same, me and the fellas are grateful to you for
lookin' after our girl."

"Glad to." I looked over at the band, inadvertently catching
Big Willy's eye. He gave me a half-hearted wave. I looked
back at Doc, who straightened to his full height. "I see you
have a keyboard tonight," I said, tipping my bottle toward an
expensive-looking black unit he had set on a metal stand moments earlier. "I'd have pegged you as a die-hard piano man."

He held out his fingers and flexed them, as if playing. "I am
but not every place got a piano. She may not be the love of my
life but that old keyboard ain't never complained 'bout bein'
my back-up sweetie. You gotta make do on the road."

"You on the road often?"

"Not so much anymore. Used to travel a whole lots—bus,
train, car. I been at this for a long time, almost thirty-five
years. Played in thirty-eight states in a dozen different bands."

"I'm impressed. That's why you're so good."

He waved away my compliment and snorted. "Sometimes bein' good means knowin' when to get out the way."

"Indi."

"Yeah, Indi," he said. "Gal gonna go places."

I noted the hope in Doc's eyes and remembered something I'd intended to ask Indi. "Why jazz and blues? Why not hip-hop or something more appealing to a younger set?"

Doc shrugged. "Hard to do when real music's in your blood." He went back to the band, and I went back to scanning the room.

A few minutes later, the ladies' room door swung open, and Indi stepped out in tight black leather pants and a low-cut yellow satin blouse. Black patent leather stilettos added four inches to her height. She wore a yellow flower in her hair, as well as a black onyx necklace and matching bracelet. She carried the garment bag, bottom-heavy with the shoe bag zipped inside it. She walked over to the table, eased me forward, and folded the bag over the back of my chair.

"You mind?" she said. "No place else to put it." She blew me a kiss and crossed over to the band.

As I sat back and adjusted my jacket against the garment bag, I glanced at my watch. The Jazz Blues Alliance wouldn't start playing for another twenty minutes. When I wasn't looking at the front door or watching people at the bar, I studied Indi as she chatted with the band. She laughed, did a mike check, and exchanged greetings with some of the patrons, who had started to gather near.

Last night, after wondering whether she was a source of stress, I had concluded the band's feelings toward her were more protective than prurient. Now I saw nothing to suggest my take was wrong. She probably found them too old to flirt with the way she kept flirting with me. All except Dix, who with his goatee and tan corduroy sports jacket looked attractive in a late middle-age professorial way. But he carried drumsticks, not a gun, like Kenny and, now, me.

Maybe Dix wasn't dangerous enough for Indi. Maybe the need for protection that inspired the band to look after her was

like a high-intensity beacon to dangerous men, an unerring
signal which drew them to her. For a moment, I turned that
over in my mind. Was Kenny just the first of many who would
stalk this woman because something about her fed his arrogant
self-importance as no other woman could? It didn't take a
psych degree to know men and women who were bad combi-
nations just keep finding each other, repeating their indelicate
and dangerous dance until the wrongness of it all consumed
them. If this was Indi's destiny, I wondered whether one of
these future stalkers would kill her then shove his gun into his
own mouth. There seemed a sad inevitability to the idea, but I
decided that, as long as I was involved, it would not be Kenny.

Then I took another pull on my Corona and almost chuckled at the realization Indi had roused *my* feelings of protective-
ness.

Amid servers bringing out platters of wings and pizza and
full-course dinners, Grace Patterson emerged from the kitchen.
She crossed toward the bar, simultaneously surveying her es-
tablishment and greeting patrons, many by name, as if they
were in her home instead of her lounge. Though several customers were twentysomethings, the Shadow had a reputation
as a grown-up night spot for people middle-aged or older, professionals and working class alike, who preferred better food,
traditional drink, and classic rock and soul to the youth-
oriented bars on Chippewa Street downtown. Like most of her
patrons—like Bobby—Grace was a Baby Boomer, a pleasant
woman with short blonde hair and rimless glasses. Tonight she
wore a long loose white jacket over a black turtleneck and
matching slacks. She went behind the bar and said a few words
to the three bartenders, two women and one man. Then she
looked across the room, saw me, and waved. After a few addi-
tional exchanges with employees and customers, she walked
over to my table.

I stood up. "Hey, Grace."

"Hi, G," she said, standing on tiptoe, then stepping back.
"Sit. Easier on my calves."

I sat, and she kissed me on the cheek. "How've you been?"

"Fine. Just working."

"Bobby says you're bodyguarding Indigo Waters. Something about a stalker?"

"An ex who won't let go."

"Indi is a nice kid, and her voice brings in a lot of business." Grace frowned. "I want her safe and I don't want any problems here. If he shows, just give me the high sign and I'll send my boys to help you hustle the creep out." She pointed toward two young men in black tees that could barely contain their physiques, one beside the door and the other near the bar.

"You got it." For a moment, I considered not mentioning that the creep was a cop who might be armed. Even Kenny wasn't stupid enough to menace a bar full of civilians, to reveal his inner stalker to a hundred or more people with mobile phone camcorders. He had no way of knowing who would be there to document the end of his career, no matter how his Police Benevolent Association rep framed it. Then I remembered what Chalmers had said last night: *Always volatile. Totally unpredictable.* And I told Grace because she had a right to know.

"Bobby didn't tell me that." She was quiet for a moment, uneasy. Then she frowned. "Figures you wouldn't have an easy one."

"Sorry," I said. "If you'd rather I took her out of here—"

She sighed and shook her head. "I told you, she's a good kid, and customers like her. This isn't her fault. I just don't want anybody to get hurt."

"I hit him with a court order yesterday," I said, dangling the only filament of hope I had. "If he respects the law he's sworn to uphold, he won't show."

She pursed her lips. "Right. You don't half believe that yourself."

"Sure I do." I gestured toward the bar, toward the laughter and conviviality. "You got way too many people here. Guys like him do their stalking with a much smaller audience."

I could see she wanted to believe in the logic of what I was saying as much as I tried to believe in it myself, but we'd both been around long enough not to try masking our doubt. *Always volatile...*

I knew Grace was happily married to Alex Reedy, an earnest man who ran his own upscale restaurant on Delaware Avenue in North Buffalo. But owning a bar had likely left her as much a cynic as being in the CID had left me. One in four women was a victim of domestic abuse. Frequently those who survived did so because somebody inched out on the ledge to help them, sometimes at great personal risk. Outgoing and strong-willed, Grace was exactly the type to step into the DMZ. Though he had seven or eight years on her, she and Bobby had been friends for a long time. I had no idea how they had come to know each other, but I suspected being a nurturer was something they shared. She just stood there, arms crossed and eyebrows raised. I wondered how many battered women she had seen over the years. How many had she lied for or hidden or given money for a fresh start in a new city? After a moment I spread my hands. "Okay. If he shows, I'll stick up two fingers. Send over your boys *and* call nine-one-one."

"Can I beat him with my baseball bat first?" Then she unfolded her arms, and her face brightened. "So where's Bobby? It's been ages since he stopped in."

"He should be here any time now."

"Tell him to forget the glasses and buy his wine by the bottle tonight. Expensive wine so I can start putting away money for repairs to this place."

"I'll try to keep it from getting to that point." I took a pull on my beer.

"I'll hold you to that," she said. "Is Bobby bringing Kayla? He told me four chairs."

"He doesn't go too many places without her."

"She's really good for him." Grace grinned widely. "And they look so cute together." Then she checked out the bar again and the band and all the activity. "I better talk to my guys and get back to work. Tell Bobby I'll stop by later."

Without waiting for a reply, she moved back into the growing swirl of customers. She threaded her way first to one bouncer and then the other, stood on tiptoe to whisper into their ears, and pointed to me.

We all exchanged barely perceptible nods to confirm our

understanding of what we would do if Kenny arrived. Presently, I saw Phoenix Trinidad at the hostess station and stood to wave her over.

Tonight, beneath the stylish black coat that fanned open as she walked, she wore a casual burgundy pantsuit and a pale blue blouse with an open collar and pearl choker. Her hair was untied and bounced about her face as she moved. Her lipstick the same shade as her suit, she smiled, and I remembered how much I had liked her smile when she brought Indi to my office.

"Evening, counselor," I said and shook her outstretched hand as she murmured a greeting.

I pivoted a chair toward her so she could sit. First, however, I helped her out of her coat, an expensive-feeling microfiber trench. Careful to keep the belt from dangling to the floor, I folded the coat over the back of the seat and took her hand— her nails matched the lipstick and the suit—as she hiked a hip onto the chair. Then I took my seat again.

"This is a nice place," she said, looking about the room like the first-timer she was. Her gaze settled on Indi and the band. She waved to her client. "So the owner is an old friend of your godfather's?"

"Yes. Bobby has tons of friends, all over town."

"Marla says the food here is good."

"It is."

She turned to face me, head slightly cocked, brown eyes so dark they caught the light like mirrors. I noticed the tiny smile wrinkles at the outer corners of her eyes.

"What do you recommend, Gideon?"

"How hungry are you, Phoenix?"

"Let's see." She scrunched her face, as if thinking hard. "I had a bagel and coffee after this disturbing phone call from a tough guy who said he might have to hurt somebody." She knit her brow in a mock scowl. "When he called back this afternoon, I was having an apple and some saltines while I did paperwork. Oh, and at Marla's I had tea and these cute little—"

"Steak," I said, putting my fingertips on her forearm to halt her recitation. "Trust me, you want the Kansas City Strip. It's good for all-day hunger and all-night sarcasm."

"What if I'm vegetarian?"

"Then I'd recommend the Texas tofu."

"They have tofu here?" Her surprise looked as genuine as her distaste at the thought of cubed bean curd. Then my alliteration registered. "*Texas* tofu?"

I laughed. "Grace would rather lose her liquor license than deal with either one."

Phoenix smiled warmly. "Then Kansas City steak it is."

"And speaking of Marla—" I hated to steer her away from her playfulness but I needed to settle the issue of where Indi would sleep tonight. What Phoenix didn't know was that if Kenny didn't come to the Shadow, and Indi got an emergency placement, I planned to sleep at her place and wait for him there. She had told me that, when they were together, he sometimes dropped by after her Saturday night gig. They'd watch late movies on cable, make love, sleep late, and go out to brunch. If he showed up tonight, as he had last Saturday night, I would cuff him, at gunpoint if necessary, and take him in for violating the court order.

"Yes, Indi can stay at Hope's Haven tonight. There's a vacancy. They have a lot of small rooms on the third floor—originally servants' quarters, some barely big enough for a bed. That's where they house displaced women and children. And the door to the upstairs is a heavy steel security model with a coded keypad for getting in and an emergency crash bar for getting out. She'll be safe."

"Good. I'll drive her there after they finish."

"I have to go with you," Phoenix said. "Security. Nobody gets in the front door after eight without a key card. Evening staff aren't permitted to answer the door and have to call the police if bell ringers don't go away."

"And you have a key card."

"I do, and the code for the third floor. I'm their lawyer and a board member."

"Should I follow you then, or vice-versa?"

She shook her head. "I'm riding in your car. I came in a cab so I could go with you."

I nodded and thought about that. As a favor to Bobby,

whose friend Jonah was a senior partner in Phoenix's law firm, I was charging Indi less than my usual rate. But fees or no fees, I wanted this job over sooner than later.

If I took Phoenix home after Hope's Haven, I would get to Indi's apartment later than I intended. Too late, and Kenny was unlikely to come knocking, which meant the entire mess would spill into next week.

I wanted to get back to my regular routines—serving subpoenas, finding witnesses, skip-tracing, surveillance of personal injury claimants, background-checking potential employees or spouses—things that paid better and didn't involve facing down cops with guns.

I looked up to resume my watch of the doorway and saw the hostess leading Bobby and Kayla to our table. Bobby was in his favorite blue suit, the gray shirt I'd given him for his birthday in August, and a cobalt tie. Beneath a short tan jacket, Kayla wore a fall dress with a dazzling pattern of browns and reds and oranges. When she went out, she dressed to be seen, as well as to distance herself from the somber robes of her profession, which she sometimes described as puritan black. They were both smiling as they joined us. I stood and kissed Kayla's cheek.

Already acquainted, Kayla and Phoenix shook hands. I introduced the lawyer to Bobby, who took her hand and offered a slight bow before drawing out the chair next to hers and helping Kayla into it. He pecked Kayla on the cheek then rounded the table to take the seat beside mine as I sat and shifted my gaze back to the door. Ordinarily, Bobby would have insisted on sitting beside Kayla, but he was too much of a gentleman to ask Phoenix to move. Also, he understood that, when I worked, my choice of vantage point was inviolable, so they ended up flanking us.

The girl with spiked hair came over to hand us menus and take drink orders. Phoenix ordered a glass of malbec, but Bobby, having seen Grace on the way inside, said, "Make that a bottle." When Kayla ordered a pinot noir, he said, "Make that a bottle too," and shrugged when I looked at him. I ordered another Corona.

"G, isn't Ms. Trinidad pretty tonight?" Kayla said after the server left.

Phoenix's cinnamon cheeks darkened as she looked down at her menu.

"Don't mind Kayla," I said. "She wants me to squirm, not you."

"She knows your life could use the touch of a good woman," Bobby said.

Just then the band plunged into its opening number, and I saw Kenny Carnahan—in blue jeans and the same dark jacket as last night—step through the front door, as if on cue.

Chapter 8

"Gideon?"

I didn't answer Bobby as I squeezed behind his chair and rounded the table on my way to the front door. Keeping Kenny in sight, I shot my left hand into the air, in hopes Grace or the bouncers would see my first two fingers. Kenny and I got to the hostess station at the same time. For an instant, he smiled at me.

In almost everyone, there is a resident mathematician who factors into an ever-shifting equation the numberless impressions taken in through the five senses. On the conscious level, we use our internal mathematics to judge whether we can cross the street before an oncoming car reaches us or sink a bank shot on a pool table or a foul shot on the basketball court. But it is on the subconscious plane that most such calculations take place. For example, glimpsing an older man with no facial stubble or neck fuzz, faint to non-existent eyebrows, and a full head of evenly colored hair whispers the word *toupee*, regardless of whether the hairpiece in question looks like a $10,000 work of art or poorly-groomed roadkill. The processing speed needed for all these data rivaled that of a mainframe computer. In most of us, then, the product of this calculus came as a first impression, a strong gut feeling, or a completely surprising epiphany.

Surprise was what I felt at Kenny's brief smile. Subconsciously, I had expected the seething rage I saw when he threw Kayla's court order to the floor or the forced *Who, me?* innocence of one too arrogant to see himself as a stalker. But there was something knowing and disingenuous about his smile. It was a smirk based in artifice. For a sliver of a second, as the music behind me rose—a tight rendition of the Shemekia Copeland song "Salt in My Wounds"—I felt on uncertain ground and wondered, *Is he fucking with me?*

"What?" Kenny said as one of the bouncers came up beside me. "I'm off the clock, just here for a beer." He unzipped his jacket. No gun under his arm or on his belt. Maybe he had a belt holster in back.

"A hundred yards, Kenny," I said. "You know she's singing here tonight, and you know you can't be here."

"Sir, I'm gonna have to ask you to leave." The bouncer was younger and broader than Kenny but about the same height. The second bouncer, who had by then joined us, was even larger. The first took a step sideways so that he was standing to Kenny's right. The second bouncer positioned himself on the left.

"So you two—you three—are gonna…what?…pick me up and throw me in the street?"

"Sir," the first bouncer said, "I am asking you, politely, to leave." Despite his youth, his voice was deep and resonant with authority. "If you don't, we'll have to call the police."

"The boss already called," the second bouncer said, his voice higher but no less firm.

"I *am* the police, dipshits, and I want a beer!" Kenny's increase in volume caused a hush to fall over the conversations nearest the hostess station but the music kept the growing tension from spreading to the rest of the Shadow.

"You're in violation of a court order," I said, giving the bouncers no chance to doubt the correctness of what they were doing. The music continued, Indi's voice strong enough to have come from a much larger body, but a barely discernible glitch in her rhythm told me she'd seen what was happening. "Judge McQueen herself is here tonight and will probably make bail impossible if you get arrested in front of her."

Kenny shrugged and held out his hands just as the bouncers stepped toward him. Each one took an arm, and, with a coordination apparently born of practice, hustled him backward toward the door. Kenny offered no resistance as they pushed him through to the front patio. But he smirked again, for barely an instant. Seeing his eyes narrow, I started toward him just as he made his move.

Kenny snapped his forehead toward the bouncer on his left, and I heard the impact that broke the man's nose and forced him to relax his grip on Kenny's arm. Before the other bouncer could react, Kenny swung his left fist into the man's right ear and snatched his right arm free. Then he whirled on me.

Whatever the system—kung fu, karate, Krav Maga, or old-fashioned street fighting—hand-to-hand combat demanded three things: total focus on the opponent, reflex anticipation of likely attacks, and heightened awareness of surroundings. Thus, in a life-or-death face-off, the mathematician nestled somewhere between the brain stem and the cerebrum became an indispensable ally, working overtime to process incoming data. Trained to respond without hesitation to the mathematician's whisper, soldiers, cops, and martial artists—from black belts to boxers to cage fighters—all knew the only real advantage was speed. So I crossed my forearms to block Kenny's incoming punch as I snap-kicked his left knee then jabbed the fore knuckles of my right hand into his throat as his balance shifted to the left.

The blow lacked enough force to crack cartilage but sent Kenny staggering backward, choking, into a mesh-topped patio table, which broke his fall. The occupants scrambled away as he pushed himself to his feet. Gasping and coughing, he seemed about to launch himself at me, so I dropped into a defensive stance. Just then, from behind, I heard a commanding alto: "Stop this!" Kayla pushed past my raised left arm and stepped between us, facing Kenny. "Officer Carnahan, stop this instant or I will personally see to it that you spend a week in the holding center while your missing paperwork is located!"

Still swallowing and trying to catch his breath, Kenny dropped his hands and glared first at us then at the bouncers— one in a chair, his head back and hands covering his nose, the other standing near the front window and cupping his ear. "Just horseplay, your honor," Kenny said after his breathing steadied. "Rimes here and me are old friends."

"I don't care if you're identical twins," Kayla said. "This ends now."

The music had stopped. I could sense patrons had clotted in the doorway and begun to spill onto the patio behind me. I heard Grace push through and glanced to my left as she went to the bouncer by the window. He muttered that he was okay and waved her toward his seated colleague. She crossed behind me and bent to check on the other man, whose head was still tilted back. She looked up and snapped an order. There was the sound of movement in the crowd. Someone pushed through to hand her a small bar towel. Gingerly, she put it over the man's nose and guided his fingertips to hold it in place.

Kenny looked past Grace and jabbed his finger at someone just off to my right. "Hey, you in the baseball cap!" he said hoarsely. "Turn off that video camera! Now!"

The honey-skinned young man with the compact digital camcorder ignored the command but took a step closer to me as if uncertain whether Kenny would attack. I saw the beginnings of a grin as he triggered the zoom button for a close-up. LJ had done exactly as I asked. He'd shown up at the Shadow and maintained a low profile while keeping his camera ready to document any disturbance. Now he glanced at me, and his gray-green eyes twinkled. He knew I'd drop by his home tomorrow and pay him well for the mini-DVD.

"A camera is the least of your worries," Grace said, standing. She turned to Kayla. "I intend to press charges against this son of a bitch."

"It's illegal to record cops," Kenny said—much too calmly. I'd have expected to see some sign of an impulse to rush LJ that was held in check only by the presence of a judge.

"Not in New York," Kayla said. "The First Amendment means something here. Besides, you're off-duty and acting like a damn fool in public, so there's no reasonable expectation of privacy and no interference with the discharge of your official duties." She shook her head. "Violating a court order. Disturbing the peace. Assault and battery. What the hell are you thinking?"

"Self-defense."

Kayla snorted. "If you're that stupid, you're on the wrong side of the badge."

Kenny said nothing, just looked at us blankly. For an instant, however, his eyes met mine, and I thought I saw a flicker of uncertainty. That was the first sliver of logic, the first glimmer that he understood reality, I had seen in him since our encounter last night. But it was replaced quickly by something else, a barely perceptible, though distinct, lack of worry. That made no sense in a man whose career was flaming out in front of an audience and a video camera. I tried to hold his gaze, to read what lay behind it.

"I advise you to go home and pack a toothbrush and clean underwear," Kayla said, taking a phone from her jacket pocket. "Somebody will be along to collect you before dawn. If you're lucky, I might forget there's a video."

Shaking his head, Kenny stepped off the patio. "See you, Rimes," he said before he shoved his hands into his jacket pockets and headed west on Hertel Avenue.

Most of the crowd drifted back inside, but I waited and watched Kenny climb into his Tahoe, parked near the start of the next block. He pulled away from the curb and spun into a wide U-turn, his thick tires thrumming as he accelerated through the changing light. He was on his way to forty as he passed the Shadow Lounge. His brake lights flashed briefly at the intersection of Hertel and Parkside, but then he chose to blow through that red light as well and disappeared on his way toward Main Street. He had driven past the lounge for show, but having passed Parkside without a right turn, he seemed headed somewhere other than Indi's apartment or his own. Kayla's call notwithstanding, I decided I would still stake out Indi's place after Phoenix and I dropped her at Hope's Haven.

When I stepped back inside the lounge, the music had not yet resumed because Indigo Waters was wrapped in Doc's arms, staining one of his pearl gray lapels with her tears.

Chapter 9

Indi had lost her spark. When she disappeared into the restroom, Phoenix followed with the garment bag. For the next ten minutes or so, Doc led the band in an instrumental and vocal medley of several blues and jazz standards. Meanwhile, almost simultaneously, two police cars double-parked out front, a blue-and-white answering Grace's nine-one-one call and an unmarked supervisor's Taurus in response to Kayla.

The uniformed cop was the older and taller of the two men who strode inside. The district commander, a slim young nicotine gum-chewer named Rogalski, was good-looking in an almost movie star way—pale blue eyes, strong nose, black hair carefully styled. He wore a well-tailored charcoal suit and expensive-looking white shirt with a navy tie. The uniform deferred to him, and Kayla stood beside me as Rogalski fired questions at me, using a stainless steel pen to write in a pocket-sized leather notebook. Next he spoke to Grace and the bouncers, continuing to scratch away. Kayla took charge when Phoenix and Indi emerged from the ladies' room, allowing Indi to answer only two or three questions before saying it was time I got her to the shelter.

I stepped outside first and scanned the street then started my Escape with the remote key. Hand inside my jacket, I walked to the car. I pulled away from the curb, eased behind the blue-and-white, and pushed my flashers button. I slid out, went back inside the Shadow, and gathered Indi's belongings.

I hung the garment bag in back on the driver's side door hook and put her shoe bag and purse on the seat. Then I held open the back door on the passenger side as Phoenix, arm around her client, led Indi out and helped her into the middle rear seat. Phoenix climbed in after her, and I shut the door. I nodded to Rogalski, who had followed them outside. He held up a finger to tell me I should wait a second before leaving. I stood beside the car as he drew near.

"From what I can tell," he said, leaning in close enough for me to smell his Nicorette tab, "this is all about a good cop who let things get away from him—you know, his feelings." There was an easy glide to his soft baritone which suggested that one reason he'd made district commander while still in his early thirties was a calming demeanor.

"Feelings are hard puppies to control," I said.

"Be a shame if it ruined his career."

I looked at him for a second then went round to the driver's side and slid inside. When I closed the door and pressed the START button, Phoenix said, "What did he want?"

"He wants Indi not to press charges."

"No fucking way," Phoenix said. "Kenny's dangerous."

No one said another word as we drove to the shelter.

Three stories of tan brick and modern thermal windows, Hope's Haven sprawled on a double lot directly across Main Street from Ladder Seven, the district fire station. Hope's Haven was brightly lit and had two aprons into the street, connected by a semicircular blacktop driveway that arced through a leaf-strewn lawn. I parked at the uppermost point of the arc, right in front of the center entrance, and followed the women up flagstone steps to a round porch bracketed by curved wooden benches. A dark plastic camera hemisphere was mounted high above the steel security door. Phoenix swiped a card through a small gray reader. Once the tiny LED indicator light changed from red to green, she held open the heavy door to let us into the vestibule, where an identical door beside an identical card reader blocked our entrance into the house itself. Another security camera housing was mounted in the vestibule ceiling.

Phoenix looked up at it and waved before swiping her card and pulling open the second door.

Inside, the walls were a warm gold. The air was laced with scented oil from plug-in fresheners. The security desk was to the right of the door. A big, balding brown-skinned man about sixty stood up behind it, his tight blue blazer open just enough for me to see the Taser clipped to his belt. He smiled. "Evening, Miss Trinidad, Miss Waters." His voice held a whisper of gravel.

"Hi, Oscar," Phoenix said. "This is Mr. Rimes. He's handling security for Ms. Waters."

Indi said nothing as I shook the man's huge hand. Maybe he looked eighty to her, but his grip told me he was a retired something—cop, soldier, boxer, whatever—who had refused to let himself go to seed. He had the steady gaze of one unafraid to face the necessary.

I doubted he needed the Taser. If somehow an abusive husband or boyfriend got inside Hope's Haven, Oscar could flatten him with one punch.

Unlike other women's shelters or health centers which depended on grants, public money, gimmicky fundraisers, and modest donations, this one was funded by a hefty endowment, which meant well-paid protection. Oscar was likely not the only formidable security officer.

"I'm going to take Ms. Waters to a room on three," Phoenix said to Oscar. Then she turned to me. "Back in a minute, Gideon."

I nodded as she and Indi disappeared around a corner.

Oscar studied me for a time, his lips pursed somewhere between contemplation and amusement. "Your mother spend a lot of time with the Old Testament?" he asked finally.

"She never told me," I said. "Guess you don't meet too many Gideons."

"Can't recall *ever* meeting one," he said. "You just look like your name, and it takes a warrior to recognize a warrior." My face must have shown my confusion. "Names are kind of a hobby of mine. Both of ours mean warrior of one kind or another, only yours is in the Bible." He fished a business card out of his inside breast pocket and handed it to me. "Ever need to talk about any of it, let me know."

The card was pale blue with embossed gold lettering: *Rev. Oscar Edgerton* centered below a simple cross and above a telephone number. No address, no King James verse, no church, no times for Sunday services or Wednesday Bible study.

"You got that slightly haunted look I see in good men who can't forget what they've seen and done."

"Like looking into a mirror, isn't it?" I said, pocketing the card in my jacket and withdrawing my own leather-covered card case. I watched his eyes move to my Glock. "Where were you a chaplain, prison or the army?"

For an instant he looked surprised. Then he grinned, revealing strong, age-discolored teeth. "Retired from both," he said. "Twenty years in army greens, twelve with a collar, and twenty years in Georgia corrections. I've killed a couple and comforted too many men who didn't deserve to die, and I've been the last measure of human kindness for a lot who did."

"And now you're here in Buffalo, protecting women and children from men who don't deserve them."

He shrugged. "God's work is more complex, my brother, than we can ever imagine. Redemption and faith form an upward spiral toward perfection." He chuckled and sat down in his net-backed black swivel chair. "And when God gives you the best woman ever, you'd be a fool not to follow her home to the frozen North if she has to take care of her elderly parents."

"Can't toss a gift from God," I said, extracting a card and handing it to him.

"Amen." He read my card. "Driftglass Investigations, G. Rimes, Licensed PI."

"Named after a book I read when I was a kid, by a black science fiction writer."

"Really? Well, you don't need to worry about Miss Waters. She'll be safe here."

"I know." I returned my card case to my pocket. "But you should know her ex-boyfriend is a cop."

"And he carries." Oscar smiled. "Don't change a thing."

"Where in Georgia?"

He slipped the card into an inside pocket. "Atlanta, born and bred. Know the area?"

"Been there a few times," I said, then added, "Indigo Waters is from Baxley."

He grinned. "Knew she was a Georgia girl first time we talked. Heard it in her voice. But Baxley's all the way 'cross the state, southeast, not too far from Savannah. Kinda small."

Just then Phoenix returned, sooner than I'd expected, and reminded Oscar her numbers were programmed into the security desk telephone. "Anything happens, call me right after you call the police," she said.

I nodded goodbye to Oscar and followed her out to my car. I held the passenger door for her. Before I could close her inside, she ratcheted back the seat, nestled into the headrest, and sighed. "I'm getting too old for this shit."

If things had been less serious at that moment, I might have told her she sounded like Danny Glover. Instead, I climbed in and started the engine. She told me where she lived. I let her talk as I drove.

"Indi isn't sure how far she wants to push this. She's afraid but she doesn't want to press charges and go to court. If we can keep him away from her for a few weeks, she says, she'll be leaving because Doc says some record company bigwig is coming to hear her, and she's sure he's going to give her a contract. She doesn't seem to understand that getting famous makes it easier for a serious stalker to find her in another city." Phoenix took a deep breath and let it out slowly. "I had to leave before I got too pissed off and told her she was being stupid. Don't get me wrong, Gideon. She might need to hear it, just not tonight."

Phoenix lived in a loft downtown, a block past the point where the subway emerged from underground to pick up and discharge passengers at street level in the Theater District. The semicircular drive to her building was off Pearl Street. I swung in and stopped at the all-glass front entrance. The lobby inside was well lit, with security camera bubbles in discreet places, glittering fixtures and trim, and a uniformed man seated at a desk. He rose and looked out at my car then started toward the twin sets of double doors. He stopped just inside the interior set and adjusted a pseudo police hat clearly too large for his head. He was pale and scrawny and probably not yet thirty. All that hung from his belt was a long blue flashlight in a vinyl holster. He was no Oscar.

Phoenix sat forward and raised the back of her seat. "Phil won't come out unless you sit here too long."

I turned to her. "What's he going to do, shine his Mag Lite in my eyes?"

She laughed. "It's a secure building. Phil is—"

"Mainly for show," I said, "or his old man is somebody important."

"Both," Phoenix said. She paused for a second or two before adding, "Gideon, thank you so much for all this." She placed her fingers on my right forearm, pressed lightly, and withdrew them. "I know we've been a pain in your ass, but you've been a real professional. Indi's safe now and Kenny is in jail, or on his way." She flashed a quick smile. "I think you can go back to your regular life. Just send your bill to my office."

I shrugged and felt myself half smile. "Phoenix, if you ever need anything—"

"You too, Gideon." She looked at me a moment, her faced faintly illuminated by my dashboard lights and her lips parted as if she were about to say something else. But then she caught her lower lip between her teeth, lowered her eyes, and turned away. "Goodnight," she said.

She opened the car door, climbed out, and pushed it shut a hair too hard. By the time she reached the first pair of glass doors, Phil was grinning as he held one open for her. From inside the vestibule, she waved to me once then passed through the interior door Phil swung open wide. Without looking back, she walked toward a trio of elevators.

When she was out of sight, I pushed the FM button and settled on a public radio jazz program halfway through the title track on Miles Davis's *Bitches Brew*. Fingers keeping time on the wheel, I pulled out onto Pearl Street, drove down to Chippewa, and turned right. A second right put me on Franklin, which would become Linwood Avenue several blocks ahead, at North Street. Another quarter mile would bring me to Indi's apartment building. I thought it might be too late for Kenny to show up, if somehow he had evaded arrest. But I'd always believed in being sure. I flipped open my glove compartment and saw I still had a banded bundle of cable ties. With a calm determination that, after tonight, I really would go back to my life, I cruised toward Indi's apartment. Her keys, which I had slipped out of her purse, were in my jacket pocket.

Chapter 10

I never heard the battery-powered lock drill they used to get inside the vestibule, but the battering ram that splintered my door at six-thirty a.m. was loud enough to wake the entire block.

I rolled out of bed and snatched my gun off the shelf below the nightstand drawer. On one knee between the bed and the wall, I had just racked the slide when the bedroom door burst open and banged into the wall. Darkness was sliced by criss-crossing beams of tactical laser sites and LED flashlights fixed to the barrels of assault rifles. Professional gear, military precision, overwhelming numbers—I let go of my Glock even before a red dot appeared in the middle of my black T-shirt.

"Police, motherfucker!" someone shouted. "Hands where we can see 'em!"

I raised my hands and awaited further instruction.

Someone found the light switch, and I winced at the sudden brightness. When my eyes adjusted, I counted six rifles trained on me, the men holding them in helmets and body armor. The man directly across from me lowered his rifle. With a gloved hand he picked up my gun from the bed and bagged it. The huge man nearest me took a step closer, his sneer visible through his plastic face shield, and drove his rifle stock into the left side of my skull.

Contrary to what happened in movies and paperback thrillers, people were not easy to knock out with a single blow. There was no descent into darkness, no "everything went black" moment. After the strike, which in my head sounded like a wet sandbag dropped onto a hardwood floor, I remained fully conscious. Within half a second, the pain began, radiating from my right ear to my eyes. It took me several heartbeats to realize I'd bitten my tongue. Blood trickled into the back of my throat as I tried to match my breathing to the murderous pulsing. If the space between the platform bed and the wall had been wider than two feet, I'd have slumped to the floor instead of leaning on the edge of the bed and struggling to keep from sliding off. I squeezed my eyes shut and grasped the bed-spread, keeping my hands where they could be seen.

"Enough, Berko!"

Somebody banged into my dresser as if shoved.

The voice had sounded familiar. I forced myself to open my eyes. Standing above me, bald head bare and torso sheathed in Kevlar, Terry Chalmers holstered his service pistol and un-hooked handcuffs from his belt. Beside him was Rafael Pinero, gun still in hand, his brown fedora an odd-looking accessory for his vest. Chalmers hauled me up onto the bed face down, cuffing my hands behind me.

"Gideon Rimes," Pinero said, "you are under arrest for the murder of Kenneth Carnahan. You have the right to remain silent…"

Kenny, dead?

I didn't hear the rest of the Miranda warning but answered yes when asked if I understood my rights. Two cops jerked me to my feet. My head was pounding now, and I felt blood on my ear and cheek. By the time they dragged me, barefoot and in running shorts, out to the hallway stairs, Bobby and Kayla were on the third floor landing.

"What the hell is going on?" Bobby cried.

Some of his tenants had stepped out to look too. Dr. Cook, the middle-aged blonde widow directly across the hall, stood robed and open-mouthed in her doorway, her fifteen-year-old daughter behind her. Outside the door diagonally across from mine, gray dreadlocks framing his long face, Fred Watkins was already in one of his kente cloth *batakaris*. A retired CPA and sometime photographer who regularly visited Buffalo's sister city in Senegal, he raised a small camera, snapped a couple of flashless shots, then slipped it behind his back before one of the cops looked in his direction.

"Shit! These cuffs are too tight!" I said, hoping the cops would concentrate on me and forget any shutter clicks they might have heard. Fred's pictures might prove useful. "Hey, my hands are going numb!"

The curious cop—the big guy who'd hit me—turned back to me. "Too bad!" he spat.

I looked through his face shield at cheeks reddened by the burst capillaries of a heavy drinker. "I'll remember you, Berko."

"Yeah? New York couldn't decide on the needle nap, so you can remember me for forty years, asshole." Berko shoved me forward as Fred retreated into his apartment.

Kayla stomped down the stairs ahead of Bobby, cinching her robe. "He's bleeding! Why is this man bleeding? Officers, if you've abused him—"

"Ma'am, please," Chalmers said, blocking her as Pinero and the others took me down the stairs. I couldn't glance back, but knowing Kayla, I imagine she tried to push past him, which made Chalmers say, "Ma'am, don't make me charge you with obstruction."

Her reply came as no surprise. "Do you know who I am? I demand to see your warrant!"

Old Sam Wingard, the maintenance man, had come out of his rear apartment on the first floor and now stood in gray work clothes near the front door, his broad brown forehead creased with worry.

As I was hustled outside and into the early morning cold, I heard Bobby shout from the stairs, "I'll call your lawyer!"

The last thing I saw before the door closed was a tear roll from beneath Sam's thick, brown-framed glasses and disappear into his drooping gray mustache.

Chapter 11

Chained to a table ring in a cold, windowless police interrogation room was hardly how I had envisioned spending my Sunday morning. The front and shoulder of my T-shirt were sticky with blood dripping from my head wound. Chalmers and Pinero let me sit for a long time without offering so much as a paper towel to stanch my bleeding. Maybe they hoped I would bleed out because of Kenny, or maybe they just wanted to scare me. Either way, I refused to give them the satisfaction. I avoided looking at the two-way mirror as I gazed about the pale green room.

Despite bravado, street cred, and lawyers, most people who sat in this stationary stainless steel chair would scare easily. But most of them weren't combat veterans who had already exhausted a lifetime's allotment of fear and just didn't give a damn. Nor were they ex-cops who understood the nature of evidence and chains of custody. And to one extent or another, most would be scared because they were guilty. I was innocent, but since my alleged victim had been on the job, the path to exoneration could be rocky. Bleeding lessening but head still throbbing, I leaned back and closed my eyes.

Kenny had failed to show up at Indi's apartment. After nearly two hours seated in the same uncomfortable armchair in which I'd slept the night before, I gave up and went home to bed. It seemed likely then he had been arrested, so when I slipped between my sheets—expecting to resurface about noon—I thought I might actually be slipping back into my life.

Now Kenny's death would delay that, for how long I had no idea. How had he died? Because they'd bagged my gun, I first assumed he must have been shot with a nine-millimeter. Terry Chalmers had gotten a good look at my carry permit Friday night at the Anchor Bar and they would have run me through the system. They had made no effort to locate my gun safe, which held two other pistols, a SIG P228 from my CID days and a .357 Magnum. They must have liked my Glock for the killing. They would submit it for ballistics testing. Once they realized it wasn't the murder weapon and hadn't been fired since my trip to the range two weeks earlier, they would have to let me go. And they would be no closer to identifying Kenny's killer.

I thought about that for a long moment. Who would want to kill Kenny? And why?

Before I could assemble a mental list of possibilities, the door squeaked open. I raised my eyelids just enough to see Chalmers and Pinero step inside, their body armor replaced by empty shoulder holsters. Chalmers wore a sky blue shirt tucked into black jeans and a loose burgundy tie. Pinero's shirt was yellow, his slacks and tie an identical shade of brown. He was bareheaded, his hair creased above the ears by his missing hat's sweat band. A toothpick in one corner of his mouth, he moved to my left as Chalmers positioned himself on my right. It was too early on a Sunday for a ballistics test to have been run. *Damn.* They were here to sweat me—a presumed cop killer. This might get ugly. For a moment the only sound was the foot-long handcuff chain ratcheting through the table ring as I shifted and opened my eyes.

"Hey, fella, we disturb your beauty nap?" Pinero said.

"Nice hair," I said.

Pinero smiled. "Least mine ain't got blood in it." He leaned in, exhaling coffee fumes into my face. "You know, when you try to catnap in custody, we kind of think you're guilty and saving your strength for what's ahead."

I squinted at Chalmers. "Does he begin all his interrogations with bits from *The Usual Suspects*?" Then I shifted my attention back to Pinero. "Ever stop to think my eyes might be closed because none of you geniuses thought to bring my glasses and I might have a hard time seeing things?" Not entirely true, but they didn't need to know that. "Or could be I just have a bad headache because some dipshit hit me." True enough.

"An ex-cop who's a cop killer," Pinero said, lips pulling into a snarky grin. "Guess it's a toss-up what happens to you in the joint, a high five or a high hard one up the ass."

"Man, I can't sit still for that," I said. "Any pointers?"

"Did you a favor bringing your ass in, you son of a bitch!" Pinero was close enough now that we were past coffee and into last night's dinner. "If we didn't, every cop in town'd be looking for you. Some of 'em are off duty—with throw-down pieces."

"Is that supposed to scare me?"

Chalmers had remained quiet, studying me. Now he moved behind me, easing Pinero away in a classic good cop-bad cop move. "Look," he said, "I know you know procedure, so I'm gonna ask you some questions straight up. Answer straight up, get your side out there, and maybe we can get to the bottom of things real quick. Okay?"

Theoretically, I could shut this down by demanding a lawyer. But I wanted more information about the murder. Of course—also theoretically—I could be killed during a struggle on the stairs or while snatching an officer's weapon. Internal Affairs would happily clear the cop who took down the killer of a decorated officer. Or maybe they would wait till I was in a cell in the Holding Center. Then I could hang myself with my T-shirt and star in two or three days of *Buffalo News* articles about suicides in lock-up, topped off by an indignant editorial decrying jail conditions. "Go ahead," I said,

"We know about the fight at the Shadow Lounge last night."

"Then you know Kenny assaulted two bouncers." I paused for a reaction that didn't come. They knew. "And I hit him in the throat to make him stop."

"Is that when you decided to meet him later?" Chalmers asked. "To settle things once and for all?"

"You make it sound personal," I said. "I was bodyguarding a stalking victim, and your boy was the stalker. There was nothing to settle. Never was."

I looked from Chalmers to Pinero, who had moved to my right, occupying the space once filled by Chalmers. Circling, to keep me off balance.

"If you know about the fight, then you must know Judge McQueen witnessed him violating her protection order and called to have him arrested." I smiled at Chalmers. "You must be Homicide. I guess you don't get to Family Court much, but I believe you met Judge McQueen."

He bit his lip as if suppressing a smile. I had my first hint that he, at least, had doubts. "Where'd you go after leaving the Shadow?"

"I took my client to a safe place, where Kenny couldn't get to her."

"A friend's place?" Pinero cut in. "A hotel? A shelter? Where?"

"Confidential," I said.

"You ain't a doctor or a lawyer," he said. "You got no privilege here."

I said nothing. Obviously, they hadn't exercised due diligence or they would have known Indi worked at Hope's Haven, a logical place for her to seek shelter. I wondered what was going on here.

"Maybe your little girlfriend did Kenny and is using you to take the fall. Ever think of that? You wouldn't be the first poor dumb bastard to go to prison for pussy."

I ignored Pinero's offer of an escape hatch, certain Oscar had kept Indi on lockdown.

"Where did you go after you dropped your client off?" Chalmers asked.

"Where did you find me?"

"What time did you get there?"

"I didn't pay attention to the clock. I was tired and went to bed."

"Is there anybody who can verify that?

"No."

"So you could have gone looking for Kenny before you went home."

"Do you have a witness that says I did?"

"We might."

I studied Chalmers for a moment, wondering if someone had noticed my car outside Indi's apartment building. Near a complex that likely housed a number of young singles who might have parties or one-night stands, there was no reason my Escape should rouse more attention than any other vehicle parked on Linwood. If somebody had taken the trouble to note my plate number and phone it in, something different was going on. Somebody was setting me up. Why else would police come after me? They had to have gotten a lead from somewhere. The fight at the Shadow had not been enough to justify a predawn raid. Maybe Rogalski, the district commander, had seen a lack of cooperation in my eyes when he hinted Indi shouldn't press charges. Maybe he had dimed me out when Kenny's body was found.

"You have my gun," I said finally. "Why don't you drag your lab rats out of bed and test it? You'll see it's not the murder weapon."

The two detectives exchanged a look.

"You're too smart to use your registered piece," Chalmers said.

"I'm also too smart to kill a cop and leave a trail of evidence to my front door, as if I never worked a homicide before. But that didn't stop you from busting it in and dragging me down here almost naked. I think I'm insulted." I let out a breath and leaned forward. "What made you think it was me? A nine-millimeter shell casing? Or a call to your tipline? What did the caller say? A cop was shot dead and he saw somebody driving away in a car like mine?"

Neither one said anything.

"And driving away from where? Where was the body found anyway?" I sat back. "I think you two got sucker-punched by bad intel, and you're starting to realize it."

"So you're saying you didn't shoot Kenny?" Chalmers asked.

"I didn't shoot anybody. Are you saying Kenny was shot?"

Again, silence and an exchange of looks. Pinero nodded to Chalmers.

"Kenny wasn't shot," Chalmers said. "He was beaten to death."

I don't think I could have hidden my surprise. Beaten? That took Indi out of the pool. "Kenny was a big guy. It would take a big guy to put a beat-down on him. Is that why you're looking at me? I jab him in the Adam's apple to stop a fight, and you think I iced him with my hands? Check 'em out." I lifted my hands as high as the cuffs and the ring allowed. "See? No skinned knuckles, no cuts."

"You coulda worn gloves," Pinero said.

"No defensive bruises on my arms," I said. "No signs of fighting at all, except on the side of my head." I dropped my hands back to the table top. "Oh, wait! That was you guys."

"We didn't say he was beaten with fists," Chalmers said.

"So now I snuck up behind a trained cop—the mayor's bodyguard, no less—and beat him to hell with a brick or a baseball bat?" I shook my head. "Kenny was no fool and he was probably armed. Whoever it was had to get behind him, and if he let that happen, he either trusted him or didn't consider him a threat." Or her—because a weapon put Indi back in the suspect pool, at least as far as they were concerned.

"Or you tricked him," Pinero said.

"Hey, here's a thought. Why not look at the prick who clubbed me? Berko, right? He's got poor impulse control."

Just then the interrogation room door swung open, and Phoenix Trinidad, in a beige pantsuit, stepped inside. "Okay, Rafael, play time is over. Gideon, don't say another word." She looked at Pinero and shook her head. "You arrested my client because of a text message on a prepaid cell phone? *Pendejo!* "

"*Vete al infierno!*" Pinero said "The tower hit was near his place."

I laughed. "You thought I invited Kenny to the OK Corral with a burner? Now I really am insulted."

"Gideon, be quiet," Phoenix said.

"We Mirandized him, counselor," Pinero said, "and he never asked for a lawyer."

The way he leaned into her space as he held up his hands told me they knew each other, well.

"Sure, and he was free to go at any time," she said. "Provided he could pull that table out of the floor and drag it out the door. You've got no case and you know it. Uncuff him."

Chalmers undid my cuffs and I stood up. I flinched when Phoenix came over and gingerly touched the side of my head to examine my gash. "Kayla said they hit you."

"They wanted to stop me from resisting arrest with my hands up."

"You need stitches," she said, starting toward the door. "I'll take you to an ER."

As we moved into the squad room, Berko, minus his helmet but still in his tactical uniform, rose from the edge of a desk on which he'd been sitting and came near. He had bottle-black hair and a thin salt-and-pepper mustache that curled with his smile. "Asshole lawyered up? Well, the CSU boys are good. It's only a matter of time before they find—"

He never got to finish his sentence because my uppercut caught him squarely below the chin and rattled his teeth so hard I felt the vibration in my elbow. One of the most satisfying punches I'd ever thrown, it sent him reeling into a padded, metal-framed chair which tumbled to the floor with him. Hands shot out of nowhere, and I was thrown face down onto a desk. Head pounding now and left cheek pressing down hard on a Plexiglas paperweight—thankfully round—I heard Phoenix cry, "Gideon!" as somebody jerked my hands behind my back and somebody else said, "Now we got you for assaulting an officer!"

"That's the bastard who hit me with his rifle!" I hissed.

Phoenix took the cue and whirled on Pinero. "Rafael, you had no probable cause to break down Mr. Rimes's door and even less to have one of your men hit him with a weapon."

"Berko acted on his own," Chalmers said. "I was gonna write him up."

"Good for you," Phoenix said. "Now, Mr. Rimes is black,

so there's a good chance of keloid scarring if that laceration isn't stitched up. Perhaps even scalp disfigurement. I'd hate to stick the city with more than an ER bill. Forget the assault charge, and I'll advise my client not to sue for false arrest, or jam up Berko with his own charges—assault, harassment..."

For a moment no one moved. Then hands fell away from my arms and back like skin off a shedding snake. Unsure who had given the signal to release me, I pushed myself up from the desktop and rubbed my left cheek. Seven or eight detectives and uniforms, their faces flushed with anger, stepped back to give me room. Turning to Chalmers and Pinero, I spoke calmly. "If I wanted to meet Kenny—to settle things, as you say—it would have been just like that, face to face."

Phoenix took hold of my arm, as if certifying for those present that she understood I was crazy and would keep me from throwing another punch. "Let's get you to a hospital." She pulled me away from the growing circle of cops.

"Gotta get my gun back first," I whispered. "It's got nothing to do with the murder."

"Gideon—"

"I'll need it," I said, still close to her ear, "if I'm going to find Kenny's killer."

Chapter 12

Phoenix was parked on Church Street, around the corner from Buffalo Police Headquarters on Franklin. She left me just inside the door as she went to get her car. Most of those who passed me on their way into or out of the building seemed to find nothing unusual about a bloody, barefoot black man in T-shirt and shorts standing by the door on a Sunday morning. No one noticed my gun because it was under my T-shirt, in the band of my running shorts, so close to my junk a pat on the back might have pushed me into a higher singing register. With my hands crossed in front of me to keep it in place, I must have looked like a near-naked church usher waiting for an offering plate at the end of a pew.

After a few minutes a white Toyota RAV4 with tinted rear windows pulled to a stop beside a parked police car. Phoenix got out after putting on the flashers. As I stepped into crisp morning air, she went around to the back and flipped up the rear door. Unzipping a soft plastic carrying case, she took out a blue emergency blanket and draped it over my shoulders when I reached the car. I climbed into the passenger seat. Grit embedded in the floor mat lightly scratched the soles of my feet, and I resisted the urge to brush them off. There was no point until I had shoes. As Phoenix had insisted before asking for my gun, I opened the glove compartment and slid the Glock inside.

Once we were heading north on Franklin, I used her white Samsung to call Bobby, who answered on the first ring. I told him I had been released and was on my way to Buffalo General's ER.

"I'll meet you there," he said. "What should I bring?"

"Clothes and sneakers would be good. My wallet, phone, leather jacket." I thought for a moment and turned slightly away from Phoenix. "My keys. And my nylon Blackhawk."

"I saw them carry your gun down," he said. "I'm surprised they gave it back."

"No reason to keep it."

"What about your glasses?"

"Yes," I said, grateful Bobby often remembered things I didn't. Then I thought about the grit and looked down. "And some wet wipes. My feet are filthy."

After I clicked off, I held out the phone to Phoenix.

"Just drop it in my purse," she said, the edge in her voice even sharper than when she left me to get the car. I noticed her hands tighten on the wheel.

Her antique white purse sat open on the floor of the passenger side, behind my left foot. I slid the phone inside and snapped the bag shut. Then I drew the blanket tighter around myself and waited.

"So what was the cowboy shit all about?" she said after ten or twelve seconds. "You just *had* to hit that guy. Who do you think you are, Clint Fucking Eastwood?"

I said nothing as she began to vent, telling me she understood violence was sometimes unavoidable.

"But this wasn't shooting two spree killers in self-defense. This was a cop, in police central no less." Clocking him had been neither necessary nor prudent. "Pinero is prick enough. You want *every* badge in town on your ass?" Giving me no time to answer, she added that if I pushed my way into the investigation and got charged with obstruction of justice or got my license pulled, there was nothing she could do about it. The more she ranted, however, the more the anger in her voice subsided. After two or three minutes it faded into something that seemed a cross between disappointment and hurt. Finally, after muttering I was clueless, just like other men, she sighed, "It doesn't matter."

"I don't particularly like violence," I said.

"But you won't hesitate to be violent."

"No, I won't. Not when I need to be."

"When you *need* to be?"

"Do you know the motto of the Army CID?"

She shook her head.

"'Do what has to be done.'" I waited for a response but she glanced over at me blankly. "Berko's a bully, a guy who got a badge to sanction his behavior. A bully has to get knocked on his ass every now and again so he'll think twice before pushing somebody else around."

"That's what you were doing?" she said after a few seconds. "A pre-emptive strike on police brutality?"

"A well-timed use of force."

"And you took no personal pleasure in dropping him?"

"Oh, I enjoyed the hell out of it." I looked straight ahead, loosening the blanket a bit because the car had begun to warm. "I'll enjoy the memory even more when they stick a lidocaine needle in my skull." I turned to her. "Now you know I don't lie to my lawyer."

Despite her anger, she laughed. "Good." After a few seconds she said, "So do what has to be done pretty much sums you up?"

"Yes," I said. "What was that between you and Pinero?"

"He told me to go to hell after I called him a jerk."

"Sounds personal."

"It is. We—we went out—years ago. Not one of my smarter moves." She drew in a breath and let it out slowly. "Maybe I'll tell you about it some time. Then you'll know your lawyer won't lie to you. Right now let's stick to the matter at hand."

"In the spirit of all this honesty," I said, "I want you to know I didn't kill Kenny."

"I know," she said. "I may think you're an asshole for hitting Berko when the cops need to staple a beating death to somebody. You have this cool detachment thing going on but it can't hide the real you. There's a difference between cool and cold-blooded. Your veins lack the requisite ice crystals for you to be a snake. You're not a murderer."

"I'm glad you see me that way but anybody can commit murder."

"Almost anybody can *kill*. Not everybody can *murder*." She turned to look at me for a second, as if she thought I might question the difference. But I knew the difference, and she could see I knew. Her eyes swung back to the street. "I learned long ago to trust my legal instincts. You were forced to kill before—to do what had to be done. If you're forced to kill again, it will bother you just as much, but you'll live with it." She hesitated, glanced at me. "There's something reassuring about you, Gideon Rimes. Maybe a quiet strength that helps you do what's necessary when others can't. Maybe a face that says you're tough but more in touch with your feelings than your ego. I don't usually find tough men so...attractive."

For two or three blocks we were quiet. Her last words hung in the air between us.

"Sorry if I make you uncomfortable," she said finally, turning right onto Virginia.

"You don't."

"And sorry if I acted like a harpy. I was starting to feel that—" Her voice caught.

"Phoenix—"

"Just forget I said anything." She swiped a backhand across her eyes. "You're not out of the circus yet. They still think you're good for Kenny. You need a lawyer right now, not complications." She shrugged. "So, if I'm your lawyer—" She let out a brief, bitter breath. "I was partly mad at myself, you know." We turned left onto Main and headed toward High Street and Buffalo General. "I was mad for talking myself out of something foolish last night. If I had invited you in for a drink, as I wanted to, it may have been a breach of ethics and probably something we'd both regret, but you would have had an unimpeachable alibi."

"You and Captain Mag Lite."

"That's right. You couldn't leave without going past Phil."

"For the record, I would have said yes—but not last night." I shifted in my seat and studied her profile. Her confession had pushed color into the one cheek I could see. Her lips were pressed together in a tight line and her eyes were fixed on the street ahead. "Last night I went back to Indi's place to wait for Kenny. I was prepared to cable tie his hands and take him in, but he never came."

"Probably because he was lying dead in the park."

"Delaware Park?"

She nodded. "Behind the Rose Garden, not far from Shakespeare Hill."

"What the hell?" What was he doing where the Shakespeare in the Park Company assembled a modular stage and performed two of the Bard's plays every summer?

"I spoke to the homicide commander before I barged into interrogation," she said, stopping for a red light at Main and Carlton. "I didn't see the phone but he told me about the message they found on it. Something like, *Need to settle up? Rose Garden, one hour.*"

"That doesn't make any sense. Why would they think I sent that text?"

"Obviously, somebody told them you had a fight with Kenny."

"Yes, but who?" I thought for a moment. "What time was the message sent?"

"A little past midnight."

"About an hour after I dropped you off."

"Yes," she said, pulling forward after the light changed. "You were sitting on Indi's place with no alibi, but by then Kenny should have been in custody."

"What time did the call come in about Kenny's body?"

"A little after one. And before you ask, the number was different. An anonymous tip on one of the few payphones left, in a plaza on Delaware Avenue."

"Was it the tipster who gave them my name?"

"I don't know."

"Indi's apartment isn't too far from the park. Neither is mine, and neither is the payphone." I considered that. "Pinero said the text message pinged off a tower near my building. There's a tower in the middle of the park."

"Which means what?"

"The text could have come from Indi's place or mine or the Shadow Lounge and hit the tower first. Hell, it could even have come from inside the park."

Lips parting in sudden realization, she turned onto High Street. "That means the killer might have sent the message while he was standing over the body."

I nodded. "And might have staged the scene before he went somewhere else and used a payphone to call it in." I looked at her as she turned into the emergency room parking lot. "The only question is, why wouldn't the killer just wait for somebody else to find the body? Why would he wait an hour and then call the tip line himself?"

Chapter 13

The ER waiting room wasn't as crowded as it must have been the night before. Those ahead of me had Sunday morning kinds of emergencies—a heart attack, a fall down church steps, a screaming baby with a fever, a rear-ender that left an elderly couple holding hands and wearing cervical collars. Apart from those who got the heart attack victim—a woman in her seventies—to the CCU, the staff moved at a Sunday morning pace too, drinking coffee, doing paperwork with little sense of urgency. Those of us seeking treatment sat on padded black chairs and bench seats, nodding off, paging through magazines, watching wall-mounted flat-screen TVs, or just staring out the large plate glass windows at the sunny fall day we were missing. I began to think I might be there till nightfall.

Bobby reached Buffalo General ten minutes after us. Having thrown on wrinkled khakis and the old brown jacket he wore when he helped Sam Wingard with yard work, he brought a paper bag into the waiting room and handed me my glasses. Stripping in a small unisex lavatory, I washed my face with paper towels and scrubbed my feet with alcohol wipes. Then I pulled on my black moleskin shirt, jeans, socks, and sneakers. The bag also had held my wallet, phone, and keys— including keys for the new front door and apartment locks Sam had already installed—along with a disposable toothbrush and a tan baseball cap. "For after they shave your head," Bobby had said, adding that my jacket and Blackhawk holster were in his car. I stuffed my T-shirt and shorts into the bag. Phoenix had taken my picture with her phone but insisted I keep my sleepwear in case we needed it for evidence.

Cleaner, if not clean, I returned to the waiting room, where now a dozen or so seats were occupied. I sat between Bobby and Phoenix on a bench seat and set the bag on the floor. I thanked her for coming to get me and driving me to the hospital. "You don't have to stay," I said. "I know you have better things to do. I can ride home with Bobby."

She shook her head. "If they come after you again or we have to sue, it's better I'm here now to make sure everything gets done right. Once you're stitched up, I'll pick up Indi and take her home. Then I'll go back to my Sunday." She studied me for a moment. "And I'd advise you to do the same. Go home and watch whatever's left of the Bills game. Let the police handle this investigation. Get in their way, and they'll probably charge you with obstruction of justice."

I said nothing.

My time in the hospital would have lasted longer than three hours and nine magazines if I hadn't balked at the skull CT the attending physician ordered after I was finally shown into an exam room. A thirty-something dark-skinned woman with big amber eyes, small deft hands, and a faintly British accent, she checked my vitals, chatted with me to evaluate my lucidity, and momentarily stiffened in discomfort when I explained I had been clubbed by a SWAT cop. After shaving the hair around my gash and cleaning it, she injected me with lidocaine and stitched the wound shut. Then she recommended the scan and apologized that getting to radiology would take a while because it was Sunday.

I shook my head—felt no pain—and slid off the examination gurney, saying I didn't have the time to wait.

She looked at me with open-mouthed horror and stomped after me into the waiting room. "Could be a concussion," she said. "Or a subdural hematoma that could cause problems later."

Just as I spun around to repeat that I needed to leave, she looked past me and smiled.

I turned to see that Bobby had risen and was drawing near, Phoenix a few steps behind him. His hand was outstretched, and I already knew what would come next. Bobby's ex-students were everywhere.

"Dr. Chance," the attending said warmly, taking his hand. "Good to see you again."

"Good to see you too, Ayodele. So you didn't remain in Nigeria, and I see you didn't go into teaching, after all. Is it *Doctor* Ibazebo now?" When she nodded, he looked at me, lips shifting from a prideful smile to the half-frown I knew only too well as the prelude to a lecture. "Did I hear something about a possible concussion or subdural hematoma?"

"Bobby, the longer I take to get on this guy's trail, the colder it'll be."

"Obstruction," Phoenix said. "How many times do I have to tell you?"

"Or maybe even an epidural hematoma," Dr. Ibazebo said. "We need to get a CT scan to be sure."

Brow knit and black frames low on his nose, my godfather looked up at me with his kind teacher's eyes. "I wonder which one will get cold faster, the trail or your body if you die from a brain bleed." Then he turned to his former student, inclining his head just enough that she understood he was bowing to her judgment. "Dr. Ibazebo, since my godson is intent on pursuing a life-and-death matter, even at risk to himself, is there any way we can expedite the CT?"

"With a head as hard as his," she said, "getting good film may be difficult. But for you I will see what I can do." Shaking her own head, she stepped into a nearby office.

Bobby turned to Phoenix. "Ms. Trinidad, if you choose to walk away now, I'm sure Gideon will understand and harbor no ill feelings. But if you continue to represent him, or choose to become his friend, please understand that he *will* investigate and will stop *if and only if* he or the police find the killer."

"I've already figured out he's stubborn," Phoenix said.

"Not stubborn," Bobby said. "Persistent."

I braced myself for the famous Calvin Coolidge quote about persistence, something I'd heard recited throughout my teens, but this time Bobby continued without mentioning a president who served nearly a century ago.

"Persistence is one of his two strongest character traits," Bobby said. "The other is loyalty. I'm sure you will agree there are worse qualities in some men, but you might find Gideon useful, especially if you continue to represent Ms. Waters and need an investigator."

Phoenix sighed, nodded, and returned to her seat. Ten minutes later, she squeezed my hand when I was put into a wheelchair and taken to an elevator. Soon I was on my back, being eased into the donut-shaped opening of a large white scan unit. It was a tight fit for a man with broad shoulders, but I kept still and cooperated, as Phoenix and the doctor had cooperated.

Talk about persistence. It was damn near impossible for anyone to win an argument with Bobby.

Chapter 14

When we left the hospital, it was half past three and still sunny enough my transition lenses began to darken. But I could feel the start of a chill through my shirt. I was grateful Bobby'd had enough foresight to bring me a cap with an adjustable backstrap. It not only covered the small bald spot around my scalp stitches but could be loosened enough not to abrade the area when the local anesthetic wore off later. Though the official CT results would take a day, Dr. Ibazebo assured me from her reading of the images there was no concussion or hematoma. Site pain was the worst I could expect. She recommended ibuprofen and bed rest.

Phoenix agreed to take me with her to collect Indi from Hope's Haven. She walked through the ER lot to her RAV4 as I crossed East North with Bobby. I traded my bag for the leather jacket and shoulder holster on the back seat of his silver Camry. As soon as I had shrugged into my rig and jacket, Phoenix pulled up next to the Camry. Promising Bobby I would come upstairs to see him when I got home, I climbed into the RAV4's passenger seat. I clicked the seatbelt and checked the charge in my phone. The battery icon was more than half green. As Phoenix headed up East North to Main Street, I took my Glock from her glove compartment and slid it into my holster.

She turned right. "You want to make sure Indi never left the shelter last night."

"I do."

"No way she got past Oscar, especially right after we dropped her off."

"I'm inclined to agree," I said. "I just want to be sure." What I didn't tell her was that I wanted to see how Indi reacted to the news of Kenny's death—if she didn't already know about it. I thought about that for a moment. If she did know, it wouldn't have come from television. It was Sunday, which meant local morning airwaves would have been occupied by network programming devoted to discussions of national politics. Afternoons belonged to football, golf, post-season baseball, and infomercials. With the exceptions of CNN and a couple other news outlets, cable networks would be full of old movies, specialty shows, and re-runs. A beating death in a Buffalo city park was insufficiently horrific for a cable news crawl, much less a full story. Even if Indi were a PGA or MLB fan, it was unlikely anyone would break into network programming with a local story best saved for the evening news broadcast. But radio was another matter. I doubted Kenny's name would have been released to the media before noon or one, which meant Indi might have heard the story at two or three—if she listened to a station with an hourly update. With communications into and out of Hope's Haven limited, the odds were good, I decided, she had not yet heard.

I didn't think Indi was involved. Still, there was a chance she had played all of us—me, Phoenix, Doc, and the band—for reasons yet unknown. Someone might have beaten Kenny on her behalf, even at her request. I wanted to hit her with the news of his death so I could study her response. She would register surprise, of course, but would it be genuine? Would there be tears, regret, relief, indifference? Whatever her reaction, I hoped it would tell me whether I should start with her or look elsewhere. It was just as likely a cop who had been shot while serving on the city's Gang Crimes Task Force might have been murdered by someone with a motive that had nothing to do with Indi.

"I know I'll have to wait somewhere downstairs while you go get her," I said, "but I'd like it if we could tell her about Kenny together."

Phoenix drew in a breath as if about to answer, perhaps to protest. Then she sighed, pressed her lips together, and nodded.

Traffic was light. Hope's Haven was a straight shot up Main. We reached it in ten or twelve minutes. Phoenix turned left into the second entrance of the semicircular drive and parked on the edge near the right side of the building. We got out, and she slung her purse over her shoulder. We walked toward the porch. Looking directly at each surveillance camera, I followed her through the security doors to the front desk.

This afternoon, the man wearing a blue blazer and a belt with a holstered Taser was a thickset blond with square-tipped fingers and blue eyes. He was about my age and his name was Don. He shook my hand as Phoenix rounded a corner and disappeared into a paneled corridor. Don led me to a mid-sized conference room perpendicular to the security desk. The room had mint-colored walls, reflecting fluorescent ceiling lights, and a gleaming mahogany table with seating for eight. A large potted plant I could not identify sat on a stand on either side of drawn dark green curtains which stretched from ceiling to floor. Gesturing me into one of the upholstered chairs on casters, Don withdrew and shut the door.

Once I was alone, I took out my key ring and unhooked the gold carabiner that held Indi's apartment keys. Then I returned both sets of keys to my jacket pocket. My head began to throb as the lidocaine wore off. I closed my eyes and tried to steady my breathing. I did not want to be sidelined by a headache. I still had things to do before ibuprofen and bed rest, at least one more place to go. Whatever Indi's reaction, I had to go to LJ's to get a mini-DVD of last night's fight. And I'd have to watch it, again and again, head pain or no—

Just then the door opened. Indi stepped inside, with Phoenix right behind her. Indi was in the same jeans and jacket she'd worn last night and carried the same garment bag, shoe bag, and clutch purse. She wore no make-up but obviously had brushed her hair, which meant she had opened her purse. I wondered if she had noticed the keys missing from the inside zipper pouch.

"She says I can go home now," Indi said. "Says you'll explain everything." She bit her lip. "So they got Kenny?"

I stood and took a step toward her. "Somebody got him," I said. "He's dead."

Indi's intake of breath was sharp and immediate. Her eyes widened and she let go of her things to clamp her hands over her mouth. She shuddered, trembled. The tears began before Phoenix and I could get her into a chair.

"What—what—happened?" she gasped.

I looked at Phoenix, who stood beside Indi's chair and slid an arm around her. "He was killed in the park last night," I said.

"Oh my God!" Indi turned to Phoenix and looked up. "Oh my God!" Then she buried her face in the jacket of the beige pantsuit and sobbed.

I crouched to pick up Indi's belongings, slipping her keys into the clutch purse before I straightened and laid everything on the table. I waited for her crying to run its course. When at last she let go of Phoenix, she slumped back in the chair and stared off at some imaginary point on the wall. Her face was slack and tear-streaked. Phoenix reached into her own purse for a wad of tissue. Indi took it, dabbed her eyes, and wiped her nose. "He didn't deserve to get killed," she said after a moment.

"No, he didn't," Phoenix said. "But you'd best believe the police will do everything they can to nail a cop-killer."

"Indi," I said, "I'm going to put all your stuff inside the big bag and then we'll take you home." Half-looking at me, she nodded. I unzipped the garment bag—which held the same leather pants and yellow satin blouse she had performed in last night—and put the shoe bag inside. "Keys in your purse?" Again she nodded. My gaze never leaving hers, I felt around inside the purse and held up the carabiner. Then I closed the purse, laid it next to the shoe bag, and zipped the garment bag shut.

"Are you ready?" Phoenix asked.

Indi sniffled, swallowed, and nodded for the third time. "Could you take me to Doc's?" she said, climbing to her feet.

There was something helpless and halting in the way she spoke, as if she were a child asking for the bedroom light to be left on. "Doc's wife likes to fuss over me and feed me—and I don't think I can be alone right now." She began to cry again.

Phoenix kept an arm around her. "Sure, we'll call ahead." Then she threw me an over-the-shoulder glance. "You drive. We'll sit in the back."

Nodding, I returned Indi's keys to her purse and made a mental note that she hadn't asked *how* Kenny had been killed.

Chapter 15

The Rogers' house, a burgundy duplex with navy trim, was on Humboldt Parkway near Utica and overlooked the Kensington Expressway. I turned into the driveway and parked behind a metallic blue Cadillac DeVille nearly forty years old.

We climbed out. I handed Phoenix her keys. Then she and I followed Indi up the front steps to a large oak door with leaded glass. To the left of the door was a wide front porch with a curtained picture window I could tell was a layered acrylic the average burglar would find too difficult to break. In front of the window was a round patio table with a pebbled glass top and four padded folding chairs. Inside the foyer were two steel security doors, each with a semicircular viewing window in the upper third. Indi pressed the downstairs doorbell, and the door to the left opened after a few seconds.

A small caramel-skinned woman in a rust-colored dress stepped into the foyer and unlocked the outer door. "You poor thing!" she said, enfolding Indi in her arms.

Indi gulped a breath, as if choking back new tears. Then Doc was in the doorway, looking sad himself as he slipped his arms around Indi and his wife and pulled them inside.

Phoenix and I followed the three of them into a wide, brightly lit living room with a baby grand piano in the front corner, a modest flat-screen TV in front of a fake fireplace, and a tan sofa set which included a loveseat, recliner, and marble-topped coffee table. Atop the piano and mantel and at

varying heights on the walls were twenty or so framed photographs, many of Doc and the JBA, as well as younger Docs
with at least four different bands, on numerous stages. As I
paused to look at a picture of a baby-faced Doc shaking hands
with Count Basie, his wife led Indi to the sofa and they both
sat. Doc moved toward the recliner—*his* recliner, I expected.

"Y'all take a seat," he said. "Lizzy, this here's Mr. Rimes
and Miss Trinidad. They been lookin' after our Indigo."

Lizzy Rogers kept one arm around Indi and reached over
the coffee table to shake our hands as Phoenix and I went to
the loveseat. Doc was still in a white shirt and striped gold tie
knotted to the neck, as if they had just returned from church.
He tugged the creases of his crisp navy slacks and sank into his
recliner.

For a moment no one spoke as Lizzy held Indi. Then Doc
leaned forward and looked at me, his face contorted. "So the
boy is *dead?*"

I nodded. He opened his mouth as if about to ask what happened, and I gave a quick shake of my head. I glanced toward
Indi to suggest I wanted to spare her the details.

Doc nodded. "Baby girl, can I get you some water?"

"Yes, please."

Doc rose. "Miss Trinidad, water or ice tea? I'm afraid we
drunk up all the coffee this morning. But I could start a fresh
pot if you want."

"No thanks," Phoenix said.

"Lizzy?"

"I'm fine, honey," his wife said.

"What about you, Mr. Rimes?'

"Sure," I said, standing. "Water would be nice."

Doc led me into a dining room with walls the same corn-
silk color as the living room. These held a dozen or so carved
African masks and more photographs of Doc, alone at a piano
or with one band or another in venues I had never seen. A couple of the backgrounds had a *deja vu* quality not unlike the
butcher-on-the-bus phenomenon, where you see a face that
strikes you as familiar and may or may not belong to someone
you've met. Some of the photos featured massive-breasted

Nona Swanson squeezed into an assortment of glittering dresses. Others put different women singers front and center, including two or three with Indi smiling broadly. Doc stepped into a white kitchen with old-fashioned cupboards and turned back to me. "Like I said, I done played just about everywhere."

I nodded. "Not just bars and nightclubs, but it looks like state fairs and public parks and even schools."

"Yep. I've played jazz piano in a bar on Saturday night and gospel piano in church on Sunday morning. When they offer you money, you play wherever they put you. " He pulled two glasses from the cupboard over the sink and a plastic Britta pitcher from the refrigerator and began to pour. "So, what happened?"

"Kenny was beaten to death in Delaware Park last night," I said.

"Beaten?" He stopped pouring and shook his head. "He was a big boy."

"Yes."

"They know who done it?"

"They think I did."

Doc studied me a moment, eyebrows raised. "I guess you big enough and you were ready to shoot him on Friday." Then he shook his head again and resumed pouring. "But you couldn'ta done it or you'd look like you went a few rounds with somebody tough as you." He handed me the first glass.

"Thanks, Doc." I took a swallow. "No, I didn't do it, but the only reason I'm not still in interrogation is Ms. Trinidad came to get me." I pulled off my cap and angled my head so he could see my stitches.

He winced at the sight, almost overfilled the second glass. "Cops done that to you?"

"Yes," I said, putting my cap back on. "One did. To convince me not to resist arrest."

"Man, that's some shit. I guess somebody musta told 'em about last night."

"They knew."

"Police brutality against another black man. You oughta sue."

I shook my head. "We made a deal on the way out."

He looked at me as if he wanted to ask what the deal was but instead took the Britta pitcher to the sink. He added more water to the filter chamber then returned the pitcher to the refrigerator. "I 'spect Indi asked you to bring her here 'cause she don't wanna be alone right now and you ain't the hand-holding type, now she don't need a bodyguard." He poured a splash of water from the overfilled glass into the sink, then wiped the side of the glass with the edge of a dishtowel hanging nearby. "She can stay with us long as she want," he said, gesturing me toward the door.

We returned to the living room. Doc gave Indi her water. She swallowed half the glass before we sat down again. She looked at Lizzy, with the discomfort of one who feared she might violate a standing house rule. Lizzy told her she could set the glass on the coffee table, as long as it was atop one of the magazines. She did.

"So what now?" Lizzy asked Phoenix.

"The police will want to talk to Indi at some point. Once I produce sworn statements from staff that she was at Hope's Haven all night, they won't consider her a suspect, but—"

"Suspect?" Indi said. "They think I killed Kenny?"

"Girl ain't big enough to beat up a hamster," Doc said. "Why, she couldn't—"

I coughed hard and gulped some water. This caught Doc's attention, and I gave him another shake of my head. He nodded and fell silent, likely believing I just wanted to spare Indi the pain of the particulars. What I wanted was for Indi to ask what happened. So far, she hadn't. That bothered me.

"They don't know who did it, Indi," Phoenix said patiently. "They'll know you didn't when I give them documentation, but they'll still want to talk to you."

"Lizzy," I said, "you should drop by Indi's place in the next half hour or so to get her some clothes. Two of the cops have already seen Doc and might recognize him if he comes near her building. Right now they don't know where she is and are probably looking for her. She's safer if she talks to them only when her lawyer is with her. If anybody interferes, call Ms.

Trinidad immediately. She *will* handle it. She's one hell of a lawyer."

Phoenix smiled at me then handed Lizzy her card. "I know one of the lead detectives, Rafael Pinero. I'll call him and try to set up an appointment for late tomorrow afternoon."

"I have to go the police station?" Indi sounded nervous.

Phoenix shook her head. "We'll do it in my office. I'll pick you up—or maybe have Mr. Rimes do it."

"Of course," I said.

"See, sugar?" Doc said. "It's gonna be okay. Got good people lookin' out for you."

For a moment Indi looked as if she might cry again, but then she smiled, and Lizzy pulled her closer. She kissed Indi's forehead and held her tight for a few seconds. Sipping my water, I realized Lizzy's expression of maternal instinct was as much for her benefit as Indi's. There were plenty of pictures of Doc around, and a few of Doc and Lizzy, including a wedding picture in which they looked about nineteen. Off in one corner hung the obligatory tri-panel of President Kennedy, Martin Luther King, and Jesus. But there were no children in school portraits, no young adults in cap and gown or military uniform, no grandchildren squirming on Santa's lap. Doc and Lizzy were childless. Lizzy's modeling of etiquette about such things as water rings on furniture, the huge plate of leftovers from early Sunday dinner she would likely prepare as soon as we were gone, Doc's references to *our little girl* and *our Indigo*, the protective impulses both clearly felt—everything was intended to fill a void in their long lives together.

"I'll call you here to let you know the time of the appointment," Phoenix said. "And I'll call Marla to let her know you won't be in for a couple days. She has a good sub list."

Indi nodded.

Phoenix stood as I downed the last of my water. "Then we should get going." She looked at me and shrugged. "I have to get my investigator home so he can get some sleep."

I climbed to my feet. "Does my new title come with a raise?"

"Depends on the quality of your work."

Phoenix stepped aside as Doc took my glass and showed us toward the door. "Don't worry, folks," he said. "We got her now, and she'll be fine."

I was sure she would.

Chapter 16

It was quarter past five when we reached my building. Phoenix kept a finger on the lock button until I promised her I would eat dinner then take a rest. "You came to my rescue today and stayed when you didn't have to," I said. "Thank you."

She smiled as I climbed out, and I remembered how much I had liked her smile that first day in my office. I waved and waited till she had driven off to walk up Elmwood to where I had parked my Escape last night. I intended to honor my promise but I had one more errand to run first.

LJ lived with his parents in a three-bedroom single family home on Admiral Road in North Buffalo. The house was white-trimmed brick with a split lawn, center entrance, and wide front porch. The railing to the right of the front door had been removed to accommodate the steel wheelchair ramp used by LJ's father—my old Buff State partner Jimmy Doran, left paralyzed from the waist down by a nine-millimeter bullet from Marv Tull.

When I parked in front of the house, I took a second to inhale deeply before I climbed out. In the wake of the shooting, Jimmy had become one of my closest friends. I saw him frequently, but I always gave myself a moment before going to ring the bell. Jimmy had never blamed me for the card he'd drawn, but he didn't need to. I blamed myself. Bobby once told me the heartbeat I always took before getting out of my car at Jimmy's was an attempt to measure my hesitation before

I drew my gun and fired at Tull and Hellman, to relive the moment in search of a different outcome. "No matter how much you'd like a chance to set things right," Bobby said, "you have to move on."

Peggy Ann opened the door for me and greeted me with her trademark smile then pulled off her sequin-studded glasses and stood on her toes to kiss my cheek. A pretty woman with milk chocolate skin and dreadlocks that smelled faintly of olive oil, she wore tan slacks and a denim top. She was in her mid-fifties, like Jimmy, but still had the figure of a woman who played tennis three times a week, which, I knew, she did.

"LJ said you were swinging by today to pick up something he shot last night," Peggy Ann said when I stepped past her into the paneled living room. Chairs and couches were against three walls, and the old hardwood floor bore the scuff marks of narrow rubber tires. "Jimmy and I had a bet about whether you would get here by dinner time, and you just made me win. I'll set a place for you."

I took off my hat, as Peggy Ann always required gentlemen to do in her home, and stuck it in my back pocket. I saw her eyes widen at the sight of my bald spot and stitches. A former nurse practitioner who had taken early retirement to care for her husband, she went up on her toes a second time to inspect the work. I bent to make it easier for her.

"What happened?"

"Long story," I said. "Tell you about it at dinner." I straightened to my full height as she dropped her heels. "And let me apologize in advance for my manners tonight. I haven't eaten anything today but chips and candy from a hospital vending machine, so I might talk with my mouth full."

"Then you'll have to eat on the back deck," she said, laughing. "Jimmy and LJ are in the office. Tell them we eat in fifteen minutes."

I went through the house to the back, to what was once a large rectangular breakfast room with six tall windows opposite the door and two on either end. Beyond the glass was the wide back yard that held Peggy Ann's vegetable garden, the swing set LJ had played on as a child, and the custom-built enclosed deck with a long, narrow year-round lap pool for Jimmy's regular exercise. All the modifications to the house—front and rear wheelchair ramps, widened doorways, the chair lift to the second floor, the back deck—had been paid for not with Jimmy's pension from twenty-five years with the state police and his disability pension from Buffalo State, but with insurance money and the proceeds of a lawsuit against the state of Pennsylvania for the security lapses that permitted Tull and Hellman to begin their spree. Despite being financially comfortable for the first time in his life, however, Jimmy was the kind of man who needed to work.

Six months after he came home from the hospital, Jimmy had an idea for a business that combined his law enforcement savvy with his son's high tech aptitude. A Buffalo State sophomore who had been given a full scholarship in the wake of his father's shooting, LJ had grasped the possibilities instantly. Over the next year the breakfast room had evolved into the office of Doran Private Security Consulting Services. Here they built custom-designed gear and gadgets for clients with unusual needs: stickpin cameras and recording devices, pocket alarms, personal GPS trackers built into everything from the stems of eyeglasses to medical alert bracelets, pepper sprayers disguised as jewelry, daggers hidden inside ball point pens. The narrow tables against all the window sills always held computer towers and flat screen monitors, circuit boards, micro video lenses, wireless button microphones, various other electronics components, and small tools beside a large lighted magnifier.

Now Jimmy was proud he had come back from the edge of death to build a successful home-based business that catered to customers from police agencies and corporate security providers to private citizens who preferred protection which extended beyond a monitored home alarm system.

Today, as usual, Jimmy's motorized wheelchair was in the center of everything, moving from one station to another as LJ—Little Jimmy—sat at one of the many computers. Having seen me on the front porch in one of the monitors, Jimmy said hi with his back still to me, then spun his chair to face me.

"Good to see you, G. What's it been, about a month?" He stuck out his hand.

"About," I said, taking his hand and, as always, making a mental note of his grip strength. I could tell from the handshake and the freckled biceps pushing the limits of his blue short-sleeved shirt that he was doing his exercises regularly. I was pleased.

"Hey, G." Grinning, LJ had turned away from his computer, and I could see Beyoncé on his oversized black T-shirt.

"LJ."

Dirty blond hair short enough to reveal touches of gray, Jimmy folded his hands in his lap and squinted up at my head. "Looks like the PI business is getting a little rougher than process-serving and motel photography."

"And *Google News* had a picture of the Buffalo cop who got killed last night," LJ said. "Looked just like the guy you had me film."

"I'll tell you all about it at dinner," I said. "Peggy Ann says it's in fifteen."

Jimmy looked at his wristwatch and nodded.

"What did you lose in the bet?" I asked.

He grinned. "The only thing I ever lose, and I lost on purpose. *Bon appetit!*"

I pressed my lips together to keep from laughing while LJ was there. Once, during a rehab session I had spent beside him, Jimmy had confided to me he was worried about sex now that he could no longer get an erection. He was afraid Peggy Ann—the woman I had seen weep with relief when the surgeon came out to tell her he would live but never walk again—would leave him now that their very active sex life had slammed into a wall. He could live without ever coming again, he said, but he couldn't live without Peggy Ann, without her touch and her smile and her laugh. "Is the old in-out all you ever did?" I asked. When he shook his head, I shrugged and said, "*Bon appetit!*" which made him laugh so hard he nearly dropped the dumbbell he was curling.

"I got your disk," LJ said, holding up a mini crystal case. "Want to see it?"

I shook my head. "I can look at it at home."

"Pop it in," Jimmy said. "We've got time."

I took a seat, and the three of us crowded around the computer. LJ did as his father asked. In a moment, his screen was filled with a wide angle image of my stepping in front of Kenny and the bouncers converging on us. The image shook as LJ hurried toward us and zoomed in, but he'd caught it all—the assault on the bouncers, my fight with Kenny, Kayla's intervention, Kenny's moving off down the street with his hands in his pockets as if he had nothing to worry about. The disk ended with close-ups of the bouncers, one with a bloody towel over his nose and the other looking more humiliated than hurt. The sound was good too, so there could be no doubt about the context in which everything had happened. I wasn't sure how any of the footage was useful now that Kenny was dead, but the video was short enough we could watch it a second time before Peggy Ann called us to the table.

On the second viewing, I realized LJ's camera work was more artful than I first thought, that his instincts were sharp. He chose his angles carefully to take the best advantage of available lighting and zoomed in and out when he felt it necessary to focus on a detail or capture a wider image. He zoomed out as Kenny sauntered away. It was then that I noticed what I hadn't seen last night when Kenny monopolized my attention.

Directly across the street from the Shadow Lounge was a man leaning against a parked car, watching at least the end of the confrontation. The man looked vaguely familiar but I couldn't decide why when he was so far away and on screen only for a few seconds.

"Roll it back," I said to LJ, then pointed to the screen. "Freeze it there." I studied the still image of a thin man in a dark suit jacket that looked too large. The face was unclear but the man was unusually tall and had gray hair. I stabbed my finger toward him. "Is there any way you can zoom in on that guy, clean him up so his face is clearer?"

LJ nodded, fingering his keyboard and moving his mouse. After a few seconds the man grew, and his facial features sharpened. "That's about the best I can do," LJ said.

The image wasn't perfect but it was good enough.

"Can you print these out for me, the original and the blow-up?"

"Sure," LJ said. Within seconds a laser printer was whispering.

"Who's that?" Jimmy asked when I showed him the sheets.

"I don't know," I said. "But I damn sure have to find out." I didn't tell them until dinner, when I explained everything, that it was the same sallow, unreadable man who had come into the Anchor Bar with Kenny and his friends on Friday night, the one I had thought of as Gray Hair.

What the hell was he doing at the Shadow Lounge?

Chapter 17

It was dark when I got home.

Sunday night parking in my neighborhood could be difficult if you planned to sleep in on Monday. It's easy enough to find metered space on Elmwood itself, but ultralight Parking Enforcement trucks began circling early the next morning, even before metered time began, so officers knew which cars to tag when the clock struck seven. I had slept only four hours the night before and had spent Sunday bouncing from police headquarters to the hospital to Hope's Haven to Doc's to Jimmy's. Now I was ready to give body and brain a rest. With Peggy Ann's matchless fried chicken salad, red bean casserole, homemade rolls, and peach pie pushing me toward slumber, I had every intention of staying in bed till lunchtime. But as I circled the block twice in search of a place to park, I noticed a man—a redhead, with hands jammed in the pockets of a blue nylon shell—standing on the corner across the street from my building, just looking up at it.

It was Lenny, Kenny's brother.

On my third sweep, I crossed Elmwood and passed Lenny. He never looked into my car. I found a spot near the end of the block and walked back up the street, glad I had asked Bobby to bring me sneakers instead of shoes. As I got closer to the corner, I tugged my cap down with my left hand and kept my right inside my jacket, near my Glock. I slowed, then stopped seven or eight feet behind Lenny and watched him for a moment. Occasionally, he glanced left or right, but for the most part he just stared up at my building, right at my second floor window, as if he knew exactly where I lived. The curtains were open, and the timer had switched on a living room lamp. Was he waiting for me to look out so he could take a shot?

I closed the distance between us and said, "Hey, Lenny."

"Huh?" Startled, he turned, saw me, recognized me.

I couldn't recall whether he was left-handed or right, so I didn't know which arm to grab. Instead, I pressed the Glock against his forehead and swiped the back of my left hand across the front of his jacket. The gun was in his right pocket, with his hand resting on the butt but his fingers outside the trigger guard. I gripped his hand and the gun, twisting his wrist a bit. "Twitch and you're dead."

He sucked in a gallon of air and began to shake. Through the nylon shell, I peeled his fingers away from the gun—a small automatic—and wrenched it out of his pocket. I slid it into the back pocket of my jeans without looking at it. Then I stepped back, pulling the barrel away from his forehead. "What the fuck are you doing here, Lenny?"

He hesitated, breathing in and out a few times to stoke his courage "What do you think, asshole?" Beer breath and slightly slurred speech. Great.

I holstered my Glock. "Are you drunk enough to call somebody an asshole when he's got a gun on you or sober enough to recognize he's not the kind of man who'll shoot you in cold blood if you do? Which is it?"

"I'm not scared of you."

Buzzed but not wasted. Good. "I don't want you scared. Scared people do stupid things. I want you smart enough to think everything through."

"What?" He narrowed his eyes at me—or tried to narrow his eyes but had trouble focusing. "What are you talking about?"

I sighed. "Look, I know you think I killed your brother, and you figure you're doing what you have to do, standing up for him and all." I shook my head. "But you're going about this all wrong."

"What do you mean?"

"You don't wait out in the open, under a street light, with a belly full of beer to kill somebody, especially a real killer. Real killers are careful. Very careful. And no matter what you see in movies, they don't talk you to death before they shoot. They shoot and move on."

"Uh huh?" He looked confused.

"I'm talking to you."

"Yeah."

"Man to man."

"So?"

"If I killed your brother, why would I talk? Why wouldn't I just kill you?"

He considered that for a moment. "Because your gun would make too much noise."

Frustrated, I took hold of his collar with both hands and shook him. "Do you see a gun in my hand now? Whoever killed Kenny didn't need a gun. A real killer could beat you to death too, or strangle you." Then I jammed a fingertip against his forehead, pushing hard. "But if I had my automatic pressed like this against your head, Lenny, your skull would act as a partial silencer because—"

I exhaled some of my tension but kept my finger in place. He began to shake again, as if my index finger actually could shoot. Even in the dim glow of the streetlight, I could see the crotch of his khakis darkening. I pulled my hand away, certain I'd left a depression in his forehead. "Do you know *anything* about guns?" I patted my back pocket. His gun felt like a pocket piece, a .380, maybe a Ruger or a Kel-Tec. "If I take this out, will I even find bullets in it?"

Lenny took a step back, and his heel caught the brick border of the lawn beside which we were standing. Arms flailing, he landed flat on his ass beside a hedge and looked up at me. His eyes welled and his lower lip began to flutter. For several seconds, he held my gaze as he fought back the tears sliding down his cheeks.

When he began to hyperventilate, I couldn't tell whether it was rage or hatred or embarrassment roiling beneath his skin. Snot bubbled from his right nostril, and he wiped his nose on his sleeve. Then he buried his face in his hands and let himself go.

"Jesus God! Jesus God! Jesus God!" he said.

I looked up and down Elmwood as Lenny's blubbering grew louder. There were a few pedestrians a block or so away in either direction, near a bar one way and a coffee shop and convenience store the other. I glanced up at a few windows and saw no one staring down at us. Cars passed, but no one slowed to investigate a scene I was sure looked like the end of a fight.

Still, there was no shortage of police cruisers in town. It was only a matter of time before one happened upon us. I had to get him off the street.

"I didn't kill your brother," I said, kneeling in front of Lenny when his crying began to subside. "I think you know that."

He sniffed hard and tried to clear his throat. "Yeah, I guess I do."

I handed him a tissue from my jacket. "I was hired to body-guard his ex."

He blew his nose. "The colored singer."

"Indigo. You ever meet her?"

He shook his head. "I didn't know anything about her till we went out drinking Friday night."

"What about your folks? Did they know?"

He shook his head again.

I thought about that as I removed more tissues from my pocket pack and handed them to him. "Let me take you to my apartment so you can clean up a little. I've got a hair dryer you can use on your pants."

"You're not gonna call the cops on me?"

"No. I've seen all the cops I need to today."

"But the gun isn't registered."

"Where'd you get it?"

"It was Kenny's. He told me it was a—a throw-down—with no number."

"Then I have a couple questions I need to ask you before you go home."

"Like what?"

"First things first." I took hold of his arm and helped him to his feet. "I can make some coffee too."

As soon as we reached the top step of my building, a white cruiser with the blue stripe and logo of the Buffalo Police Department slid past. I was relieved the uni behind the wheel didn't slow down or even glance my way. The motion of a single car was no guarantee my address, description, and status as a suspected cop killer had not yet been furnished to the entire police force, but it gave me hope Chalmers and Pinero were as competent as I expected they would be. Good detectives followed the evidence, and when we parted company this morning, I was confident the evidence was leading them away from me. Still, there were a few cops like Berko, for whom everyone was guilty and being deemed otherwise was just proof the criminal justice system was hobbled by technicalities. However small the number of Berkos in the department, the right word planted in the right ear in the right cop bar could leave me dead on the wrong side of any street. And my concern was not paranoia. *Somebody* had made sure Kenny's nitwit brother had my name and address.

I put my cap on the stainless steel coat tree by the door. Then I steered Lenny past the bookcases, free weights, and heavy bag fixed to a tubular steel stand in my living room and down the corridor to my bathroom. I sat him on the toilet lid and got a towel and washcloth from the étagère above the tank. Opening the vanity below the sink, I took out a small blue hair dryer, which I plugged into the mirror's outlet and set on the bottom shelf of the étagère.

"I'll put on some coffee," I said. "The kitchen is off the hall to the right."

Lenny nodded, and I left him in the bathroom.

I turned on the kitchen light and added water to the Keurig coffee maker Bobby had given me for my last birthday. Then I chose the last K cup of dark roast from the storage carousel, popped it in, and put a Buffalo State mug from the cupboard under the spout. As I heard the hair dryer kick on in the bathroom, I took out Lenny's gun and sat in one of the two wooden bistro chairs at the dining counter. The gun was a Ruger LCP, a reliable subcompact that weighed less than a ribeye steak at Outback. I expected the olive drab green frame was intended for the camo crowd the same way the pink polymer frame I had seen in catalogues was supposed to appeal to women. The serial number stamp on the left side of the frame had been gouged into illegibility. I ejected the magazine—full—and slipped it into my jacket pocket. Examining the view hole beside the extractor and finding no round in the chamber, I set the gun on the counter and removed the folded papers from my inside jacket pocket. I opened them both and studied them for a long time, then folded them again and put them on the counter beside the gun. I wanted Lenny to tell me who Gray Hair was, but that would not be my first question.

By the time Lenny joined me, his coffee had cooled. He sat across from me and gulped it black, then set down the empty mug and accepted my offer of more. Clearly, this was not his first attempt at instant sobriety. I stood and started another K cup, French vanilla this time.

"I didn't kill your brother," I said while the coffee brewed, "but I'd like to find out who did. You okay with that?"

He nodded.

"I was a cop myself. I don't like blue funerals either." His eyes followed me about. I was pleased he was able to focus. "I can't help thinking whoever killed your brother took advantage of his situation with Indi. I'm part of it now and I want to make things right."

The second cup was ready. I set it in front of him and sat down. He sipped this time.

"I need to ask you some questions," I said, leaning forward and folding my hands on the dining counter.

"But I don't know anything about who killed him."

"'Course not, or you wouldn't have been waiting to shoot me."

"Sorry."

"No problem." I slid the empty gun to him. "Tell me about this."

He picked it up between his fingertips and looked at it as if he were in awe of it. I decided it was a good thing he hadn't

had six in the box and one in the chamber. A guy like Lenny—
with too much beer, too little familiarity with firearms, and a
fully loaded gun in his pocket—stood a better chance of shooting off his own dick than defending himself.

"What do you want to know?"

"You said it was your brother's. Do you know how he got
it?"

He set the gun down and picked up his coffee cup. "No."

"How did you come by it? Kenny give it to you?"

He shook his head. "I knew where he kept it, in his room."

I remembered Kenny's address on the order of protection.
"You share the apartment on Jewett?"

"He doesn't—didn't live there anymore." Lenny took a
second to steady himself and wiped his still dry eyes, perhaps
to forestall the start of new tears. Then he fortified himself
with a good swallow of coffee. "He moved back home about
six months ago."

Six months without filing a change of address? "Back
home, as in with your folks?"

"Yeah."

"Where?"

"Richmond Avenue, near Lafayette."

Walking distance, I thought. "And you live there too?"

"Until I finish school. I'm working on an accounting degree
at D'Youville."

"Big houses on Richmond."

"Not all of them."

"Why did Kenny move home? Money problems?"

"Yes, but not his. Our parents have had it rough the past
few years."

"How so?"

"My father lost his job over ten years ago. McGoldrick Materials. They just packed up and moved to Mexico, and then
Vietnam. Left him and a couple hundred other guys with the
shit end. I mean, he got the job right out of high school, and
there he was at fifty-three with no severance, no medical, no
pension but a flimsy 401K he said he started when Reagan was
president." He stopped, eyes widening. "Hey, one night I

clicked past this old movie on AMC with somebody named Ronald Reagan. Was he related to President Reagan?"

"Same guy," I said.

"The President of the United States was a movie star? No shit!"

"He left office before you were born," I said, smiling at the thought of what Bobby's face would look like when I told him about this. "So, your dad—did he find another job?"

"He worked every now and then, at stores or bars or temp places in storefronts. Being at McGoldrick helped him move out of the First Ward and buy the house on Richmond but nobody was gonna give a real job to somebody his age. Fortunately, the house was paid off so they stayed there and got by the best they could. Kenny was a patrolman then and helped any way he could—at least that's what they tell me. I was just a kid, in seventh or eighth grade, so I don't remember much, except I had to go to a public high school instead of staying in Catholic school." He bit his lip. "And I remember when Mom got sick. Cancer."

"I'm sorry."

"She got better, but hospital bills wiped out the 401K and what little savings they had. They got a home equity loan to last them till Dad turned sixty-two and got social security. Then early this year Dad had a stroke, and now he's in a wheelchair, and his social security isn't that much, and his medical bills just keep piling up. I wanted to drop out and get a job but Kenny said he would beat my ass if I did. So he moved back in and started paying for things out of his salary." Lenny ground his right fist into his left palm. "And now he's gone."

For a time we just sat there. Slowly, rage rose in Lenny's cheeks.

"Fucking McGoldrick!"

The family-owned company had closed while I was overseas. I remembered Bobby mentioning it in one of his emails. Now I wondered what materials McGoldrick had made but decided not to ask. In Buffalo the closing of a factory and displacement of its workforce was a too-common story for which no one had been able to craft a happy ending.

"I understand your brother was shot in the line of duty," I said. "Tell me about it."

"That was about five years ago, before Mom got sick. Kenny was part of this special cop group who went after gangs and drugs and stuff. The guys from the other night, the big colored dude and the Puerto Rican with that hat—they were part of it too. GC-something."

"GCTF. The Gang Crimes Task Force," I said.

"Yeah, that was it, a task force." He inhaled deeply through his nostrils. "He was outside his place one night—"

"On Jewett?"

He nodded. "I think on his way inside, when somebody rolled up on him and pulled the trigger."

"Just like that?"

"Just like that. Good thing for him another car went by and scared them off."

"Anybody ever charged with the shooting?"

"No but everybody said it was no secret who ordered it."

"Who?"

"Some gangbanger named Quick. Colored guy."

Lorenzo Quick, leader of the Nightwalkers, a Buffalo-based street gang that had begun with drugs and prospered so much it was called a nascent *Cosa Nostra* back when I was in the CID and regularly got e-circulars about crimes involving military personnel abroad, in places like poppy-rich Afghanistan. I had read other reports when I was at Buff State, where the administration was concerned the renewed popularity of heroin would impact the student body. Owner of a dry cleaning business, Quick was smart and careful. Very careful. Though suspected of ties to everything from complex smuggling networks to dozens of unsolved murders, he had never been arrested. He had faced questioning on numerous occasions, his lawyer beside him, and was released without charges every time. Whenever he denied involvement with a gang called the Nightwalkers, he flashed his biggest smile—which revealed canine teeth capped with what appeared to be gold vampire fangs. Yes, Lorenzo Quick could have had Kenny killed with half a nod and taken a nap afterward.

When my silence became uncomfortable, Lenny said, "Hey, you don't mind I said colored, do you? I mean, some prefer black or African-American or whatever. My folks use colored because they say they can't keep up with what to call...you people."

"I'm just thinking," I said, certain now I understood why Kenny never introduced his family to Indi. "So Chalmers and Pinero go on to be homicide detectives and Kenny ends up driving the mayor around. How did that happen?"

He shrugged. "No idea but Mom was real happy he was off the street. And she thinks the mayor is a nice lady. She stopped by today and hugged Mom for a long time and said the police would spend whatever time and money it took to find the killer."

I unfolded the sheets of paper still between us and tapped the blow-up of Gray Hair. "Can you tell me who that is? He was with you the other night."

"Mr. Osterman," he said, without hesitation. "I don't know his first name. He used to be a cop but now he's in business."

"What kind of business?"

"I don't know but he wanted to offer Kenny a job."

"Full time or part time?"

"Full time, at double what he was making as a cop."

I thought about that a moment. Then I said, "Last question, Lenny. Who told you where I lived?"

It was Lenny who tapped the picture this time. "Mr. Osterman."

Chapter 18

I slept till ten-thirty and woke then only because Bobby let himself in and called out that he would make coffee— something he did when he had something important to tell me. I hoped it wasn't a lecture because I hadn't come up to see him last night, as promised. My head was throbbing slightly when I sat up. I touched my stitches just enough to calm the itch. Then I put on my glasses, slipped on my bathrobe, and went out to the kitchen.

Already sitting at the dining counter with a manila envelope and a folded newspaper at his elbow, Bobby seemed dressed for work: tan sports jacket, khakis, and a pale blue shirt with a rust-colored tie. Most likely he had a board meeting some-where or a guest lecture or a lunch date. Like many in his gen-eration, he was as busy in retirement as he had been during his career.

"You never came upstairs last night, but I heard you talking to someone so I knew you were okay. How are you this morn-ing?" Sipping coffee from a Buffalo Museum of Science mug, he gestured toward my already filled Far Side mug, which de-picted one bull looking on with interest as another blew up an inflatable cow.

A fan of cartoonist Gary Larson, Bobby had given me that mug before I left for the army.

"Mild headache and itchy stitches," I said, taking the other bistro chair. I picked up the spoon beside the mug and stirred in hazelnut creamer and took a swallow. "Sorry about not coming up but I had to take my visitor home and I got back late."

"Who was it?"

"Lenny Carnahan, the victim's brother. He came to shoot me because somebody told him I killed Kenny."

"But you talked him out of it."

"I did."

"And took his gun."

"It's in my gun safe."

"And took him home."

"To express my condolences to his parents. They're nice people."

"Now you need to talk to whoever sicced Lenny on you."

"I do."

"I don't know whether these make things harder for you or easier." He slid the envelope and the newspaper to me. "You tell me."

I opened the envelope first. It contained large prints of four photos Fred Watkins from across the hall had taken of my arrest. The blood on my head was visible in all four.

"I thanked him for you," Bobby said. "I don't know if you can use them."

I shook my head. "The cop's being written up, and thanks to Phoenix, the city's paying my ER bill."

Bobby tapped the newspaper. "What about this one?"

I unfolded the Monday morning *Buffalo News* and saw the headline: *Mayor's driver found murdered in Delaware Park.* The subhead read: *Decorated officer was in a barroom brawl shortly before his death.* Below the subhead was a poorly lit color cell phone photo in which the faces were unclear but the situation apparent, Kenny falling into the patio table at the Shadow Lounge and me in a fighting stance. The caption read: *Having attacked the two bouncers who tried to make him leave the bar, Officer Carnahan was struck down by another man. Witnesses indicate a domestic dispute was the cause of the confrontation.* The insert box below the caption held a smaller photo of the lighted crime scene in the park: *Body found at one a.m.*

"They don't name you in the article," Bobby said, "but they make it sound like you're part of a lover's triangle."

I glanced at the byline. Amanda Corso. I had first noticed that name in the paper a few months after my return home. Her primary beat was the local political scene, not crime and the courts. In one of our beer-and-darts outings, Danny Green, the mayor's husband and my brother-in-arms in Iraq, had warned his wife that Amanda Corso was a young gunslinger, not to be trusted. Ironically, when Danny died a year later, in a fall down the basement stairs of the Green home, it was Corso who won a state AP award for her coverage of his funeral. If she was assigned to the Carnahan murder, the story was already political.

"This makes it easier," I said to Bobby.

"How?"

"The angle of this picture means it had to come from across the street, and the man who most likely took it is the same man who gave Lenny this address."

"Does he have a name?"

"Osterman," I said. "No first name yet. But I bet Amanda Corso knows it."

Bobby smiled. "And you're going to get this visceral J-school apostle to reveal her sources how?"

"I'll give her a better story. But if she doesn't come through, I can have LJ—"

The land line in my bedroom rang at that moment and I went back down the corridor to answer it.

The woman's voice on the other end was crisp and efficient: "This is Mayor Green's office calling for Mr. Gideon Rimes. Is this Mr. Rimes?"

"It is."

"Mayor Green would like to see you in her office this afternoon."

"The last time I cashed a paycheck the mayor's name wasn't on it," I said. "Is she in the habit of summoning private citizens as if they work for her?"

"I will share your concerns with her," the woman said, as if Ophelia had told her any resistance on my part would be only for show. "Now, would one o'clock be convenient?"

"One would be fine."

"We'll see you then," she said, breaking the connection.

"Ophelia wants to see me," I said when I rejoined Bobby.

"Of course she does."

"What's that supposed to mean?"

"You know perfectly well what it means."

I did. When Danny was alive, we all went to one city bar or another for beer and electronic darts eight or nine times a year. It was a night off for whichever bodyguard was on duty because the mayor was certainly safe in the company of two very large combat veterans, one of them armed. Sometimes Ophelia used these occasions to press flesh or pose for photos with the bar owner while Danny and I shared a pitcher and played. Sometimes she joined us. Twice, to my surprise, she brought along attractive City Hall staffers she hoped would be good dates for me. But Ophelia was better suited to politics than matchmaking. The clerk from vital statistics was too needy in the wake of her own recent divorce, and the Common Council aide was already in a relationship with her married boss. I had no desire to step into either mess. At Danny's urging, Ophelia abandoned her attempts to "fix G up."

In the year following his death, I had joined the mayor for dinner on several occasions and escorted her to a few high profile public events, where I stood well behind her as various leaders of Buffalo's financial, political, and cultural communities expressed their sympathy. Twice she offered me a job in her administration. Once, near the end of that year and after our last attempt at beer and darts without Danny, she invited me into her bed—as Bobby had predicted she would. Because my idea of friendship meant wives of close friends were off-limits even after divorce or death, I declined all three propositions. "Yes, because of Danny," I said that night. "And when you run for re-election next year, you don't want your love life to become a distraction." Once it was clear her opponent would be the blustery conservative Councilman Wreck-It Rick Merlotta, I was glad to be a distant planet in her solar system.

"I'd better get a move on," Bobby said, breaking the brief

silence between us. "Today I'm giving a Brown Bag lecture at the Central Library, but you should—"

"On what?"

"The lecture? Oh, the many film adaptations of L. Frank Baum's Oz books."

"You mean they are more than three?" *The Wiz* with Diana Ross and Michael Jackson was the last movie I saw with my mother before she died, and, of course, I had seen the Judy Garland film on television many times. When I was in my teens I sat through a black-and-white silent *Wizard of Oz* Bobby had come across on VHS only because his parallel narration made it interesting. "See the Tin Man," he said, excited. "That's Oliver Hardy of Laurel and Hardy. And did you notice the Cowardly Lion is black? The actor's name is Spencer Bell but the credits list him as G. Howe Black. That's what passed for humor in 1925."

"There've been Oz films for more than a century," he said now. "America has folk tales and tall tales but Baum's books are the only quintessentially American fairy tales."

"I might just come hear you," I said. "Noon, right? I can walk from the library to City Hall."

Bobby shook his head. "You have a reporter to annoy but you might want to call Mira first. That's the other reason I came down. When you didn't answer her text a couple hours ago, she figured you were sleeping and didn't want to wake you. She called me instead, in case you didn't see the text."

I said without hesitation, "She did the Carnahan autopsy."

Bobby nodded.

Chapter 19

Mira Popuri, five years my junior, was the only person I ever called my sister. Her parents, from different castes in a part of India where such things still mattered in spite of modern laws, had come to the United States when her mother was pregnant. After several young couples in their area had been murdered for marrying outside their castes, the Popuris had been granted asylum. That Mira's father was a chemist and her mother a physician likely played a role in the decision.

While her father rose to a full professorship at Buffalo State and served on the faculty senate with Bobby, her mother became Evelyn's gynecologist. Like all paths to friendship, the relationship between the Chances and Popuris was cemented brick by brick over time, so that when her parents died in a plane crash in South Asia, it was only logical that nine-year-old Mira, who had no other relatives, stay with the family who cared for her whenever her parents were away. That the Chances already had guardianship of a well-adjusted teenager earning decent grades helped speed the process of Family Court's appointing them Mira's guardians.

Death, as Bobby often said, always led to new life.

With bright, curious eyes and undeniable intelligence, Mira took to her new family with apparent ease, especially to her new big brother, who took her where she needed to go, played endless games with her, and watched her whenever Bobby and Evelyn were out. We bonded, in part, because we were both orphans and understood loss on a level most children couldn't. For her first couple months in our home, Mira came to me when she couldn't sleep, when dreams of her parents woke her up and made her cry. She could have gone to Bobby and Evelyn but didn't know them well enough yet. If her father had been the type of man who did not enjoy being awakened in the middle of the night, maybe Bobby was too. So she slipped into my room and shook my shoulder until I roused and turned on the light. I wiped her eyes with tissues and let her talk until she fell asleep then carried her back to her room.

Four years after she came to us, I enlisted in the army. It was Mira who cried the hardest when I left for boot camp. In the early years, I couldn't time my leaves to attend her high school and college graduations, but I saw her whenever I made it home. I was there after Evelyn passed so together we could hold Bobby up for the funeral. Soon after, as I was making my transition from combat zone MP to CID detective, I got a special furlough from my new CO to attend her graduation from the University at Buffalo medical school. Perhaps because her parents' remains were never recovered from the mountains where their airliner went down, Mira went on to specialize in forensic pathology. After a residency in Cleveland and a divorce in Maryland, she returned to Buffalo five years ago—a brown-skinned, green-eyed, dirty-blond toddler in tow—as an assistant county medical examiner.

Mira and I had no reason to discuss her work in other than general terms. I was not a city police officer or county sheriff, much less a homicide detective. Sometimes, when the person on her table was a child or had suffered too much, whether from disease or at the hands of someone truly evil, she unburdened herself over drinks or dinner.

Only once had she shared portions of official autopsy reports with me. She had done the postmortem on Solange Aucoin, and one of her associates had handled Marv Tull, the victim and killer in the Buffalo State incident that had led to my career change. The downward track through her brain, Mira showed me, indicated Mademoiselle Aucoin had died instantly when the bullet that entered her left eye severed her brain stem and blew out her cerebellum. But my center mass shot had not granted Marv Tull the same abrupt oblivion. It had taken him six minutes to drown in his own blood. "You couldn't have done anything to save her," Mira had told me that night as I nursed a cognac. "But in a way you made him pay for what he did to her."

Now Mira had texted *Urgent u call* and called Bobby as a contingency, apparently to discuss Kenny Carnahan's autopsy.

I used my cell to call hers, and she answered on the second ring.

"Urgent?"

"Hey, G," she said. "Well, not urgent. Timely, if the cops are looking at you for this murder and you're digging into it outside official channels." That confirmed she had talked to Bobby yesterday afternoon. Likely she had offered to do the autopsy so someone else could spend Sunday evening with his or her family. "But first, how's your head?"

"Throbbing and itching," I said. "Are you calling to confirm my guilt or innocence?"

"I can't confirm either one, at least not scientifically," she said. "Or officially," which meant the conversation we were having never happened—just as well, since few knew of our familial relationship. "But I know you. If you put a guy on my table without a bullet in him, I'd expect a broken jaw or a broken nose."

"Without a bullet? Jesus, I put one guy on your table—or your colleague's table—and now I'm Wyatt Earp?"

She laughed. "I'm just saying this isn't like anything you would do. The victim here was struck with some kind of metal bar or rod that drove skull fragments deep, *very* deep, into the brain. The COD is blunt force trauma. Not your style at all."

My pocket notebook was open on the counter, my pen moving. "How many blows?"

"One or two."

"You can't tell for sure?"

She sucked her teeth. "There's a single point of impact. Either the killer was strong enough to kill him with one blow or got lucky and put a second in exactly the same place."

Unlikely, I thought. *A single swing with enough strength to kill.* "Any indications of the killer's height?"

"The vic was struck in the crown, so his back was to his killer."

"I figured as much," I said. "Or he would have pulled his gun. I think he had it in a back holster."

For a moment she didn't speak. "Were you there? When the body came in there was an empty belt holster in the small of his back. His gun was bagged at the scene."

"I had a run-in with him earlier that night. A gun wasn't obvious. Had to be in back."

"Right," she said. "You trained detectives are a pain in the ass, always figuring things out before I finish talking." Then she resumed her answer to my question. "The angle of impact can suggest a killer's height, but we have too many variables here to be precise—the slope of the ground, the distance between killer and victim, the angle of the victim's head at the moment of impact, the length and angle of the killer's arms, the length of the bar."

I waited to make sure she had finished her answer. "So what's your best estimate?"

"Average height. Sorry."

"At least I'm a couple inches taller than average," I said.

"Somebody your height still could have done it. You know, variables—"

"Right." I sighed. At least it was unlikely Indi had done it. She lacked the height and the upper body strength. "What about the weapon itself? Some kind of bar or rod, you said."

"Round, not flat or hexagonal like some pry bars, probably eighteen to twenty inches long, three quarters of an inch wide. But it could be a bit longer or a bit shorter."

"I know, variables. Tool marks?"

"The comparisons aren't finished yet but there are no impressions of lettering or traceable manufacturing marks or flaws. The upper edge of the impact depression did indicate the bar had a wider curve at the top."

I considered that for a moment. "Some kind of tire iron or lug wrench?"

"Could be. I'll let you know when we have something de-
finitive."

"Thanks." Then I remembered Lenny and the Ruger LCP.
"One more thing. Any impressions on either leg to show the
frequent use of an ankle holster?"

"No, only faint lines to show he wore over-the-calf socks
regularly." She paused, and I could almost see her forehead
scrunched in thought. "What an odd question. He was the
mayor's driver. Why would he need a back-up piece?"

"He was a street cop. When he was on the Gang Crimes
Task Force he got shot—"

"In the chest. Odd angle. I made a note of the scar. He was
lucky with that one."

I thought about that before I said, "I'm just wondering
about old habits."

"Speaking of old habits," Mira said, "it's been a long time
since we had you over for dinner. Shakti saw Grandpa Bobby
and Auntie Kayla just two weeks ago but he hasn't seen his
Uncle G in nearly a month. What are you doing Wednesday?"

It had been too long since I'd read a bedtime story to seven-
year-old Shakti, whose innocent take on the world was especially refreshing to cynics like his mother and uncle. "Having
dinner at your house," I said, "if I'm not in jail. What can I
bring?"

"How about ice cream for dessert and Bobby's DVD of
Tombstone—Wyatt."

"You got it—Doc."

After I hung up with Mira, I called my office and punched
in my voice mail code. Three messages: Saturday, a sales
pitch—despite my being on all the no-call lists; Sunday afternoon, LJ telling me my mini-DVD was ready; early Sunday
evening, the smoky voice of *Buffalo News* reporter Amanda
Corso seeking confirmation of a Saturday night confrontation
at the Shadow Lounge. "Someone gave me a cell phone picture of a fight. If you were part of it, if it's you in the picture, I
need to know what happened. Even if you weren't there,
please get back to me ASAP to clear that up." She left work
and cell numbers. "Thanks."

I made more coffee and thought about the message from Amanda Corso as I drank it. Lack of confirmation of my identity was the reason my name wasn't in the paper. For her to call me meant she had exhausted other possibilities—probably Grace and her bouncers. The bouncers didn't know me, and Grace would likely say I was just a Good Samaritan. If Corso got word I had been interrogated, she would have talked to Chalmers and Pinero, but the story hadn't mentioned a police interview at all, which meant Chalmers and Pinero had said nothing. If she printed my name because she got it from a single source, she would have had to print the source's name as well. Rogalski, the district commander, had questioned me and hinted Indi should not press charges. Corso would have gone into print with the word of a district commander but hadn't, so he wasn't her source. That meant Osterman, who gave Kenny my address and probably gave Corso the cell phone picture and love triangle story, had been unwilling to go on the record.

Who the hell was Osterman and why was he setting me up?

I called the *Buffalo News* city desk and was put through to Amanda Corso. The voice mail recording had not been a fluke. She sounded like Lauren Bacall. I could have wallowed in that voice, but I didn't give her a chance to do more than identify herself. "Gideon Rimes," I said, shedding my robe as I turned on my shower. "I'll be there in half an hour."

Then I hung up.

Chapter 20

There was an empty space near the Naval and Military
Park, which offered tours of a battle cruiser, destroyer,
and submarine anchored in the Canal Harbor. I parked
and locked my gun in the glove compartment. Then I walked
along Marine Drive, passed the fountain in front of the Court-
yard Marriott, and crossed Washington Street to One News
Plaza. When the bald retiree at the lobby security desk checked
my ID, I told him I had come to see Ms. Corso. He made a
phone call, gave me a visitor's pass, and pointed toward the
elevators.

I got off at the newsroom floor and walked past the mounted displays of blown-up *Buffalo News* front pages which covered signature news events both before and after my birth,
among them the Hiroshima atomic bomb, the JFK assassina-
tion, the first moon landing, the resignation of Richard Nixon,
the Nine/Eleven attacks, and the election of Barack Obama.
Then I stepped into the newsroom, a sea of desks beneath fluorescent lights, with people moving about, talking on the telephone, fingering computer keyboards. I scanned the room,
waiting to be seen, and finally locked eyes with a petite, dark-
haired woman in a gray blazer, stylish jeans, and expensive-
looking gray shoes. She walked toward me.

"Mr. Rimes?" A bit less Bacall in person but definitely the
same voice.

"Ms. Corso," I said, sticking out my hand.

She had pale skin that was cool to the touch, a large mouth

with burgundy lipstick, and dark blue eyes. "You didn't give me a chance to say we could do this over the phone," she said, releasing my hand. "You didn't need to come downtown and hunt for parking."

"I got lucky and found a spot at Canalside," I said. "I thought you might appreciate another perspective on what happened with Officer Carnahan at the Shadow Lounge."

"Are you saying you're the man in our blurry picture? You look like him."

"I'm saying you might want to interview me before I confirm or deny anything."

For a moment, she said nothing, assessing me, seeking to get a read on what I could want so badly I came all the way downtown to get it.

"Come with me." She led me into the depths of the newsroom, to a cluttered desk with a computer monitor whose frame was decorated with post-it notes. Picking up a white mug with a bold blue BN on one side, she took a sip without offering to get coffee for me. "Okay, you got your interview— or your chance to tell your story, since we both know you don't really give a rat's ass if I ask you anything."

"Ask me a question," I said.

"All right." She set down her mug, flipped open a reporter's notebook, and picked up a pen. "I'm guessing if I start with the picture, you'll just walk out."

"Correct," I said, noticing her gray nail polish matched her blazer and her shoes.

"I looked you up. Former army cop, now a PI who doesn't get in the news much."

"Don't much care for publicity."

"Before that you were at Buffalo State and got involved in a shooting—"

"One reason I avoid publicity."

"Is your friendship with Mayor Green another?"

I took a deep breath. "I served in Iraq with the mayor's husband Danny. I was one of his pallbearers. I think you mentioned the gold piping on our white gloves in your article. After his death, I was one of several people who escorted the mayor when she needed a companion for some event. We are friends but the truth is, she's my dead friend's widow."

Corso nodded and moved on. "Were you on a job Saturday night or on your own time?"

"On a job but that's off the record."

She pressed her lips together and shook her head. "It doesn't work that way. You have to say off the record first. And I hate it when people think they can go on and off on a whim. It's one or the other, or the interview is over." She closed her notebook and sat back.

Toothy smiles are awkward and always make me feel like an idiot when I hold them too long, but I gave her my best effort. "Then you have no interest in learning how you were played? How we both were?"

She frowned. "What are you talking about?"

"Osterman," I said. "The ex-cop who took that picture and gave you my name."

Like any trained reporter, she was good at hiding her reactions to the unexpected, but the momentary parting of her lips told me I was right. Osterman was her source. Though he had preferred to remain anonymous, her "bystander who witnessed the altercation" must have come across as unimpeachable, or her article would have taken a different tone. So far, Corso had reported only the facts, but they were facts so simple her piece had almost written itself. And her mention of a possible love triangle told me she was hungry for a story of *domestic dispute* to have some connection to the killing. Reporters who reached conclusions too soon, like detectives, ran the risk of having their judgment unhorsed when the course they built from too few facts was half a furlong from a brick wall. Because I had mentioned her source by name, she was already seeing that possibility.

"I think Osterman told police I killed Kenny Carnahan," I said, "which made them bust down my door yesterday and drag me down to Franklin for a sit-down in the box." I pulled off my baseball cap and tilted my head.

"Jesus!" she said.

"When a cop gets killed, the rules of the manhunt change."

I put my cap back on. "But this goes beyond that. Osterman is also the guy who gave Carnahan's brother my name and address. When I got home last night, I found little brother waiting outside to shoot me."

Now her eyes widened, and she opened her notebook again. "You have my attention."

"Good." I let my response hang in the air a second. "But some things have to be off the record to protect my client. You ask the question, and I'll say *off* or *on*. How's that?"

"Too much wiggle room. I can't write half a story."

"Look," I said. "I have a client to protect, one who has nothing to do with the murder. And I don't want Carnahan's brother to get jammed up because he lost his head. He's just a kid. He's off the record completely and so is my client's name or I walk."

She appeared to think for a moment then nodded. "I'll keep him off and her name out of it, but if you try to screw me over, I will fuck you sixty ways to Sunday. Understand?"

"You might have to get in line."

She picked up her mug again. "So what happened with little brother? Just curious."

"I disarmed him and we had a nice talk."

"You took his gun from him and *talked* to him?"

I shrugged. "We talked for a long time. Then I took him home and had a talk over coffee with his parents. They all know now I had nothing to do with Kenny's murder."

She raised her pen above her notebook. "So what happened Saturday night?"

"I was on a personal security detail. Carnahan came into the Shadow Lounge and had a confrontation with the bouncers. The owner is a friend of mine, so I stepped in to help."

She bared her teeth in a cross between a smile and a sneer. I noticed one of her upper front teeth was slightly crooked.

"I warned you not to waste my time, Rimes," she said. "I know Carnahan did the same thing Friday night at the Anchor Bar but went outside before things got physical. The common denominators here are you and a certain singer who was keeping company with him. Indigo Waters. Yes, I already know who she is, but I will keep her name out of it—if you level with me." She took a breath. "You were there to protect her from him, right?"

"Yes," I said, confident now she would tell me everything Osterman had told her. Her story had said nothing of the Anchor Bar, which meant in the absence of a nine-one-one call or more witnesses than an anonymous source, she had been unable to confirm the incident. That, I realized, was what she really wanted from me, enough gas to drive a series of articles.

"You served him with an order of protection to keep him away from your client."

I nodded and thought, *Good old Osterman.*

"But the next night he came looking for her anyway, and things got nasty." Taking my silence and downward glance as a *yes*, she scribbled something in her notebook. "Had he been abusing her—physically, I mean?"

"Not that I know of," I said. "Not yet."

"But being an ex-cop yourself, you thought it might get to that point."

"Only a matter of time." I leveled my gaze at her. "Stalkers escalate."

"I know," she said, pausing a heartbeat and biting her lower lip. "So there was never anything between you and Ms. Waters? No love triangle or even the possibility of one?"

I shook my head. "Osterman fed you a bullshit sundae."

"Even if some guy named Osterman is my source, I couldn't tell you."

"Did he tell you he was with Carnahan at the Anchor Bar on Friday or did he say he heard about it from somebody else and put two and two together?"

She said nothing but her pen stopped moving and her eyebrows rose a notch. Score.

"He came in with Carnahan, little brother, and a couple of off-duty cops who thought they were going to meet Kenny's girlfriend," I said. "Don't you find it at all curious that your source is with Carnahan when he's served in one bar, then is outside taking cell phone pictures when he violates the order of protection in another? And why bring all this to you? Why not to Dennis Quinnell or Kevin Michalski? Don't they do major crimes reporting?"

Corso looked at me for a long time. Neither one of us broke eye contact, but I couldn't get a read on what she was thinking. The faint tension in the corners of her mouth suggested controlled anger. With all I had told her about Osterman, it had to be clear to her now that he had used her. Maybe she was trying to figure out his agenda, or maybe she was uncertain because she realized I knew more than she thought I did—or should— and she was trying to figure out *my* agenda. Or maybe she was just pissed that a couple of ex-cops who might have some personal beef had put her in the middle. The longer we gazed at each other, the more convinced I was somebody was going to feel her wrath. I needed it to be Osterman.

"It's a safe bet Osterman didn't tell you he offered Kenny Carnahan a job."

Her brow knit. "A job? With CitiQuest?"

Now it was my turn to hide surprise, but I wasn't sure I could. It was all I could do to keep my mouth shut. CitiQuest Investigations and Security was Western New York's leading private investigation agency. While Driftglass was a one-man operation with yours truly as sole proprietor, CitiQuest was a closely held concern owned by a former military contractor named Zack Briggs. It had dozens of employees and computer-networked branch offices in Rochester, Syracuse, and Albany. CQIS provided the usual range of items on the PI menu, from subpoena service to marital and non-marital surveillance with the latest high-tech toys to private and employer-driven background checks to personal protection. But CitiQuest clients tended to have much more money than mine—corporations, larger law firms, pivotal civic organizations, the independently wealthy—and CitiQuest's personal security consisted of bodyguard teams that covered the likes of visiting rockers, presecret service presidential hopefuls, and film stars in town for a movie shoot.

If he could recruit Kenny and offer him double his salary, as Lenny had said, Osterman's name must be in a secure box near the top of the CQIS organizational chart.

"Of course CitiQuest," I said. "Does Osterman have some other gig I don't know about?"

Corso sighed and shook her head. "You didn't know about *this* gig, Rimes. You took way too long to respond." She leaned her desk chair back, gazed up at the ceiling for a moment, then sat forward. "I bet you don't even know Osterman's first name, do you?"

"No." I put on my best *you-got-me* face. "I was hoping you would tell me."

She sucked her teeth. "You got the name Osterman from little brother?"

"Yes."

"Damn." She sighed again. "I don't like to be played, by anybody, but I walked right into this. Kudos to you for getting me to tell you something about him."

"Knowing who's setting me up gets me closer to why."

She nodded. "I think my story just got more complicated. And complications always take time." She closed her notebook and put down her pen. "But I think you're right. Vince Osterman is setting you up, maybe to get killed when you don't even know who he is. And the bastard used me to do it. Showed me his goddam CitiQuest ID card and said he just happened to be outside when it started. He recognized Carnahan from when he did a security gig for some bigwig who met with the mayor. Then he heard about the Anchor Bar from a friend who was there and knew Indigo Waters, and he figured there was a connection."

"What was his reason for not wanting to go on the record?"

"CitiQuest operatives like to keep a low profile, and there is a conflict of interest. The *News* sometimes uses the company when it has security concerns, like the threats Dennis Quinnell got for his series on Southern Tier biker clubs. We try not to quote CitiQuest in a story unless it's unavoidable."

"What's Osterman's role in CitiQuest?"

"His card didn't say, but if he could offer somebody a job..." Drumming her fingers on the cover of her notebook, she sighed. "My editor is going to shit a porcupine unless I can get her a better story. And if Osterman has enough of a hard-on for you to get you taken out, there must be a better story here."

"Like why? And why me? If he wants me dead, why doesn't he just take a run at me himself?"

"Something tells me you're the kind of guy who'll figure it out." She took a business card from an acrylic holder near her keyboard and held it out to me but pulled it back when I reached for it. "My iPhone's the second number," she said. "I expect you to keep me in the loop on this. Only me, not those shiny pricks on TV or the half-assed neighborhood beat guys who write for the weeklies. Just me. Clear?"

"Or you'll fuck me sixty ways to Sunday."

Amanda Corso studied me for a long moment then smiled again, revealing another centimeter of her crooked tooth. "I just might—if you don't end up dead." She handed me her card. "Good luck, Rimes."

Chapter 21

City Hall was less than a mile from the *News*. It was warm enough to walk but too early for my meeting with the mayor, so I headed north on Washington to the Central Library, where Bobby would begin his talk in a few minutes. On the way I left LJ a voice message, asking him to dig up the deepest information he could on Vince Osterman and CitiQuest.

I spotted Bobby seated near the far front corner of the Ring of Knowledge, an open space in the center of the library's main floor. Intent upon the notes in his lap, he didn't see me, so I slipped toward the back and stood half-hidden by one of the pillars flanking the escalators. No point in distracting him.

Home to lectures, readings, film showings, book displays, panel discussions, cultural performances, and media events, the Ring was the library's version of a public square. Any patron walking from one side of the building to the other had to pass whatever program was in progress and could stop to take part. Fifty or so padded tubular chairs were usually there, in one configuration or another. Today they were in semi-circular rows and were already occupied by a dozen or so adults and about thirty squirming grade-schoolers on a field trip. The area's centerpiece, in front of the panoramic display case, was the Ring of Knowledge itself, a sculpture consisting of five massive blocks of greenish glass cut into arcs and arranged to resemble a circular stone bench. Six kids sat on the Ring, waiting for the talk to begin.

At noon, a white-haired man in a tan sports jacket went to the lectern in front of the display case and identified himself as Jay Perrin of the library board. He welcomed everyone to the Brown Bag lecture. Then he launched into Bobby's bio—his years at Buffalo State, the breadth of his articles and monographs, his frequent op-ed pieces in the *Buffalo News*, his service on various community boards—including the library's—his undying curiosity. The adults murmured admiration when Perrin described Bobby's stint on *Jeopardy*. "I'd sure hate to play trivia games with somebody whose brain is like a lint trap." When the chuckles subsided, he nodded. "Let's give a warm welcome to Dr. Robert Chance."

The applause was loud enough to hide the whirring of the movie screen which dropped from the ceiling as Bobby rose and moved to the lectern.

The talk lasted half an hour but began with Bobby's five-minute re-enactment of the one Oz film everybody knew, the 1939 MGM spectacular with Judy Garland. His Dorothy and Glinda impressions weren't particularly good, but he nailed the Wicked Witch and the Munchkins who sang "Lollipop Guild" and had the kids laughing with his Cowardly Lion and starting at his sudden "Pay no attention to the man behind the curtain!" Once Dorothy was back in Kansas, he recited a brief biography of L. Frank Baum and explained how he had come to write his Oz books. Showing stills and film clips from as far back as 1908, Bobby talked during the silent clips, which featured a lot of jerky dancing, and let scenes from later Oz films end before he commented on the Turkish version or those featuring the Muppets or Tom and Jerry. By the end, he was hoarse from performing so many voices but still obviously delighted. I had met former students who told me how mesmerizing Bobby was in class. I had seen it myself many times in his off-campus lectures. What students never understood was that the magic they saw when he taught was just a by-product of the joy Bobby derived from life itself. Like Mira's son Shakti, he kept my cynicism in check, and I loved him for it.

When hands shot up for the Q and A, I backed farther away from the Ring and took the down escalator to the Ellicott

Street exit. Then I walked up to Main and down Court to Niagara Square and City Hall. By twelve-fifty-five I was stepping into the second floor executive suite, where I took off my baseball cap and gave my name to the receptionist, a well-dressed older woman whose voice I recognized from her telephone call. A few minutes later, I was ushered into the mayor's private office.

She was standing in front of her neat, glass-topped wooden desk, eyeglasses dangling from a neck chain. A tall woman with healthy bronze skin, short black hair, and shoulders made wider by well-tailored pantsuits, Ophelia Green was three or four years my senior and had a politician's smile made sensual by a small beauty mark just above one corner of her mouth. Today's pantsuit was autumn brown but the glow was missing from Ophelia's skin. She looked more tired than when last I saw her. Smiling faintly, she stepped forward to kiss my cheek, even before the receptionist withdrew. Then she gestured me into a visitor's chair and circled the desk to sit down. I crossed my legs and put my cap on my knee.

My last visit to this office had been more than a year earlier. The paneled walls held even more framed handshake pictures—Mayor Green with the county executive, both New York senators, the governor, members of congress, community leaders, the owners of the Bills and Sabres, athletes, visiting celebrities. There were plaques and citations and letters, as well as a blow-up of the *Buffalo News* front page that announced her election win.

Part of one wall was devoted to her family, with pictures of Danny in his dress uniform, in his tux at a party fundraiser, and in cargo shorts as he tended a grill at a public cookout. Danny's large friendly eyes and thin brown-skinned face lived on in their son Drake, here and there framed in his lacrosse uniform, his NYU graduation gown, and in a page from the Harvard Law yearbook. I wondered if his resemblance to his father ever pained his mother.

"How's Drake?" I asked.

Ophelia's face brightened. "Good. He interned for Congressman Gill this summer."

"Complete waste of time," I said. "When has a black man from Harvard law ever made it big in DC?"

The mayor laughed. "A mother can dream." She leaned forward, hands folded on her desktop. "You look great, G, except for those stitches."

"Kitchen hazard," I said. "The next time I bend over to pick up something that slides out of my freezer, I'll try to remember the door swings shut on its own."

"Really?" She folded her arms and raised an eyebrow. "I heard it was a cop named Berko." Then she unlocked her arms and exhaled. "If it matters, he's been reprimanded."

"Thanks." I wondered who had told her. "I guess you really do know everything that goes on in this town, Madame Mayor."

She waved a dismissive hand at me. "Madame Mayor? Come on. We're old friends. You know all my nicknames."

I did. In childhood, she'd been called Opie, from OP, though I didn't know whether it had come from her given name alone or from her maiden name, Plummer. Close friends called her Phee, and Danny had called her Pheely. One or two of her nicknames might have been suitable for a small town mayor but not for the chief executive of New York's second largest city. So, despite the tragedy of her Shakespearean namesake, she was simply Ophelia when her title wasn't used. She was Buffalo's own one-name celebrity.

"Somebody has to show you respect during this campaign," I said.

She pressed her lips together and nodded. "I think it's obvious by now I don't know everything that goes on around me. I never saw this Kenny thing coming. I didn't know he was so out of control. And now he's gone." Her eyes moistened, and she wiped them.

"It's not your fault, Ophelia."

"But it's the kind of thing Councilman Merlotta will have a field day with," she said. "He'll say my staff is out of control, even though Kenny was one cop of four on my security rotation, and nobody else in the whole executive branch has more than a parking ticket. He already says my spending is out of

control, even though I've never had a budget deficit and reve-
nues are up. If I show any spine in our debate next week, he'll
say *I'm* out of control and unfit to lead." She brought her fist
down hard but stopped an inch above her desktop, locked forearm shaking. "Bad enough, he spends all his time in office un-
doing inner city recovery programs. Now his numbers are up
because he gets a lot of press for saying a lot of nothing. You
don't give Wreck-It Rick a sledge hammer like this and expect
him not to use it."

Ophelia had been elected because of her promise to rede-
velop the largely black East Side, which had seen new home
construction but hadn't blossomed in the city's two-decade
renaissance. The gateway to downtown had gentrified with a
medical corridor comprised of hospitals, high-tech device
companies, and UB's new medical school. Farther downtown,
the Theater District had new upscale apartments and hotels.
The hockey-themed Harbor Center stood alongside Key Arena
near Canalside. South Buffalo had benefitted from Solar City,
a still-new solar panel factory. The West Side had grown with
immigrants from Central and South America and refugees
from Iraq, Somalia, Nepal, and Myanmar. Straddling the North
and University Districts, diverse North Buffalo was still solid-
ly middle-class. When national news stories compared Buffalo's poverty to worse-off places like Detroit, the stats came
from the impoverished core of the East Side. Rick Merlotta
had built his public persona fighting every initiative from
Mayor Green's office and now based his campaign on her ina-
bility to produce change. Having served with him on a non-
profit board, Bobby once called Merlotta a pathological control freak to his face. *Anybody who can cause Bobby to lose
it...*

"You didn't give him anything," I said. "He's crazy and
everybody knows it."

"But he keeps getting elected by people who think his pop-
ulist bullshit means he's looking out for the little guy when
he's really securing his own business interests. Two at-large
terms on the Board of Ed, with no program improvement but
more charter schools on land he owns. The law department

said there was no conflict of interest because he turned over management of his development company to his son. Give me a fucking break."

"A technicality with a monogrammed T-shirt and a vanity plate."

"Yes, and then there's his two terms on the Common Council with nothing to show but gridlock. Political kabuki of the worst kind."

"That's why they started calling him Wreck-It Rick." In this case, *they* was *Artvoice*, a weekly alternative newspaper that specialized in Metro Buffalo's active music and theater scenes but also covered local news and politics with the irreverence of the independent.

"Once he started making noise about making a run at Governor Brown," Ophelia continued, "Bart Weston had to find some way to neutralize him so Republicans across the state wouldn't get burned in his wake if he financed his own campaign and actually got the chance to take his clown show statewide. I can almost hear that smarmy little shit now: 'Hey, Rick, how about Mayor of Buffalo? We almost never win that one, but there's a woman in there, and we think you can take her.' So those damn *You're in Rick Country Now* and *Let's Take Back Our City* signs are everywhere."

"Let's take back our whatever," I said. "Code which undergirds bigotry, class rage, fear of change, and a longing for a time and place that never was."

"You sound like Bobby," she said. "I guess wisdom does rub off."

"Bobby's a natural-born teacher." I felt myself smile. "He can't help but teach, every time he opens his mouth, and you can't help but learn, whether you want to or not."

She nodded. "You were lucky to have him. You and Mira."

"I hated hearing that when I was a kid. I was really angry my parents weren't coming back. But, as a man, I know how lucky I was. Am." I pulled my cap into my lap and uncrossed my legs. "After I had my first firefight in Iraq and killed somebody I saw fall, I called Bobby on a sat phone. I had to talk."

"He talked you through it."

I shook my head. "He let me tell it and reassured me it was a good shoot and told me he would have been devastated if things had gone the other way."

She nodded. "Kenny's parents are devastated."

"I met them last night," I said. "His mother thought you were very sweet to come to their home. His father didn't say much. He just sat in his chair, looking kind of helpless and small." Her puzzled look asked for an explanation, so I gave one. "I ran into his brother. We talked and he took me home so I could offer my condolences."

She looked at me, waiting for more details. When none came, she sighed. "How's the girl? Miss Waters."

"Quite upset. She didn't want Kenny following her around but she did care for him. Her lawyer has arranged a police interview later this afternoon."

Ophelia nodded again, locked her fingers across her abdomen, and leaned back. "Commissioner Cochrane has assured me the department will spare no effort to find Kenny's killer. It's hard enough when a brother in blue is lost in a shootout or a traffic stop gone bad, but in those cases the killer is almost always taken down or taken out at the scene." She sat forward, a stiff index finger jabbing the desktop. "But this guy got away, and the police want to find him before cops come from all over the country for Kenny's funeral."

And before the election, I thought. "How can I help you, Ophelia?"

"I want to hire you," she said.

"For what? I can't interfere with an ongoing investigation, and the department has more resources than I do." I sat forward. "And I'm still a suspect."

"No, you're not. The commissioner knows you're my friend and told me about Berko. The corporation counsel thinks you might file another police brutality lawsuit the city doesn't need, right on the heels of the Kozlowski decision."

Archie Kozlowski was a supermarket produce manager who had been in a persistent vegetative state ever since two cops, one off-duty and one on, had shoved him down a flight of stairs to break up a bar fight. That Kozlowski had not been part of the fight left the city on the hook for a multi-million dollar settlement with his family.

"Which means what?" I asked.

"I want to put you on retainer as an independent investigator for the mayor's office."

"What?"

"You have CID experience in homicide investigation and a master's in criminology. We're calling you a consultant because you have extensive CID contacts, which could prove useful if this killing had anything to do with Kenny's time on the GCTF."

"That sounds shaky even to me."

She shrugged. "The commissioner hated the idea but the corporation counsel loved it if it would forestall a lawsuit." She pulled a sheet of mayoral stationery from a file folder and handed it to me. A check was attached. "You're not to interfere with the investigation itself but this letter, signed by the commissioner, the corporation counsel, and me, gives you access to everything that makes it into the murder book put together for this case."

I studied the letter, looking for any traps—unintentional and intentional—into which I could fall. Citing my credentials, it named me as a private contractor who would bill the city for investigative services whose costs exceeded the impressive retainer. As long as I didn't file a lawsuit or obstruct the police investigation, I was on safe ground. Folding the letter and check, I slid them into my inside jacket pocket. Then I gazed at the mayor for a long time.

"What am I really looking for, Ophelia?"

She took a deep breath. "You'll know it when you find it."

Chapter 22

At three-twenty I parked in front of the Rogers house, instead of in the empty driveway. The Cadillac might be in the closed garage, but if Doc was out, he would certainly not want to park his vintage car on the street. Lizzy opened the door and left me in the living room. A moment later, as I gazed at one picture or another, Indi came in with Lizzy a step or two behind her.

"Don't she look nice, Mr. Rimes?" Lizzy said.

In a modest mauve skirt, white blouse, and slip-on half-heels—all of which appeared brand new—Indi looked "presentable" but uncomfortable. Lizzie had dressed her and done her damnedest to mask Indi's natural sexuality, as though her police interview would be easier if Chalmers and Pinero understood what a nice girl she was.

"Yes." I didn't have the heart to tell Lizzy her effort was about as effective a mask as Clark Kent's glasses. "Where's Doc?"

"Getting stuff for that old piece of junk. Oil and fluids and more new tools and God-knows-what-else before he locks it in the garage and covers it up for the winter."

"I saw the car the other day," I said. "An old Cadillac in almost mint condition."

"He spent a lot of years fixing it up—restoring it, he says." She dismissed his efforts with a wave of her hand and jerked a thumb toward the baby grand in the corner. "That's his child, his baby," she said with no trace of irony. "The car is a ragamuffin he picked up on the street, nursed back to health, and just can't bring himself to leave out in the cold."

"It's a classic and might be worth a lot of money someday."

"Someday?" Placing a hand near the collar of her teal housedress, she laughed. "Neither one of us got *that* much time left." She sighed. "I thought he left the grease monkey work behind when he retired from his brother's garage. But it gives him something to do when he's not doing his music. Keeps him out from underfoot."

I smiled then looked at Indi. "Ready?"

She shrugged. "Guess so."

"You'll be fine," Lizzy said, kissing Indi's cheek.

We took the Kensington Expressway downtown and exited at Goodell, then crossed Main Street to Franklin, and parked half a block past Landsburgh, Falk, and Trinidad at three-fifty. We climbed out. I zipped my leather jacket a third of the way up so my Glock wouldn't be visible on the street. At first, Indi said nothing on the walk back to the office, something I attributed to nerves. We mounted the stone steps to the sprawling brick house that had been converted to a law office, but Indi stopped moving when I held the leaded glass door for her.

"I'm scared, Rimes," she said. "I'm scared they'll think I had something to do with what happened to Kenny."

I let go of the door and waited till the hydraulic closer had cut us off from the inside. While she couldn't have killed Kenny herself, she could have used someone else to do it. The idea posed a lot of problems but I was still open to the possibility. "Did you?"

She shook her head.

"Then tell the truth."

Just inside the front entrance was a receptionist's desk built into the oak-paneled wall. The young redhead seated there swiveled away from her computer and stood as we stepped inside. Supporting her weight on a black quad cane, she looked at me and smiled. "Mr. Rimes? I'm Eileen. I'll take you right back." She led us past what once must have been a parlor but now had closed sliding doors with a gold nameplate: *Jonah Landsburgh.* Phoenix's office was a converted sitting room at the rear of the first floor. Its sliding doors were open. In a blue pinstripe suit, Phoenix sat at the desk across from the doorway, shelved law books behind her. Chalmers and Pinero were already in the two leather client chairs facing her, and on the cushioned window seat to my right was Jonah Landsburgh, who had about five years and ten inches on Bobby. With his mane of unkempt white hair, he reminded me of Spencer Tracy in *Inherit the Wind*, only he was much thinner. As Eileen announced us, Phoenix and Jonah both stood. Chalmers and Pinero turned to look at us. Eileen withdrew, closing the sliding doors behind her.

"Hello, Gideon," Jonah said, circling behind Pinero to take my hand. "Been a while."

I pulled off my cap. "Yes, it has." Our last encounter had been one of Bobby's semi-annual low-stakes poker games. Most of the fifty bucks I'd lost had gone to Jonah.

He narrowed his eyes at my stitches. "Phoenix said they whacked you pretty good."

"I'll live," I said, avoiding the temptation to look at Pinero and Chalmers.

But Jonah glared at them for a long moment before taking Indi's arm. "Miss Waters, why don't you sit here?"

He steered her to the window seat. When she sat, he sat beside her, pushing his wire-rimmed glasses back up on his nose. Phoenix resumed her seat as well, and I took the only vacancy, a black plastic folding chair to the right of her desk, which gave me an unobstructed view of everyone in the room. Jonah held my gaze long enough to give me a flicker of a smile then brushed something off the sleeve of his gray suit jacket. Message: he was there not only to support his junior partner but also to unsettle the two detectives.

"First some ground rules," Phoenix said. "This is a voluntary interview. Detectives Pinero and Chalmers are here to ask my client, Indigo Waters, about the murder of Kenneth Carnahan. The detectives are already in possession of sworn affidavits from various staffers at Hope's Haven that Miss Waters was in the shelter at the time of the murder and thus could not have committed it. However, as an intimate of the deceased, she may possess relevant information, even if she is unaware of its importance to the investigation. So, Miss Waters, you are to answer questions truthfully, but, for the protection of your constitutional rights, you must stop speaking if I tell you to stop. Detectives, if I determine that, for whatever reason, the interview must end, it is over, period." Phoenix spoke as if giving background to Jonah but I suspected a hidden recorder was capturing everything so they could review the details later. She wouldn't reveal that to the detectives, who could subpoena the recording. "Gentlemen, you may begin."

Pinero, whose fedora was in his lap, leaned forward and placed a pocket digital recorder on the desk. "May I, counselor?"

"You may not." Phoenix picked up the recorder, made sure it was off, then set it back down out of his reach. "This is informal."

Pinero sat back and appeared to think for a moment. Then he took a deep breath and leaned toward Indi. "Miss Waters, how long were you acquainted with Kenneth Carnahan?" he said too gently.

Indi looked at Phoenix, who nodded, then turned back to Pinero. "Since July. The first time I saw him was when we— me and the band—we were doing a Canalside gig for the Fourth. Kenny was there with the mayor and her people. It was a hot day, and I was kinda sweaty after our set. When the mayor came onstage to shake our hands, she said we all looked like we could use a drink. Kenny got us cups and a pitcher of lemonade."

Chalmers studied Indi and took notes as Pinero eased into his next question: "When was the next time you saw him?"

I realized the two men had the subtle body shifts and non-verbal communication cues of long-time partners. They had worked out their questions in advance. It was Pinero's turn to play the good cop. One would signal the other when it was time to go off-script. Then Chalmers would take over and press Indi as hard as Phoenix would allow.

"He showed up at the Anchor Bar two or three weeks later, on a Friday night," Indi said. "He sat right in front of the bandstand, smiling at me while I sang. I didn't recognize him and thought he was acting real weird, but after our first set, he came up to me and asked if he could buy me a real drink this time instead of lemonade." She smiled, somewhat sadly. "Then it clicked and I said yes, rum and Coke. At the end of the second set, he asked me for my phone number."

"How soon after this did you start dating?"

"Another week or two."

"How soon before you were intimate?"

"Don't answer that," Phoenix said. "We'll concede my client and Mr. Carnahan were intimate. The precise nature of their intimacy is a private matter and irrelevant to your investigation."

Pinero looked at Phoenix for a long moment—his lips pursed, her eyes unblinking—and I had a glimpse of the difficulty they would have had forming a friendship, much less a relationship. '*Not one of my smarter moves*,' she had told me.

"Fair enough, counselor," he said at last, maintaining only part of his artificial cool. "What *is* relevant is how long the intimacy continued before Ms. Waters got an order of protection and whether she was intimate with anybody else at the same time." He shifted his gaze to Indi. "So, Ms. Waters, how long were you...together...before you started feeling Mr. Carnahan was getting too attached?"

"About two months," Indi said, sitting back and looking up as if cycling backward through a mental calendar. "Then he started talking about marrying me and having coffee-colored babies and shit—excuse my French."

"Marriage and babies didn't interest you?" Pinero said, regaining his rhythm with a deft sincerity that would have made his advanced interrogation instructor proud.

She shook her head. "I had plans—I got plans—for other things."

"Bigger things, but then he started stalking you."

"Yes."

"How?"

Indi shrugged. "First it was, like, too many phone calls and text messages telling me he loved me and couldn't live without me. Then he started showing up at my door late at night without calling and sometimes I'd even have—" She hesitated. "Some mornings, I'd come downstairs and find him sitting in his car, smiling and waiting to drive me to work."

"Did he threaten you?"

"Not right away." Her face contorted a bit. "Actually, he never really threatened me at all. Things just got real creepy, and it started to *feel* dangerous. The more I told him I wasn't ready for what he wanted, the more it felt like he was about to explode. I told my supervisor at work, and she put me in touch with Miss Trinidad."

"And during those two months you were intimate with Mr. Carnahan, were you intimate with anybody else?"

Indi stiffened, as if indignant, and looked at Phoenix, who nodded she should answer. Indi looked down, and Jonah put a hand on her shoulder, which completed the transition of her indignation to embarrassment. "Yes," she said, her cheeks darkening, as if the drawer full of sex toys I'd found in her room was sitting on the desk for everyone to see.

Pinero leaned closer to her and looked into her eyes. "I need the name and address of everybody you had sex with while you were having sex with Mr. Carnahan."

Indi's voice fell to a near whisper. "Everybody?"

"Yes."

"What if one of them is married?"

That peaked my interest because I remembered most members of the Jazz Blues Alliance were married. Earlier, I had dismissed them as too avuncular to take Indi to bed, but drummer Dix Danishovsky was younger than the others and remained an outside prospect.

"We can be discreet," Pinero said. "Nobody's wife has to know."

"Unless it turns out the husband is involved in Kenny's murder," Chalmers said.

Indi swallowed. "What if it's a woman who's married?"

The room was quiet a heartbeat or two longer than it should have been.

Phoenix and I exchanged glances, as did Chalmers and Pinero, who had raised his eyebrows. The only one who showed no reaction was Jonah Landsburgh, the old pro.

"Same deal," Pinero said finally.

"No one's judging," Phoenix added.

"All that matters is the truth," Chalmers said, shoulders tense with anticipation.

Indi looked across the room and into my eyes. I smiled at her and nodded, and she smiled back, something everyone couldn't help seeing. Then she turned to Pinero and gave up two first names and two full names, and locations rather than addresses. Jervis and Tony were college kids with whom she'd had one night stands and whose surnames she didn't know. Carter Boyle lived over a bakery in suburban Amherst, and Alfreda Winstone shared an East Side single family home with her minister husband Eric and their toddler son.

"Did any of your other...contacts...ever meet Kenny, coming or going? You know, get confronted by him outside your place, maybe have an argument?"

"No, never."

Chalmers glanced at me twice during the revelations. I could see his train of thought was riding the same rails as mine. The one-nighters had no motive to kill Kenny and were likely too young to have suckered him into the park, let alone gotten him to expose his back to one of them. Winstone and Boyle had each slept with Indi three or four times during her two months with Kenny, hardly the kind of escalating passion that led to murder. Winstone was on the down-low and had a child, a baby. Even if she envisioned a future with Indi and knew about her involvement with Kenny, she had no reason to kill a man about to be arrested for violating a court order. Carter Boyle was an unknown who would certainly be investigated, as would Indi's other three lovers and Reverend Winstone, but nothing looked promising. As he jotted notes, Chalmers let his shoulders sag a bit.

Pinero's next several questions explored Indi's background and her move to Buffalo. She told them about growing up in Baxley, where she was a standout in her church choir, and earning an early childhood degree in Augusta, where she was a soloist in the Paine College Concert Choir. She met Doc Rogers during one of his solo piano tours, when he shared the stage with the Concert Choir. He complimented her on her singing and told her to look him up if she ever got to Buffalo because he could help her find work there and had industry connections in New York and Chicago. Pinero passed the closing to Chalmers.

"Is there anything at all you can tell us that might help in our investigation?" Chalmers said simply.

When Indi shook her head, the two detectives looked at each other then climbed to their feet. Chalmers closed his notebook, stuck it in the back pocket of his jeans, and zipped his leather jacket. Pinero put on his hat and retrieved his digital recorder, which he slipped into the inside pocket of his topcoat. They thanked Indi and both lawyers and slid open the doors to leave. Pinero ignored me, and Chalmers shot me a sidelong glance.

I stood and held up a finger to Phoenix to signal that I would be right back. I followed Chalmers and Pinero past Eileen's desk and called their names when we were all outside and the front door had closed behind me.

Pinero turned to face me and put his hands on his hips. "What do you want, dipshit?"

I handed him my letter from the mayor. He skimmed it, which told me he had already been informed of its existence. "Ain't this about a bitch. Can't settle our contract but she can sure figure out ways to waste our time." He passed it to Chalmers, who barely glanced at it but gripped it hard enough to crumple the edges before handing it back and folding his arms across his chest. Pinero spat on the sidewalk as I smoothed, folded, and pocketed the letter. "Why can't you just be happy you're not a suspect?"

"No, he's gotta be a consultant," Chalmers said. "CID contacts my ass. You been out of the army for years. This letter just uses the CID as a cover so you can spy for the mayor. And what was all the smiley-poo with Waters? You tapping that? I didn't think so when we had you in the box, but now—" He clenched his teeth, the muscles along his jaw tightening. "You got some nerve slipping into a case by going behind the prima-ry's back."

"This wasn't my idea," I said. "The mayor's a friend of mine. She—"

"I don't care if she licks the shit off your dick—back door man." Chalmers leaned too close. "We're not about to let you fuck *us* in the ass because *she* can't sit still."

"I know you were stoked for a hard run at Indi," I said, locking eyes with him, "but it's not my fault she didn't give you any juice. So, you make your play, I'll make mine. If I obstruct, arrest me and charge me." I looked at Pinero. "Turn on your recorder and I'll say it again. If I obstruct, arrest me. If you're worried the corporation counsel might get his balls knotted in his G string, record me saying I will not sue the po-lice." I stepped back. "And I smiled because she trusts me, and I wanted her to talk. I hoped she'd give you something."

For a moment we looked at each other without saying any-thing. Then Pinero turned to Chalmers. "Bro, I could shoot Berko for putting us in this spot."

"That asshole." Chalmers nodded. "I'd help you reload."

"It's got nothing to do with Berko," I said. "Last week I was hired as a bodyguard but that changed over the weekend because somebody killed Kenny and tried to set me up for it. That made it personal. I want to know who and why. Now I have four clients who want me to investigate the same crime. I don't want to cross your wires but you need to know I do what I'm hired to do."

Chalmers frowned. "*Four* clients?"

"Mayor Green, Miss Waters, and Mr. and Mrs. Carnahan." I waited a couple seconds for the final two clients to register before adding, "The Carnahans are *pro bono*."

Chalmers looked away for a moment and sighed. "Rimes, you want to see the murder book, you gotta come downtown. You get to look at it for an hour—with one of us there—but you don't get to put anything in it. You come up with some-thing on your own, a lead or a name, give it to us and step off. No Hardy Boys or Sam Spade shit. We will not be asking for your opinions or taking you to witness interviews or using you…How do they say it in the movies?…to go places we can't go? We go everywhere, we're not offering rides, and we won't be giving you any credit when the case is closed."

"I don't want credit, and I'll see the murder book when I see it," I said. "Right now I want to know if Lorenzo Quick's name is in it."

They studied me for a moment, as if uncertain what to think of me now that I had offered a name. Chalmers broke the silence. "What do you know about Quick?"

"When I was with the CID, his name was linked to drug smuggling involving military personnel. I hear he may have ordered the hit on Kenny when you were all on the GCTF."

"God, I hate guys who think they're smarter than everybody else," Pinero said. "But you do get cool points for surprising us. We interviewed Quick yesterday. We got nothing to connect him to this. Anyway, it's not his style to have somebody beat to death."

"When Quick wants you dead," Chalmers said, "your dying is an object lesson to others who might cross him. Everybody knows who did it and nobody has the proof. But our GCTF days are long past. He's got no reason to move on any of us now."

"But the fucker did like that we remembered him," Pinero said. "Didn't you think so, Terry? Just sat there next to his lawyer, smiling that nasty little vampire smile. Oh, man, I wanted so bad to yank out his canines with pliers."

My next question pivoted away from Quick. "Anything new on that burner?"

Chalmers shook his head. "We tried calling it, texting it, GPS tracking. Phone's dead, probably smashed."

"So you're coming up on your first forty-eight with no hook to hang a theory on," I said.

"Oh, we got a theory," Pinero said.

"The phone makes it premeditated, not random, but looking at previous cases gets you nowhere, especially with Quick, so you keep coming back to Indi."

"Pretty much," Chalmers said.

"Indi couldn't have done it. She was on lockdown. No way she got past Oscar."

"Oscar Edgerton," Chalmers said. "We got his statement."

"And she lacks the height and upper body strength for the angle of the fatal blow."

"Now you're reading official autopsy reports before they're made public?" Chalmers whistled a long note. "The mayor is going out on a limb here. I really gotta go to the PBA."

"Wasn't Ophelia," I said.

"Waters coulda hired it out," Pinero said. "Might not have the money, but she's good to go between the sheets. Hell, sheets might even cramp her wild child style. Men have killed for less than pussy that blew their world off its axis."

"So much doesn't add up," I said. "When did she set up the hit? She was with my people all day Saturday and then with the band till Ms. Trinidad and I took her to the shelter. They take away cell phones there so women with second thoughts can't call their abusers. If Indi couldn't call the killer, how would he know the hit was on?"

"Coulda been there waiting at the bar," Pinero said. "Followed Kenny."

I couldn't recall noticing anyone who left when Kenny drove away. I would have to check LJ's video again. On my earlier viewing, I had focused on only one person, Osterman.

"She could just be the inspiration," Chalmers said. "Means we still got people to see: the band, Kenny's friends, the girl's fuck buddies." He sighed. "Anything else, Sherlock?"

"What can you tell me about Vince Osterman, the older guy riding with you and Kenny Friday night?"

Chalmers shrugged. "Nothing to tell. He was homicide before my time. Retired when I was in patrol and went to work for a private outfit."

"Did you know him? Was he part of GCTF before you guys got there? Did he ever work a case when one of you or Kenny was first on the scene?"

Chalmers chuckled, and Pinero let out a full-throated laugh.

"You might've been good at the CID," Chalmers said, "but don't lose your car keys, man, or you'll wear out your shoes."

Pinero smiled and bumped fists with his partner. "Osterman was out with us because he's Kenny's *padrino*, his godfather."

Chapter 23

During our brief post interview conference, I shared Pinero's speculation Indi had hired someone to kill Kenny, but Jonah dismissed it with a snort. "He's got no foundation, and nothing means nothing."

Phoenix agreed and said Indi was free to resume her life but might want to avoid getting involved with anyone for a time. "This has been hard, and I know you had feelings for Kenny. Give yourself time before you hook up with somebody new."

I drove Indi to her apartment building and waited in my car while she went upstairs to change. Then I took her back to the Rogers' house, where she would dine with Doc and Lizzy before band practice. The old DeVille was in the driveway, with a green Jeep Liberty behind it. I parked in front of the house and walked Indi to the door. Lizzy answered the bell and hustled us inside, as if I were a teenager caught stealing a kiss.

Looking tired, Big Willy, the sax man, was seated on the couch. He wore a too-big gray Dickies work shirt, blue jeans, and a soiled gray baseball cap on his head. The shirt's sewn-in name tag read *Simmons*, and the cap said *Leland Rogers' Auto Repair*. The Jeep, I guessed, was Big Willy's. Leland was probably Doc's brother.

Big Willy smiled and stood to pull Indi into a hug. "Baby girl, how things go with the police?"

As if uncertain how to answer, Indi stared up at me. Just then Doc, white shirtsleeves rolled up, came from the rear of the house and slipped a nervous arm around his wife's waist. I looked from one expectant face to another and wondered if Indi knew how loved she was.

"Everything's fine," I said. "Sooner or later, they'll interview everybody who saw what happened Saturday night—and that includes the band—but Indi told them the truth, and they know she's innocent." I kept the notion of a hired killer to myself. No need to dampen the joy in Lizzy and Willy's faces and the relief in Doc's until Chalmers and Pinero came up with something solid and made a move—which I considered unlikely. "There's nothing to connect her to the crime."

"Course there ain't," Doc said. "She didn't do it. They gotta railroad somebody else."

Lizzy clapped her hands together. "Then we're gonna have a special dessert tonight to celebrate. I made it 'cause I had faith the cloud of suspicion would be lifted." She turned to me. "Mr. Rimes, would you like to stay for dinner?"

"We got plenty," Doc said before I could answer. "Big Willy always joins us on practice nights 'cause, since Isabel passed, he got nobody to cook him a down home meal no more. Lizzy always makes enough for him to take two plates back on upstairs."

Big Willy was not only Doc's tenor sax player but also his upstairs neighbor and had retired from the same auto shop. I wondered if they were lifelong friends and what it would be like to have one.

"And if the special dessert is her sweet potato pie—" Indi said, grinning.

"Indi, invite that nice lawyer, too," Lizzy said. "Maybe Mr. Rimes'll pick her up."

"Thanks, but I can't stay tonight," I said. "I have another commitment."

"Then another time, and you bring Miss Trinidad," Doc said, pumping my hand. "After all y'all done for our girl, it's the least we can do for you. Thank you."

As I moved to the door, Indi threw her arms around my torso and embraced me as a child would embrace her father. She held on for a long time, as if attaching herself to me would somehow protect her from the unintended consequences of her

interview—suspicions of an accomplice that would keep her in
police sights, angry lovers who would never again slip into her
bed, publicity that might scuttle Doc's efforts to steer her toward the majors. Then she let me go and stepped back, her
eyes wet but happy. Lizzy kissed my cheek. Big Willy clapped
me on the back, half as hard as I would have expected from a
man his size.

Once I was back in my car, I unfolded and reread the note
Phoenix had pressed into my hand as she held the front door
for Indi and me.

> *Gideon, thank you for being the single constant in
> this mess. I'd like to cook dinner for you tonight, if
> you're free. 7:30. My place. Unit 11C. Bring wine,
> white or blush. If you can make it, just nod. If not, next
> time you'll have to ask me.*

On the front steps of the law office I had looked over my
shoulder just enough to see Phoenix, framed in the leaded
glass door, smile when I nodded. Now, I smiled myself but
made no move to start the car.

It had been nearly a year since I'd had a date, if that was
what this dinner would be. My last relationship and the marriage that preceded it had both ended badly. Tired of life on
post after six years as a military spouse, Lisette demanded I
leave the army two years before I was eligible for my pension.
When I refused, she detached herself from me emotionally and
eventually began seeing an unmarried captain with a higher
pay grade. Confronted off-post and in civilian clothes, I broke
his jaw in a fight but faced no disciplinary action because his
contract contained a morality clause and my finger rested on
the trigger. Stalemated, we both walked away from Lisette.
When Alicia, the Buff State admissions advisor I'd been seeing for seven months, could no longer fall asleep beside me
after I killed a spree killer, various friends attempted to play
matchmaker, so often pairing me with women in need that I
grew skeptical of anything but infrequent casual encounters.
From the start, however, I had been attracted to Phoenix, had

felt connected to her self-assurance and distinct lack of need. I sensed we were both in that space between casual and serious where anything could happen.

Before I could imagine the possibilities, though, there was something I needed to settle. I pressed the *START* button, pulled away from the curb, and turned right onto Utica. The Escape's built-in blue tooth automatically synched with my mobile phone whenever I was in the car. I was about five blocks from Main Street when I gave a voice dial command. "Call Lenny Carnahan."

My dashboard display screen lit up with the number I had stored in my phone the other night, and a moment later Lenny's voice filled the car. "Hello."

"Hi, Lenny. Gideon Rimes. Can you talk?"

"Let me just step in the other room."

I waited a moment, then said, "I need to ask you something."

"Sure."

"Somebody told me Mr. Osterman was your brother's godfather."

"What?"

"Mr. Osterman—first name Vince, by the way. Was he Kenny's godfather?"

"No." For a moment, he said nothing, as if stunned at the nonsense of my question. "Kenny and me, we have the same godfather—Mom's brother, Uncle Patrick. He's in the other room right now with Mom and Dad and Father Ryan."

"Was last Friday the first time you met Vince Osterman?"

"No, Kenny introduced us a few months ago."

"Did you always call him Mr. Osterman?"

"Whenever I did, he said to call him Oz, but I felt funny doing that because…"

I remembered being Lenny's age, on the bridge between childhood and adulthood, and understood the discomfort. "Because he was older and it seemed disrespectful."

"Yeah. Everybody else called him Oz. I just sorta spoke without using any name."

"Okay. Thanks, Lenny. Call me if you think there's something I need to know."

I clicked off and began to consider why Kenny would tell Chalmers and Pinero Vince Osterman was his godfather. The only reason to lie about the nature of a relationship was to keep hidden the true nature of the relationship. Osterman had offered a Kenny a job with CitiQuest. Why would that be such a secret? Kenny was an underpaid cop with financial problems, a hero for getting wounded in the line of duty. A new position that alleviated his money concerns, especially one with a respected private, was certainly news to be shared with family and friends and the media—unless there was something shady about the job itself, perhaps something illegal. Maybe CitiQuest operatives provided more than security to their big name clients. They wouldn't be the first handlers to supply drugs and hookers and clean up after the rich and famous. Maybe Lorenzo Quick was part of the supply chain. Had Kenny figured that out and decided not to play along with the man who had tried to kill him before?

As I crossed Main Street on the way to Elmwood, the display screen signaled an incoming call from Mira. I pressed *ANSWER*, and her voice vibrated through the speakers: "Hey, big brother."

"Hi, Mira."

"You always sound so far away when you're in the car, so I'll make this quick. The tool mark analysis came back. Looks like the murder weapon was a common breaker bar, which gave the killer enough leverage to cause death with a single blow. A breaker bar is used for—"

"I know what it's used for," I said.

"'Course you do," she said.

"I know, I know, trained detectives are a pain in the ass."

She snorted. "You never cut Bobby off when he starts a recitation."

"Trained professors are a pain in the ass too, but they're harder to stop, once they get going. That's something a trained pathologist should know. There's got to be something in there, a special battery or spare lung that makes them just talk and talk and talk."

Mira's laugh was loud enough to produce static. I heard her explaining to Shakti Uncle G had said something funny. Then, composed, she came back on the line. "There was no oil or metal debris at the point of impact so the bar was probably new, though I'd leave the purchase search to the police. Breaker bars are less common than screwdrivers but still too common to make a search easy, especially when most of them are cheap enough to buy with cash."

"Thanks, Mira. See you Wednesday. Give Shakti a hug for me."

At home, standing beneath the pulsing shower head that made my lacerated scalp sting but the rest of my body tingle, I thought about Vince Osterman, Lorenzo Quick, and the breaker bar that killed Kenny. My brain tried to connect the three in various ways but every configuration felt forced, unsupported by what I knew. Why would Osterman offer Kenny a job and then kill him? If he had done so at Quick's request—or set Kenny up for one of Quick's men to take him out—there was a complex conspiracy at work. But why a breaker bar instead of the typical small-caliber double-tap to the head? How can you send a warning with a weapon of convenience? Was Quick an active partner, an investor who put money into CitiQuest to launder it, or just a thug whose name had come up? There was nothing to connect him to anyone but Kenny. So, why Kenny? Why now? When I added Indi to the mix, my ideas just got messier. What could she have to do with Osterman or Quick? And there was the recurring question. Why would Osterman set me up for Kenny's murder?

I hoped that, when I got LJ's CitiQuest report, things would start to make sense.

Chapter 24

At seven-fifteen I parked on Pearl Street, half a block from Phoenix's loft. I carried a bottle of pinot grigio and a mixed bouquet wrapped in white paper to the front entrance. Stepping inside the first of the glass doors, I pressed a black intercom button. The uniformed guard at the desk was older and bulkier than Phil but flabby pink jowls made him look less than formidable. Putting aside a copy of the latest *Men's Health*, he flipped a switch on his desk console and leaned toward a speaker.

"Gideon Rimes to see Ms. Trinidad in Eleven C," I said when asked to state my business.

The guard looked at a sheet of paper then nodded and buzzed me into the lobby, which had gold trim, two crystal chandeliers, and a faux marble floor. After sizing me up—perhaps against the wine and flowers in my arms—he went back to his magazine without unholstering his Maglite, and I went toward the elevators. One opened the instant I pushed the call button.

I rode up, surrounded on all sides by ghostly burnished steel reflections of myself. On the eleventh floor, I stepped into a rectangular beige hallway with a mahogany door at either end and three widely spaced doors facing the elevators. The center door carried a brass *11C* above a peephole. I took a deep breath before knocking.

A few seconds passed before locks clicked and the door swung open. In black stretch pants, an untucked denim shirt, and slip-on sneakers, Phoenix stood there smiling. "You're here," she said.

"I am." I handed her the wine then the flowers.

"Thank you." Her breath caught as she peeled back the white paper. "These are too beautiful to be from a supermarket." She turned aside to let me enter and closed the door behind me. "Where did you find a florist after business hours?"

"Maureen's, over on Ellicott."

"Don't they close at five?"

"The owner was there working late and let me in when I tapped on her window." I shrugged. "She's an old friend of Bobby's."

"'Course she is." Chuckling, Phoenix told me to hang my jacket on one of the wall hooks by the door.

When I did, she looked at me so long I thought something was wrong with my black shirt, black jeans, and light gray pullover. "Should I be wearing a tie?"

"Your gun," she said.

"In my safe at home."

"I think this is the first time I've seen you without it."

"Do I need it?"

She laughed. "No. I like you defenseless." Then her smile faded. "But if you didn't wear it because you thought it would bother me, don't worry. My dad was a cop. I know there's nothing magic about guns. It's just too many are in the hands of assholes."

I nodded.

She led me into her loft—a split-level affair with high ceilings; hardwood floors; tall windows along the far wall; a glass-topped dining table, already set for two, in one corner; and a steel-framed sofa and chair, facing built-in bookcases on either side of a crackling fire that my nose told me was smokeless gel fuel. On the mantel stood a sizable flat screen television, a cable box, and a Blu-Ray player. The elevated floor at the far end held a large bed in one corner and a cluttered desk in the other. I followed her around a granite-topped island into a kitchenette with stainless steel appliances and more granite surfaces. She put down the wine and bouquet and got a glass vase from the

cupboard above the sink. She half-filled the vase with water,
pulled kitchen shears from a cutlery block, and trimmed the
flower stems.

"Nice place," I said as she arranged the bouquet in the vase.

"Thanks."

"And something smells good."

"Ready in five." She handed me the vase and asked me to
put it on the table.

I carried the vase, the wine, and a corkscrew into the dining
area and set them on the table, which already held unlit candles, a bread basket, and a large bowl of salad. I uncorked the
wine to let it breathe. Then I went to the corner windows. It
was dark outside but Phoenix hadn't yet closed the vertical
blinds. I saw a long swath of downtown: Main Street with auto
traffic synched to subway trains rising to street level or heading back underground via the portals near the theaters. Street
lights and restaurant signs and bank logos. Lighted condos,
hotels, and closed office buildings stretching toward Seneca
Tower, which straddled the tracks near the end of the line. Off
to the right, sodium-lit Niagara Square with the gleaming Robert H. Jackson US Courthouse and the art deco City Hall. In
the distance, the edge of the harbor.

"Beautiful view," I said, turning to see Phoenix setting a
casserole dish on the table.

"Yes. I almost never close the blinds."

"Except when you want to sleep in."

"Usually only Sunday morning." She smiled as she took
her seat. "Unless I have to get somebody out of jail."

"Sorry. I'll try not to make a habit of that." I took the seat
perpendicular to hers and spread the cloth napkin on my lap.

"And I'm sorry I brought it up. I meant to set ground rules
at the door." She put a match to the candles, the flame illuminating the blue nail polish on her thumb. "No talk tonight
about that confused child and her goofy love life."

"Amen," I said, pouring the wine.

We found plenty of other things to talk about during dinner,
which consisted of spinach salad, an angel hair pasta bake full
of bacon and chicken in Alfredo sauce laced with hickory bar-

becue sauce, and a dessert of fresh strawberries. At first our conversation was superficial—food, music, books, and movies. She enjoyed the soul food and Latino food of her youth but liked to experiment with all kinds of dishes now, especially Italian.

"As you can tell," she said.

Like mine, her tastes in music and books were eclectic. And despite her response to my knocking Berko on his ass, she liked Hollywood action films, found them cathartic. After dessert, we touched on politics and current events, discovering many shared sentiments, including lack of faith in organized religion, dislike of TV reality shows, and mistrust of the marriage of money and power. Then we moved on to the more personal.

Phoenix told me about herself. She was the only child of a Puerto Rican policeman and a black nurse he met when he responded to a burglary call. Phyllis Carver had come home from the second shift at the old EJ Meyer Hospital to find her apartment ransacked and her late mother's jewelry among the missing items. There were fewer black and Latino officers back then, and Phyllis found herself relying on Julio Trinidad, not only for updates on the investigation but also for reassurances her new locks were strong and reliable, that she was taking the right precautions to remain safe. She had no idea how low a priority such a robbery was to the department, but Julio, armed with her pictures of the missing pieces, investigated on his own time. He recovered most of the jewelry at two city pawn shops and managed to track down and arrest the burglar himself. His initiative, he had told her often, had won him his three greatest joys—a detective shield, a wife, and a bookworm daughter who had been inspired by her parents' sense of justice and service to attend law school.

"They're both gone now," she said.

"Much too soon, I'm sure," I said. "I'm sorry."

"Thank you." She looked down a moment then up. "My only living relative is Tia Rosita in Ponce, Puerto Rico. I try to visit her once a year."

I told her about my parents' deaths, growing up in Bobby's

house, Mira and Shakti, and my time in the army. Some of this she knew from Jonah but was surprised to learn I had been married. I told her about Lisette but said nothing of my fight with her lover. Instead, I shared details of my time in Iraq, which brought us back to politics and an empty wine bottle.

After I helped her load the dishwasher, she opened a bottle of malbec. We took fresh wine glasses to the coffee table, and she turned off the lights. The loft now lit by whatever illumination came from outside and the still-bright gel fire, we sat on the couch and sipped wine and talked for two more hours about everything but Indi and Kenny and case details I would share with her another time. It was a relief to push Osterman and CitiQuest and the breaker bar, and Lorenzo Quick, to the back of my brain. It felt good to exchange memories and observations and details of things read and seen with someone who enjoyed conversation and witticisms and being in another's presence. Before I knew it, the digital display on the cable box read eleven-forty. With the last flickers of the gel fire sputtering wisps of alcohol into the air, I told her I ought to get going because she likely had to get up early. It was then that she pulled my face to hers and kissed me, lightly at first, then deeply and hungrily.

"You taste good," I said when, finally, we pulled apart. "And you smell good too. What is that perfume?"

"It's not perfume. It's grape seed lotion." She traced my lips with her thumb, her eyes searching mine. "From a winery in Monroe County." Her fingers slid through my curls but skirted my stitches, brushed the edge of my ear. "You know, you don't have to go."

"Good, because I'd really like to stay."

She bit her lip. "I don't usually do things like this with men I've just met. But I like you and feel more comfortable with you than I've felt with anybody in a long time. Before we go any farther, though, there's something you ought to know. And after I tell you, if you need time to—to think about things, I promise I will understand."

"All right."

She pulled away and switched on a table lamp beside the

couch. Then she took a deep breath and caught her lower lip between her teeth again, so hard that, for a moment, I thought she would bleed. "My name wasn't always Phoenix. I changed it, legally, a long time ago."

"Okay."

"I was Phyllis, like my mom." She shrugged and gave a brief nervous laugh. "I guess after twenty hours in labor…"

I nodded. "She wanted a junior."

"My mother died young," Phoenix said. "Younger than I am now. So did her mother and her sister and her mother's sisters." She began to unbutton her shirt but held the sides tight, revealing only a sliver more of her smooth cinnamon skin. "I knew breast cancer was hereditary long before anybody talked about BRCA gene mutations. I decided I didn't want to die that way."

"So you had a preventive mastectomy," I said.

"Mastectom*ies*," she corrected, fingers lingering on the second last button. "I was always slender and small-breasted. I figured I could still wear my double A cup in public. This was when I was an undergraduate, before there was gene testing, before insurance paid for preventive surgery, before recon-struction was required by law. It was like somebody put a gun to my head and said, 'Your tits or your life.' I've met men and even women who don't understand what I did, but we spent everything we inherited from my mother, my dad and I, choos-ing my life. I couldn't afford cosmetic surgery…"

The moisture in the corners of her eyes made me want to tell her scars wouldn't bother me, but I sensed she was headed elsewhere and waited. Having undone the final button, she opened her shirt, exposing her chest to me. If there were scars, I couldn't see them. Where her breasts had been were the arcs of two large fiery wings of red and gold and green against a cinnamon backdrop, between them the head and body of a screaming bird, below the curled talons the swirling plumage of ignited tail feathers. The bird's eyes were black and fierce, its golden beak sharp and merciless.

"But you could afford a tattoo," I said. "It's beautiful. A phoenix."

"I rose from my own ashes—or from the ashes of the women in my family." She leaned back against the arm of the couch. "I had to tell you. It's not the kind of surprise—"

I shifted to her and cut her off with a lingering kiss. Afterward, she pulled off my glasses and put them on the coffee table. I peeled the shirt from her shoulders and traced the tattoo with my fingertip. I found the scar tissue hidden in the artwork and felt her tremble, whether from my light touch or scar sensitivity I could not tell. I let my lips wander over her face and neck and chest, my hands over her torso and the stretch fabric sheathing her legs. I inhaled the smell of the grape seed lotion that clung to her skin.

"You don't have to do this," she whispered.

"Neither do you," I whispered back.

"But I want to."

"Me too, and I'm really glad you chose to live."

Her arms went round me and pulled me in for another kiss. Soon she began to pull my sweater over my head. Her fingers worked on my buttons, and her hands slid inside my shirt. She opened it wide, fingertips making circles in my chest hair, lips finding my nipples. We kissed and touched and explored for a long time, disrobing in unhurried stages. When we were naked, she stood and switched off the table lamp. Then she took my hand and led me across the room and up the single step to her bed. For a moment we just stood there, gazing at each other in the pulsing glow of light that came through the windows.

"Are you sure?" she said. "Some men find it hard not to have a breast to hold or…you know."

"I'll find other parts of you to hold and…you know."

And I did.

Chapter 25

NPR's *Morning Edition* woke us at six-thirty. Sunrise was still an hour away. Outside lights had lessened during the night, and the loft was dark. Beneath the covers, Phoenix lay pressed into my spine, her left arm curled around my torso. She detached herself, stretched, and sat up as I turned onto my back. For a moment she was just a silhouette, looking down at me, saying nothing. I groped for her right hand and brought it to my lips. Then she turned on a bedside lamp, and I saw her smiling. Fingers in my hair, she kissed my nose and told me to get coffee while she showered for work. "The Mr. Coffee is always on a timer. I fill it every evening when I get home." As I sat up, she slipped out of bed and disappeared down the step and around the corner to the bathroom. *Always on a timer.* Information I would need if I were invited to sleep over again. I thought about that as the shower began to hiss.

While a local news reporter interviewed a woman whose name I didn't catch about something called Sunrise Village, I stood and went to the corner windows. I seldom got a chance to see a waking city from such a vantage point and stayed there for a minute or so, naked and shivering, only my feet warm beside the baseboard heating unit. Then I went to the couch, where my clothes were heaped on the floor and my glasses lay on the coffee table. Once dressed, I carried last night's wine glasses to the kitchenette, washed them, and set them in the rack. The Mr. Coffee was on the counter, its glass pot full. I got two blue UB Law mugs from the cupboard and set one beside the coffeemaker. The other I filled and topped off with caramel creamer from the refrigerator. I got a spoon from the flatware drawer and stirred. After rinsing the spoon and putting it in the rack, I carried my coffee back to the windows and looked out again.

Sipping, I reviewed what I would need to accomplish today. As soon as I got home I would log onto a specialized search engine and delve into Vince Osterman and CitiQuest. But I wanted more than public records before I confronted Oz to ask why he had taken my picture and given my name to Amanda Corso and the police. I wanted things LJ was more gifted at finding: private files, emails, cached audio and video, hidden financials. I had left my phone on vibrate and hadn't heard it buzzing in the night but I took it from my pocket and checked it anyway. Nothing from LJ yet, and it was too early to call him. No texts or voice mails from anyone else either. I wondered where Chalmers and Pinero were in their investigation, what their next step would be. They had ruled out Lorenzo Quick, but I wasn't ready to do that without at least reviewing their notes. I wondered how they'd feel if I went to see the murder book this afternoon. But maybe they needed today to do more interviews, to initiate a purchase search for the breaker bar. Wednesday afternoon or even Thursday morning might be a better time to annoy whoever lost the coin toss to babysit me.

I heard the shower shut off. A few more minutes passed before I heard the hair dryer whining like a miniature jet engine. Then the bathroom door opened and Phoenix stepped out in a long white terry robe and fuzzy blue slippers. She went to the kitchenette and filled the mug I'd left on the counter for her.

"That's a lot of coffee," I said. "Do you make that much every night?"

"I wasn't sure how much you would want."

She winked at me, and I smiled when I realized I hadn't seen her prep the Mr. Coffee because she had done so before I knocked on her door last night.

"If you want to take a shower, there are towels—"

"Thanks, but I'll shower at home—you know, fresh clothes." I swallowed the last of my coffee. "I will use your bathroom, though." I went to the kitchenette, rinsed my mug, and put it in the sink. Then I made a show of kissing her cheek. "Can't hit you with morning breath and coffee breath at the same time."

"I put out a toothbrush for you," she said. "Still in the package."

"You think of everything."

"I try." She took a hefty swallow as I started toward the bathroom. "And I bet my coffee breath will beat yours anytime."

When I returned, she was at the stove, scrambling eggs and sprinkling in shredded cheese. Two glasses of orange juice and two plates were on the island, and between the settings sat a plastic container of mini-croissants. "Sorry I don't have any bacon," she said.

"This is fine." I perched on a metal stool. "I hope I'm not keeping you from work."

"I'm usually at my desk by seven-thirty. This morning, I'll be there by eight. And I'm not due in court at all today. I just have a ton of paperwork to do." She switched off the burner and turned to the island, frying pan in one hand and spatula in the other. "Besides, who would write me up for being late? I'm a full partner in a small, unusual law firm." She pushed the eggs onto our plates. "I have a lot of latitude."

"Unusual how?"

"Jonah was a one-man operation for most of his career. Him, his secretary Kathleen, who eventually became his wife, and the occasional investigator."

"Sounds like Perry Mason." I ate a forkful of eggs.

She laughed. "He always says watching that show when he was an undergraduate inspired him to go to law school." She sat and picked out a croissant. "He had a serious heart attack about fifteen years ago, and Kathleen demanded he take on associates. So who does he pick? Two idealistic kids just a few years out of law school. He said we reminded him of himself, smart but naïve. What he didn't expect to get was so diverse a firm." She took a bite, then explained. "Jonah is Jewish. Kathleen was Irish Catholic. Eileen, our paralegal-slash-receptionist, is their niece on Kathleen's side and has a spinal disorder. Cameron Falk and I are both mutts. Cam's father is white, his mom second generation Japanese. They're lovely people who didn't bat an eyelash when their son came out in his freshman year of college."

"That is pretty diverse," I said. "Even if Eileen didn't use a cane, you'd have an office where protected classes outnumbered individuals."

She laughed. "Eileen will be happy you noticed her. She said you were cute."

"For an older guy."

"She didn't say that!"

"But she meant it. She looks younger than Indi. A woman her age thinks babies and puppies and old people are cute, not hot." I took a sip of juice. "Cute means I say funny things when she volunteers to feed me pudding in the Alzheimer's ward."

Phoenix laughed again and swatted my arm. "Oh, stop."

"I like your laugh," I said. "If I didn't say so before, I feel comfortable with you too."

"Good. I don't wear these fuzzy slippers for just anybody." She picked up her juice glass but held it without drinking, and her voice took on a more serious note. "You know, even if I felt typical morning-after awkwardness, I'd say last night was fine. No strings, no guilt, no second thoughts. Just a much needed good time."

"But since neither one of us seems to feel awkward this morning..."

"Then last night was wonderful." She sipped her juice. "Still no strings and no guilt. If that was it, fine. But I wouldn't mind seeing you again."

"I'd like that." I looked at her for a moment then washed down the last of my food with the last of my juice. "But now I should get going. I've got a few things to take care of today, and my car probably has a ticket by now."

"You parked on the street and it's past seven." Phoenix

grimaced. "Sorry. That's one thing I didn't think of. I get two spaces in this building's underground ramp. Next time—and I do hope it's in the not too distant future—"

"How about Saturday night? I owe you a Sunday sleep-in, and I'll make brunch."

"Then I'll text you the entry code and my slot numbers later this week." She studied me for a few seconds. "Do your errands today have anything to do with Indi?"

"I guess they involve her indirectly." I shrugged and gave her the short version of everything I had done since she dropped me off on Sunday: the trip to the Doran house for the Shadow Lounge mini-DVD, Lenny Carnahan and the Ruger LCP, Lorenzo Quick, Vince Osterman, Amanda Corso, CitiQuest, Ophelia's retainer, Mira and the breaker bar, the lie Kenny told about Osterman being his godfather, and the warm welcome I would get from Chalmers and Pinero when I went to see the murder book. I finished with, "But most of all I want to find out why Osterman set me up."

Phoenix was silent for a long time. When she spoke, she did so softly, her words almost feathers caught in the updraft of all I had told her. "You don't fuck around, do you?"

"A quality I hope you'll come to appreciate."

She half-smiled and shook her head. "This is—this is all just crazy." She stood and moved behind my stool then slipped her arms around me and rested her cheek against the back of my head. I closed my eyes and inhaled the scent of grape seed lotion already applied. "Be careful, Gideon," she said. "Please."

Chapter 26

I spent the morning perched on a bistro stool at my dining counter, Lenovo laptop open, blue BuffaLove mug and pocket notebook at hand. First I logged into KeyBank and paid the parking ticket that had been on my car. Then I pulled up IntelliChexx and got to work.

Vincent C. Osterman, sixty-five, had retired eleven years ago after thirty years with the Buffalo Police. He'd spent most of his twenty years as a detective in homicide, where he'd earned commendations for distinguished service. Twice married, twice divorced. Two sons from his first go-round—one a Seattle neurosurgeon, the other a Virginia Tech engineering professor—and no children from his second. No felonies before retirement, as expected, and none after. Apart from his appearance over the years in various newspaper accounts of police cases or trial testimony, his online activity footprint was small—no Facebook or other social media, few pictures, no articles or blog posts or comments. A decade-old *Buffalo News* filler noted he had taken a position with the newly expanded CitiQuest but offered no details.

We shared membership in state and national professional investigators' associations, but each link to Osterman went to the CitiQuest site, which labeled him a "senior investigator with thirty-plus years in law enforcement." No real estate activity since the sale of a small west side house and subsequent purchase of a waterfront condo nine years ago. The condo was in a high-rise that looked beyond the means of the average civ-

il service retiree, and his car was a fully loaded Cadillac Escalade, so whatever Osterman did for CitiQuest, the job paid
well.

Next I dug into CitiQuest. It was a privately held company
with no apparent outside investors. In addition to the *About Us*
link that offered the company philosophy and listed services,
the web site had the obligatory flattering bio of founder Zack
Briggs. A native of Wheatfield, a town near Niagara Falls, he
had excelled in history and sports in high school. After ROTC
at St. Bonaventure, he went into the army as a second lieuten-
ant and served with distinction in the first Gulf war. Retiring as
a ranger captain before the turn of the millennium, he part-
nered with three other retired rangers and two retired navy
SEALs to establish LibertyQuest, a private military company
later well-positioned to offer contractual security services in
Iraq after the fall of Saddam Hussein. Two years into the
war—six or seven months, I recalled, before a little-publicized
incident which left an Iraqi couple and their two sons dead—
he sold his share of LibertyQuest to investors and came home.
Settling in Niagara Falls, he began CitiQuest. Three years later, he relocated the company to Buffalo and opened branches
across the state. With degrees in military science, criminal justice, and business, he was a church-going family man and ded-
icated professional who wanted "to give as much back to
Western New York as the community has given him."

Photos interspersed throughout the bio showed a tall, fit-
looking man in his late fifties with sandy hair and a smile that
advertised everything but his dentist's name. In some he posed
with local luminaries or celebrities who'd engaged CitiQuest's
services. In one he sat in shirtsleeves at a circular console that
looked like a high tech movie set. In another he was surrounded by a diverse group of employees who seemed captivated by
his presence. The last photo was an Olan Mills-style portrait of
Briggs with his wife Michelene, a younger woman whose
dress was blue and hair platinum, and their son Paul, a blond
boy of seven or eight.

I ran Zack Briggs through IntelliChexx and came up with
nothing but an ex-wife and two speeding tickets, all pinpoints

in his rear view mirror. Buffalo-born Michelene Briggs, nee Bello, forty-one, had no felonies or misdemeanors but did have a UB law degree and served as CitiQuest general counsel. In my notebook I wrote: *Ask Phoenix if she knows M. Briggs.*

Phoenix. I got up, made another cup of coffee, and thought about her as I drank it.

After my parents died, I lost my natural childhood inclination to dream of happily ever after. Throughout my teens, it was Bobby who kept me from surrendering to full-blown despair. Life, he said often, was a balance between hope and hopelessness, between the real and the possible, between our better and worse selves. But when I went to Iraq after several years in the army and witnessed firsthand the futility of a mismanaged war, any hope I risked feeling curled in upon itself like an ingrown hair. By the time I reached the CID, my path to pessimism was already framed and full of gravel. Since then, it had been cemented block by block by nearly every investigation I undertook, by my failed marriage, by Jimmy's shooting, by spree killer Jasper Hellman's attempt to sue me for leaving him with a colostomy bag.

Bobby liked to say it was the people we loved who saw us through life, who gave us meaning amid madness and purpose amid pain. The people we would happily die for were the ones who most inspired us to live. In that department, I counted myself lucky. In country, all that kept the in-growth of hopelessness from festering was the warrior brotherhood and a handful of close friends like Danny. Back in the real world I was anchored and even buoyed by Bobby and Kayla, Mira and Shakti, Jimmy and Peggy Ann and LJ. Now Phoenix was stepping into the mix in a way the others couldn't, offering me a balance I had lacked for some time. I felt a strange blend of exhilaration and fear. I knew better than to rush things, even when they felt so easy and comfortable and right. Still, I wondered if I could wait till Saturday to see her again.

When the BuffaLove mug was empty, I filled it with water and left it in the sink. Then I returned to the Lenovo and tapped it out of its sleep mode. My next subject would be Kenny Carnahan. If CitiQuest wanted to hire him at double his police salary, he must have had talents that made him worth the investment.

Because his death certificate had yet to become part of the public record, IntelliChexx listed Kenneth P. Carnahan, thirty-three, as a City of Buffalo employee who lived in a Jewett Avenue apartment. Parents James I. and Mary—nee McCarthy—Carnahan. Uncle Patrick J. McCarthy. Brother Leonard E., a decade younger. Kenny had no active social media presence of his own but was tagged in several photos on his brother's Facebook page. I looked at all the photos, learning more than I cared to know about Lenny's love of beer, his college classmates, and his lack of a life plan. As I expected, there were no pictures of Indi, but in three Kenny had his arm around a young, auburn-haired woman tagged as Karen O'Brien. I pulled up her Facebook page. Her profile picture showed someone in her late twenties, with green eyes, freckles, and full lips. Her cover photo put her at a desktop computer. The *About* page noted she was a Daemen College grad and a manager for Rich Products. No mention of relationship status but thirty-plus condolence messages suggested she was involved with Kenny:

> *My deepest sympathy, KO. This is hard but your friends will see you thru.*
>
> *Karen, so sorry for your loss, you need me girl, im there.*
>
> *if theres anything we can do just call or text.*
>
> *U been thru so much together. Now this, no fair.*
>
> *Cops got a dangerous job nobody appreciates. So sad.*
>
> *True true true. The job was always the thing made it hard for you both.*
>
> *Put your faith in God, girlfriend. I'm praying for you.*
>
> *You'll see him again. Somewhere, KO, he is waiting for you.*

KO's response deepened my curiosity:

Thank you, everybody. Thank you so much. Kenny was a good man with a hard job. Been apart awhile but we went thru so much together we always believed we'd be together again. We just never thought it would be on the other side. Will post funeral details when I have them. Pray for his mom & dad. Thank you. Love you all.

According to IntelliChexx, Karen M. O'Brien was thirty-one and lived in the same Jewett Avenue apartment as Kenny Carnahan, her residency, like his, stretching back more than six years. Lenny told me Kenny had moved back in with his family six months ago, which meant he and O'Brien had lived together a long time before parting ways. They had been together when Kenny was shot and for years afterward but had never married. If her Facebook post was truthful, she had expected they would reconnect. I wondered how O'Brien felt when she learned the man she had likely nursed back to health hooked up with a sexy blues singer who so obsessed him he was talking about marriage after only two months. Would KO be angry enough to kill him, or have him killed?

I jotted a note to interview Karen O'Brien then went back to searching Kenny.

Like many cops, he began his career working the hours and days avoided by officers with more seniority. Overnight and weekend shifts are often busy and give younger cops a chance to bump up their early career arrest stats, but Kenny's were within the average range. Then a brief undercover assignment led to a commendation and his attachment to the plainclothes Gang Crimes Task Force. One of three uniformed officers so assigned, Kenny was popular with GCTF leaders and seemed on track to get a detective shield early. But he was sidelined by a bullet. Newspaper articles reported his girlfriend had found him on the sidewalk after the shooter drove off. I double-underlined *Interview KO* then turned back to the computer. After two months of recovery and physical therapy, Kenny returned to work on light duty. I could find no chain of circumstances that led to the front seat of the mayor's car or justified his promised salary at CQIS. With any luck, LJ would unearth a transfer request or a secret memo or a special assignment to complete the picture.

My final search that morning was Lorenzo Quick. There were two in New York State, one in Brooklyn, one in Buffalo. The Buffalo Quick owned QuiClean, a trio of one-day dry cleaning storefronts. I had known I would find no arrests, and the intelligence circulars that suggested his involvement with the Nightwalkers during my CID days were classified. But I was surprised at the sparse information between high school in his native Chicago and the QuiClean site, which had no CEO bio. Two years in the army with service in the first Gulf War, a GI Bill MBA. But no marriages or relatives or community milestones. A newspaper article about the dry-cleaning business that noted the expansion from one site to three. The reporter called Lorenzo Quick "a very private, hard-working businessman who keeps to himself." Publicly, he was a silhouette behind the plastic bags on a motorized garment rack.

At a quarter to noon, I closed my Lenovo and made lunch. LJ called as I took the second bite of my peanut butter and jelly sandwich. I washed it down with iced tea and touched the answer icon on my screen.

"Hey, G. How you doin'?" His tone was light, therefore promising.

"Good, LJ. Just having some lunch."

"I can call you back if you don't want it to get cold."

"No problem. It's PB and J."

"Grape or strawberry?"

A question for the ages. "Grape," I said.

"I don't get you grape people. Strawberry's got so much more body."

I laughed. "Got something for me, LJ?"

"You asked me to dig into Vincent Osterman and CitiQuest." His voice took on a more serious note, his idea of businesslike. "Which report would you like first?"

"Osterman," I said, only because I'd opened my notebook on the page headed Oz.

Most of what LJ said about Vincent Charles Osterman I already had. Listening, I chewed my sandwich as noiselessly as possible. After a few minutes, with only a quarter of the sandwich left, I put it down to pick up my pen. Phone records suggested Osterman's relationship with each of his sons was limited to the occasional phone call. An email exchange between two of his associates wondered if it was a coincidence that both of his wives sustained black eyes from walking into the edge of a door, but there had been no investigation of either claim. Internal police memos had noted four complaints of police brutality over two decades. The infrequency and variations in circumstances and ethnicities of the complainants had been judged insufficient evidence of a pattern. No report had made it into his personnel file until the fifth incident, the year he retired.

"It was one of those stupid traffic things," LJ said. "Kid cuts him off and Osterman puts a bubble on his unmarked car. He chases the kid down, lights flashing, and pulls over a red Maserati."

"No shit? I think there's only one or two Maserati dealers in this whole area."

"One," LJ said. "In Williamsville."

"So what happened?"

"The kid says Osterman dragged him out of the car and started punching him. Osterman says the kid got out and told him to suck his dick, then lunged at him."

"Lunged?"

"His word, not mine."

"Probably a sliver of truth in both statements but he does seem to have anger issues." I scanned the notes on my Oz page. "And there's no newspaper story about the incident?"

"Osterman couldn't have been that good a detective if he didn't figure out a red Maserati plus blue eyes equal money. Money kept it quiet and money cost him his job."

"Forced retirement or the wrath of God comes down on the city."

"Yep. He should have asked for the kid's license before starting a beat-down."

"What was the name on the license?"

"McGoldrick," LJ said, and I could almost see him nodding. "Lance McGoldrick. The name even sounds like money."

I didn't need to flip back to the Lenny page to remember my talk with him. "The same McGoldrick family that closed a factory about ten years ago?"

"Yeah. Dad says they were in Buffalo a long time and helped pay for a lot of public buildings and monuments and stuff."

Had Oz been at least partly responsible for McGoldrick Materials leaving Buffalo and putting Kenny's father and two hundred others out of work? Or was the plant closure just a coincidence? Had a shared hatred of McGoldrick brought Oz and Kenny together? "Anything else about Osterman?"

"Went to work for CitiQuest less than a year after he retired. Now makes about 125K, plus profit-sharing. A high five-figure bank balance and a Canadian beach house."

"His job title is senior investigator, but what does he really do for them?"

"The CitiQuest network has some sick encryption, G."

"Sick but not incurable."

"Nope." He let the word hang there a second like the Cheshire Cat's smile. "Memos make Vince Osterman sound like some kind of troubleshooter. Special problems. Not a problem solver, but a problem eliminator."

"I see you've been watching James Bond movies again."

"I think they're kind of corny, but Dad loves them, and Mom gave him this complete Blu-Ray set a few years back. It's something we can do together."

"Anything to say it's Osterman's job to hire people?"

"Not really."

"Supposedly, he offered a job to Kenny Carnahan."

"The dead cop." He paused a moment. "Guess that brings us to CitiQuest."

Again, his recitation mirrored what I had but I listened patiently, waiting for new bits of information. I put away the last of my sandwich and drank some iced tea. I knew Zack Briggs had gotten out of LibertyQuest with a nice sum of money, and the company had collapsed within two years, but I was surprised to learn the Freedom's Tide mercenary group had grown out of its wreckage. LJ found no link between the Tide, reportedly training independent militias in Africa and the Middle East, and CQIS. There was no record Zack Briggs had spoken to his LibertyQuest partners ever again, even by telephone, since selling his share of the business. Some of the memos he wrote made him sound bombastic, even clueless. His wife, on the other hand, came across as shrewd and calculating enough to keep the business afloat.

"What do you have on her?" I asked.

"I didn't go too deep on her. Only child. Father died before she was born. Mother worked as a secretary in several different companies. Pretty lady and real smart but no prom queen. They were far from rich. She had to fight her way through, from grammar school to law school. She worked jobs from high school on but still managed stay on top in school and snatch every scholarship she could. And she earned a lot as a lawyer before she hooked up with Briggs. Like I said, real smart. After they swapped rings, it was her idea to make the move to Buffalo and expand."

"Interesting." I scribbled a note on my CitiQuest page. "Can you go deeper?"

"Sure. I got an hour between classes this afternoon."

"No rush. And I take it you've looked at the financials."

"Course. The public and the private are just about identical."

"Any shadow investors or secret money?"

"Maybe at first, when he had all kinds of paper from selling his part of Mercs-R-Us. Would have been easy then for rich guys to hide money in his set-up funds. If they're part of it now, the records are someplace I can't get to them."

"Anybody got anything offshore?"

"Osterman transfers money into a Canadian checking account to cover beach house expenses, usually a grand or two at a time. Nobody else has anything I could find."

I heard papers shuffle and asked, "Anything else?"

"You said Osterman offered Carnahan a job."

"That's what Kenny's brother told me."

"I got a payroll list right in front of me that says Carnahan already worked for CQIS. He started drawing a paycheck in July."

Chapter 27

At one, shaved and showered and wearing clean jeans and my leather jacket, I left my apartment for my one-thirty appointment with Karen O'Brien. On the phone KO—as she told me to call her—had sounded almost pixielike, but her demeanor was all business. Because the day was so packed and she had already spoken to a detective, she would give me fifteen minutes while she ate a light lunch. If I was even a minute late, I'd have to wait for her to get back to me. A short drive up Elmwood to Ferry and over to Niagara, where Rich Products was headquartered. Plenty of visitors' parking, KO said. There was no way I'd be late.

I went around the corner toward where I'd parked and pushed the *UNLOCK* button on my remote. Before I could reach my Escape, three large men in leather coats and gloves climbed out of a black Lexus SUV parked two spaces ahead of me. The younger two—kids really—were hatless and bald. The oldest man was darker and taller but all three were of medium height, like Kenny's killer. Each kept a hand inside his coat as if holding a gun.

"Gideon Rimes."

The voice was a controlled baritone. The man who spoke was the oldest and seemed in charge. He had not asked a question, so there was no point denying my identity.

"Yes?" I glanced at the plate number, memorized it.

"My employer would like to meet you, sir." He gestured toward the open back door with his free hand. I could see a fourth man behind the wheel, gloved hands at ten and two.

"I don't suppose he'd accept my card and call for an appointment."

"No, sir, he would not."

"And I don't suppose I can reach for my phone to cancel my one-thirty."

"Do reach for your cell, sir, but hand it to me. I will turn it off and it will be returned to you undamaged after your meeting with my employer." There was an unsettling contrast between the friendly smile bracketed by a salt-and-pepper mustache and the flatness in the eyes beneath the brim of a leather Greek fisherman's cap. "And your gun. Take it out slowly, using only a finger and thumb. Hand that over as well, and it too will be returned afterward."

I gave him my Glock first, then my phone, and he put them both in his right coat pocket after he produced a rubber-tipped stylus and turned off the phone without removing a glove. No fingerprint on the screen. Damn.

"And your keys," he said.

I held up my key ring. "Mind if I lock my car first?"

"No need. Wouldn't want you to try something foolish like the panic button." He took the keys and handed them to one of the younger men. "My associate will follow in your car."

As the kid with my keys moved away, I said, "You're very polite. I appreciate that."

The man in the Greek fisherman's cap shrugged. "Never a point in being rude."

"I can put in a good word with Mr. Quick. Get you named Employee of the Month."

The smile faltered a bit. "Please get inside, sir."

So, it was Lorenzo Quick who had sent a car for me. No need for a plate number now.

As my Escape started, I got in the back seat of the Lexus and slid over to the window. The driver was a skinny kid in a leather coat and baseball cap. He looked straight ahead but I could see his sunglasses in the rear view mirror. The remaining younger man got in beside me, hand still inside his coat. Greek fisherman's cap, with my gun well out of reach, took the front seat. The driver clicked something—probably a child lock so I couldn't open the door—and cranked the car. We pulled away from the curb, and I let out a long, slow breath.

"Do you gentlemen have names? I'd like to know who's going to kill me."

"First, let me assure you we intend you no harm," the leader said, turning to face me. His expression left no doubt they would harm me if they needed to. "And there is no need for names. It's unlikely we'll ever meet again so you won't have to rack your brain remembering what I'm called. My employer simply wishes to speak to you."

"Why? I've never met Mr. Quick. What does he want with me?"

"Again, there is no need for names. All will be clear soon enough."

Lorenzo Quick was smart enough to thrive without ever being arrested, but he knew he was on the radar. I doubted his men would shoot me in the car in the afternoon in the middle of the Elmwood Village and create a forensic nightmare— or worse if a stray bullet passed through a window and hit a bystander. My mind ticked ahead to when it was time to get out of the car. Would I have a chance then to disarm the younger one and take his gun before the others could shoot me? An action movie shtick that bore little resemblance to real life might be my only chance. But there was also the guy in my car to consider.

Then it hit me, and I relaxed. "It was my computer search, wasn't it? Your employer has no online presence but he's got umpteen alerts that go off when somebody searches for him. So he reverse-searches me back to my IP address and figures we need to talk." Quick would demand to know who'd hired me, what I knew, and who shared that knowledge. Only then would he decide what to do with me. If I proved no threat, would he throw me back like a fish below the legal size limit or would he gut me on the spot, triple-wrap me in plastic, and dispose of me before anyone noticed? I was glad I hadn't asked LJ to dig into Quick. Jimmy and Peggy Ann would be inconsolable if their son simply disappeared one day.

"As I told you, all will be clear soon enough." The leader said nothing more but continued to look at me as if daring me to make a move.

I glanced out the back window and saw my Escape was behind us, two cars back. Then I looked out the side window at the homes and businesses we passed.

We drove north on Elmwood for nine or ten blocks, then turned right onto Bidwell Parkway. We followed Bidwell to Soldier's Circle and rounded it onto Lincoln Parkway, which ran parallel to Elmwood. At Forest, we crossed to the access road side of Lincoln and turned left into an overgrown drive. The massive stone house was diagonally across from the Delaware Park Rose Garden, where Kenny's body had been found, and about half a block from the rear of the Albright-Knox Art Gallery, where cousins Hellman and Tull dumped their stolen car before walking to the front of the building and crossing the street to Buffalo State. I couldn't help thinking how ironic it would be if I died here, between where I had been accused of killing one man and where I actually had killed another.

The driver pointed a controller at a tall iron gate. It opened slowly to admit us and closed after my Escape pulled in behind us. We crept into a large, tree-filled yard surrounded by tall wooden fences, then stopped.

"We're here," the oldest man said. He opened his door and got out, as did the driver and the man beside me. The driver let me out only after the fourth man had joined them, and the first thing I noticed was the two security cameras covering the yard. The windows on the first floor were barred, even those on the far right too small for anyone to squeeze through.

The four men surrounded me as if they were secret service agents and walked me toward a solid steel door. The door opened before we reached it. A petite dark woman in black shirt and pants stepped outside to hold it for us, and for a moment I thought she was Indi. But she was a few years older than Indi. Her lips were less full, her body less curvy, her hair shorter, and she offered only a flicker of a smile to the man in front. Our cluster entered a long, lighted corridor that forced us into a single file. The woman closed the door after we were inside and squeezed past us to reach the front. I watched for tells that would reveal the nature of her relationship with the man in the Greek fisherman's cap—a touch, a look, a bitten lip—but she spoke to him evenly. "He's already in the water."

Water? I thought about the small windows I'd noticed outside and wondered if Quick had an indoor swimming pool.

We continued along the corridor to the end. I smelled chlorine before the woman opened the glass door on the right. There was a pool inside, about fifteen by twenty, framed by a three-foot wide ceramic tile deck. The room was warm but not steamy. The windows I'd seen outside were above head height. Sitting at the far end, legs dangling in water, was a tall and muscular mocha-skinned man in red trunks. He had close-cropped black hair and a trimmed mustache that circled his mouth and ended in a sharp Vandyke. We filed in along one wall as he slipped into the water and walked toward us. The water just covered his chest, which meant the pool was about five feet deep. He said nothing as he looked up at me, just smiled. He looked about fifty but his teeth were flawlessly white—except for his canines, which were long, though not long enough to interfere with eating, and capped in gold.

"My employer would like you to join him in the pool for your meeting," Greek fisherman's cap said.

"Do I get to undress?"

"Of course." Grinning, he pulled over a sturdy plastic stool so I could sit. "If you'd like, we can have your clothes steamed while you talk. Won't take long to freshen them up."

"No, thank you. They're right out of my closet, fresh enough." I took off my jacket and shoulder holster. The driver stepped forward to take them. Then I sat and untied a sneaker. As I undressed, the driver continued to drape my clothes over one arm, and one of the bald kids picked up my sneakers and socks. When I stood I was wearing only my boxer-briefs.

"Those too," the man in the cap said as the woman snapped on a pair of latex gloves. "And please sit back down."

I stepped out of my shorts and handed them to the driver. Then I sat again and went through a mental checklist of what they would find in my clothes and wallet: pen, pocket note-book with case notes in a personal shorthand it wouldn't take a genius to decode, a few coins, fifty or sixty dollars, driver's license, PI license, carry permit, business cards. I was glad I had left Ophelia's letter at home. There was nothing to identify anyone I cared about except an "in case of emergency" card with Bobby's name and number.

The woman positioned herself behind me and ran her gloved fingers through my hair as if massaging my scalp. Next she probed the skin around my stitches, pressing just hard enough to cause me pain. I clenched my teeth against it and kept my seat. After she explored each ear canal and my arm-pits, she took my glasses and told me to stand and face her. I did so. She took hold of my penis and gently palpated the sides, then lifted my scrotum and did the same to my testicles. Her touch was clinical, not in the least arousing. It was appar-ent she had a lot of practice checking people before they en-tered the pool. I turned my head to one side and coughed. No-body laughed—but when I glanced at my examiner I saw a hint of a smile. Before I could smile back, she spun me around. The reason for her lapse in seriousness was clear when she probed my rectum, which made me suck in a breath too deep to hide my surprise. Until that moment I had felt no humilia-tion, only a simmering indignation.

When she peeled off her gloves and nodded to the man in the water, I looked at him and said, "Next time I'll have to get extra pay for that one. It's only fair."

His smile widened and he gestured me into the pool. The others left with my clothing, and Greek fisherman's cap went to stand by the door. I slid into the warm water a few feet away from Quick and circled him a bit so I could keep an eye on the man at the door too.

"Gideon Rimes," he said. His voice was rich, resonant. "Born in Buffalo. Enlisted at eighteen. Worked your way into the MPs. Career army cop. Two tours in the sandbox. On the first you butted heads with the CIA man who wanted to use...*enhanced interrogation*...on the prisoners in your care. Both of you were reassigned—him to another detention center, you outside the wire to training the Iraqi police. Punishment, but it led to a Bronze Star and Purple Heart. After your second tour you went stateside and got bumped into CID because your complaint a couple years earlier helped your immediate superiors dodge Abu Ghraib blowback. Retired after twenty. Signed on as a cop at Buffalo State. Quit after a nasty fatal shootout with a couple of crazy crackers on a killing spree. Now you're a PI. Married briefly. No children. Closest relative, your godfather, Dr. Robert Chance."

I said nothing but continued to stare at him.

"All that came in the time it took one of my tech people to eat a ham sandwich." His volume dropped a notch or two. "But you don't scare easy, do you?"

"When a mortar shell takes out a latrine where you just took a dump," I said, "you learn when to be afraid and when to let go. Since you seem to know everything about me, Mr. Quick, I'm just waiting for you to make your point."

"I was over there for the first go-round, so I understand," Quick said. "But you're wrong. I don't know everything. Sure, I got some idea who you are and what you can do—that shootout was some serious shit. And I know one person you love, not everybody. But fuck all that. What I really want to know is who hired you to dig into me and why."

"You've got people tracking you all the time. Cops, the Bureau, even DHS, if the old CID circulars I saw meant anything to the brass. You kidnap them at gunpoint too?"

"When my associates invited you here, did you see a gun?"

Invited? I opened my mouth to protest but hesitated when I realized I had not seen a gun. His thugs had held their hands inside their coats *as if* they were carrying, but no one had shown me a weapon or even pointed a finger at me. It would be hard to call this a kidnapping with four witnesses testifying they were unarmed when they "invited" me to meet their boss. There was no struggle, no physical altercation. To any passersby, I had gotten into the car of my own free will. No names, no guns, no fight, no clothes, no listening devices. Lorenzo Quick's reputation for hyper caution was well deserved.

"All right, I didn't see a gun. But why do you want to waste time talking to me when people who'd love to arrest you are swarming around your foundation like carpenter ants?"

"I *know* what *they're* looking for. Drug deals, money laundering, human trafficking, smuggling, RICO violations, bribes, unsolved hits—things they'll never find with internet searches and attempts to get inside my home." He narrowed his eyes at me and his voice grew quieter, more serious. "What I *don't* know is what *you're* looking for and who sent you to find it."

"So you're going to threaten me or my loved ones if I don't cooperate."

"There's never a point in acting rude."

The same thing Greek fisherman's cap had said to me. However paranoid he was, Quick had such tight control of his people they quoted him, in an almost identical rhythm. At least one did. Apart from the woman's single sentence, all the others had said nothing but had remained calm and detached throughout our encounter, as if taught how to be that way. It occurred to me Quick's face-to-face crew was likely very loyal and very small, a tight band whose activities were so shrewdly interconnected the criminals doing grunt work far down the chain had no idea who they were really working for.

"Then you invited me here to satisfy simple curiosity?"

He smiled again, those damn vampire fangs gleaming. "Yes."

"Nobody hired me to look into you," I said. "I was hired to protect a woman from a stalker. The stalker was a cop named Kenny Carnahan who got shot five years ago during his time on a gang task force. The cop talk then suggested you were behind the hit, or the trigger man yourself, but nobody could prove anything. When Carnahan turned up dead a couple days ago, the two detectives on the case looked at me for it. Then your name came up in discussion."

"Pinero and Chalmers," Quick said, sucking his teeth. "Those pricks need to get laid more often. Maybe then they wouldn't have such a hard-on for me—" He spread his hands apart. "—me, a simple dry cleaner." He moved close enough to me to study my stitches. "They did that to you? Those boys must be changing their style."

I shook my head. "An eager SWAT guy jumped up on adrenaline."

He nodded. "I take it *you* didn't kill Carnahan if you're thinking I did."

"No. I would have if he forced me to, but I wouldn't have beaten him to death." I studied Quick's face for a reaction to this detail about the murder but he gave none. "You know, Chalmers and Pinero don't really think you did it. They say it's not your style."

"But you couldn't take their word for it."

I shrugged. "A good investigator does his own investigating."

"Now that you've met me, now that you've...investigated, what do you think?"

"I doubt you did it. It was a killing far too careless for a man so careful he has people strip-searched for bugs and holds his meetings in a swimming pool."

He leaned closer, his voice dropping to a whisper, his dark eyes flat as a shark's. "What would you say if I told you right here, with no possible way to record it and no one else to hear, I did it?"

"I'd say you were fucking with me to see what I would do."

He stepped back and grinned. "Might be."

"Just so you know, if I thought you really did it—you, a simple dry cleaner—I'd try to find a way to prove it."

"If somehow you managed to leave."

"True, but making me stay might not be...cost effective."

"Rimes, the mayor can't protect you here."

I refused to take that particular piece of bait and didn't break eye contact with him. He wouldn't have needed tech people to find my friendship with Danny and Ophelia.

We gazed at each other for a long time, neither of us blinking, neither of us moving. It was clear he was still trying to make up his mind about me, whether I was a threat, whether my association with the mayor would make me too much trouble to kill. For my part, I was calculating my chances of getting to Quick's throat or eyes if he signaled the man in the cap to pull the gun I knew was under his coat even if I hadn't seen it. I would certainly die, but if I didn't have time to get Quick into the line of fire, I might still crush his windpipe, or rake out an eye so he would live with the memory of how close I'd come to taking him down.

Just then my certainty of having some impact faded because Quick's hand came up from beneath the water with a black Sheffield folding knife that must have come from the pocket of his swim trunks. He opened it and studied the carbon blade for a long moment then used the tip to clean his left thumbnail. He held up the blade again, turning it this way and that as he looked at me. Finally, he let out a deep laugh and shook his head. "You should see your eyes, man. Hard as flint arrowheads and you didn't flinch a hair." He closed the knife and returned it to his pocket. "Damn! A tough motherfucker to the end. I like that."

For the first time, I forced myself to smile back at him. "And now that I've met you, I don't think you shot Kenny either."

"Why not?"

"Because you're a tough motherfucker yourself," I said. "Not the kind who leaves something unfinished."

"You're smarter than you look, Rimes." He nodded as if in approval. "I hope you've enjoyed our conversation as much as I have. But savor the memory because it's unlikely we will ever meet again." Smile fading, he curled a finger at the man still standing by the door. "Get him a towel and a robe and take him to the changing room so he can get dressed." As Greek fisherman's cap opened the glass door and stepped into the corridor, Quick looked at me and said, "Say hello to the mayor for me." Then, as I climbed out and stood dripping on the deck, he plunged beneath the surface and swam to the other side of the pool.

Twenty minutes later I pulled over on Bidwell Parkway half a block before Elmwood and took a few deep breaths to steady myself. When at last a tension that felt like wet cement in my gut drained out of me, I used the Swiss Army knife I kept in my glove compartment to open the duct-taped plastic shoebox they'd given me when I got into my car. Inside were my notebook, mobile phone, and wallet—money and cards intact—and my Glock, empty clip beside it and loose bullets rolling about. I loaded the magazine, slammed it home, and slid the gun into my holster. I got out and pocketed my wallet, cell, and notebook. Then I dropped the shoebox into a yellow waste can bracketed to a nearby streetlight. Maybe I should have had somebody dust everything, but I was certain the only prints found would be mine.

Chapter 28

After I rang the bell, Peggy Ann smiled at me through one of the sidelight windows, but something in my expression made her smile fade. She let me in without a word and made no effort to kiss my cheek.

I slipped my arms around her, and she let me ease her head to my chest. "I'm not crashing for dinner," I said. "I had a bad encounter with somebody this afternoon and I need to see friendly faces."

She nodded against my jacket, her glasses shifting. "Somebody dangerous?"

"Very."

She hugged me hard for a long moment. Then she stepped back and smoothed her tan housedress and looked at me.

"Is Jimmy free?"

"He's with a client right now, but he shouldn't be too long. Meanwhile, mister, you're coming to the kitchen with me. You need more than a friendly face."

I followed Peggy Ann into the kitchen and sat at the semi-circular table that had been specially designed to accommodate Jimmy's wheelchair. She pulled a vanilla creamer from the fridge and set it on the table. Next she scooped coffee from a canister into a Mr. Coffee on the countertop. Then she got two mugs from a row of hooks just above the sink and two spoons from the drawer beside it and sat across from me.

"LJ still at school?" I asked.

"Yes."

"Good."

She narrowed her eyes at me. "What is it, G? What aren't you telling me?"

"I'll tell you everything when Jimmy joins us."

"Got something to do with LJ?"

"No, and I want to keep it that way."

The vanilla creamer made the coffee sweeter than I usually like but the presence of a friend countered the extra sugar. I wanted to put her mind at ease, so I began to tell Peggy Ann about Bobby's Wizard of Oz library lecture. Though she seemed hesitant to engage in small talk at first, when I shifted the topic to my dinner with a woman I wanted to see again, her face brightened. She began to press me for details. I was half-way through a description of Phoenix when Jimmy's motorized chair whirred past the kitchen doorway, and he offered a brief nod. Walking behind him was a lanky middle-aged man in a shabby sports coat. The man could have been a store owner in search of a reliable do-it-yourself security set-up or a suspicious husband in need of a voice-activated digital recorder to conceal in the bedroom when he was away. Whatever the case, confidentiality was guaranteed. Jimmy would never share the details of the transaction with anyone, not even Peggy Ann.

A moment later, in shirtsleeves and loosened tie, Jimmy rolled into the kitchen and stopped by the sink. "Mind if I join you?" He reached up and unhooked a cup, then rotated over to the coffee machine and poured. Bracing his mug on the armrest, he steered his chair into his slot at the end of the table. "So what's up, G? I saw you on Monitor Two. The way you hugged Peg says something's wrong."

"Ever hear of a guy named Lorenzo Quick?"

Jimmy shrugged and took a sip. "Name rings a bell."

"I first heard about him when I was in the CID. And we used to get confidential circulars at campus police headquarters. Suspected drug dealer. Head of the Nightwalkers. Never arrested."

"Right, right," Jimmy said, nodding. "Gold vampire teeth. So what about him?"

"He had me kidnapped at gunpoint this afternoon."

"*What?*" Peggy Ann said as Jimmy said, "Jesus!" and leaned so far forward in his chair it looked as if he were attempting to stand. Almost simultaneously, Peggy Ann asked if I'd been hurt and Jimmy started to ask if I'd called the police.

Then he narrowed his eyes at me. "You didn't go to the police, did you?"

I held up a hand. "I'm fine. I'll tell you everything and then I'll tell you why I'm here, but I'm fine." When they were ready to listen, I recounted the details of my investigation and the path that led me to Quick. I described my abduction and saw their eyes widen when I told them about the examination I underwent before going into the swimming pool. I said Quick was a disciplined sociopath, a snake in swim trunks who wouldn't hesitate to strike when cornered. I waited until the end to explain how his people had reverse-searched me to my home.

Peggy Ann saw where I was headed before Jimmy. She sat up straight and jabbed her finger at me even before I finished. "Did you have LJ digging into him?"

Jimmy's intake of breath was audible.

"No, and I never will. That's what I want to talk to you about." I folded my hands on the table and looked from Jimmy to Peggy Ann and back. "LJ's good at what he does, the best I've ever seen, but I can't be the only one he's doing jobs for so he's got to be careful. Phantom servers, ghost IP addresses, rerouting, piggybacking on international networks—whatever he needs to do, Jimmy. You've got to make sure LJ covers his tracks and then covers the covers. Sure, it's a long shot the average search target would have people as good as Quick's but we can't take that chance."

"He has to see the danger," Peggy Ann said. "He doesn't now because he's young and grew up sheltered. And he's cocky because he knows he's smart. But he has to see the danger, to see some of these men as the animals they really are, the way both of you do."

"Okay," Jimmy said. "I'll talk to him. Limit his searches to basic background checks until we know more about what we're digging into."

"A basic background check is what I did," I said. "He can't even do that for a guy like Quick. People with a public presence are probably safe. Google hits are okay. Start there, but if a general search doesn't turn up much, run it by me before you give it to LJ. Anything."

"And no hacking unless *you* know the target is safe," Peggy Ann said to her husband.

"You're right, Peg."

"I mean it, Jimmy. No more midnight cyber walks for fun. I can't—can't have—" Looking unsure what else to do, she stood up. "I can't have something happen to him too." She put her arms around Jimmy and rested her cheek against the top of his head. "If I have to, I'll take every goddam computer out of his bedroom."

For a time none of us said anything.

"We need to teach him," I said finally. "If he's going to do any kind of security work, even on the tech side, he's got to learn to observe and assess. To be mindful and anticipate situations the average person would never imagine. To check out everything with his danger detectors on full. We need to teach him, you and me, to think like a cop."

Just then we heard the front door unlock, swing open, and bang shut. Still embracing her husband, Peggy Ann tensed visibly. Jimmy called out, "LJ? We're in the kitchen."

"Hey." LJ appeared in the doorway, backpack slung over one shoulder. His wrinkled hipster sports jacket covered a blue and orange Buff State T-shirt and the hems of his skinny jeans rested atop his black sneakers. He took one look at the three of us frozen into what must have seemed a strange tableau. "Who died?"

"Nobody," his mother said, going to him and hugging him. "Nobody died."

His eyes questioned his father and me. We exchanged looks with each other then looked at him and shrugged. LJ sighed and shook his head. "Glad to see you too, Mom."

Peggy Ann stepped back. "Are you hungry? Want a snack before dinner?"

"I'm fine. It's almost four-thirty and I have to work on

something before we eat." He looked at me. "You gonna be here awhile, G? I spent an hour in the lab and I got something for you, but first I gotta Skype with this girl in California." He turned to his mother. "And before you start talking about girl-friends, it's a joint schools computer thing. We're doing a long distance research project together."

"Is she cute?" Jimmy asked.

"I'll find out in about ten minutes. We just got each other's info today and swapped an email. Didn't get to Facebook yet." He turned to me. "So you're okay with waiting a bit?"

I had asked him to find out more about Michelene Briggs but hadn't expected him to get back to me so quickly. "Sure," I said.

"If you're seeing this girl for the first time," Peggy Ann said, "you really need to do something about your hair." And she followed LJ out of the kitchen.

When we were alone, Jimmy shifted his attention to me and said, "The stuff about a rectal probe. Did that woman really stick a finger up your ass?"

"And didn't even offer to buy me a drink."

Chapter 29

It was about nine when I parked on Pearl Street and called Phoenix's cell phone.

"Hi," she said, somewhat breathless, as if she had run across her loft to answer. I wondered if she had already assigned me a ringtone. "I didn't expect to hear from you tonight but I'm happy you called."

"I know we said Saturday, and I don't want you to think I'm crowding you—"

"I don't think that at all."

"I need to talk to you about something."

"Sure. Go ahead."

"Not on the phone. I'm downstairs in my car."

For a moment there was only stillness then an exhalation. "I'm in my pajamas."

"I've never seen you in pajamas."

"I have an early day tomorrow. I'm in court and I'm still prepping."

"I didn't come to spend the night. This won't take more than a couple minutes."

She laughed. "Not exactly the most romantic proposition I've ever heard—"

"That's not what I meant."

"I know. All right, I'll call the desk and have them let you in."

Phil, the gaunt guard from Saturday, buzzed me in before I touched the intercom. He seemed surprised when I greeted him by name. "Ms. Trinidad speaks highly of you," I said.

His cheeks darkened a bit. "She's a nice lady...Mr. Rimes."

"I'll tell her you said so."

Phoenix was standing in her doorway when I stepped off the elevator, and we both said hi at the same moment. She wore a teal silk lounge outfit with long sleeves and billowy pants. She was barefoot, her toenails the same deep blue as her fingernails, and stepped aside to let me in. Only when the door was closed did she pull me to her for a long kiss.

"I'm glad to see you," she said afterward.

"I'm glad to see you too."

She led me into the loft, lit only by the table lamps beside the sofa and lights beyond the uncovered windows. I saw the bouquet I'd brought yesterday was still on the dining table. A hopeful sign that maybe tonight I wouldn't ruin my chances with her. We went to the sofa. Papers were spread out on the coffee table, amid them an empty wine glass.

"I'd offer you wine," she said, moving a pen and yellow legal pad from the sofa to the coffee table, "but then I'd have to drink with you, and another glass will make me too sleepy to finish my work. If we have coffee, I'll never get to sleep and court will be a bust. But I can offer you ice water or juice."

"I'm good."

She nodded and sat on one end of the sofa, gesturing me toward the other. Tucking her right foot under her left thigh, she looked at me. "So, what's up?"

"I have something to tell you." As I spoke I noticed a slight tensing of her jaw and realized she was as nervous about what my visit might mean to our prospects as I was. "But first I need to ask you a question, to...to clarify how it was you brought Indi to me."

Her brow knitting, she shrugged. "I told you. Indi came to me because she was being stalked, and I'm on the board of Hope's Haven. I talked to Jonah, who recommended you."

"Because of my friendship with the mayor."

"Because he's an Ophelia Green supporter who thought having a stalker drive her around might be embarrassing if it came out in the middle of an election season."

"Apart from the three of you, who else knew about any of this?"

"Nobody from me or Jonah."

"Somebody from the board or your firm?"

"No." Her denial was emphatic.

"Do you remember what I told you this morning about my investigation?"

"Of course I do." Her annoyance was evident when she began to speak in what I thought must be her *I'm-not-stupid* tone. "Kenny's brother wanting to shoot you, the gang leader who's never been arrested, the man who's setting you up—"

"From CitiQuest. Is there any link between CitiQuest and Hope's Haven or your firm?"

"I'd have told you." For a moment she looked sad, uncertain, hurt. "This morning I would have told you anything." Then she pressed her lips together and narrowed her eyes at me. "Gideon, are you suggesting some kind of malfeasance here? Accusing Jonah or me of colluding with the man trying to set you up?"

"No, not at all." I reached for her hand, which she let me take, but the taut muscles in her fingers let me know she was ready to pull it away instantly. "I believe you, Phoenix. I just want to understand something that came up today. I'm looking for any connection I can find, however flimsy. I'm not accusing. I'm fishing."

"So fish someplace else. Hope's Haven vets and hires its own security staff, like Oscar, the man you met Saturday night. And our firm is too small to do business with a showboat outfit like CitiQuest." Her face softened a bit. "What happened today?"

"For starters, that gang leader's people picked me up this afternoon and took me to meet him."

Phoenix stopped breathing for several seconds, her eyes never leaving mine but blinking rapidly. Her fingers tightened around mine, and I could feel her pulse in each of them. She swallowed. "Baby…"

Last night, in the middle of things, she had called me baby, and I had liked it.

"Baby, what did they do?"

"Mainly they tried to scare me, and made a decent effort." I described the car ride and the house and the swimming pool meeting, but I omitted details of the poolside exam because I didn't want her to think of it the next time she saw me naked— if there ever was a next time. "I don't think Lorenzo Quick killed Kenny," I said when I finished. "He's far too careful."

"Doesn't matter. Kidnapping is a crime, even if you're held for only a short time." Her free hand took my free hand, and she leaned closer. "Have you filed a complaint yet?"

"No."

"B District Station is just a block away from here. I can put on shoes and a coat and go with you right now."

"No, I'm not going to make a complaint."

"Gideon—"

"They didn't hurt me, and they didn't threaten me."

"The threat was implied."

I shook my head. "It's my word against theirs it ever happened at all." I slid to her, put my arms around her, and inhaled the smell of her. "You know better than I do how far an allegation like that would get."

She turned her face up to me. "Yeah. It just feels so personal, so...creepy."

"Because it happened to somebody you know."

"And care about." She lowered her eyes. "Now I'm worried."

"Quick is a bad man, maybe the worst, but I'm no threat to him. Once he realized that, he sent me packing. He's got no reason to stir things up by hurting me. He knows about Ophelia and Bobby but he doesn't know a thing about you or anybody else important to me." I leaned back and lifted her chin to look into her eyes, which had begun to fill. "If it makes you feel better, I'll tell Pinero and Chalmers but I won't make a formal complaint." I almost said, *Then, if something happens*—but I stopped myself.

She wiped her eyes on her sleeve. "I'll still worry."

"Don't," I said. "Anyway, Quick isn't who I came to talk about."

"Who then? What's his name from CitiQuest?"

"Yes, and the mayor."

"I don't understand."

"You remember LJ."

She thought a second. "The young man who shot the video. Your partner's son."

I nodded. "LJ is gifted when it comes to computers and sometimes I hire him to look into things for me."

She laughed. "I hate euphemisms. Just say he's your hacker. Yes, hacking is illegal but you have attorney-client privilege here."

"Okay, he's my hacker," I said, spreading my hands. "I stopped by Jimmy and Peggy Ann's today to make sure he never hacks Lorenzo Quick and ended up staying for dinner, for the second time in three days. LJ had some new information about CitiQuest. That's why I had to ask you what I did, to make sense of it."

"What new information?"

"First, one final question."

"Gideon—"

"Last one. I promise. Do you know a Michelene Briggs? She's CitiQuest's general counsel and the CEO's wife. If my math is right she was a year or two ahead of you in the UB law school. Her maiden name was Bello. Tall. Blonde."

"The law school has a lot of students at any given time, up to five or six hundred." Phoenix chewed her lip for a moment and began to nod slowly. "Bello. Briggs. I think I met her but I don't really know her. I may have seen her at some ABA function but I couldn't tell you what she looks like. Blonde? I'm not sure. I've had no professional contact with her." She looked at me. "But for some reason I think her friends call her…Mickey?"

I nodded and summarized my lunchtime conversation with LJ: Vince Osterman's background and Kenny's name on the CitiQuest payroll, how Zack Briggs founded CitiQuest and moved it to Buffalo. "That was plenty but when I got to the house and saw what else LJ had, things finally began to make sense."

"Mickey."

"Michelene Bello," I said. "An only child. Father died before she was born. Raised by a single mother who worked as a secretary. That's the official story. But LJ hacked into her social media history and tracked her to Backstory Mine, one of the DNA testing sites. He got into her account and found a surprise familial link. Turns out she's not an only child and her biological father's not dead. DNA matched her to a half-brother, another person who thought he was an only child. Her father may not know he's got a daughter, but her email history confirms she and her brother have had an unpublicized relationship for almost nine years."

"Who's the brother?"

"Anthony Merlotta."

Her eyes widened. "You mean—"

"Yes, the son of Councilman Wreck-It Rick Merlotta. The son who manages Merlotta Development while his father holds public office. The same Merlotta Development that uses CitiQuest to provide security for its holdings." I shook my head. "This was never about Indi and Kenny or Kenny and Quick. It was always about Ophelia and the mayoral election."

"Embarrass her. Make her look corrupt or at least too incompetent to control her staff. Erase the Democratic advantage."

"Exactly."

Phoenix stood and circled behind the sofa, for a time lost in thought. Then she turned to me, folded her arms, and looked down at me as if her anger were looking for another way to get out. "So you thought Jonah and I were part of this?"

"No," I said. "I thought you or Jonah could have been used. And maybe Indi. Unlike Kenny, she wasn't on the CQIS payroll, and LJ couldn't find any bank deposit that suggested a payoff."

Phoenix finished rounding the sofa and passed the coffee table. She moved to the mantel and stood with her back to me, gazing down at the unlit fireplace. "Did you check my financials too?"

"No. I trust you. I've never trusted Indi. She's too immature. It doesn't look like she's part of it—"

"But you'll make it your business to find out for sure."

"I will."

"Do you think Merlotta's behind it or is it just his kids doing him a favor?"

"I don't know?"

"And why would they kill Kenny?"

"Don't know that either—if they did kill him. I plan to see them tomorrow."

"Mickey *and* Anthony?"

"Mickey first, and Osterman. Maybe Anthony later."

"Jesus." Phoenix took a deep breath and circled the coffee table back to her seat. She slumped against the armrest and said nothing for nearly a minute. Then she leaned forward and swatted my arm. "Damn you, Gideon. How the hell am I supposed to finish my work now?"

"Sorry."

"Tonight is shot. I can't focus on something like a slip-and-fall lawsuit after all this. I'll have to set the alarm for five and finish in the morning."

I got to my feet. "I *am* sorry. I had to talk to you before I go to CitiQuest tomorrow. I never intended to throw you off your game."

"So where do you think you're going now?" She reached for my hand and tugged me back down to the sofa so that I was perched on the edge as she slid down and stretched out. "I said I'd set the alarm for five, so you won't have to worry about a ticket." She pulled me to her and began to kiss my neck, chin, and cheek. "By the way," she said, lips moving from one side of my face to the other, "did you get a ticket this morning?"

"I don't remember," I said.

Chapter 30

Michelene Briggs's shoulder-length hair was so blonde it was nearly white in the afternoon sunlight pouring through the plate glass windows behind her antique desk. She stood when I was shown into her corner office, on the tenth floor of the Donat Building, which overlooked the inner harbor. She came round to shake my hand. Her lipstick matched her tailored burnt umber business suit. Her skirt stopped at the knees, revealing long legs well-muscled from running or dancing, or maybe kick-boxing. In heels, she was more than six feet tall. Her grip was strong, and even her half-smile radiated power. I was duly impressed.

"Please have a seat, Mr. Rimes," she said, returning to her own.

I unbuttoned my suit jacket and sat in—rather, sank into—the thick leather seat of the wood-framed client chair facing her desk. I scanned the office. Perpendicular floor-to-ceiling windows in place of outside walls, interior walls with shelves full of books and pictures, plaques and awards. To my left was a narrow second door of dark pebbled glass. Plastic camera bubbles were mounted near the ceiling in two corners. Instead of industrial carpet, the floor was covered with the kind of tiles used for radiant heating systems.

"So," Briggs began, "how may I help you? Ordinarily, I don't see people on such short notice, but you were so insistent on the phone. A matter of some urgency, you said."

I took the mayor's letter from my inside pocket and passed

it to her. She read it before I could lean back, eyes snapping from side to side with a speed that matched Bobby's, which meant she was clocking around 800 words a minute. Smart. Almost certainly smarter than the husband who had written some of the silly memos I had read. I began to suspect Michelene Briggs was the power and the soul of CitiQuest.

"Where's Mr. Osterman?" I asked when she returned the letter. "As I said on the phone, this involves him too."

"Mr. Osterman is with a client and will join us when he's finished." Her voice was controlled, somewhat husky. "Though I can't see how any of this involves him. Your letter says you're here on behalf of the mayor to investigate a homicide, the murder of a police officer. While such a loss is tragic, I can't quite grasp how it's a matter of urgency for a private company like CitiQuest—unless the police, the district attorney's office, and you, a private contractor, are all coming up dry and need some high tech help. We have done contractual work for special prosecutors in the past, but we never play the subcontractor for a lone wolf private eye." She smiled broadly, flawless teeth adding wattage to an already well-lit room. "But if what you're really looking for is a better-paying job—"

I was tempted to ask if there was an opening. Instead I watched her carefully. "So you have zero interest in finding out who murdered one of your employees?"

The smile froze for a second then transformed into lips parted in confusion. Her eyes narrowed, and I could see she was considering which way to pivot. "I don't understand."

But the awkward shift in her expression told me she did understand. She knew Kenny was on the payroll but was reluctant to admit it. Why?

The pebbled glass door to my left opened. Vincent Osterman stepped into the room, rubber soles making almost no noise as he moved toward Briggs's desk and straightened to his full height behind her chair. His suit today was charcoal, a better fit than the other one I'd seen him wear, despite the bulge beneath his left armpit. He said nothing.

"Oz," I said. "How nice to see you again."

He stared at me for a long moment. Finally, he moved

around the desk, and I tensed as he reached toward me. As requested, I was unarmed and would have to rely on my speed and my hands. Instead of throwing the punch I anticipated, however, Osterman flicked my left lapel aside and snatched the pen from my shirt pocket. For a time he studied it, lips stretching into a self-congratulatory grin that showed slightly graying teeth. Then he dropped it to the floor and crushed it beneath a twisting heel. When he was done, he bent and picked up the wreckage and handed it back to me before returning to his place behind Briggs's chair.

"I wouldn't offer Rimes a job just yet, ma'am," he said. "Reports of his skills as an investigator are greatly exaggerated."

"A literate thug," I said. "Imagine that." I held up the broken pen and examined the micro lens just above the pocket clip. Crushed. I pulled the smashed black barrel apart, bits of plastic falling into my lap, only to reveal stray wires and a destroyed USB connector. I looked at Osterman. "Do you know how much this cost?"

"If it's the 32-gig model, about three hundred," he said. "You're in our house trying to shoot a secret video? Bill me, but don't be surprised if I sign my check *Fuck You*."

I leaned forward and put the ruined spy cam on the desk near her laptop. Then I stood and locked eyes with Osterman, who unbuttoned his suit jacket. "Maybe I'll just put it on the tab you started when you told the police and the press I was Kenneth Carnahan's killer."

He began to move but Michelene Briggs stopped him with an uplifted hand. Her face had remained impassive during our testosterone spray-off. Now her glacial blue eyes fixed me where I stood. Even with the possibility of violence in her office, she showed no trace of discomfort or fear. That meant she knew everything, and I was likely one hidden button-push away from being seized and ejected by "security"—perhaps even "disappeared."

"Suppose we drop the pretense," she said. "Why are you really here, Mr. Rimes?"

I angled my head and pointed at my stitches. "I got that

from a SWAT cop who broke down my door and arrested me
for murder—on a tip from your pet gorilla here—no, your pet
chimp. Gorillas don't commit murder. Chimps, on the other
hand—"

"The finer points of primatology aside, you want to know
why Mr. Osterman would do such a thing." She lowered her
hand and leaned forward on her elbows. "Do you have any
proof it was my associate who told police you might be a killer? Even if you're in possession of, say, a nine-one-one recording, is it a crime to give police a tip during an active investigation? Is it even grounds for a civil suit? No." Control reestab-
lished, she sat back and folded her hands in her lap. "Here under false pretenses and you dare suggest Mr. Osterman, a decorated retired law enforcement officer, could be guilty of murder? That might be actionable if repeated in public or in print."

"Why would I kill Ken?" Osterman said. "He was a friend
of mine."

"Your godson, according to the detectives you were hanging out with Friday night."

"You don't need to say anything, Oz," Briggs said. She
touched his arm, as if to offer support but the gesture came a
second too late to be anything but part of her performance.

"I can't incriminate myself when I have no knowledge of
the crime. He's not a cop, Mrs. Briggs, even with a letter from
the mayor. Let's just get this over with."

Osterman hadn't been here when I showed the letter. I
wondered how many other men were watching this stab at
drama on monitors in the room behind the pebbled glass door.

"All right, but I am the company lawyer," she said, too gently. "When I say stop—"

Osterman nodded. "Ken wasn't my godson." He shrugged.
"Don't know where they got that idea. He was a good kid. I
met him when I was on another job, security for a high tech
investor who was meeting with the mayor. We got to be
friends."

"And you recruited him for CitiQuest."

Osterman shoved his hands into his trouser pockets. I could
see the Beretta logo near the bottom of the pistol grip beneath

his left arm. "Like I said, he was a good kid, smart and ener-getic, the kind we're always looking for."

"So you put him on the payroll."

Before Osterman could answer, Briggs scowled at me. "How do you know that?"

"A shot in the dark—a bull's-eye, given your reaction when I mentioned he was your employee." I said nothing about Kenny's having been on the payroll since July.

She studied me a moment, perhaps considering whether I'd actually breached CQIS data security or was just cocky and dumb-lucky. Then she drew in a deep breath and slipped back into her reluctantly cooperative executive act. "Mr. Carnahan worked for us part time on a case-by-case basis, until he could leave his job and join us here full time. We kept his employment secret because, as I'm sure you know, departmental regulations limit the moonlighting cops can do. Poor guys can't get a raise and can't work on the side for real money."

Osterman shook his head. "That's why I retired when I did. I saw where things were headed and knew it was time to go."

Now I resisted the urge to ask him about Lance McGoldrick's red Maserati. Instead I said, "Kenny was going to be full time after the election?"

"He didn't want to leave the mayor until the time was right," Briggs said.

"Of course," I said.

The time would be right when Ophelia's reelection train derailed, leaving Merlotta an express run into office and his associates a clear path at whatever they hoped to gain. I doubted Briggs and Osterman had killed Kenny. They'd had no reason to shoot their own election strategy in the head—unless somehow Kenny had threatened to expose them. If his last performance at the Shadow was any indication, however, that was unlikely. And his family still needed the money, according to Lenny. But the police had broken into my home early Sunday, which meant if Osterman gave them my name he had to know Kenny was dead soon after it happened. Had he used a burner to text Kenny to meet him in the park and then discovered the body? He would have realized on the spot that with Kenny poised to become the mayor's martyr, they needed a back-up plan. What could top having a friend of Mayor Green arrested for killing her bodyguard? He wouldn't have needed to stage the crime scene, just to drive to a payphone and wait awhile before calling the tip line. I thought about all that for a moment and decided it made sense. I was a convenient Plan B.

"Look, I did give your name to the cops," Osterman said, as if he were reading my mind. He tried to sound contrite. "But all I said was you were in a fight with Ken."

"Because you were there and saw it and even took cell phone pictures."

He sighed, pulling his hands from his pockets and folding his arms across his chest. "Yeah. I was out with him. We were headed to a new place for some craft beers. He stopped when we reached the Shadow Lounge and told me to wait in the car while he ran inside to get something from a friend. I had no idea what he was doing."

"When did you learn Kenny was dead?"

"The supervisor who came to the bar—Rogalski. We go way back. I talked to him after you left with the girl. Later, when the body was found, he called me. Got me out of bed and asked if I thought you were good for it and if I thought you were dangerous. I told him I didn't know, just that you fought Ken. Truth is, Rimes, I wasn't looking to jam you up."

I could have asked Oz how he got home when Kenny drove off and left him but since Oz owned an Escalade and was standing beside a bronze Escalade in LJ's video, I knew the answer would be a lie. I could have asked why Rogalski, on night duty at D District, would bother to call Oz at all about somebody he'd never met when he had my name and address from our earlier meeting. I could have asked why Oz gave Lenny Carnahan my address, but I already knew that answer. Whether Lenny killed me or I him, the blowback would settle on Ophelia. Whatever Oz said would be more misdirection. So many lies, I wondered if I should applaud his *wasn't-looking-to-jam-you-up* act as a courtesy. Instead, I just nodded. When good old Oz smiled, I half-expected him to go classic Hollywood on me by sticking out a paw and saying, "Put 'er there, pal." Before he could embarrass himself with such a shtick, I said, "One more question."

They exchanged looks. "Sure," Osterman said.

"Did Indi know?"

He blinked hard, as if puzzled I'd have the nerve to undercut him by asking such a question. But showing no confusion about the name, Briggs dropped her mask altogether and in full frown started to climb to her feet as Osterman said, "Who?"

"Indigo Waters, the singer you paid Kenny to stalk so he could embarrass the mayor. Did Indi know what was going on?"

"Enough, Mr. Rimes!" Briggs said. "Leave now and take your absurd allegations with you, or we will have you arrested for trespassing and sue you for slander."

"Does *we* include your brother Anthony—and your father?"

As the pebbled glass door swung open and two muscular young men in brown blazers came in, Briggs's face registered its first genuine emotion since my arrival—astonishment. "*What?*"

Blazer One and Blazer Two grabbed my arms, and I said, "You heard me, Mickey."

Chapter 31

At six, with a bag of Perry's Panda Paws ice cream in one hand and Bobby's *Tombstone* DVD in the other, I wiped my sneakers on the welcome mat and rang the front doorbell of Mira's Williamsville cottage. The door flew open. There stood my nephew in jeans and a Bills jersey, taller than he'd been just a few weeks ago and grinning to show me the absence of two bottom front teeth. Shakti was a beautiful boy with a lighter shade of his mother's rich brown skin and his father's green eyes and dirty-blond hair. He hugged my waist, then pulled me inside.

I set down the bag and DVD and hung my leather jacket on the coat tree.

"Uncle G's here!" he announced.

"Inside voice, honey," Mira said as Shakti led me through the dining room and into the kitchen. In jeans and a sleeveless yellow tee, my sister was at the stainless steel stove, stirring a pot of spaghetti sauce with a wooden spoon. A foot shorter than I, she smiled up at me, and I pushed aside her thick black hair to plant a kiss on her cheek. "Guess who chose the menu."

"Spaghetti is my favorite too," I said to Shakti as I moved to the fridge and put the ice cream in the freezer. Then I pointed to a glass bowl on the counter. "You make the salad?"

"I helped," he said.

"He washed the cherry tomatoes, shook in the croutons, and set the dining room table," Mira said. "I don't know where I would be without him."

Shakti looked puzzled. "Yes, you do, Mommy. You'd be lost. That's what you always say."

Mira's cheeks darkened, and I said, "She sure would."

Dinner was all about Shakti. As we ate the spaghetti and meatballs he loved—and the garlic bread and salad he didn't—he produced schoolwork he had piled on the sideboard to show me. There were math and vocabulary worksheets with *Excellent!* or *Perfect!* scrawled across the top in red. There were several pictures he'd drawn to illustrate a story his class had read. There was a more elaborate crayon and paint picture on construction paper he had done in art class and a mini-greenhouse with a seedling poking through soil in a large clear plastic cup covered with Saran Wrap. When he finished with school, he moved on to his karate class and his piano lessons. Then he told me about his friends and their pets and their toys and the games they all played together and the videos they liked to watch. When we got to the ice cream, he began to talk about the fun he and his mother would have in Toronto this weekend: a hotel with a pool and a park with ziplines even for little kids and pandas at the zoo and a stage play with songs about a magic place...

"*Babes in Blunderland*," Mira said, calming Shakti's excitement by mussing his curls. "Two children go through a magical cave and come out the other side in a topsy-turvy town."

"Like Bizarro world," I said, nodding. "How's Julie?" Julie Yang was the live-in mathematics graduate student who doubled as Shakti's nanny.

"She spends hardly any weekend time with her new boyfriend because the chief keeps calling me in."

"I thought you volunteered last Sunday."

"I did, when Bobby told me what happened to you. But that made four in a row. I told Dr. Owens I needed a body-free weekend, so Friday morning we're both playing hooky."

After dinner Shakti put on his pajamas and we turned on *Jeopardy*, one of the TV shows mother and son enjoyed watching together. It always delighted my nephew to see his mother call out a question before the contestants, and my participation this evening was an added treat. After Final Jeopardy, he took my hand and pulled me down the hall to his room, where I waited while he brushed his teeth and used the toilet. When he returned, I tucked him in and read him two Dr. Seuss books before I kissed him goodnight and turned off his light.

"He still likes *Sam-I-Am*," I said when I re-entered the living room.

"Always has," Mira said. "He identifies with how Sam annoys you with questions." She was already seated on the couch, two uncapped bottles of Purple Haze on coasters on the coffee table and the dishwasher thrumming in the kitchen. The sepia montage of the DVD's main menu was looping on the wall-mounted flat screen TV. The volume was muted. I sat on the opposite end, and we both picked up a Purple Haze, clinking bottles before we drank.

Mira swallowed. "Bobby said you had a date the other night, with a lawyer."

"I did."

"How was it?"

"Nice. We're going out again Saturday night." I took another pull and added, "Her name is Phoenix Trinidad. She's pretty, smart, a full partner. I think you'll get to meet her."

Grinning, she made a show of clinking my bottle again, then half stood to examine my stitches. Gingerly, she pushed aside the hair around them. "So how's your head?"

"Better but still a bit itchy."

She sat back down. "And the investigation?"

"This morning I went to see the murder book," I said. "Rafael Pinero was pissed he had to babysit me, but he didn't hold anything back. You ever talk to him, or his partner in homicide, Terry Chalmers?"

"Sure, they're good cops." Then she pursed her lips as if in thought. "You didn't tell them about us, did you?"

"No, I wouldn't embarrass my secret weapon."

"It's not embarrassment, and I'm not your secret weapon. But I do need to keep a professional distance, even if they don't still think you're good for this."

"They are good cops," I said. "They've done serious leg-work, interviewing Kenny's friends, his old girlfriend, a lot of people he arrested. Their notes are thorough, but they've hit a lot of dead ends." I told her I was still thinking about the text exchange on Kenny's cell. *We need to talk*, Kenny's phone said. The burner's reply: *Settle at Rose Garden, 1 hour.*

"How tall is the old girlfriend?" she asked.

I thought back to the Facebook picture of Kenny with his arm around Karen O'Brien. "I haven't talked to her yet, but she was a lot shorter than Kenny, probably too short for the angle of impact."

"Variables," Mira said and took another swig. "So why haven't you interviewed her? I mean, if he dumped her for this blues singer, there's your motive."

"I got sidetracked."

"You? You're like a dog with a bone Super-Glued to his canine teeth."

I had told Jimmy and Peggy Ann the full story of my visit to Lorenzo Quick's house because the event was still so fresh in my mind I needed to tell somebody. I had given Phoenix a truncated account and assured her Quick had no further interest in me because I needed to be honest but not frighten her away. Now I gave my sister the same sanitized recitation I had given Bobby that morning, implying it was a legitimate interview that ran so long O'Brien said I'd have to reschedule. Consciously—perhaps conscientiously—I made the story less dangerous each time I told it. It was bad enough I had given Jimmy, Peggy Ann, and Phoenix cause for concern. Mira and Bobby had known me the longest and would worry the most. I loved them enough to spare them whatever pain I could. "I will get to her," I said. "But yesterday I found another thread to pull." Then I recounted my visit to CitiQuest.

"So Wreck-It Rick's got a love child," Mira said when I finished. "I didn't see that one coming."

"It's not public knowledge. I'm not even sure *he* knows it. But his children seem determined to put him on the second floor of City Hall."

She leaned back, crossing her sock-covered ankles on the

coffee table, and rolled the Purple Haze bottle back and forth between her palms. "I wonder why."

"I don't know yet but I will." I winked at her. "While Osterman was busy finding and destroying a dummy spy cam, I fixed a thumbnail stick-on bug under the armrest of my chair. It's sound-activated with a six-hour charge and a 4G transmitter. It's been dumping into LJ's cloud account since I was there. He'll start listening tonight and call me tomorrow if anything is worth following up."

Mira smiled and shook her head. "You're still one sneaky SOB, aren't you?"

"You know that better than anybody." I nodded toward the dissolving sepia shots of the Earp brothers and Doc Holliday on the TV screen. Mira laughed as she pressed PLAY on the remote and raised the volume. As the pre-credit black and white images flickered and Robert Mitchum began his narration about the Cowboys, we brought our bottles to our lips.

Tombstone was our movie. It had been released the year I went into the army, a choice that had left Mira in tears. She was just starting high school then and beginning to distinguish herself in science class. In fact, she had tested out of her freshman earth science course in the first two weeks and was placed in sophomore life sciences. In December, when I came home on leave between basic training and advanced infantry training, she was at first cool toward me, as if angry I had left and would leave again. But she was angrier at some of the boys in her biology lab. They had seen *Tombstone* and couldn't stop quoting it. When she asked what it was about, one boy said she wouldn't understand because she was a girl. She stomped into our kitchen that day, determined to see the movie. Because it was rated R and she was only fourteen, Bobby and Evelyn both said no, she couldn't go. She protested it was unfair the boys were saying, "I'll be your huckleberry" when they didn't know what a huckleberry was and she did. Bobby smiled at that, but Evelyn still said no.

So that night, when our godparents were asleep, Mira tapped on my door.

The next Saturday I borrowed the car and took Mira for

lunch at the area's newest shopping mall, the Walden Galleria near the airport. I was in my uniform, and she emerged from the food court restroom wearing lipstick, eye shadow, and high heels. Arm in arm, as if we were a soldier and his date—we must have looked more ridiculous than I remember—we went unchallenged to a bargain matinee and got lost in *Tombstone*. Afterward, Mira scrubbed off the make-up and put the high heels back in her oversized purse. When we got home, we fought the urge to discuss our shared transgression by exchanging smiles over dinner.

Though he didn't ask, Bobby suspected what we'd done, and we confirmed it years later, but Evelyn never found out.

Some people never missed the pre-VCR annual broadcast of *The Wizard of Oz*. Even after DVD and Blu-Ray players, others never tired of commercial-saturated holiday showings of *It's a Wonderful Life* or cable marathons of *A Christmas Story*. Mira and I never tired of *Tombstone*, our secret that became an experience we shared off and on for years. Tonight, as always, we laughed and talked our way through it, quoting favorite lines a second before they were delivered, replaying and high-fiving favorite scenes, and, without saying so, reliving the moment that had cemented in place the final brick of our relationship.

A week after we saw the now-classic western the first time, I had to leave for AIT. We all piled into the car for the trip to the airport, me in uniform riding shotgun, and Evelyn and Mira in the back seat. In front of the *PASSENGERS ONLY* sign, I set down my army duffel bag and looked at the three of them. Bobby and Evelyn took turns embracing me, and Evelyn handed me a plastic bag of fresh-baked peanut butter cookies. Lips pressed together in a tight line, Mira stood off to the side and was the last one to put her arms around me. She kept her face nestled against my chest for a long time. When I asked if she were upset with me for leaving again, she shook her head. Then she went up on her toes to kiss my cheek and whispered in my ear Morgan's words to Wyatt after Virgil decided the Earps must become lawmen again: "Gotta back your brother's play."

When I stepped back and looked into her large wet eyes, I knew we would be brother and sister for the rest of our lives.

Chapter 32

When I woke I had two text messages from late last night, and a third came in while I held the phone.

Phoenix: *Voir dire today. Trial starts tomorrow. Likely end Friday. Up late prepping & thought of you. Saturday at 7? Made reservation for 8 at a bistro walking distance from my home. Can't wait for Sunday brunch. I hope to be good and hungry. :-)*

LJ: *On campus til 3, then ur office. Got my laptop.*

Bobby: *I made cheese biscuits. If you're awake, come up and have some.*

After brushing my teeth and washing my face, I pulled on a blue running suit and sneakers. Despite the sunny October weather, most of my recent workouts had been indoors with my weights and heavy bag. Today looked like a good day for an overdue run. And running was a good way to digest biscuits. I got *Tombstone* off my counter and went upstairs to Bobby's apartment. I opened the door with my key and called out, "It's me, Bobby."

"In the kitchen," he called back.

I slid *Tombstone* into its slot on the alphabetized DVD rack and walked through the living room library into the kitchen. Seated at his dining counter with a mug of coffee, Bobby was in his white bathrobe. He looked up at me through glasses riding low on his nose and smiled.

A large plate of warm biscuits flanked by two smaller plates was in the center of the counter. A folded-over section of the morning newspaper was in his hand. "Get yourself some juice or coffee if you want," he said. "How's Mira?"

"She's fine." I got a glass tumbler from the cupboard and a bottle of apple juice from the fridge. "She's taking Shakti to Toronto for a three-day weekend." I sat across from him.

"Good. She works too hard."

"Look who's talking." I poured juice. "Retired, and almost every morning you dress like you're going to work, then head off somewhere for a meeting or a talk." I took a swig. "If Mira doesn't know how to take it easy, it's because she had you for a role model."

"But I'm in my robe today."

"Good. *You* work too hard." As he laughed, I picked up a cheese biscuit, bit into it, and let it start to melt on my tongue.

"How are you?" Bobby asked. "I know you had dinner with the lovely Ms. Trinidad the other night but you never told me how it went."

"We're going out again this weekend."

He nodded. "Kayla won our bet. She was sure once you two spent a little time around each other, you'd test the waters, so to speak, within a week. Given your usually cautious nature, I thought it would take two or three weeks." He sighed as if lamenting his loss. "But I'm glad you're seeing her again."

"Sometimes you just know a person is a chance worth taking." I finished my first biscuit and picked up a second. "What did you lose?"

"The cost and choice of our next weekend getaway. I wanted to drive to Stratford before their season ends this month but I think Kayla would prefer theater in New York to Shakespeare in a Canadian town, which means airfare and a more expensive hotel."

"Sorry."

"Why? You weren't the fool who made the bet."

"No, you're the fool who gets a romantic weekend with Kayla no matter who wins."

Bobby smiled and sipped his coffee. He seldom bet on anything outside low-stakes poker games with friends he would give more than nickels if they truly needed money. Often he described the state lottery as a pension plan for the stupid. The only bet worth making, he told me when I lost ten bucks on a Bills game as a teen, was one where losing felt almost as good as winning.

He set down his cup. "And how's your investigation?"

I told him about Osterman and Briggs and the plan to undercut Ophelia's reelection. "I know, the whole thing sounds crazy," I said when I finished, "a long shot at best. But there must be money in a Merlotta victory for somebody. I still need to figure who and what."

"Pretty far-fetched," Bobby said. He slid the local section of the Buffalo News across the counter and tapped an article below a picture of a white-haired man shaking hands with a bald man as a woman and a younger man stood by smiling. "Then again, maybe not."

The article described the efforts of white-haired Congressman Hunter Gill to secure for Buffalo funds from a massive federal project. With support from agencies that included the Departments of Energy, Interior, Transportation, Commerce, Labor, Homeland Security, Health and Human Services, and Housing and Urban Development, as well as the National Science Foundation and various economic development agencies, Sunrise Village would be the largest attempt ever to build self-contained renewable energy model neighborhoods. Six solar-powered villages were to be built from the ground up in urban areas with significant neighborhood decay: two in the west, two in the south, and two in the north.

Having been under the radar in its years-long planning stages, the project, if successful, would have an impact not only on the future of energy, housing, and labor for the nation, but also for each Sunrise Village host city, which stood to get an infusion of half a billion dollars or more.

"Winning any elected office brings with it a measure of power," Bobby said, taking another sip of coffee. "Isn't half a billion dollars more than motive enough to try a crazy long shot when you own a development company ready to make construction bids for the money?"

"And everybody's playing the game," I said. "Ophelia told me Drake interned for Gill just this summer."

"But Ophelia's angling to get the money for Buffalo, not the family business."

"So you think Merlotta himself is in on this plan to scuttle her."

"Technically, Rick doesn't run the company now. His son does, and it makes sense he'd want his father in office to grease the skids." Bobby's brow creased. "As for going after the mayor *sub rosa*—" He exhaled heavily. "Rick denies conflicts of interest bigger than Santa's ass. He's a windbag and a control freak. He dismisses awkward racial and cultural remarks by saying he refuses to be politically correct—which ought to be career suicide in a city with so many minorities and immigrants. Yet somehow he keeps *Rick Country* alive. It's just not his style to be secret. He completely believes in whatever he's doing. He's always right, not the least bit subtle. Say whatever comes to mind, even if you don't have the facts."

"What do you mean?"

"Back when he was on the Board of Ed, he asked some friends how their daughter was faring as a teacher. When they told him she didn't get along with her principal, he said, 'Don't worry. We'll fire the bum!' without knowing the principal was a friend of his who'd supported his board run." Bobby shrugged. "That's the Wreck-It Rick I know and love."

I felt my eyebrows go up. "Love?"

"I could've said 'loathe,' to be cute, but I kind of like his sincerity. Bigoted, maddening to work with, and that 'my-way-or-the-highway' crap has no place in City Hall. But if he ever gets off his elevated *equus* and thinks before he speaks, he might actually do some good."

Still smiling inwardly at Bobby's use of the Latin word for horse, I asked, "Do you think he knows Mickey Briggs is his daughter?"

Bobby was quiet for a few seconds. "I doubt it. If he knew, he would make it public so he could have his 'I-made-a-youthful-mistake' moment and get past it."

I thought about all that half an hour later when I started my run—up Elmwood to Buffalo State and the Albright Knox, then around the lake in Delaware Park and back. I was certain Merlotta didn't know what his children had been up to. They'd set up the play but, in the wake of an unexpected murder, had been unable to pass him the ball. If Kenny were in jail instead of a morgue drawer, Rick Merlotta would have been all over the airwaves the past four days to proclaim Ophelia's incompetence in all matters administrative. Because so far he had said nothing, it was likely he was being used too. By the time I reached Hoyt Lake in the park, I began to think of him as another victim.

Chapter 33

At three-thirty, sitting at the desk in my small office which overlooked Elmwood Avenue, I handed LJ a small bottle of root beer from the bar fridge underneath. It was a warm enough day that I had one of the windows open, and the breeze stirred the white curtains Mira had given me a year before to replace the blinds I never dusted.

"I put in a lot of extra time," LJ said. "My bill might be higher than usual."

"No problem," I said, twisting the cap off my own cream soda.

LJ nodded as we both took sips. He mouse-clicked the *PLAY* arrow on his laptop screen. The speaker crackled with my voice: "You heard me, Mickey."

I remembered offering only token resistance as Blazer One and Blazer Two dragged me to the elevator, pinned my arms to my sides all the way down to the ground floor, and shoved me out the front door. Now I heard Briggs's office door close, too hard, as Osterman went back inside.

BRIGGS: "How the hell did he know?"

OSTERMAN: "Prick's guessing. He doesn't know shit."

BRIGGS: "We've been so careful—"

OSTERMAN: "He said it himself, Mickey. He's shooting in the dark, trying to protect his friend, the mayor. Kenny couldn't have told him."

BRIGGS: "Only the two of us know."

OSTERMAN: "Doesn't matter. A uni who subbed on her protection detail thought Rimes was putting the wood to Green a while back. If we get proof of that, we shut down whatever he says about how we're the ones fucking the mayor."

A sound of something—a palm or a book—hitting a desk blotter, hard.

BRIGGS: "Damn it, Oz!"

OSTERMAN: "What?

There was a tuning fork sound of a padded desk chair rolling into the thick plate glass behind her, probably as Briggs stood up.

BRIGGS: "I'm not talking about who's fucking Ophelia Green! The problem is who's fucking us. Didn't you hear what that bastard said?"

OSTERMAN: "Something about your brother and your father. Proves he got bad intel."

BRIGGS: "What if it was good intel?"

OSTERMAN: "What do you mean? He might get lucky? Only a matter of time till he gets something real?"

BRIGGS: "There's only one way he could've gotten anything at all. Somebody hacked us. Our network. My email."

OSTERMAN: "Then we've got his ass on so many violations, it'll cost him his license. And CitiQuest can sue him into the welfare line."

BRIGGS: "If it gets out, and he's the one who hacked us."

OSTERMAN: "But this time it's bad information. A gift-wrapped lawsuit, you ask me. We shut him down before he can get something real and hurt us."

BRIGGS: "We can't. No matter what, this will cost us more than it costs him."

OSTERMAN: "I don't understand."

BRIGGS: "Maybe he hacked my brother."

OSTERMAN: "But you don't have—You have a brother? A brother nobody knew about?"

BRIGGS: "Yes."

OSTERMAN: "Well, who—wait a minute. What was it he said? Anthony…Anth—Holy shit! Tony Merlotta is your brother?"

BRIGGS: "Yes."

OSTERMAN: "I thought he was a just client, just a rich guy paying us to help get his father—Your father? Jesus God, Mickey!"

BRIGGS: "Rick doesn't know. Tony and I found each other through DNA. Only the two of us know—and now you."

OSTERMAN: "And Rimes."

A long silence.

BRIGGS: "The question is, what does the low-rent cocksucker want?"

OSTERMAN: "If he's still chalking his cue in the mayor's center pocket, it's obvious what he wants, to get her re-elected."

BRIGGS: "He's a one-man operation in the increasingly complex field of professional security. A lone wolf can't make much. He must have a price."

OSTERMAN: "I doubt it."

BRIGGS: "Maybe you can put the fear of God into him. You're good at that."

OSTERMAN: "I doubt it would work either, not on him."

BRIGGS: "If he gives this to the press, no reporter will give him up in court, and the story will hurt us more than anything we can do to him."

OSTERMAN: "Not everything—"

BRIGGS: "Oz, over the years I've handed you problems I hoped you could make go away, and you always do. I've never asked how you do things, and I won't start now. Somehow, we need to make this go away."

OSTERMAN: "I understand."

LJ clicked on the vertical *PAUSE* bars and looked at me, pleased the stick-on bug worked so well but worried about what he had heard. "You got 'em, G! The sticky bug worked great. But I didn't know city politics got so vicious. These people—Mickey and Oz—they seem so much worse than I thought when I was digging up their information."

"Mickey and Oz. They sound like Disneyland on the Yellow Brick Road."

"They sound like bad people."

"What makes you say that?"

"The way they talk about you. Her tone of voice, like she hates the air you breathe. The way he gets calm when he understands he's gotta do something about you." He shook his head slowly. "These are real bad people. Dangerous. G, you gotta take this to the police."

"I can't do that yet. There isn't enough here, and dirty politics isn't illegal."

"But it sounds like Oz is gunning for you, man. You gotta be careful."

"I know." I took out Phoenix's business card and slid it to him. "Anything happens to me before this gets out, you get this recording to her. She'll know what to do. Understand?"

He nodded and put the card in his wallet. "The stuff about you and the mayor—"

"Not true. Her husband was one of my battle brothers in Iraq. That's it."

"Just wondered."

I sighed, let the tension out. "You told me it would last six hours. What else you got?"

"I think the guy leaves at this point but it's hard to tell."

"Rubber-soled shoes," I said, remembering.

"Then there's some intercom noise and a secretary bringing in things to sign. Lots of computer keystrokes and a silent patch, so the bug shuts off." LJ hit the FAST FORWARD double arrows and kept his eyes on the digital counter at the bottom of his display window. "Comes back on with her telling somebody she's not to be disturbed, and she makes a phone call. I know it's the phone and not Skype or Face Time because I can't hear the other guy." Then he stopped and clicked *PLAY*. The speaker crackled with the sound of a door closing and Michelene Briggs's high heels clacking across the tile floor.

> BRIGGS: "May I please speak to Mr. Merlotta...Yes, I'll hold...Tony? Hi, it's Mickey, and we've got a problem...No, I couldn't. Your cell might not be secure...There's this lone wolf PI who somehow figured us out...Yes, the DNA...A big black guy named Rimes...I don't know for sure what he wants but he's a friend of Ophelia Green's...My guess is one of us has been hacked...I already sent a memo to IT to get on it, and I deleted my SAVE folder...No, we pay our IT people well enough not to consider offers like that. Besides, this guy doesn't have enough to buy my people a hot dog...Of course, he could be working for somebody with money but I can't imagine who...Embarrassing? You'll be embarrassed, and maybe Rick. For me and Zack it would be devastating. Who'd trust their security to a security company that can't secure itself? This could ruin us...No, goddammit, you need to check your end!"

Remembering the terror I had seen in his mother's eyes the other day, I motioned for LJ to stop the playback. "And you've covered your tracks so they can't walk it backward to your house?"

LJ looked hurt. "Give me some credit, G. I did the hack at school."

"Which means they can track you to your campus computer account."

He offered me a feral smile and shook his head. "I got three accounts, mine and two made-up students. Rollo Weed did the hack and the sticky bug download. Come midnight Rollo will disappear like Cinderella's carriage horses. I'll keep Lotta Bottoms for another time."

"Rollo Weed?" I said. "Lotta Bottoms? Who are you, a wannabe Ian Fleming?"

"Gotta play, man. It gets lonely in Nerd Land, and the mind tries to compensate."

"You need to get out more."

"I need to get laid more." His shoulders sagged. "I never said anything about that Skype thing for school a couple days ago."

"The girl from California. I was there for dinner, remember? Your mom asked you about it."

"And I blew her off like it was nothing but the girl who came on-screen was to-die-for hot. A little older than me but *damn*. Just looking at her I could barely breathe. And I thought maybe, just maybe, if the project went okay, you know, we could *talk* a little. Get to know each other. Yeah, I'd travel across the country to meet somebody like *her*. But then her husband and son came in and wanted to say hi to the guy in Buffalo. A jock with a chest like Superman and a toddler in an Elmo shirt."

We sat there for a few seconds. Then I put my hand on his shoulder. "LJ, with your double major it will get better. In another year, you'll be doing all this for a law enforcement agency, hacking under a warrant and impressing the hell out of your boss. And real women, not girls, like smart men. Trust me, real women are better."

He chuckled, almost bitterly. "You sound like Mom." Then he exhaled and clicked *PLAY* again.

BRIGGS: "You came to me, remember? Over two years ago. You came to me and asked what we could do to make sure the mayor doesn't run again, or win if she does...Sure, and I got on board and put Oz right on it...He used to be a cop and has lots of connections...I never ask how he does things...Threats, lawsuits, overdue client bills, women blackmailing my husband—Oz makes them all go away and tells me only what he thinks I need to know...No contact between the two of you and plausible deniability for me...I did wonder

about that but it only made her more sympathetic to vot-
ers...One thing he did share was that he paid a girl to
hook up with Drake Green when he worked in Hunter
Gill's DC office. But she couldn't seal the deal...No, I
don't know how it was supposed to play out—maybe a
sex scandal or the boy getting caught with his hand in
the office safe. Whatever it was, the kid turned her down
because he's got a girlfriend. Zack could take a lesson
from him...So the other weak spot in the mayor's orbit
turned out to be a cop who needed money, and Oz
worked him beautifully...Had Ken date this singer and
start stalking her and violate an order of protection...Of
course, Oz didn't kill him but he did find the
body...They agreed to meet because Ken was skittish
about going to jail—You see, the judge who signed the
protection order was on the premises when he violated it
and ordered his immediate arrest, so no chance for a
voluntary court appearance and contrition...Yes, ironic.
When Oz got to the meet Ken was already dead...He
tried his best to turn lemons into lemonade by hanging
the murder on the lone wolf, who's a friend of the
mayor, maybe even her fuck buddy. But it didn't take.
Must've had an alibi...He thought Ken's brother might
go after Rimes but apparently he didn't...Yes, Oz
knows about the DNA and is trying to neutralize it...For
starters, Green's sex life could body-check news of a
surprise bastard...Best of all would be a photo of something like the chaste widow giving her friend a blow
job...But if Oz can't contain it we need a contingency
plan...Oh, I'm sure he'd take the fall for the right
price...What do you mean, accessory?...I agree, who
better than an ex-homicide cop to stage a scene, but
there's no evidence he ever did anything more than dirty
tricks for us...If he did that, we have no knowledge of
it, and it's on him. But if our relationship gets
out...You're right. Rimes'll need proof to go to the
press...Deny, deny, deny—that's one way...Distant
cousins? The press would dig into it, but it could work.

Without access to our actual DNA profiles nobody will know the difference, and the Merlotta campaign can even spin the whole thing as a dirty trick by Green's people...Yes, I do feel better now. I always do when I talk to you."

LJ stopped the playback. "There's a couple more meetings and some phone calls and other stuff that has nothing to do with you." His voice rose briefly with excitement. "But Dr. Zee and the Truth Train are coming next March and CitiQuest is doing the security—" And then it returned to its normal cadence. "—near the end, her husband comes in and says he's leaving for Albany and will be back on Monday. She says fine like she really doesn't give a shit, and he kinda slams the door on his way out. A few minutes later, she buzzes her secretary and says she's going home. That's it. There may be enough juice left to get a little more tomorrow morning but don't count on it after the bug sits there all night."

I sat without speaking for a long time. I was sick of being called a lone wolf and that's what I planned to tell LJ if he asked why I was so quiet. But he just ejected the flash drive and handed it to me as I continued wrapping my brain around what I had heard: '*Oz makes them all go away...plausible deniability...who better than an ex-homicide cop to stage a scene...*'

Perhaps Tony Merlotta had suggested Osterman killed Kenny for wanting to back out of their deal. Perhaps Chalmers and Pinero could use the recording as a battering ram through their dead end. My thoughts, however, were barreling down another highway. '*I did wonder about that but it only made her more sympathetic...*'There wasn't enough in this one-sided conversation to reopen an investigation or have the court order an exhumation. But something gnawed at my gut like an unfed carnivore coming off a long fast—the possibility that Vince Osterman had tried to throw Ophelia Green off her game by murdering her husband Danny and staging it as an in-home accident.

Chapter 34

Sitting in my Escape, I was listening to the second hour of NPR's *All Things Considered* when a yellow VW Beetle stopped in front of Indi's Linwood Avenue apartment building. She climbed out of the passenger seat and hoisted a large canvas carry-all to her shoulder. Then she bent to say goodbye to the woman behind the wheel. As the Beetle pulled away, Indi turned toward the front door of her building. I got out and walked toward her.

"Hi, Rimes," she said, her momentary surprise replaced by a grin. "What are you doing here?"

"I need to talk to you about something."

Grin widening into a smile, she was quiet a moment. "I got rehearsal tonight, and I usually have dinner with Doc and Lizzy. But I don't have to eat with them. You could drop me off there later."

"All right," I said.

"Well, all right then." She handed me her carry-all, whose shoulder strap had slid off the smooth brown leather of her jacket. "And the price of admission is carrying this for me."

The bag was heavier than I expected, and when I slung it over my shoulder, it made several noises that suggested a variety of children's musical instruments from small drums and xylophones to cymbals and maracas. "Gotta love music day," I said. I followed her into the building and clanked and rattled up three flights to her apartment.

"You can put that over there," she said, indicating bare

floor beside the armchair. She closed and locked the door as I set down the bag then shrugged off her jacket and hung it on one of the hooks on the back of the door. She turned to me, and I could see what looked like paint splotches and crusted milk stains on her pink shirt and blue jeans. "Make yourself comfortable. Been a long day. The kids just kept climbing all over me. I need to use the bathroom and hop in the shower for a minute. Can we talk after that?"

"Sure."

Throwing a smile over her shoulder, she started toward the bathroom.

I took off my jacket and dropped it on the armchair. Then I walked to the window and pushed aside the navy curtains to look out onto Linwood. I stared down at the street for a few minutes, half-expecting Osterman's bronze Escalade to cruise past. Since my meeting with LJ, I had been thinking of all the possibilities. If Oz decided the best way to make the Rimes problem go away was to make a run at me himself, I would have to be ready. But he must be smart enough to anticipate I'd have a way to get the whole story out if I disappeared, and he had to know Mickey Briggs would make him the fall guy if their political hijinks reached the press. No doubt he would face his all-for-show termination, and hefty addition to his regular pension, with aplomb. But what if he liked his job enough to look for another way to shut me down? He could hang around Ophelia's home, hoping I'd show up for a rendezvous, but that stakeout would prove boring, and eventually the mayor's security team would notice him.

Or maybe he would try to get to me through someone I loved.

I tended to keep my personal relationships private. Apart from court records naming Bobby and Evelyn as my legal guardians, which Oz could find if he had any idea where to start, there was nothing immediately accessible that defined my relationship with Bobby as anything more than landlord-tenant. Even if Oz stumbled onto Mira, she was on her way out of town with Shakti first thing Friday morning. Newspaper accounts of the Buffalo State shooting carried Jimmy's name along with mine. Everyone in area law enforcement knew about Doran Private Security Consulting Services. I supposed our friendship was known to some on the job, but I hoped not so many that Jimmy and his family would occur to Oz before he considered other targets.

"Don't sweat it," Jimmy had said when I dropped LJ off earlier and told him of my concerns. "Our alarm system has a direct-to-police panic button, and Peggy Ann and I both spend a lot of time at the range."

I had gone shooting with them and knew that unlike the average cop, who didn't get enough time to practice, they were both excellent shots. Next, I thought of Phoenix, but because we had just begun she was unlikely to be on anyone's radar yet. Apart from Chalmers and Pinero, then, there was only one other person Osterman could be certain I knew, Indi.

The question I was here to answer was whether Indi knew Osterman and had been part of the plan all along. If she didn't know Oz, perhaps she knew Mickey Briggs or Tony Merlotta. Then I remembered Rick Merlotta's book, which I had seen in Indi's bedroom.

I went to the bathroom door and heard the shower running. I considered knocking and asking permission to get the book but decided I could get it and go before Indi knew I was in her bedroom. I slipped into her room and circled the bed, crouching to sort through the books piled on the floor. I found the trade paperback *A Vision for the City of Buffalo* and stood with it in my hands. I opened it, hoping for a personalized inscription but finding only an illegibly scrawled *Richard Merlotta*. As I turned to go, I saw myself in the dresser mirror, my black nylon shoulder holster a stark contrast to my faded gold shirt. My reflection was flanked by photographs wedged into the mirror's frame. I was drawn at once to the pictures on the left showing Indi as a teen, singing in what must be her school and her church. I stared at them for a long time and blinked. *Son of a bitch!*

At that moment, the door opened and Indi stood there wrapped in a towel, droplets of water clinging to curls that stuck out of her plastic shower cap. If she was at all surprised

to find me in her bedroom, she masked it with a smile as invit-
ing as any I had ever seen. For more than a heartbeat neither of
us spoke as I stared at her face, almost seeing its truths for the
first time, and thought, again, *Son of a bitch!*

"I showered as fast as I could," she said, "and here you
are—comfortable, I hope."

She dropped the towel and crossed the room to me quickly—but not so quickly that I didn't take in the curve of her
hips and her well-muscled legs and the swell of her breasts, her
already erect nipples a shade or two darker than her whipped
chocolate skin. She tossed aside her shower cap and pressed
her damp body against mine, pulling my face down to hers for
a hard kiss that tasted of toothpaste and mouthwash and ended
with my lower lip bitten and the bitterness of blood on my
tongue.

Dropping the book, I stepped back and held her at arm's
length. "Indi, that's not why I came."

"You didn't come to come?" She laughed at her own joke
and even as I gripped her biceps used her fingertips to tease
my elbows and triceps through my shirt. "Why not? You don't
have to guard my body anymore. Now you can have it." She
rotated her hips toward me, and I noticed the tight curls of her
pubic hair had been trimmed to a thin treasure trail that began
just below the curve of her belly and ended in a point just
above the hood of her clitoris. "Why don't you get that gun out
of our way, so I can unbutton your shirt? We don't have to be
strangers anymore."

"Indi—"

"I can make you happy, Rimes. You don't have to love me
or marry me. But I can make you stupid happy." She ran her
tongue over her upper lip. "All you have to do is do me, right
here, right now—hard, soft, kinky. You can have me any way
you want, any way you been thinking about since the day we
met." Her expression flickered between playful desire and a
mounting desperation I could not define. She tried to push in
for another kiss.

Maybe she was hungry for affection because she had grown
up without her father. Maybe she was a narcissist, afraid of

what would happen if she stopped being the center of the world. Maybe she just liked to screw and was unashamed of her desires. I didn't care. Someone more qualified would have to consider all that if she ever sought therapy. I was here for another reason. The rage I felt at what might have happened to Danny rose inside me like a putrid hash, impossible to digest, and with it irritation at myself for not anticipating what Indi would try. I squeezed her biceps hard enough to make her wince and shoved her onto the bed with enough force to make her bounce. "I'm not here to fuck you!"

For a moment, she sat propped on her elbows, stunned, unmoving, blinking in a way that made me think she might cry. But she drew in a deep breath and clamped her teeth on her lower lip. Whether hurt or angry, she shed no tears and made no effort to cover herself or close her legs. "Is it Miss Trinidad?" she said finally. "I saw how she was looking at you the other day and how you were looking right back. But I thought I might still have a shot at a hook-up." When I said nothing, she huffed and made a show of examining her arms. "You coulda bruised me, you know. I wouldn't mind bruises, if—" Her voice cracked a bit, and she drew in a long breath as she looked off to one side. "It is her, isn't it?"

Surprised by her perceptiveness, I said, "I'm sorry if I hurt you, Indi, but my personal life is not your business." I took the bottom edge of the flowered quilt and draped it over her as best I could then sat on a corner of the exposed sheet. "I'm here because I found out some things about Kenny, things I need to tell you. But first, I have to ask you what you know and who you know to figure out if your life is in danger too."

She sat up and scooted back to the headboard, pulling the quilt around herself. "Now you think somebody wants to kill *me*?" There was no challenge in her voice as the thwarted seductress dissolved into a wide-eyed young woman, processing what she had just heard. "Why?"

"Maybe you're a loose end. Maybe it would divert attention from the other story."

"I don't understand."

"Tell me about Oz," I said, studying her face, looking for

twitches or tells. "Did he ever pay you for anything?"

"Oz?" She frowned, and a filament of indignation slipped into her voice. "I don't know anybody named Oz. And if he said he paid me for something he's a goddam liar."

"Right now I'm asking the questions," I said. "Osterman? Vincent Osterman?"

"I don't know who that is."

"He was at the Anchor Bar Friday night. Older man, a white guy, tall and thin with gray hair. He came in with Kenny and his crew. Did Kenny ever mention him?"

"I said I don't know him!" She took a breath as if steadying herself. "Jesus, Rimes. I didn't know any of those guys, and nobody ever gave me money."

"Not even Kenny?"

"Not even Kenny." Now she glared at me, voice rising. "Somebody said his friends were all cops. Maybe this Oz is a cop. Why don't we call nine-one-one and find out?"

She started to slide toward the edge of the bed but I pushed her back against the headboard and held her there with one hand. At first she resisted, her hands coming up, red nails toward my face, but something in my eyes must have kept her from scratching me.

"I told you, *I'm* the one asking the questions now." I kept my voice level but tight. She dropped her hands and her lower lip began to quiver, as if, finally, it sank in that I was twice her size, angry, armed, and capable of hurting her. I felt like a bully for scaring her but nothing focused the sober mind like fear, and I needed her to be afraid of telling me anything but the truth. "Now, did you ever meet a lawyer named Mickey Briggs, a woman?"

"Never heard of her." Indi's voice was almost a whisper.

"What about Anthony Merlotta?"

"Who?"

"Anthony Merlotta." I withdrew my hand from her shoulder and reached down to pick up the book. I held it out to her but she made no move to take it. "Anthony—Tony—is Rick Merlotta's son. The guy who's running for mayor? He wrote this and signed it. You ever meet him or his son?"

She shook her head and adjusted the quilt to cover her breasts again. "It's Kenny's book. Was Kenny's book. He left it here one night." Her eyes finally moistened, though whether from the fear I had tried to instill or from a memory of Kenny I could not say. "I don't know any of these people, not a one. Are they the ones who want to kill me?"

"*Might* want to kill you," I said, setting the book on the bed. "And I'm sorry to be an asshole, but I just found out they might have murdered one of my best friends."

"Oh, God! I'm so sorry." She put a hand on my forearm without hesitation, an honest gesture of comfort, and I appreciated it. "But why would they want to kill me?"

"Maybe you're easier to get to than I am."

"I still don't understand. How does that hurt you?" She wiped her eyes, narrowed them at me, and smiled. "It's not like we hooked up or anything."

I couldn't help smiling back. "They're not aware of the other people in my life, just you, and I do care about what happens to you." I let that admission hang there a second. "I know something about them they want to keep secret."

"Something they'd kill to keep secret."

"Possibly. I came here to find out if you know it too."

"But I don't." She sat forward. "Did Kenny know? Is that why they killed him?"

"Could be part of it but not all of it. If they killed him—*if*—it was probably because of something he didn't want to do for them anymore."

I looked at her and wondered how to tell her Kenny's feelings for her had been a sham. When the story broke it would embarrass her publicly, perhaps hurt her. Right now I needed to put it into an Indi-friendly context.

"I think Kenny was a good guy," I said, "better than this will make him sound. But he needed money. People who need money do things they regret. His parents had bills they couldn't pay, and he wanted to be a good son."

"I never met his parents." She shrugged. "He talked about them sometimes, said they were old and sick, but he never said he wanted me to meet them."

"Didn't that strike you as odd if he wanted you to have his coffee-colored babies?"

"He said they were a little prejudiced." She held up her thumb and forefinger with less than an inch between them. "Not a lot, just a little."

"Indi, Kenny was paid to go out with you."

"What?"

"Vince Osterman—Oz—paid him to go after you." I could see she didn't believe me so I plunged ahead and gave her no chance to object. "Look, at first, I wondered if Oz was paying you too, to go along with it, but I believe you. He didn't need to pay you. He had Kenny, a cop who knew what to say and how to behave to make his stalker act seem real."

Indi said nothing as she considered this, perhaps remembering moments with Kenny that didn't feel quite right or things he'd said that struck her as less than genuine. Brow knit, she looked crestfallen. "So he didn't really give two shits about me?"

"I think the original plan was for him to ask you out and, when you said no, to keep pushing until you filed a harassment complaint." I took one of her hands between mine. "But you said yes, which changed the game. Now he had to act possessive, so scary you'd want to get away from him, and he'd keep showing up so you would file an order of protection."

"Why?"

"To embarrass the mayor. To make it seem her people were out of control."

"Bullshit!" She laughed and withdrew her hand. "That's the dumbest—"

"The election is a few weeks away. The polls have Merlotta running close behind Green but gaining points. Oz works for a company that was hired to change the odds. Oh, and there's half a billion dollars at stake."

"Half a *billion*?"

"Yes. Merlotta's people want it."

She stared at me and drew the quilt even tighter, as if it were some kind of protection against the grime of the real world. "Then why would they kill Kenny if he did everything they asked?"

Had Kenny done everything? How far had he been willing to go for his new job and whatever signing bonus his charade brought in?

Mickey Briggs had hinted at a reluctance on Kenny's part. It was possible he'd had second thoughts because, as a cop, he wasn't thrilled about the weekend jail crowd. He could have been making his way back to Karen O'Brien and thought jail would ruin things. Or he could have gone along with stalking Indi because Oz had something on him, but in the end he had stood his ground. Those scenarios, however, weren't Indi-friendly.

"I think he wanted out," I said after a time. "The truth is, Kenny gave way more than two shits about you. I think he wanted to stop because he liked you enough not to go on hurting you."

Chapter 35

Indi called Doc and said she'd be late for rehearsal. After she emerged from her bedroom in black jeans and a cream blouse, I took her to Elmwood Taco & Subs. She ordered a chicken quesadilla, I had a Philly cheesesteak sandwich, and we shared waffle fries and a chocolate chip thumbprint cookie the size of a small cake.

During the meal, she said nothing about what I had told her. Instead, she explained how the Jazz Blues Alliance was auditioning a new sax player tonight because Big Willy needed time off for surgery.

"What kind of surgery?"

"I don't know," she said. "But he's supposed to be off about two months."

I thought about Big Willy, who looked as if he had *serious* health problems, and had a feeling he'd be gone from the JBA longer than two months but kept that to myself. "So who's the new guy?"

"A friend of Teddy's. They were in another blues band together years ago. I think he's a retired music teacher."

"Will he be ready to play the Anchor Bar tomorrow night?"

"Won't have to. They got another band this Friday. Doc and Big Willy knew about the surgery for a good while but they didn't tell the rest of us till the other night. So we get a week off to work with this new guy or find somebody else if we don't like him. Then we got a few weeks of steady gigs to get in shape for Doc's friend from New York."

"The record executive who's going to give you your big break," I said.

Indi smiled sadly. "Big Willy told me he's so sorry he can't play that night. But he should be up and around by then and promised he'd be there. He says he's proud to be my good luck charm."

"You don't need luck, Indi. You're a great singer."

"Thank you." She lowered her eyes momentarily, as if embarrassed, then met my gaze. "Will you come? You and Miss Trinidad?"

"I can't speak for Ms. Trinidad," I said, "but I'll be there if I don't have to work. Just let me know what day."

It was dark when we reached the Rogers' house. I parked four doors past it. As we walked back, I saw the glowing tip of a cigarette brighten and hold—a final drag—then fade to an ember. Faintly backlit by light seeping through the closed front drapes, someone tall stood on the porch and flicked the butt away. Even before we got close enough to see, I knew it was Big Willy. He was taller than anyone else in the JBA and the only obvious smoker. In dark clothing that hung loose and a baseball cap, he moved to the top of the steps and greeted us with, "How you doin', baby girl?"

"Just fine," Indi said.

She went up the steps first, and I followed. Big Willy bent to let her kiss his cheek, then stepped aside as I reached the top.

"Evenin', Detective."

"Big Willy," I said.

"Doc said you'd be late, Indi. Somethin' 'bout you havin' dinner with Mr. Rimes?"

"He wanted to give me his final report," Indi said, without missing a breath. "How's Teddy's friend?"

Big Willy sighed. "He ain't played yet—that asshole just talk, talk, talkin' 'bout all the shit he done. I known Tank for years. He'll get the job done but he don't know when to shut up. That's why I stepped out, 'fore my mouth got me in trouble." He chuckled then coughed and cleared his throat. "'Course, he ain't nowhere near good as me."

"Nobody is," Indi said. Unzipping her jacket, she turned to me. "You coming in?"

"And get Tank even more wound up because he doesn't know me?" I said. "I wanted to see Doc about something but, for now, I'll just talk with Big Willy."

"You don't have to wait. It's okay if you come in now."

"Right," Big Willy said. "Doc don't mind if a friend watches."

Doc considered me a friend. I thought about that.

"But if you have to go, thanks for the food and the ride," Indi said. "And for telling me everything. You were right. Me and you are better this way." She came to me and stood on her toes to kiss my cheek. Her lips and the tip of her nose were both warm as she slid to my ear and whispered, "When you nail those motherfuckers, I want to know."

I nodded, and Indi pulled away from me. She pushed open the door and went into the foyer. Before the outer door closed, I caught a glimpse of Dix, just inside the inner door, his arms open and ready to embrace Indi when she stepped inside.

Big Willy lit another cigarette and looked at me as he took a drag. "She hit on you?"

"Yeah," I said. "I told her I was a better friend than booty call."

He nodded and exhaled a cloud of smoke. "The girl got issues. Hornier than half the young bloods I ran with when I was her age."

"Why do you think she's like that?"

"She country," he said. "She come from the backwoods to the big city and lost her damn mind."

"Buffalo isn't exactly a metropolis."

"Compared to Baxley, Georgia, it's Man-Fuckin'-hattan." He frowned at me as if I were stupid not to have realized that myself.

I leaned against a porch post and gazed into the sky. "Never been to Baxley."

"Blink once, you miss the *Entering Baxley* sign. Cough and then blink again you miss the *Leaving Baxley* sign. Which is why I worry about what'll happen to baby girl when she actually do get to New York. I'm scared it gonna eat her alive."

"You think she has a real shot with Doc's producer friend?"

"Man, it's a lock. Ain't you heard her sing the other night, or is your ears fulla wax? A real shot? Shit, the blues just waitin' for a voice like hers."

I shrugged and glanced at him. "I don't know anything about the music business."

"We do—me and Doc—and this guy comin' to see her, Triplett, is big time." Big Willy took a long drag and blew smoke toward the street. "Back in the day, we cut a couple LPs with him and his father. Didn't get too far in the sales department but we did get some respect and enough money to help Doc's brother finally set up his auto shop."

"Leland's," I said.

"Yep. We was partners but we both worked there when we wasn't on the road."

"Car repair and music. That's an odd combination."

"Blues couldn't pay all the bills but it's somethin' we just had to do." He paused, as if giving me time to understand his need to make music. "We tried day jobs and we could get to weekend gigs in Rochester or Cleveland but the steel mill and the Ford plant kinda frown on you takin' time off to play Tuesday in Detroit. The shop was the way we did it all." He took another pull and exhaled. "Now that Indi 'bout to get where neither one of us got, Doc might have to go with her for a time, to make sure Triplett and his people look after her right."

"You and Doc must go way back."

"To kindergarten, Rimes, all the way back to kindergarten." He grinned. "To old Miss Hoffman, who looked like a giant pale scarecrow with a puffy white helmet."

I chuckled. "You're a lucky man, Big Willy. Must be nice to have a lifelong friend. I wish I did. My folks died when I was young and I didn't make friends easily."

"Doc and me been together since 'fore Leland was born. Same classes all through school, music lessons with the same teacher. Started our first band at ten. When you together that long, you stop bein' friends and become brothers, with no secrets between you."

I nodded, and, after a moment, said, "Indi says you'll be off a while, for surgery."

He waved a hand in dismissal. "Just old man shit."

"You have no secrets from Doc, but what about Dix and Teddy?" I pulled away from the porch post and turned to face him directly. "Do they know how serious it is, or is Indi the only one in the dark?"

Big Willy stared at me without answering and took a long final drag then flicked his cigarette toward the street without looking away from my face. "What you mean?"

"Your clothes and your skin are both loose," I said, "as if you've had recent weight loss. I never see you without a cap and I see no fringe of hair around it, but in some of the pictures on Doc's wall your hair is pretty thick. And your eyes show a bit of jaundice. So I'm thinking some kind of cancer maybe and chemotherapy. You smoke but it's probably not lung cancer because you can still blow a mean saxophone."

"Pancreatic," he said after a few seconds.

"And they've been working to shrink the tumor to an operable size. Dix and Teddy and Lizzy know all about it, don't they? But Indi is so self-absorbed she missed the cues."

His voice went even lower than usual. "You think you pretty smart, don't you?"

"Not as smart as all that, or I'd have realized some other things much sooner."

"Like what?"

"Like I wonder if Doc ever told Indi he's her father."

"Shit!" He rubbed his fingers over the stubble on his cheeks. "How you figure that out?"

"Pictures," I said. "The official story is that Doc met Indi when he played at Paine College and invited her to come to Buffalo. But Doc and Indi both have pictures of the same church in Baxley where Indi made her mark as a young soloist. Doc has a picture of himself there, and Indi has two of herself there at different ages. There's no picture of them together, but they're in the same sanctuary with the same choir robes and the same mural of Jesus surrounded by children. What would bring Doc to a town of less than five thousand? One possibility was a child, so I took a closer look at Indi and started to see the pieces of Doc that are in her, like the flare of her nostrils and the shape of her chin. And I remembered how uncomfortable he looked when Teddy called her Wonder Pussy. Still, I wasn't sure I was right so I planned to surprise Doc with the same question I asked you. You confirmed it."

"I ain't confirm nothin'," he said.

"Yeah, you did with your reaction and even before that by telling me you'd been to Baxley. So I repeat my question: does Indi know Doc is her father?"

Big Willy let out a long breath. "No." He moved toward the patio table on the porch and sat in the first chair he reached. "Doc met her mama in Atlanta. Fine ass Ruth. When she got pregnant, she went home to Baxley, so whenever we hit GA, we made a side trip to see her and the baby. Early on she told her church Doc was her cousin from DC, and he played for them when he was in town on a Sunday. But as Indi got older, Ruth wouldn't take him home 'cause she didn't want the girl confused, so they'd meet up at a motel outside town."

"They kept screwing," I said, "even though the only way Doc could see his daughter was to sit in a back pew like a visitor. That must have eaten away at him, especially if he was paying child support."

"Yep. Indi didn't really meet him till she was in college and got a half scholarship 'cause her mother passed. But Doc kep' on sendin' money to help cover things, and a friend at the school let him know how she was doin'. She never knew it was him payin' for her."

"He never told her the whole truth?"

Big Willy shook his head. "We went to play there a couple times during her last year and she sang with us. Nona was too sick to travel then. Doc said Indi oughta come up here. Then Nona died, and he sent Indi a letter offerin' her a job."

I could hear the notes of a tenor sax filling the house and realized Tank finally must have stopped talking. I raised the volume of my voice. "Do Dix and Teddy know?"

Big Willy shook his head again. "They wasn't with us way back when. They come into the band a few years 'fore we played the college. They met Indi when we did."

"But Lizzy knows."

He closed his eyes a moment and nodded. "Yes."

"And she accepts Indi because she couldn't have children of her own."

He nodded again.

"Do you have children?"

He shifted in his chair. His eyes narrowed and his face took on a pained expression. "Me and Isabel, we had a son, Walter, but he got killed in the First Gulf War. I couldn't protect him on the other side of the world." His eyes moistened and he bit his lower lip.

"I'm so sorry," I said.

"Only baby I care 'bout now is the daughter of my brother from another mother."

I took a deep breath and let it out slowly then launched my last probe. "So when Doc killed Kenny Carnahan he was protecting his only child."

Big Willy wiped his eyes and said nothing for a few seconds. Then he smiled. "Doc didn't kill that boy. I did."

Bingo, but not quite the verification of my theory I had expected. I pulled over one of the padded chairs and sat facing him. "Tell me what you used as a murder weapon."

"A breaker bar." He looked at me as if daring me to challenge him. "Used to use it on my old Lincoln."

"Where is it now?"

"It went for a swim, at Niagara Falls."

I knew what Big Willy was hoping to do and why, and he knew I knew. The question that hung between us was whether I would let him do it. I turned it over in my mind, all of it. As Doc's best friend, he almost certainly had been in the park that night—and therefore was an accessory—but he was likely too tall to have struck the fatal blow himself. The angle of impact was wrong—though, as Mira had said, variables made it possible. With his illness, Big Willy might not have had enough strength, but again variables came into play. The two of them

probably had flanked Kenny to demand he stay away from
Indi. Kenny had faced Big Willy because he was the taller of
the two and presented the more visible threat—which meant he
hadn't seen the breaker bar under Doc's coat or up his sleeve.
At the moment of impact, Kenny may have been reaching for
the gun holstered in the small of his back or he may have been
reasoning with two old black men who didn't especially
frighten him.

It didn't matter, because his real misjudgment was the
speed of someone who'd spent his entire life calculating time
on a keyboard, from complex classical music to blues to intri-
cate jazz rhythms. It did not occur to Kenny that a man in his
sixties could move as fast as Doc must have.

"How did you get Kenny to go to the park?"

"He went on his own. He came back after you took Indi
away. Got outta his truck and went over to this brown Escalade
and start talkin' with the man behind the wheel."

I nodded. Osterman had been there, probably waiting for
Kenny. "Then what?"

"I was comin' out the bar with my sax case and followed
him when he drove away. When he parked, I got out and went
over and told him he better leave Indi 'lone. He call me a ol'
fool and turn to walk away. And I hit him. Didn't know he was
dead till the next day."

Big Willy's story was a perfect fit. Osterman had made the
appointment verbally and chosen the park because police
would be looking for Kenny. When he found the body later, he
sent both texts and drove away until it was time to make the
nine-one-one call from a payphone.

"So he was out of his truck?" I said. "When did he get
out?"

"Soon as I walk over!" Big Willy sucked his teeth as if irri-
tated. "The fuck! Cop kill a black man don't get this kinda
shit! They ask what happen and he say the nigger went for my
gun and they say, okay, good shootin'. They can't take a black
man's word he kill a cop?"

"If you get mad when they question you, they might think
you're lying, to protect somebody else." I waited a few sec-

onds for that to sink in. "When did you get the breaker bar out of the back of your Jeep?"

He smiled, finally getting it. "When I put my saxophone case in it."

I continued wrestling with his effort to take the fall for Doc. He could sell his story to Chalmers and Pinero, only if he maintained consistency in the retelling. Or would they be so eager to make an arrest they would overlook flaws in the confession? Of course, the plan to torch Ophelia had set everything in motion. When it hit the news, it would explode in Briggs and Osterman's faces like a gun with a stone in the barrel. And it would support Big Willy's claim. Kenny had been lured to the park by his handler, and Big Willy had followed him.

The pivotal question, however, was whether I could let an accessory who didn't understand how weak the evidence really was take the blame. I thought about the district attorney and realized that, faced with my choice, he would cut a deal. The first one who flipped would get some kind of pass—a lighter sentence or even a walk—because imperfect justice was better than none. I was making a deal too but the terms were inverse: the first one to confess freed the other. In this case, the confessor might not even live to stand trial. And what of the man who had killed to protect his daughter? Would he kill again? Or would he just make music and help the child he'd been unable to nurture find her better self? I thought of the closure an arrest would bring Ophelia and the Carnahans. Moreover, an arrest would give Amanda Corso the leverage she needed to usher Briggs and Osterman's election scheme into the light and keep it there. But first Big Willy would need a lawyer.

"You don't have to do this," I said finally.

"Gotta be done. I made my peace with it." Big Willy got to his feet. "But 'fore we go, I gotta talk to Doc, 'splain things." He gazed down at me for a long time, tired eyes full of sympathy for whatever he saw in my face. "Ain't you got nobody you'd kill or die for?"

"Yes," I said, picturing them, all of them. "Ever read *A Tale of Two Cities*?"

"Prolly in school." He shrugged. "Can't 'member none of it, though. Why?"

"You remind me of somebody." I sighed and stood. "Talk to Lizzy too. I'm sure all this will be news to her. And Indi. She said you're her good luck charm. She doesn't need to know exactly how but I think it's better if she hears about this from you." Thinking of the two calls I had to make, I took out my mobile phone. Before I keyed in the first number, I looked at Big Willy as he opened the front door. "By the way, the breaker bar was brand new, so you never used it on your Lincoln."

Chapter 36

The headline read:

Arrest made in Carnahan killing.
Musician confesses to private investigator.
BY AMANDA CORSO
NEWS POLITICAL REPORTER

Last night held a welcome surprise for city homicide detectives investigating the beating death last weekend of off-duty Buffalo police officer Kenneth Carnahan, 32. Detectives Terrence Chalmers and Rafael Pinero had gone home after another day of conducting interviews and reviewing evidence. They were called back to work shortly after 10 p.m. by night duty officers who notified them a saxophone player had come forward to confess.

Willy P. Simmons, 65, of Buffalo, arrived at police headquarters at 9:45 p.m. in the company of his attorney and a private investigator. Police spokesman Jay Park said Simmons confessed to confronting Carnahan in Delaware Park last Saturday night over Carnahan's relationship with a singer in Simmons's band. After an argument, Simmons allegedly struck the victim once with a tire iron. The blow proved fatal.

"Their relationship was troubled," attorney Jonah Landsburgh said of Carnahan and singer Indigo Waters. "After two straight nights of angry words and dis-

rupted band performances, my client sought to reason with a man he felt posed a danger to his friend. It was never his intention that anybody get hurt."

Simmons reportedly first confessed to Gideon Rimes, a private investigator hired to bodyguard Waters after she filed an order of protection. After Carnahan's death, Rimes continued to protect the singer during the investigation and was present when Simmons felt he must...

Chapter 37

Amanda Corso's story of Big Willy's confession and arrest made Friday's front page so that by Saturday morning, everyone at Kenny's funeral must have known his death had resulted from a relationship dispute. The article stopped short of calling him a stalker and did mention he had been cited for taking a bullet in the line of duty. The follow-up, still being sourced as mourners took their seats to pay their final respects to a hero, would not appear until Sunday.

The service was held at St. Joseph's Cathedral, next door to police headquarters on Franklin Street. The entire block had been closed off to regular traffic as police vehicles from around the country took their places in two lines that would follow the hearse and family limousine now in front of St. Joseph's through the city to Holy Sepulchre Cemetery on Harlem Road. There were cruisers and unmarked cars in a wide assortment of colors—black and white, black and silver, green and yellow, gray, brown, gold, Buffalo's own white and blue, Erie County's white with black and red door markings, and New York State's blue and gold—as well as tactical patrol SUVs with various styles of push bumpers and PIT bars, from tubular wraparounds to grille mounts that looked like twin battering rams. On the sidewalk across from police headquarters, a line of motorcycles from too many departments to count stretched down to Swan Street and around the corner.

I parked several blocks away and walked to the cathedral.

The sprawling interior held a shifting sea of dress blue and dress black with smatterings of gray, green, and brown from assorted state and county law enforcement agencies, and even a clot of red jackets worn by RCMP officers from Canada. In my blue suit, I was not the least out of place. Surrounded by floral arrangements, the flag-draped coffin was in front of the marble stairs which led to the chancel and the altar. I took an aisle seat in the back, near the loft that held the massive pipe organ. I was too far away to recognize anyone in the front. As mourners filled my pew and the crowd swelled to standing room only, I read the funeral program.

The cover picture of a smiling Kenny was one I'd seen on Facebook, only here his brother Lenny had been cropped out. The obituary noted Kenny's family, his schools, his years in the navy, his decade with the police, and his love of football. As expected, it made no mention of Indi but did note his "special friendship with Miss Karen (KO) O'Brien." Having missed my chance to interview KO earlier, I wondered if it would be worthwhile to try again. In the wake of Big Willy's arrest, would it even matter? I checked the order of service to see if "special friendship" meant O'Brien would speak, but her name wasn't there. Bishop Lang and Father Ryan would conduct the traditional funeral mass. But between the communion and the final commendation of the spirit, because of the "special nature" of Kenny's public service career, there would be "brief remarks" from those who knew him. Listed were three men whose names I didn't know, and three dignitaries whose names I did: Commissioner Cochrane, Common Council President Peters, and Mayor Green.

The service was long, and, in a smaller building, would have been unbearably hot with so many people packed inside. But the doors were open on this warm October day, and the cathedral was not far from the usually breezy waterfront. Also, high vaulted ceilings and white walls seemed to help keep the interior cool. After communion, taken by fewer than half the mourners, speaker after speaker—including a childhood friend and a watch commander—rose from a front pew and went to the microphone near the casket to praise Kenny as a son and friend and to salute his service as a police officer. After sharing two anecdotes furnished by other officers, Commissioner Cochrane spoke of Kenny as a valued member of the Gang Crimes Task Force, an assignment for which he took a bullet to the chest. "But thanks to faith, family, and modern medicine he made a full recovery," Cochrane said. Then he looked at the casket. "Technically, that case is still open, Ken, and although the man who killed you is now in custody, we will never stop looking for the man who shot you. You did your duty to the fullest. We will follow your example and continue to do ours." As the commissioner returned to his seat, the applause went on so long the council president stood at his pew for nearly a minute before his name was called. It was clear Peters knew Kenny only as part of the mayor's security team, for his remarks were awkward and generic, lasting less than the time he had spent waiting to deliver them. Then it was the mayor's turn.

Ophelia rose, planted a kiss on the American flag covering the casket, then went to the microphone. From where I sat, I couldn't be certain her black dress was the same one she had worn to Danny's funeral but I thought it might be. I knew her appearance here was, in part, political, but there was genuine grief in her voice as she recounted how safe Kenny had made her feel when he was beside her at public events. Over the years, she had come to know all the officers assigned to her, but Kenny stood out for his enthusiasm, his ready smile, and his obvious joy at being alive. She would miss him, she said, for his many kindnesses, his professionalism, and his willingness to deviate from planned itineraries whenever she felt a craving for her favorite iced cappuccino between engagements. After the brief laughter, she looked at the right front pew, beside which sat a wheelchair. "Mr. and Mrs. Carnahan, you raised a fine son into a fine man I was proud to call not only my protector but also my friend. Thank you." Then, wiping her eyes, she went back to her seat.

The pipe organ filled the cathedral with a recessional hymn, and everyone stood. Kenny's casket was wheeled up the center aisle. His family followed, Lenny pushing Mr. Carnahan's

wheelchair and Mrs. Carnahan walking with the help of a man
and woman who flanked her, each with an arm around her
waist and a tight grip on her biceps. I thought the man must be
Kenny and Lenny's godfather, Uncle Patrick. Even at this distance, I could see the woman was younger than he was and
wondered if she might be Karen O'Brien. Her hair was the
same color I had seen in Facebook photos, but shorter, and her
height was about right.

The recessional, however, was slow, and my curiosity had
to wait for satisfaction. Mourners who had aisle seats reached
out to pat shoulders or squeeze hands as the group passed. A
few stepped out of their pews to offer full embraces. When,
finally, they were six or seven pews away, I knew the woman
was O'Brien.

Two pews away, Lenny noticed me and looked surprised to
see me. Then he nodded and grinned. Mr. Carnahan looked
vacant and lost, even more shrunken in his chair than he had
seemed the other night. His loosely knotted yellow tie was the
only splash of color in the whole group. Mrs. Carnahan sobbed
non-stop, her sagging shoulders giving the impression she was
being dragged along. I could see her resemblance to the man
holding her right arm. As they passed, Lenny started to lean
toward me, and I mirrored his action.

"You got him, man!" he whispered.

I couldn't tell whether she heard, but having witnessed our
interaction, O'Brien stared at me for a long moment, probably
wondering who I was.

It took a long time for the cathedral to empty and the visiting officers to reach their vehicles. Cluster after cluster of people gathered on the sidewalk or in the street to talk. Because I
wasn't going to the cemetery and my car was three or four
blocks away, I made my way through them but it was slow
going. As I drew alongside the family limo on the street side,
the back door opened. Karen O'Brien swung her legs out and
stood up.

"Len said you're Mr. Rimes. I'm KO." She extended her
hand, the nails a bright red. Despite its apparent sadness, her
voice still had the faintly helium quality I had noticed in our

phone conversation. "I talked to you the other day but you never made it to my office."

"Sorry, but something beyond my control took me in another direction."

She shrugged. "That's all right." She was pretty in a pleasant-but-somewhat-shy-and-self-conscious way. While puffy, her striking green eyes actually glittered. The freckles visible through her make-up did nothing to diminish the seriousness with which she carried herself. She was nothing at all like Indi, and I wondered why she and Kenny had separated. "Whatever it was must have led you to the killer. Len says you're the man who caught him."

Something flipped in my gut. It took me a second to speak. "How can I help you?"

"I'd still like to talk to you, if you have time."

"Sure. When?"

"Today if possible?" She lowered her eyes as if embarrassed. "I was a wreck at work all week. I could have stayed home, but we had a project deadline, so I just worked through the tears. Now my boss wants me to take some time off." Her smile was crooked, and she seemed to know it. It disappeared almost before it registered. "I'm flying to San Francisco in the morning to stay with my sister for two weeks."

"I have plans tonight," I said. "And I imagine after the cemetery you'll have lunch with the Carnahans and spend most of the afternoon at their house."

"Len said you were there the other night. You can stop by if you'd like. After what you've done for us, I'm sure no one would mind."

Us, I noted as I shook my head. "I'd rather not intrude."

"Then I can slip out for a little while. Are you free about two? Spot Coffee on Elmwood?"

When I nodded, she flashed her awkward smile again and sank back into the limo. Before I closed her door, I bent to look inside and offered my final condolences. Buckled in on the curb side and slumping, Mr. Carnahan gave no response. Beside him, his still tearful wife smiled at me and, when I declined her invitation to drop by, said, "Then God bless you, Mr. Rimes."

Despite sitting low in a jump seat, Lenny looked more adult than I'd ever seen him. "Thank you, for everything," he said.

Closure.

On the way to my car, I called Phoenix and told her about the funeral. Then I listened as she told me about Big Willy, who had spent the night in jail but had been transferred to Erie County Medical Center in the morning after vomiting blood.

"He's stable now and under guard, but he won't be arraigned until Monday. They may have to find a judge who'll go to his hospital room to do it. Meanwhile, doctors at ECMC are trying to get his records from Roswell, and his oncologist is screaming bloody murder to every elected official he can get on the phone."

"I know two he missed."

"Jonah's filing to get him taken to Roswell, where he's supposed to have surgery on Thursday. He's trying to get the charge reduced from second degree murder to manslaughter or involuntary manslaughter. Right now, though, this is all one giant mess." For a moment Phoenix said nothing. "Gideon, are we doing the right thing here?"

"I don't know. This is what Big Willy wants to do, but I don't know if it's right. We can talk about it tonight."

"That's not what I want to do tonight," she said after a moment.

"I'm so glad."

"Good. Then I'll see you at seven."

Chapter 38

Karen O'Brien had changed out of her black dress into brown slacks and a stylish green jacket. She sat across from me at a small table in a well-lit corner of Spot Coffee, eyes still puffy and hands wrapped around the bowl-sized cup of chamomile tea I had just set in front of her. She hadn't eaten much at the Carnahans' because her stomach was bothering her and now she hoped the chamomile would calm it. When I asked how long she had known Kenny, she pressed her lips together as if struggling with the question.

For a long time she said nothing, eyes downcast but occasionally rising to scan the coffee shop. It was filled with people of various ages, many of whom lived in the Elmwood Village. They looked like students, academics, artists, actors, urban professionals, retirees, and those seriously down on their luck. There were pockets of conversations, both lively and subdued. Stuffed armchairs were occupied by persons with a coffee cup or a pastry in one hand and a book or a magazine in the other. Seated at the wooden counters that ran the length of the front windows were people hunched over laptops, a few wearing headphones. There was a steady stream of foot traffic in and out of both the corner door and the center door.

I wondered if KO were missing Kenny, glimpsing him amid the regulars. Or maybe she was just nervous at being here with me. In any case, I waited, sipping my coffee.

"Me and Kenny were together off and on for years," she said, finally. "We first got together in high school. My all-girls school would hold these dances and invite the boys from his school. We met when he was a senior and I was a junior and we just hit it off." Her voice drifted into a slightly higher register as she reminisced. "We were sort of pre-engaged when he graduated and joined the navy. We did a lot of emailing when he was at sea and a lot of Skyping whenever we could. Anytime he got leave—" She reddened a bit and looked away. "We broke up a few times after he came home for good and dated other people, but somehow we always found our way back to each other." I saw in her eyes a flash of delight, as if we were old friends reconnecting. "We had this special bond, like we were each other's destiny."

I set down my cup. "You said you got pre-engaged. Did you ever get engaged?"

"No."

"When did you start living together?"

"After he was on the force three years and I was at Rich for one. My grandmother—she raised me—died around then. With my only family gone, moving in with Kenny seemed the logical thing to do."

"You lived together a long time. Then you broke up. What happened?"

"The usual stupid shit." She lowered her eyes again and smiled her awkward smile. "We were in different places in our heads—you know, where we were going as a couple. We argued a lot, mostly over things not worth arguing about. His work didn't give him enough overtime and we both worked wild hours. We stopped talking like we used to, stopped going out, stopped being…intimate." She bit her lip and looked up. "I don't want you to think we stopped caring for each other, Mr. Rimes. We still loved each other but things just got harder over the past few years—though a lot of it, I think, was Kenny worrying about his family."

"Lenny told me his parents needed money and Kenny wanted to help." I leveled my gaze at her. "You're saying driving the mayor didn't give him enough money to do so."

"Exactly."

"When he wanted to move back home and help his folks, why didn't you move with him? The house is big enough. You have no other family, and you could have saved a lot of money together. Mr. and Mrs. Carnahan seem to think the world of you."

"They've always been very sweet to me." She took a long swallow of tea and briefly closed her eyes as if willing it to the right place to soothe her stomach. Then she dabbed her lips with one corner of her napkin and wiped her eyes with the other. "Kenny said no. He said he didn't want to carry our shit into his parents' house. He said we needed time apart, time for us to learn to appreciate each other again, maybe for him to catch up."

"Catch up with what?"

"With his parents' bills. With his career. With me."

"He felt he was being left behind? His career was stalled but you were moving up?"

"Yes."

"Any idea why he slipped off the fast track?"

"He got shot." She took a quick gulp of tea. "Things were never the same after that, but before he left I thought what we shared getting through it was making us stronger."

"How have you managed without him? The apartment must be expensive for one."

"My friend from work, Zaida, moved into the second bedroom." She shrugged. "We do okay as roomies."

"And you've gone on with your life—working, hanging with friends, dating?"

"Yes." She chuckled nervously. "Girlfriends and a passable frog now and then can be entertaining while your prince tries to get his head straight."

"Very practical," I said, wondering how she could be so practical about someone she loved when the average person couldn't. "When was the last time you talked to Kenny?"

She answered without hesitation. "About a week after he moved out."

"Did he say anything then about getting a new job?"

She shook her head. "He said sooner or later he would have

to because he was going nowhere but he didn't have any prospects when we talked."

"So he never mentioned a Vincent Osterman—Oz—to you?"

"No. Who's that? He's not mixed up with that man…Simmons?"

I shook my head. "Oz hired Kenny for a side job."

O'Brien looked relieved. "Good. He deserved a chance to show what he could do." She drank more tea then leaned forward and lowered her voice. "What they said in the paper, about Kenny and that singer. Was all that true?"

"Enough of it was, but it was complicated."

"Is she pretty?"

"She is."

"Is she nice?"

"Yes."

She nodded, chewing a lip as if in thought. "Did he—hurt her?"

"No." For a moment I wondered if Kenny had hurt *her*.

"But the man who killed him thought he would."

"Yes." I waited, still hoping she'd get to her point, to why she had asked to see me.

"Then it's like he's a victim too." She sat back, index finger tracing the rim of her cup, and let out a long sigh. "It's all very sad. Two lives ruined. Maybe hers too."

"What about yours, KO?" I put my hand over hers and stopped her moving finger. I tried to keep my voice as calm as possible. Whether it was resignation or detachment, her shifting mood bothered me. I wondered if she had taken something that was just kicking in. "What about your life? It was ruined too. At least a part of it was by what happened."

Looking alarmed—perhaps guilty—she withdrew her hand. "What do you mean?"

"You loved Kenny. You got pre-engaged and moved in together and seemed to be planning for the future. You said he was your destiny and even took care of him when he got shot. Now he's gone. It's got to be terrible for you, and I am so sorry. I'm concerned about you. I hope you're talking to somebody, a priest or a counselor." I took her hand again, held it between both of mine, and stared into green eyes that looked almost backlit. "But you asked me to meet you, and so far you haven't told me why."

"I thought—I thought you'd want to know more about Kenny."

"I do, but what do you get out of this? You didn't come here after a man confessed so I could tell you how pretty Kenny's other girlfriend was. What do you need to ask me or tell me? How can I help you? Whatever it is, I *will* keep it between us."

She hesitated, looked about, as if seeking an offstage rescuer who had missed his cue. "Len—" She swallowed. "Len told me what happened Sunday night."

"He did?"

"Yes. He told me everything."

Everything included that he had wanted to kill me and had pissed his pants after I disarmed him, so I doubted he had told her everything. I released her hand and folded my arms. "What did he say?"

"He said he drank too much and took one of Kenny's guns—the little one—and went to your place to shoot you but you talked him out of it—and he gave the gun to you."

Close enough, so I nodded.

"I was wondering about the gun."

"The little one." Arms still folded, I rested my elbows on the table. "You know it?"

"Cute. Small enough for a pocket or purse. Kind of camo green?"

"Okay. What about it?"

"What did you do with it?"

"Let's just say that where it is now is a better place than Lenny's pocket. Why?"

"At the funeral the commissioner said…" Her voice dropped to a whisper and she looked about as if making sure no one was listening. A desperation I had not expected slid across her face. "Look, I don't know how all that *CSI* stuff works, but if the police get that gun and they still have the bullet, they might find my prints or DNA or something—"

I sat back, dropping my hands to the tabletop, and whispered, "Aw, damn, KO!"

Now she took both my hands in hers. "I didn't mean to. Please believe me. It was an accident. He took the gun off a wannabe thug and used it to teach me to shoot. I carried it in my purse for protection. One night we got home from a movie, and I dug in my purse for my keys and—" She threw her hands up as if she had been helpless to stop it. "It just went off."

"You couldn't register a gun without a serial number," I said. "He told you to take the gun inside and hide it and then claimed it was a drive-by. But the bullet hit him at such a weird angle." The rising panic in her eyes told me I was right. "The angle looked so wrong to the ballistics guy, he knew something was off. Still, Kenny stuck to his drive-by story. He got himself a medal—and a shadow of suspicion that derailed his career."

"I gave it to him when he got out of the hospital," she said. "He said he destroyed it, and I believed him—till I had my heart-to-heart with Len." She scowled, eyes filling and lips quivering. "Don't you see? If he had come back to me, he'd have brought it with him and I'd be safe now." Squeezing my hands this time, she swallowed and leaned close, and I smelled chamomile. "I'll pay you whatever I can," she said. "Do whatever you want. I just need to get it back."

Chapter 39

At six-fifteen, dressed in a black turtleneck, black jeans, and a tan suede sports jacket, I left my apartment and put a duffel with clothes for tomorrow on the back seat of my Escape. Then I drove up Elmwood to the Lexington Co-op and bought what I would need to make Sunday brunch. Afterward, I turned left out of the Co-op lot and headed back down Elmwood, toward Phoenix's downtown loft. Had I resisted the sudden impulse to add mimosas to the brunch menu, the evening might have played out differently.

I found a parking spot outside a liquor store near Summer Street and went inside to get champagne to mix with the orange juice I'd already bought. When I returned to my car, I opened the rear driver's side door and braced the bottle behind my duffel on the back seat. Before I could withdraw and straighten, I heard a shuffle of feet behind me and felt a fist pile-drive into my right kidney. My legs buckled but I caught myself and was turning to see who had rabbit-punched me when a fist connected with my jaw and sent my glasses spinning away. I slumped again, but this time my attacker caught me under one arm and pushed my back door shut. A brick red SUV slammed to a stop beside the Escape. The man holding me up jerked open the back door and shoved me inside. Then he climbed in after me, keeping me face down against the far door with a gun pressed against the back of my head.

We took off, my legs scrunched between the seats and the muzzle pressure steady.

"Check that cocksucker for a gun," the driver said. "And get his phone."

The voice was unmistakable. For two days I had been looking over my shoulder for a well-appointed bronze Escalade. It had not occurred to me Osterman would use something like an old red Pathfinder to follow me and make his run at me or that he would do so around sunset on a busy street. Everything had happened so fast I dismissed hope that witnesses—if there were any—would lead to my rescue. I was on my own.

As a gloved hand groped inside my sports jacket and came out with my Glock and my mobile phone, I tasted blood and realized I had bitten my tongue. I coughed and turned my head to spit. "I think I might be sick."

"Man up, Shaft," my assailant said. But he pulled back enough for me to move.

Shaft? I thought. *Really?* And gulped air as if working to keep food down.

"You're not gonna be sick, but by tomorrow you will be pissing blood." His voice sounded familiar too but I couldn't place it. "Here's his gun and his phone."

I turned my head enough to glimpse my Glock change hands over the top of the seat.

"Toss the phone," Oz said.

I heard a power window open and stay down long enough for my phone to hit the pavement, then close.

"Nice piece," Oz said. "A baby Glock. Perfect for what I have in mind."

I coughed and spat again and did my best to make retching noises. I spat blood and saliva on the seat and the floor and tried to make myself throw up, but I hadn't eaten since noon and didn't have anything in reserve. I hoped the gagging sounded as bad to them as it did to me.

"Jesus!" the man with me in the back seat said. "Maybe he *is* gonna be sick!"

"He's playing you, Berko. Asshole's smart. Check him for a back-up piece."

Berko? The cop who'd clubbed me with the butt of his assault rifle?

"He wants to leave DNA in the car because he knows by tomorrow he won't be pissing anything," Oz continued. "He'll be rat food." Oz's laugh was simultaneously throaty and tinny. "The thing is, Rimes, after this piece of shit goes back to the chop shop where I got it, it will cease to exist, which means any DNA inside it will be lost. So go ahead and throw up. Maybe I'll make you lick it off the floor mat before I double-tap you between the eyes."

I hoped he wouldn't use my Glock for the double-tap. Nothing was more humiliating than being executed with your own gun.

The gun barrel now behind my right ear pulled away. How far, I could not tell. Berko was quiet a moment. Then with his free hand he patted me down. "He's clean."

My breath caught, and I swallowed as I struggled up onto the seat. I looked at Berko for a long time. He pulled off a black ski mask and stared back, neither of us saying anything. He was dressed not in SWAT gear but in dark civilian clothes and leather driving gloves. His too-black hair was tousled and stuck out in unruly shocks, but his salt-and-pepper mustache was a straight line. Even with narrowed eyes, his ruddy face was unreadable. He stuffed his ski mask into a jacket pocket. I wondered if he had come into this thing thinking Osterman wanted his help with a basic beat-down he couldn't administer alone. I knew Oz had more in store for me than a beating or a prosaic drive-by, and now Berko must be wondering why Oz had used his name. But he kept his SIG Sauer Parabellum leveled at my chest.

"I guess you owed me that shot to the jaw," I said, as another block slid past. "Mind if I wipe my mouth? I want to get the taste of blood off my lips."

"Go ahead, but slow, and keep your hands where I can see 'em."

I leaned against the seat back and dragged the sleeve of my jacket across my mouth while I checked my teeth with the tip of my tongue and thought about things. No breaks or cracks I could discern, but I'd bitten my lower lip as well as the side of my tongue. The bleeding was lessening in both places and the pain had dulled but my jaw would be swollen. And my kidney throbbed. If I lived till morning, I would look like a beaten boxer, face out of alignment as I teetered over a toilet, pissing blood. I gazed at Oz, his gray hair curling from beneath a black knit watch cap and his driving gloves at nine and two on the wheel. If not for the big SWAT man, I would have thrown an arm around his throat. I turned back to Berko and kept my eyes on him. "How many cops you got on the CitiQuest payroll, Oz? They go a few years without a contract and you come calling with candy and flowers?"

"He tries something stupid, shoot him in the knee," Oz said. "I want to punch his time card myself."

"Gonna do to me what you did to the mayor's husband? Hard to pull that off with a bullet in my knee, but, hey, who better to mask murder as an accident than an ex-homicide detective?"

Berko's mouth fell open and his eyebrows climbed as high as they could. This was clearly news to him. As I thought, he hadn't signed on for murder and now looked surprised Oz hadn't immediately denied killing Danny Green. It was one thing to learn someone you knew intended to commit a murder, quite another to realize this killing might not be the first bullet point on his homicide resume. The question now was whether Berko would have any second thoughts that gave me a chance or would he warm to the idea and step across the line himself. His silence offered no hints but I knew he had to be thinking it through.

"You talk too fuckin' much," Oz said. "And don't worry about me making anything look like an accident. By the time you hit the table, cause of death won't matter."

"Kinda tough to hide a body big as mine," I said.

"Not if you know where." Oz chuckled. "You brought this on yourself, Rimes, with your little stunt back in Mickey's office. I gotta hand it to you. I didn't even think of a second bug till that bitch Amanda Corso played me the recording over the phone and asked for a comment." He glanced back at me. "I'm going to enjoy putting her down. And your little cunt singer too. Both with your Glock. That ought to stir things up."

I realized he was buying himself time to disappear. If Amanda Corso and the singer featured in her last two articles were both found dead the same Sunday her final story made the front page—and their killer was the investigator who had provided information for one and protection for the other—the police and the local media would spend days if not weeks sorting everything out. The new murders would cast doubt on everything Amanda Corso had written about the Carnahan case. The massive manhunt for me would play out on television with an immediacy that jacked up advertising rates. The *Buffalo News* headline might read, Hero Ex-Cop Sought in Two Murders. Some enterprising reporter would come up with a pulpy name for me like the Detective of Death. Tip line calls would have law enforcement agencies all over the area scrambling to keep up with sightings. More than a few black men would be rousted, regardless of whether they were my size, age, or complexion. All that would give Vincent Osterman time to slip out of town, if not out of the country.

Your best plan yet, Oz old buddy.

I remembered that, like many Buffalo area residents, he owned a Canadian beach house, probably in nearby Ridgeway or Crystal Beach, and had a Canadian bank account to cover the property's expenses. He probably had a Nexus pass in his Escalade, wherever it was, for quick border crossings. It was also likely he had already transferred his savings into his Canadian account. I would still be warm but buried in some out-of-the-way place and Amanda and Indi would still be warm on the floors in their homes when Oz turned on the computer in his cottage and bought a ticket to, say, Brazil or Costa Rica. He could drive to Toronto and leave his car at the airport. By Monday or Tuesday he could be in Rio or San Jose, arranging another bank transfer. Most of the places he could go would have extradition treaties with the United States, but extradition would come into play if, and only if, he was charged with a crime. As things stood now, in the wake of failed dirty tricks, he could decide to retire again, this time overseas, where American money was more than welcome and went farther. He could dispose of his property online, and have his pension deposits forwarded to wherever he settled. Then he could live out the rest of his days in luxury.

We drove past the beginnings of the Saturday night logjam on Allen Street, where the bars and restaurants were already beginning to fill, and turned left on Virginia. Then we were passing private homes as we headed toward Main. I wondered what Berko would do if I tried to open the door and jump. I would have to be impossibly fast. It was growing darker but was not yet dark enough for me to do anything that couldn't be seen, and fumbling for the door handle in the dark would give Berko ample time to shoot—if he wanted to. Still, I studied the handle, attempting to memorize its height and placement, just in case an opportunity arose. At that moment, Berko jabbed my right biceps with the muzzle of the SIG. I turned to look at him. He was grinning as if disbelieving my stupidity. He pointed his gun toward the door handle and gave a slight shake of his head. But he kept his silence.

"You're gonna leave Mickey holding the bag for everything you set up?" I said to Oz. "Election manipulation, attempting to tangle the mayor's son in a sex scandal, the Rick and Tony Merlotta connection to money for Sunrise Village. And she doesn't know for sure what you did to Danny Green but she suspects. If they exhume Danny and rewrite the COD, do you think she'll go down as an accessory without implicating you? Unless you're planning to settle in a place like the Congo, you can be extradited."

"Think you got it all figured out, huh?" He sucked his teeth in dismissal. "Mickey can take care of herself. Been doing that a long time. Broad can talk her way out of anything. All this is just a minor embarrassment. You know nothing in your recording is grounds for any legal action. CitiQuest will go under, but she'll come out on top. Always does. As for her father and brother, fuck 'em. Business is business and when it's done it's done."

I hoped Berko noticed that Osterman had taken a pass on his second chance to deny killing Danny. Berko looked at him then looked at me, and I wondered what was going through his mind. He said nothing but I could see tension at the corners of his mouth. Anger, maybe, but at whom? Confusion from getting too much information to process? Uncertainty about the truth? Or could it be the first glimmer of fear born of that uncertainty?

"So where does that leave Berko?" I said. "Accessory or loose end?"

We crossed Main Street and turned right on Washington before Oz answered. "Berko and I have an understanding. From time to time he does things for me and knows better than to ask questions when he counts the cash."

"But until now those things haven't included murder, have they, Berko?" I tried to hold his gaze, to keep him seeing my face while there was still enough light. "You've been sitting here listening to Vincent Osterman plan three murders. That makes you—"

"Vincent Os—shit!" Oz said, almost swerving. "Is that prick wired?"

"No," Berko said, his eyes never leaving mine. "I checked him. Remember?"

"But he's a sneaky—"

"I said he's not wired!"

Berko didn't shout but he was loud enough that no one spoke for a few seconds.

I tried to draw Oz's attention away from him. "Nobody wears a wire on a date if he wants to get laid."

Oz laughed. "So who's your date, tough guy?"

Berko just stared at me, SIG still at the right height to put one in my heart.

"You plan to kill two women I'm not involved with, and you expect me to tell you the name of my date?" I steadied my voice as I spoke to Berko. "This is the guy you're working for? Now he wants to kill a woman with no connection to this case other than saying yes to a first date with a guy she just met."

"He's playing you," Oz said.

"Damn right, I'm playing you. I'm betting on you. Those things he had you do? I bet they didn't include killing another cop." Now I lowered my voice. "Yeah, I talk too much and I try to be a smart ass, but I'm retired from the job, just like your buddy Oz, only I was Army CID. Yeah, I was pissed off you hit me when you took me in, and I hit you back first chance I got, but I understand why you did it. You thought then I was a cop killer. You know now I'm the guy who brought the cop killer in. I caught a killer." I cocked my head toward Oz. "He is a killer. Tonight will make it four—that you know of." I drew in a long breath. "You're a cop, Berko, not a murderer. You know what cops call guys who kill more than three people. Serials."

"Shoot him in the knee," Oz said. "He's really pissing me off."

"No," Berko said.

"No? Are you forgetting—"

"I said no! I don't care what you got on me. There's a limit to what I'll do for you, and we just hit it. You said you wanted me to tune up an asshole and when you told me who and where, I said yeah. But then you called me by my name when I was wearing my mask. Why? Now I find out you're gonna *kill* him—*and* two others. That makes me a loose end. You gonna try buying me off, or do you plan to use his gun on me too? Give him a hat trick. Make him a cop killer, after all, so nobody thinks of you and whatever the hell he's been talking about." He shook his head. "After all the shit I done for you over the years."

"Berko—Greg, listen—" Oz began.

"What the fuck is *wrong* with you? I was your friend, your goddam friend! Now I'm disposable muscle?" Berko gulped a couple deep breaths but the SIG never shifted. "Look, I know you can ruin me, stop me getting my pension, but now we got a stalemate because I can ruin you too. So, let me tell you how this is gonna go."

"Oh, *you* have a plan?" Oz's sarcasm made Berko's jaw clench.

"No." Berko forced enough calm into his voice to sound dangerous in his own right. "You're the man with the plan. I'm just the man with the gun. My gun says I'm not part of your plan anymore."

"Which means what?"

"I get to walk away from this and we're even—for everything."

We continued down Washington Street and at Sycamore cut over to Michigan as Oz thought it over.

"All right. How?"

"Almost dark enough now," Berko said. "We'll go where you said. Then you'll both get out of the car and walk away from it. You can hold your gun on him but I'll hold mine on you. If you shoot him before I drive away and pull me in deeper, I will shoot you. Clear?"

"What if he runs to make me shoot him just so you shoot me?"

"Okay, I'll make him take off his shoes. Hard to run barefoot where we're headed. If he can see where he's going without glasses." He sighed. "Jeez, man, I want out, and this is the only way I can figure out how to do it so you don't shoot me too. Don't bother telling me how you'd never double cross me. Maybe it gives him a piss-poor chance he wouldn't get if I actually was your accomplice, but if his chance keeps me alive, I'm all for it. Besides, how far can he get without shoes? You'll be the one with the gun. Does that work for you?"

"You didn't ask if it worked for me," I said. "Oz, how about you give me my gun back and see if I'm any good with no shoes and glasses?"

"Fuck you, Rimes," Oz said without looking over his shoulder.

Berko glanced at him but not long enough for me to make a move. "You want to take him out, Oz, you'll give me five seconds to punch it and get outta there. He gets away from you barefoot out there after a five-count, it's on you. That's the deal. Take it, or I force you over right now and I walk away. Good luck getting him where you want him without me."

"All right."

"Good. I'll give you one hour. Then I'll return the car and leave it by the gate with the keys inside and drive away with my ex-brother-in-law Pete."

"He still work out of C District?"

"Yeah, and he will be pointing my AR-15 with a night

scope, so don't even think about trying to fuck me on this. You gotta run, run. Just don't come back. I ever see your back-stabbing face again, I will shoot first and claim self-defense."

Oz was quiet a moment. "Sorry you feel that way, pal, but I can live with it. I got no plans to come back."

"Good," Berko said, sliding as far away from me as possible. "Okay, Rimes, slip off your shoes. One at a time. Then your socks. Left hand only and no sudden moves."

They were brown suede loafers that matched my already ruined sports jacket, and I did as ordered. Beside me the automatic window went down halfway.

"Now throw everything out."

Again, I obeyed.

We were all quiet for the rest of the ride—each of us, I was sure, calculating the odds of his own survival. Berko's looked pretty good because he had his SIG, and I was Oz's primary concern, which made Osterman's chances about as strong as Berko's. My odds, on the other hand, were bleak. Everything depended on whether I could maneuver barefoot. Not easy to do and reach the necessary speed but not impossible either, though my bare feet were already reacting with discomfort to grit ground into the floor mat. Once I was outside, I needed to get out of pistol range for just a few seconds. I took heart that I still had a chance, courtesy of Berko.

But when we crossed the Ohio Street Bridge, and I realized where they were taking me, even that sliver of optimism vanished.

Chapter 40

The birthplace of the grain elevator, Buffalo was the world's largest storehouse and leading exporter of grain well into the twentieth century. Positioned at the eastern end of Lake Erie and the western end of the Erie Canal, the city was, for Atlantic shipping, a gateway to the Great Lakes. As more shipping channels were built and routes changed, many of the city's grain elevators fell into disuse and were eventually abandoned. For years, the concrete silos sat empty and decaying near the inner and outer harbors. Then, in the early twenty-first century, city planners found other uses for them. One cluster of towers, across the river from Canalside, was used as a massive outdoor screen for laser light shows and classic movies. Others were reconfigured for flea markets, poetry readings, concerts, art exhibits, and guerrilla theater. While reuse had brought life to many silos, others were still empty and in varying states of disrepair. Collectively, the grain elevators were called Silo City.

When we approached the chain link fence that separated several silo clusters from the street, I knew it was in one of these Vincent Osterman intended to hide my body.

Oz parked in front of a double wide gate six feet tall, his headlights illuminating the padlocked chain that held the gate closed. He got out, undid the padlock with a key from his pocket, and pushed open one side. Then he returned to the Pathfinder and threw it in gear.

"I'll leave it open so you can get out," he said to Berko as he drove through the gate. "Pull it shut on your way out and I'll lock it when I'm done."

With only the occasional light fixed high on the wall of this or that building, it was dark inside. We inched forward, headlights hitting gravel and garbage, tufts of weeds and rusty steel girders. Small dark outbuildings were scattered here and there, beyond them the silhouettes of tall grass and an elevated track bed. Oz changed to parking lights, and the car crunched forward slowly, nothing but a short amber glow ahead of it. We moved steadily, as if he knew exactly where he was going. He couldn't have chosen a more convenient place to kill me. The key probably meant CitiQuest had the security contract for the property. If there were infra-red surveillance cameras, either he would take me to a corner that lacked them or he would somehow disable them.

Even if there were no cameras, I was certain Oz had already chosen the unused silo that would receive me through a broken ground level window and serve as my resting place until at least next spring, maybe even longer if that particular tower was near the bottom of the renovation list. All he needed to do was shoot me and push me in. *He'll be rat food,* Oz had said. After I hit the concrete floor several feet below, rats and insects and bacteria would have all the time they needed to convert me from a fresh kill to a winter buffet.

After we had gone about two hundred yards, Oz turned left into a space between two long silo clusters that faced each other across an unlighted stretch of gravel and grass fifty or sixty feet wide. He drove to a spot halfway in and shifted into park.

"Oz, you first," Berko said. "Get out and leave the door open and stand where I can see you."

As Oz climbed out, the dome light revealed my Glock tucked into his belt. He would have to shoot me with a separate gun and leave mine with my body to make his cover story tidy. I had seen no shoulder rig but couldn't tell if his piece was in a back holster or a pocket.

Berko gestured with the SIG. "Now you, Rimes."

I opened the door and held it as I stepped onto gravel, aiming to give my feet time to adjust to points and edges and shifting stones. I must not have been moving fast enough, for Berko nudged me away and climbed out behind me. He slammed the door.

Zipping his jacket closed, Osterman backed up a bit because I was within five feet of him and might chance rushing him for my gun. "What next, Berko?"

Berko positioned himself so he could hold his gun on both of us as he moved to the front door. He climbed onto the rocker panel and stood up, aiming at us over the top of the window frame. "Walk around to the front, Oz, over to the passenger side. Then turn and walk five paces straight ahead, like you're going down the road. Stop and put both guns on the ground, his and yours. Then walk five more paces."

"What? You said I could hold him at gunpoint."

"I lied. Put both guns down. Don't worry. You'll be closer to them than he will."

Oz complied, glaring at both of us as he did so. Before his face left the amber glow of the parking lights, I had no doubt he would try to track and kill Berko just as soon as he was done with me. He stopped after five paces and crouched to put the guns on the ground but I had no way of telling whether he had actually done so. Berko shifted his gun to his left hand and reached inside the Pathfinder to turn on the headlights, then the high beams. Oz shielded his eyes. Only one gun was visible on the ground. It looked like mine.

Berko raised his SIG. "Both guns, Oz, or I swear to God I'll drop you!"

Wincing, Oz crouched to put another gun beside mine. I couldn't tell what it was.

Berko cut the brights. "Okay, Rimes, walk to the front on the driver's side."

I did so, willing myself to ignore sharp stones and occasional pieces of glass.

"Stop there," Berko said. "Now start walking away from the car, ten paces straight ahead. Try to get near those guns, I'll blow you away."

Caught in the low beams, I saw elongated shadows and couldn't tell exactly where the guns were. Oz and I were both shielding our eyes now so we could watch each other as I sidled forward. He glanced toward what I thought must be the guns, maybe calculating how long it would take him to reach them and fire. I looked to my left at the nearest end of the building, estimating how long it would take me to get there and round the corner.

"Good," Berko called. "Now turn and walk five paces away from Oz."

I backed away from Oz, squinting back and forth between him and the lights into which Berko had seemed to disappear. Berko said nothing about my not having turned. When we were situated kind of like the three-way gunfight at the end of *The Good, the Bad, and the Ugly*, Berko told me to stop. Then he must have dropped into the driver's seat because I heard the door shut. The high beams came on again, blinding us both. The Pathfinder shot backward, kicking up gravel as it went. I was certain Oz would go for the guns the instant the lights were no longer on us, but I was wrong. As my eyes struggled to adjust when Berko reached the end of the path and spun away, I saw Oz reach around to his back and bring out another gun. He waved it wildly, his own eyes still compensating for changes in light. I took off in the opposite direction, toward what I remembered was the end of the nearest building.

A back-up piece. Imagine that.

I was almost at the corner when Oz fired. The first two shots zinged past on my left, smacking high into concrete. The third sailed past on my right and maybe even reached the nearest bend in the Buffalo River a short distance ahead. Oz was trying to fix the position of an indistinct moving figure maybe forty feet away from him and would swing back toward the center before he squeezed the trigger again. I veered left and had just reached the corner when his fourth shot tagged my right shoulder.

Momentum carried me forward, and I went down with a grunt just past the corner.

Though I had felt the punch, I wasn't certain I had been shot. At first I felt stunned, knocked senseless. Then came the burning and the spreading numbness. *I could die here.* For a moment, I flashed ahead to my own funeral—Kayla struggling to hold Bobby up, Mira clutching Shakti so tightly he couldn't breathe, Peggy Ann following Jimmy down the center aisle with LJ in tears a few feet behind them, Phoenix standing beside my casket in the front of an empty, unfamiliar church— except there would be no casket or church and for those who loved me, or might come to love me, no closure. My agnosticism and Bobby's aside, there would be no church because there would be no funeral until there was a body. Until I was found.

No—

I tried to move, grateful the bullet wasn't a hollow point. I couldn't tell what caliber it was or whether it was a through-and-through. I could barely feel my right arm, but that side of my body ached. Taking a deep breath and using my left arm to push myself to my knees, I scuttled around the corner and backward toward the building. I sank to my butt in the weeds and listened as I struggled to control my breathing and adapt to the pain. I heard nothing but crickets and river water lapping against pilings and the faint sounds of distant traffic.

I knew Oz was listening too, hoping to get a fix on any movement or respiration. His eyes must have recovered by now, and any second he would start moving toward me to find out whether he had hit me and what he must do to finish killing me.

With my gun arm useless, I would need a few extra seconds. I drew my right leg up toward my chest, despite the pain shooting through my side. With my left hand I reached around to the ankle holster I had started wearing after LJ and I concluded Oz might come after me. I undid the strap as quietly as I could, afraid he would hear the release of the snap, but I barely heard it myself. Earlier, I had reassured Karen O'Brien I would dispose of the Ruger LCP she had accidentally discharged into Kenny's chest. Now I slid it out of the holster and tried to get a feel for its weight, to balance it with my left hand. I was glad I already had a bullet chambered because there was no way I could rack the slide with one hand. But I wasn't used to shooting with my left hand, especially a subcompact with a two-finger grip. I might need a second or two longer than usual to aim. If I lived, I promised myself I'd find Berko and thank him for leaving the gun on my ankle when he patted me down. What if Oz hadn't revealed his intention to kill me until *after* I was frisked? But I pushed that question aside in the face of another problem: I heard footsteps in the gravel.

Laying the LCP flat on my left thigh, I undid the safety. I closed my fingers around the grip and lifted the gun, rotating my wrist to get used to the feel. Then I waited.

The footsteps scraped nearer, slowly. Oz was being cautious because he couldn't be certain he had hit me. If he'd missed, I might come charging at him out of the weeds. I had at least forty pounds on him, and he had more than twenty years on me. He had to know that in hand-to-hand, the odds were in my favor. Therefore, he would be pointing his gun ahead of him and would stay far enough away from the silo walls that he'd have time to pivot and shoot before I could reach him. When he made it to the corner, he would be a dark target perhaps twenty feet away. Without my glasses and shooting with my left hand, I would need more than a little luck to take him out.

The first glimmer of that luck was actually a glimmer of light, a pale white LED beam that swept the ground far enough ahead of Oz I could see its perimeter as he crept closer. Of course. He had no idea I was armed and was using a pocket flashlight to find me. If he remained true to his police training, the gun would be in his right hand at, or above, chest level. The flashlight would be in his left, to the right of the gun, his right hand resting on the top of his left. His elbows would be out and up as his body formed its own isometric shooting framework. That meant when he got to the corner and turned—

Oz appeared and wheeled toward me. The light was right where I anticipated it would be, and I fired at the darkness below it.

Even as the flashlight beam jerked up, then spun and fell, and I heard the breath knocked out of him, I fired again and again and again at the same spot. He went down on his back, his right foot pointing skyward beside the fallen flashlight.

I still had two rounds left and pointed the Ruger at the foot, waiting for it to move. I hadn't seen a vest under his jacket but I couldn't be sure how badly I'd hurt him. If, for some reason, he tried to stand, I would have to estimate where his head was for my last two shots. If I missed, and his gun was within reach, I was screwed. So I waited, watching Oz's foot for the slightest twitch, listening for any hints of respiration, ragged or otherwise. I didn't know how long I waited before I knew he was dead—maybe a full minute—but I got to my feet, my right arm feeling like a slab of meat, and went to where Vince Osterman lay. Still holding the gun, I picked up his flashlight with my thumb and pinky and shone it at him. Only then did I put the Ruger in my back pocket.

The fabric of his black jacket was soaked in three places. The two in the abdomen were my first two shots. The wet patch in the chest must have been the third, meaning he had been hit as he staggered back and started to fall. The fourth shot caught him in the throat and put him on his back. I stood there looking at him for another minute as my mind churned through possibilities of what to do next.

Finally, I knelt beside the body and pulled off his left glove and held it with my teeth as I worked my fingers into it. I angled my right shoulder away from him. So far, my blood was soaking into my jacket and shirt but I didn't want to deposit any on Oz. I was leaving more than enough trace here but I knew the elements would neutralize whatever was outside, long before the place was classified a crime scene. That would happen maybe next spring, when somebody found Oz at the bottom of one of the silos. By then it would be a forensic nightmare: rodent DNA, insect larvae, bat guano, dust and dirt, flesh which had frozen and thawed at least a couple times during the winter, the body's own microorganisms consuming it, trace evidence on clothing from every place he had been the day he died, many months before. It wasn't that such evidence couldn't be sorted out. It was a matter of time and money when pinpointing the time of death beyond a wide window was difficult if not impossible. More obvious clues would be pursued first, and the most solid lead would be the presence in the body of four slugs that matched the bullet taken out of Kenny Carnahan. I could almost see Chalmers and Pinero in a piss-off with Lorenzo Quick and his lawyer.

Not a bad reconfiguration of your plan, Oz old buddy.

First, I used the flashlight to locate my shell casings and put them in the left side pocket of my jacket. Then I went through his clothing. I had no interest in his wallet so I pocketed it without opening it. I was happy to locate a cheap cell and even happier my bullets had missed it. Also, I found keys and a microfiber cloth designed to clean eyeglasses but useful for fingerprints when necessary. It smelled like gun oil. I used it to pick up his gun, a foot away from his right hand. It was a small caliber Browning automatic, which I slid into my jacket pocket too. When I was finished with him, I walked back to where he must have stood when he fired and found three of his four shell casings. Pocketing them, I went to where he had seemed to put down the guns. The only gun was my Glock, which, with some difficulty, I jiggered into the Blackhawk holster under my left arm. The other thing had only appeared gun enough to fool an eager-to-leave Berko. It was a gun-shaped clip-on holster just the right size for the Browning.

Oz, you sneaky bastard.

My feet were numb now and surely bleeding, but the blood flow in my shoulder had begun to slow. The throbbing told me the bullet had torn into muscle and bone but I could not estimate the damage. I began to feel my fingers again but they were still useless for what I had to do. I hobbled back to Oz and dragged him by the jacket collar to the nearest ground-level window. That took a lot out of me, and I took time to catch my breath as I looked about with the flashlight for something to break the window. I found a twisted piece of rusted metal and used it to clear the frame of glass. It took time for me to work Oz into the window head first using only my gloved left hand but, after a point, gravity took over. I winced at the sound of him thudding head first to the concrete floor.

Hoping the cell was the cheap burner it seemed, I pulled off the glove with my teeth and spat against the taste of leather and gun oil as I called Bobby. "It's me. I've been shot, but I'm okay. I need a ride." I told him where I was and not to call the police. "I'll explain everything on the way to the hospital. Come alone and flash your lights when you get here." Clicking off and holding the flashlight with the glove wrapped around it, I followed the sound of water against pilings to the edge of the river. I took Oz's gun and wallet and all the shell casings from my jacket pocket and the LCP from my back pocket. I ejected the Ruger's magazine. One-handed, I wiped both the gun and the clip with the microfiber cloth and gave each an underhanded toss into the water. Then I did the same with the Browning, the phone, and every casing. The last things that went into the river were the wallet and the glove.

My walk to the gate was slow because I was tired and used the flashlight to pick my way through the gravel. When I got there I didn't need to figure out which of Oz's keys went to the padlock. Berko had driven off without bothering to shut the gate. The open lock still hung in the chain. Closing the gate, I threaded the chain through the frame and slipped the lock through two links. I braced the loop of the lock against the frame and pushed until it clicked. I wiped the chain and lock. Then I wiped the keys and flashlight and tossed them and the cloth into different parts of the tall grass. Finally, I sat down in front of the gate to wait for Bobby.

Soon the Camry's lights flashed. I stood up, with some difficulty. Bobby pulled into the driveway beside me and jumped out. "Jesus!" he said as he rushed to me.

Putting my left arm over his shoulder, he helped me into the passenger seat. I refused the belt because the strap would cut into my shoulder. Bobby went round to his side and climbed in.

"Jesus, Gideon!" As he backed into the street, his expression was a mixture of worry, confusion, and relief. "What the hell happened! Miss Trinidad's been calling me, worried sick, and Kayla said she saw your—"

"They took me," I said, placing my left hand on his arm before he could shift gears.

"Took you? Who took you?"

"Two men. In ski masks. They took me right by my car on Elmwood. But they didn't bring me here. All right? They took me somewhere else, to—to LaSalle Park, and beat me but I fought back and they shot me when I tried to get away. But I still got away, and they drove off. I borrowed a cell phone and called you. *That* is what happened. Okay? "

He hesitated. "Are these men still a threat to you?"

"No."

Bobby looked at me for a long moment. Then he nodded and squeezed my left hand with his. "But you will tell me the truth later."

"All of it," I said, slumping against the seat. "I did what had to be done."

"Of course you did." Gently disengaging my hand from his arm, my godsend of a godfather put his Camry in drive and hit the gas.

Chapter 41

Most of Sunday was a haze.

There had been surgery the night before. Anesthetic that left me disoriented. A blood transfusion. Antibiotics. After surgery there was sleeping off and on, drifting in and out. IV lines and medical chatter. Beeping machines. Murmurs of background television. Ice chips to suck. Strange dreams and visions fueled by familiar voices that seemed to cling to unfamiliar clouds.

KAYLA: "Who would do this to him, Bobby? Kidnap him and shoot him like this."

BOBBY: "The kind of work he does, sometimes a man makes enemies."

SAM WINGARD (maybe): "Something to do with that article in the News today?"

KAYLA: "Exposing dirty tricks in a rich company? No better way to make enemies."

BOBBY: "Possibly, but it could just as easily be random."

KAYLA: "What a world we live in!"

SAM (maybe): "Wonder why he call you 'stead of nine-one-one."

BOBBY: "He knew I'd get to him faster than any ambulance."

I wanted to say something to Bobby and Kayla and Sam—maybe. I wanted to tell them I was fine and would be fine and I tried to lift my head up from the pool where it was floating but I couldn't hold it up above the warm water very long. I let go of it and it sank back down as I heard someone repeat that I could get this thing at a low-low price if I called now.

PHOENIX: "I thought you all might like some coffee."

KAYLA: "Thank you, dear."

SAM (maybe): "Thanks, ma'am."

BOBBY: "Yes, thank you, Ms. Trinidad."

PHOENIX: "Call me Phoenix, please."

I wanted to tell Phoenix how sorry I was for missing our date and not making love to her again because I very much liked how she made love to me and very much looked forward to making love and making brunch for her and making love some more, but something happened, and I got shot and somebody died, maybe the man behind the curtain, the man I paid no attention to, but I couldn't be sure because I could no longer tell what was real and what was a dream.

PHOENIX: "If you need to go home and sleep, I'll be here when he wakes up."

SAM (for sure): "Ma'am, Dr. Chance ain't goin' nowhere till that boy open his eyes."

BOBBY: "They said he'll recover, but I'll wait till I can ask him how he feels."

SAM: "Doc, lemme go on back to the 'partment house, case somebody need somethin'."

BOBBY: "Thank you, Sam."

KAYLA: "The police are here again. They want to get a statement when he wakes up."

PHOENIX: "Judge, let me handle them. As his lawyer, I'll ask them to hold off a day."

KAYLA: "Phoenix, we didn't call you here in the middle of last night as G's lawyer."

BOBBY: "I figured they wouldn't let you in."

PHOENIX: "Well, who did you say I was?

BOBBY: "I kind of told them you were his—fiancée."

I wanted to ask Phoenix if, for now, she would have and hold this turbulent man, not marry him, but just be there for him because sometimes he had to be violent and didn't really like it and needed to be held afterward and she seemed the perfect person to hold him.

By mid-morning, I was awake, fully aware the walls of my private room were robin's egg blue, and fully aware of the pain that confirmed I had been shot and operated upon. The first face I saw when I bobbed to the surface of the warm pool in which I had been sleeping belonged to Dr. Ayodele Ibazebo, Bobby's former student.

Before blinking and seeing her, I had heard a mild British accent reassuring those in the room I would be fine, that I had lost a lot of blood and my body had pushed through on adrenaline, so now I needed rest. She was examining me and frowned when my eyes opened. "Last Sunday, I stitched that hard head of yours after someone hit you. Last night we took a bullet from your shoulder and picked glass out of your feet. Your father is a good man who does not deserve the grief he will face when he cannot save you from whatever it is you do. Get a new job." Then she stepped back as Bobby, Kayla, and Phoenix gathered around me.

I couldn't recall how long we talked before I drifted off to sleep again.

The next time I woke, Bobby was there alone and said he had put my Glock and the holsters in the gun safe, as I had asked. Then I told him everything about last night. When I finished he asked why I had bothered to conceal a clear case of self-defense.

"There are too many bends in the truth," I said, "to benefit anyone. It's bad enough that, one day after his hero's funeral, Kenny has been exposed as part of a plan to unseat the mayor. Now a retired decorated cop will be unmasked as an attempted murderer. Then there's my having killed him with an unregistered firearm. If police had the Ruger, Kenny's shooting would be reopened and Lenny and KO drawn in, maybe arrested, hurting the Carnahans even more. And the investigation would dog Berko, who'd made it possible for me to save my own life. Ophelia doesn't need any of that," I said. "Neither does the department or the city."

"The article was kind to Kenny," Bobby said. "He was a reluctant participant drawn in because his folks needed money but he was on the verge of pulling out when he died."

"I'll have to read it," I said. *And thank Amanda Corso.*

Just then Mira and Shakti appeared in the doorway. Her hair unkempt and her face paler than I had ever seen it, Mira let go of her son's hand and came to my bedside. Shakti ran into Grandpa Bobby's arms. He looked over at me with a child's mix of curiosity and fear and waited for his mother to take the lead.

"I go away for one weekend, out of cell range for three goddam days, and you get yourself *shot*?" Mira said, eyes flicking between me and the monitors that showed my vitals. "We're at breakfast and getting ready to go to the Toronto Zoo and Bobby leaves a message at the front desk saying to call him because you've been *shot!*" She flashed Bobby an angry glance. "Then he won't answer his damn phone because he's in the damn hospital and it's off. So I'm driving like Batman on the QEW, where it's always rush hour, even on Sunday morning, but I don't have a Batmobile and I'm not in range till we hit customs at the Peace Bridge, and I think to call Kayla and she says you're here." Eyes tearing up, she mouthed, "What the *fuck*?" Then she put her face beside mine on the pillow, and her voice cracked. "You tell them I have permission to see all your records. All of them. And don't you ever scare me like that again, you...you snorkelhead!"

His mother's pent-up emotions at last discharged with a word he himself had coined at the beach last year, Shakti came over to the bed. "Can I hug you, Uncle G?"

"Not now, buddy," Mira said, wiping her eyes and sitting up. "It would hurt Uncle G if you squeezed him too hard and we don't want that, right?"

"Didn't exactly shoot myself, you know," I said to Mira, and, to Shakti, added, "You can hug me but only on this side." I raised and wiggled the fingers of my left hand. As Shakti eased himself into my waiting left arm, I caught sight of Phoenix in the doorway, smiling. I wondered how long she'd been there. "There's somebody I want you both to meet."

In the early evening, after Bobby finally went to get some sleep and Mira took Shakti home, Phoenix went to her office for files she needed to review. Before I could drift off, two police officers came to take my statement. Sergeant Spina, a tall brunette in her mid-thirties, studied me as I spoke. Her lanky sidekick Fritz may have been a rookie. He took notes on a clipboard as I recounted leaving a liquor store on Elmwood and being forced into the back of a van at gunpoint by two men in ski masks.

"They threw my phone out the window and put a pillow-case over my head. One drove and the other pressed the gun to my head. He said he'd double-tap me in the head if I moved," I said. "He punched me a few times. Then he took my socks and shoes and jabbed something that felt like glass into my feet." I winced and took a deep breath. "When the van finally stopped and the asshole took off the pillowcase, I saw it was dark. I didn't know where we were but figured it was where they planned to dump my body. So when he opened the door and started to get out, I went for the gun. We fought for it and it went off inside the van. Then we tumbled out, and the gun fell to the grass. Before the driver could get out, I kicked it under the van. I got in one good punch before I took off. Maybe broke the asshole's nose. I was running when they shot me."

"How far did you get?" Spina asked.

"I don't know. Maybe forty, fifty feet."

She pursed her lips. "Lucky shot to hit a moving target in the dark at that distance."

"Lucky it wasn't center mass," I said. "I stumbled but kept running. I saw the water and realized it was LaSalle Park. I made it back to a line of parked cars and knocked on a window. Scared the hell out of this couple making out, but the kid let me use his phone."

"You called Dr. Robert Chance and not nine-one-one. Why?"

"My godfather. He raised me. He has a weak heart and nearly had a heart attack last week when cops busted down the door to arrest me for a murder I didn't commit."

She nodded. "We checked you out, sir, and we know all about that."

"Then you'll understand why I wanted to talk to him my-self. And let him know that I was okay. No blue uni at the door. He said he was on his way, and I said I'd wait for him."

"You had to know GSW surgery would be reported and you'd have to talk to us."

"Of course. I'm talking to you right now."

"And the kid with the phone?"

"A gunshot victim standing by his car? Took off the minute he got his phone back."

Spina turned to Fritz and glanced at his notes. "They have one gun or two?"

"Only one that I saw."

"Describe it."

I tried to shrug and clenched my teeth at the pain. After a second I said, "Small, black semiauto. Maybe a .22 or a .25? How big was the slug they took out of me?"

"A .25," Spina said. "Perfect for his promise. I guess you didn't kick it far enough under the van." She paused. "Tell me about the van. You get a plate number?"

I shook my head. "White. No seats or windows in back, like a panel truck. Single dome light. Dirty as hell. I don't know the make. It drove off when I got to the other cars."

"They didn't rob you. This seems personal. Any idea who did this or why?"

"No." I looked toward the window. The blinds were open. I could see that, after a week of sunny fall days, it was raining. I bit back a smile. "In my line, I do meet unsavory people. I've done security and been attacked by drunks. Served subpoenas and been attacked by recipients. And some of the matrimonial work? I've been threatened by fat old farts with boxer shorts around their ankles. I can't imagine anybody like that—" I shook my head.

"What can you tell us about these two?"

"Didn't see much of the driver. The man with the gun was my size. Raspy voice."

"Was he right-handed or left-handed?"

"The gun was in his right, so I guess right."

"Are you right-handed or left?"

"Right."

"What about the thing he did to your feet? Never heard of that before."

"Me either, but if I find him before you do, I'll be sure to return the favor."

Spina bit her lip. "Sir, I have to ask. Do you have some idea *where* to look for him?"

"No." I sucked my teeth and sighed. "I'm just talking because I'm pissed."

"You have every right to be pissed." She took the clipboard and flipped pages. "We talked to Dr. Chance and your stories are consistent. We found your car right where you said it was. Broken glasses underneath. A smashed cell phone farther down the street. GSR on your left hand fits a face-to-face struggle with a right-handed shooter whose gun goes off. The clothes they cut off you are filthy, grass-stained, and bloody, like you were rolling in dirt and got shot. Your injuries support the details you gave us. The only thing that doesn't make sense is why you called your godfather and not us." She looked at me for a few seconds then sighed. "Ken Carnahan was a friend of mine. We were at the academy together. You brought in the man who killed him. In my report, I think I'll say you showed the same stamina that got you a Purple Heart." Smiling, Spina tore a slip of paper from the clipboard and put it on my nightstand. "A case file number, if you think of anything else or want an investigative update. We'll look into this, Mr. Rimes. We'll be in touch if we get something solid, like a hit off the bullet or a van with gunshot damage, or a broken nose in an ER."

"But you doubt anything will turn up," I said and thought, *Who better to stage...*

"Truthfully, sir, probably not. Even if the gun has a body on it, it could be a dead end, the way guns change hands nowadays. But that thing with the feet is one for the books."

When the two officers turned to leave, I saw Phoenix, about to enter the room, step aside to let them pass. She watched as they went down the corridor, turning to me briefly and putting a finger to her lips. A moment later the elevator bell rang, and she came to the bed.

"I should've told the desk you were off limits till tomorrow. You still look like shit."

"Had to talk sooner or later. Were you there long enough to protect my rights?"

"Quite a story." She set down her briefcase and pulled up a chair so she could sit close. "I hope you're going to tell *me,* at least, what really happened."

In a low voice I did just that, even as one of the machines to which I was tethered with an IV line sent the next shot of pain killer into my bloodstream and the pull of sleep grew strong enough to slur my words.

When I finished, Phoenix looked at me for a long time then shut her eyes and shook her head. Slipping away and fighting it, I wondered if I had lost my chance with her, if what I had done would be too much of a moral compromise for her to accept. After all, she was an officer of the court. However well-intentioned my motives, my manipulation of evidence was still obstruction of justice.

But Phoenix opened her eyes and wiped them. "Thank God he's not coming back for you. I was going to pay Oscar to sit outside your room tonight but I'll call and tell him it won't be necessary."

"See, I told you I won't lie to my lawyer," I said.

She shrugged. "Apparently I'm more than your lawyer." Then she smiled and leaned over to kiss my forehead. "Your lawyer wouldn't be able to get a recliner wheeled in here so she could spend the night next to you. But I can."

I would always remember waking up Monday morning and seeing Phoenix still asleep in the recliner not three feet away.

Chapter 42

Before I was released Thursday morning, I had cards and calls and several visitors.

On Monday, Jimmy and Peggy Ann promised to take me shooting so I could learn to use my left hand until I regained full range of motion in my right shoulder. LJ offered to install a new streaming service on my Lenovo so that during my recuperation at home, I could watch movies still in theaters.

Terry Chalmers accepted the explanation that I was unarmed for my date and speculated Vince Osterman may have been one of my kidnappers because he transferred money into a Canadian bank and dropped off the grid after the *News* exposed him as a political trickster. As long as no one had died, the commissioner preferred limited public discussion about a corrupt ex-cop who'd misdirected an investigation. Thus my case became a low-priority. "But Cochrane knows Osterman," Chalmers said. "Tells me he's a class-A dick who made enemies on the force and on the streets. Sooner or later, somebody will balance his books." Chalmers raised his right hand for a fist bump, which I completed with my left. "I didn't say this when you brought Simmons in, Rimes, but you must've been a helluva cop."

Having said next to nothing during their visit, Rafael Pinero added, "Still is."

Rolling his toothpick from one side of his mouth to the other, he pushed his hat up and smiled down at me. Then he leaned close and whispered that getting shot was easy compared to what he would do to me if I ever hurt Phoenix Trinidad.

Ophelia Green swept in after lunch on Tuesday and took the armchair by the window when I asked what she had suspected when she retained me as an investigator.

"For months, sabotage whispers were bouncing off the walls in City Hall," she said. "I told my immediate staffers and my son to watch for traps everywhere they went. I didn't warn my security detail because they're supposed to be non-political and…well, the police contract was still unsettled. My campaign couldn't get a handle on anything solid. When you called me about Kenny, I wondered if that was it, if it was coming from the department."

"You couldn't involve police in party politics," I said. "Whatever spy you had in the Merlotta camp couldn't find anything, and using campaign funds to hire a PI would be a problem." I let out a long breath. "But Kenny's death gave you an opening. Then I got arrested and released and stepped right into your marionette harness."

"Don't be angry," Ophelia said. "I thought you might find police fingerprints on this, maybe even the commissioner's, not CitiQuest's. Zack and Mickey Briggs have been to my house, for Christ's sake. Now she's resigned and he's filed for divorce. And Tony Merlotta has been replaced by a VP his father can control. I am in your debt, G. Thank you."

I said nothing.

"Rick says he never knew he had a daughter, much less what she was up to." Ophelia grinned. "He says he's still in it to win it, but the polls say I spanked him last night."

Having watched the debate, I agreed. For a moment I wondered if I should tell her what had really happened to Danny, but that wasn't what she'd sent me to find. Now I saw how radiant she looked, with the afternoon sunlight behind her, and decided knowing would do her no good.

On Tuesday evening, I thanked Amanda Corso for editing the transcript and shaping her article to make Kenny look regretful and Oz more a ruthless schemer than anything else.

"You know, I think the bastard really might have killed people," she said, sounding enough like Lauren Bacall that I realized at least some of it was an act. "Before he disappeared, he even threatened *me*." Having heard a rumor I'd been roughed up by an ex-husband who'd paid heavily after my matrimonial photographs were introduced in court, Corso asked to interview me for a series on the life of a PI. I declined. When she pressed me, Phoenix asked her to leave, and the two exchanged a look that would have made cage fighters cringe.

Wednesday, Karen O'Brien and Lenny Carnahan came to thank me again for what I'd done for his family. His mother had interpreted Corso's articles to mean that, had he lived, Kenny himself would have exposed Briggs and Osterman and thus had died a hero. No one challenged her perception. When I saw them seated side by side, leaning close and deferring to each other, I realized how likely it was Lenny and KO would get together—he at last on the cusp of responsible adulthood and she settling into a family that already embraced her as a member. *She'll mother him*, I thought. *But it might work.* As they were leaving, KO bent close to plant a kiss on my cheek, and I whispered, "Gun's gone," which made her smile.

Among the get-well cards was one from Lizzy Rogers, who penned an addition to the commercial message: *Doc is heartbroken about Big Willy and blames you. But he's a good man. One day the Lord will take the bitterness away, and he'll thank you as I do now.* A note with no return address or signature came via Jasper Hellman's contacts outside prison: *So happy to hear you got shot. Hope you get a shit bag too.* There was nothing from Indi.

Of course, Bobby came every afternoon, bringing my spare glasses, my mail, and cards from various tenants in the building. He also brought me a replacement mobile phone and loaned me his iPad so I could check email and surf the web. He was there to ask the right questions when doctors came to discuss my progress.

He was there to take notes when the physical therapist discussed the particulars of the treatment that would follow my release. "I'll take care of getting you there," he said after the woman left. "When I can't take you, I'll find somebody who can."

On Wednesday evening, my last night, Phoenix was sitting on the edge of my bed, holding my hand, when Bobby arrived with Kayla. Before long Mira came with Shakti, and Jimmy's chair whirred in a few steps ahead of Peggy Ann and LJ. As Shakti crawled onto the bed on my left side and hugged me, my visitors spent more time talking to each other than to me. As they shared stories and laughter, much of it at my expense, my nurse brought in a marble cake and paper plates. I realized Bobby had thrown together this impromptu party in my hospital room because Jimmy would be unable to get up to my apartment. But it was more than an early welcome home celebration. Bobby understood I wanted Phoenix to find her way deeper into my life. These were my family, the gatekeepers who would have to welcome her before she could feel she belonged, and the man who still cherished his role as my father had gathered them together to accelerate the process.

Chapter 43

The Friday after Ophelia Green won reelection in a landslide, I was back at the Anchor Bar. This time Phoenix was with me. We sat at a corner table, sharing a plate of medium wings and drinking Coronas. We were both dressed in jeans and knit sweaters. My Glock was on my right hip under the sweater, in a cross-draw holster so I could pull left-handed. We had heavy fall jackets folded over the backs of our chairs because for days the air outside had shown enough bite to tell us we had crossed another mile marker in the march toward winter.

Across from the bandstand, two balding middle-aged men in custom-tailored suits sat at the table I had occupied before. According to Lizzy's note, the dark-skinned man in wire-rimmed glasses was named Triplett and his translucent associate was named Kitzwilliam. Neither had finished his complimentary martini or order of wings. They had come from New York City to see Indigo Waters sing, not to eat or drink. Between them sat an expensive-looking digital recorder. Each had in hand a small notebook, as if planning to record personal impressions. From the instant Indi opened her mouth, however, to the last song of the first set, they sat transfixed, heads and fingers moving almost involuntarily, pens untouched. From my seat, I couldn't see whether they even remembered to turn on their recorder.

Even though Indi's name had last appeared in the newspaper a week earlier and her last television interview about Big

Willy had aired two weeks before that, the bar was more crowded than usual, as had been the case in all the JBA's recent gigs. There was nothing like a cocktail of sex, politics, and murder to elevate someone's profile. Even if Indi had been a wretched singer, crowds would have come that first week or two to see for themselves why she had been stalked and whether she was a victim or a temptress. That she was a wonderful talent with genuine stage presence kept them coming beyond the scandal's expiration date.

Indi was dressed in a gold gown that complimented the rich darkness of her skin and formed a striking contrast with the band's matching blue suits. When she finished her set and withdrew to resounding applause, the JBA improvised, giving each musician a solo that kept the audience clapping and tapping. Teddy Evans worked his bass as if it were a dance partner he hoped to seduce, and Dix Danishovsky tore into his drums with a fury that left him red and glistening with sweat. The aptly named Tank Truesdale was no Big Willy Simmons, but the short, thick man handled his sax with a heart that reflected years of experience. As usual, Doc Rogers closed the set with a virtuosic display of his speed and range.

When the lights came up and the chatter grew louder, I kissed Phoenix on the cheek and said I would be right back. On my way out of the dining room, I passed the table where Doc, sweating heavily himself, had taken a seat to talk to Triplett and Kitzwilliam. Our eyes met as I passed, and his mouth tightened.

When I entered the barroom, the other members of the band were gathered at the nearest corner, drinking water or soda. Teddy and Dix smiled and shook my hand—because I hadn't taken *their* lifelong friend to jail. They introduced me to Tank, and I told them all they sounded fantastic and the New York guys looked impressed.

Then I excused myself and went to the far end of the bar, where Berko was waiting for me—as I had told him to do when he called. Cheeks unshaven and mustache untrimmed, he wore a hunting jacket and cap.

"Kid can really sing," he said when I sat next to him.

"Couple guys from New York are here to check her out for a record deal."

"No shit?" He took a sip of whiskey. "Good for her."

The bartender slid into view. I ordered two more bottles of Corona with lime.

Berko was quiet for a moment then took another sip. "I called you 'cause there's something I gotta know."

I looked at him. "Are you wearing a wire?"

"No." He chewed his lip then sighed and lowered his voice. "If I was wearing a wire, I'd never admit I helped kidnap you but had no idea Vince Osterman intended to kill you. And I'd never say I chose not to arrest Osterman and instead left you with a gun in an ankle holster so you could defend yourself. I'd never say my participation was to keep Osterman from talking about—"

"Enough," I said. "I don't want to know what he had on you. It's not my business."

"Thank you."

I shrugged. "Don't sweat it, but let's not use any more names here. Not that a wire would get much with all this noise. And thank *you*. You saved my life, even though you did take my socks and shoes."

"Sorry about that."

"So what do you want to know?"

Before he could answer, my Coronas came. I pushed the lime wedges into the bottles and put a fifty on the bar. "If my friend here wants another drink, it comes out of this," I said to the bartender. "If he stops with this one, all the change is yours." When the man thanked me and moved away, I turned back to Berko. "So what do you want to know?"

"I got thirty years next month, and I'm gonna put my papers in." He downed the last of his whiskey and smacked his lips with satisfaction. "I'm using up leftover vacation first. My ex-wife's family has a hunting cabin in Livingston County. I've been staying there."

"That's great," I said, meaning it. "On the job your whole life, you deserve to retire."

"Ah, the job has changed over the years." Berko held up a

finger then pointed to his glass when the bartender saw him. "Things ain't as clear as they used to be. You never know when you're crossing some line or stepping on the wrong toe or stomping in political dogshit. Not like it was when my father and grandfather wore the badge. Things were simpler then."

"Police work has changed," I said. "Including simple assumptions and hunches—like who's probably a criminal and who's going to have your back. One thing I liked about being an army cop was there were no simple assumptions. Nothing to follow but evidence."

Berko picked up his fresh glass of whiskey and took a sizable swallow. "One thing hasn't changed, though. You could die on this fucking job, and nobody would fucking care but another fucking cop."

"Truth." I clinked one of the Corona bottles against his glass and drank. "Dangerous, thankless work most cops do with honor for shitty pay. But some get desperate or hungry, or worse, and lose their way."

"You saw him, how he looked at me that night. Like he'd kill me first chance he got." Berko swallowed without drinking. "I want to know if it's safe. What happened after I left?"

"I got away." Now the hunting cabin made sense, and I felt sorry for Berko.

"You got away." He scowled. "That's it?"

"I got shot in the process, but I got away."

"What happened to *him*? He left his car at a chop shop as collateral for the vehicle we used that night. I know for a fact that vehicle was towed and he never got his Escalade back."

"He's gone." I stared straight at Berko. "Detectives told me he transferred money out of the country and disappeared. Nobody is looking for him—or his associates—because nobody knows anything he can be charged with. He said he was leaving and left. He's gone."

"Are you worried he might come back?"

I thought about that a moment and shook my head. "Have a nice retirement, Berko. And thanks again."

Coronas in hand, I started back toward the dining room and

came face to face with Doc. "Looks like your friends from New York are in love."

His tie, the same shade of gold as Indi's gown, was loosened and he had been smiling when he turned and saw me. Now his smile vanished, and, for a long moment, he just stared at me, as if shocked I dared to show my face. He began to tremble with whatever was boiling inside him and motioned me into the photograph-lined corridor that led to the restrooms and the kitchen. "You coulda left well enough alone," he said under his breath.

I kept my voice equally low, pausing as people passed. "The police wouldn't have. They have an excellent cold case squad. Sooner or later, probably after Big Willy was in the ground, they'd have put it all together and tapped on your door." As a man left the washroom and sidled past on the way back to the bar, I thought of Big Willy, now metastatic and under guard at Roswell Park Cancer Institute. He was not expected to live long enough to face trial. "This was Big Willy's call, Doc. He loves you and wants you and Indi to have a chance he and his son never got, to form a friendship that could be the best part of both your lives." I turned slightly as another man came near and slipped into the restroom. "Looks like you spent real money tonight on suits and gowns to give your only child the chance of a lifetime. That's what fathers do. But I bet she still has no idea why *you* did it." His downcast glance confirmed I was right. "There's one thing you can't tell her, ever. What you *can* tell her you *should*. Now that she's about to need her father's love and guidance more than ever, don't you dare throw away Big Willy's gift."

I moved away before he could say anything else and returned to my table.

"That didn't take long," Phoenix said. "How's Berko?"

I sat down. "Scared Oz will come back for him. He's been living in the woods."

"Seriously?"

I nodded. "I tried to reassure him without telling him the whole story."

"Did it work?"

Before I could say I thought so, applause rose and Indi returned to the stage, bowing and smiling. Now she was in a gown of sparkling blue that matched the band's suits, with gold trim that matched their ties—Doc really had spared no expense. He gave a three-count, and the music began. The second set was even more dynamic than the first as Indi shifted effortlessly between jazz and blues, commanding the audience's attention with the ease of the superstar she might yet become. As she had the first night I worked as her bodyguard, she finished with an "At Last" that produced a seismic response. When it was over and the crowd was filing out, Phoenix and I neared the table where Doc and Indi were talking to Triplett and Kitzwilliam.

She didn't see us, but Doc did. We made no effort to get her attention and Doc made no effort to point us out to her. He returned to the conversation. By the time we made it past their table, both were breathless and smiling.

"He still hasn't told her," I said as we shuffled toward the door.

"He must have his reasons," Phoenix said.

The night was brisk and cloudless, the sky full of as many stars as one could see amid the ambient light of a city. Phoenix shifted to my left side and slipped her arm into mine as we headed toward her RAV4 at the far end of the parking lot. Pressing the remote start, she turned to me. "Give it a minute to warm up," she said and kissed me for a long time. Then she put her head on my shoulder, and we resumed walking.

The last residue of my anger at Doc drained away. Now I wondered aloud why he wouldn't tell Indi he was her father.

"It could be more complex than we think," Phoenix said.

"Lizzy knows and already treats Indi like a daughter."

"Maybe Indi's been angry all her life that her father wasn't there for her and now Doc's scared of rousing those feelings. What if being afraid is the key? If his entire understanding of being a father is based on fear of discovery, maybe fear is the filter for all his feelings about Indi. He's always afraid *for* her and *because* of her, and therefore always afraid *of* her."

"Could be." Then it hit me. "But maybe he's most afraid of being left behind."

We reached the RAV4. I held open the door. Phoenix slid behind the wheel.

"The way Doc and the band played tonight," I said as I dropped into the passenger seat, "you'd have thought they were the ones auditioning." The cold air blasting through the vents began to warm. "Maybe they were, or maybe Doc was."

"What do you mean?"

"Imagine spending your whole life hoping for the one big break that leads to the stratosphere. You work hard, traveling and playing everywhere. You get all kinds of respect. You know people, superstars, but you never get to be one. You never quite make it to the top. 'The race is not always to the swift, nor the battle to the strong—'"

"Aren't you full of surprises?" Phoenix said. "An agnostic who quotes the Bible."

"Ecclesiastes is my favorite part," I said. "Anyway, you attach your dream to this talented but immature child and hope, when she shoots to the top, she'll take you with her."

Backing out of the space and joining the line of cars waiting to exit, Phoenix could see it now and nodded. "To keep riding her coattails, you can't give her a reason to take the scissors to them." She exhaled heavily. "Fatherhood is complicated."

"All this was about fatherhood, about fathers and children." I resisted the urge to hold up my fingers one at a time as I spoke. "Doc bringing Indi to Buffalo to give her a career boost and killing to protect her and maybe protect his chances with her. Big Willy taking the fall after he couldn't keep his own son safe from war. Kenny joining CitiQuest to help after his father's stroke. But the thing that set it all in motion, that made victims of Doc and Kenny and the rest of them, was Mickey and Tony's plan to get their father elected so he'd get them an inside track to federal money. This was always about what fathers and children do for each other, how far they're willing to go."

"You forgot Bobby," Phoenix said. "He was willing to go pretty far for you."

"I never forget Bobby," I said. "I'm always surprised at how much he'll risk for me."

"You'd risk just as much for him."

"More, I hope."

We were four cars away from the exit now. "My place or yours?" Phoenix said.

Left on Main would take us toward her loft downtown. Right would lead toward my apartment in the Village. We had toothbrushes in each place but had not yet graduated to drawers and closet space. *Patience*, I told myself and leaned back as we were three cars away from the street, then two. The increasingly warm air felt good.

"I have this fantasy of making love with you on the roof of my building," I said. "On a night like this, when the sky is full of stars."

"Not tonight, Nanook," she said. "I like you but I'm not gonna freeze my ass off for anybody's bucket list. Let's save that one for when the temperature is in the eighties. Like next summer."

Just what I hoped she'd say. "Okay, I have another fantasy for a night like this—"

Phoenix laughed. "If you want to do it by my fireplace again, just say so."

"So," I said, and she turned left.

About the Author

A lifelong resident of the Nickel City, Gary Earl Ross is a retired University at Buffalo professor, novelist, public radio essayist, and playwright.

His sixty-plus short stories have appeared in many magazines and journals, as well as anthologies, among them *Intimacy* (2004, Penguin/Plume), *Wicked: Sexy Tales of Legendary Lovers* (2005, Cleis), *Medium for Murder* (2008, Red Coyote Press), *Darker Edge of Desire* (2014, Cleis), and *Buffalo Noir* (2015, Akashic).

His historical novel *Blackbird Rising* was published in 2009 by Full Court Press, a small Buffalo publisher, and his plays, most of them mysteries, have been performed in various US, Canadian, and English cities, as well as in Shanghei, China, Manipal, India, and Almaty, Kazakhstan. *The Guns of Christmas* and *The Mark of Cain* won, respectively, the 2015 and 2016 Emanuel Fried Outstanding New Play Award. *Matter of Intent*, performed in Buffalo in 2005 and London in 2009, won the 2005 Emanuel Fried Outstanding New Play Award and the 2006 Edgar Award from Mystery Writers of America. For more information visit www.garyearlross.net.